Flora Pearce was born in Heath End, Staffordshire, the village portrayed in *No Work Today*. Her parents kept the local shop and it is her father, George, former miner and coal merchant, who by his wonderful recall supplied much of the background for this novel.

Flora Pearce now lives in Dorset with her husband, Dennis, and is currently at work on her second novel.

NO WORK TODAY

FLORA PEARCE

Futura

A *Futura* Book

Copyright © Flora Pearce 1987

First published in Great Britain in 1987
by Futura Publications
This edition published by
Futura Publications 1994
Reprinted 1995

*The character of Mary Ann is loosely
based on the author's grandmother.
All other characters in this publication are fictitious
and any resemblance to real persons, living or dead,
is purely coincidental.*

ISBN 0 7088 3589 9

Printed in England by Clays Ltd, St Ives plc

Futura Publications
A Division of
Macdonald & Co (Publishers)
Brettenham House
Lancaster Place
London WC2E 7EN

To George, my father,

with very much love.

Thanks, Dad.

Heath End did (and does) exist.

Mary Ann Lived there.

The rest is fictitious.

PROLOGUE

'THERE WAS A village? Here?'

'I'll say there was.'

Mitch could not hide the disillusionment he felt as he cast his eyes over the unbending grey road, lined with identical buildings, identically-placed windows staring back at him with cold square eyes. Occasionally a car would back out furiously to join the never-ending line of irritable traffic, but not a soul moved on the rectilinear pavements.

You would think from the way Gran and Great-Uncle Ben carried on about Heath End it would be something special.

'You can't tell from what you see now,' said Paul, feeling sick in the stomach. It was all so different.

Once there was a village with a heartbeat pulsing loud enough to be heard in Brum, a village filled with life, variety and caring people. If it had not been for the planners leaving The Red Cow standing he would have been unable to pinpoint for Mitch where they had all lived.

He could read his grandson's thoughts. When you have come all the way from Canada and you have only one month in England it seemed a cruel waste of time to spend some of it gazing at a faceless road. Mitch was anxious to be off, to tour York, Stratford, London, Bath. He was poised for flight, physically and mentally, just like Ben used to be, his heels hardly touching the ground. Even his voice, despite its Canadian accent, sounded like Ben as he asked with thinly disguised impatience. 'But nothing ever happened here, did it, Grandad? *Did* anything ever happen here?'

'No . . . perhaps you're right.'

One day he would tell him.

CHAPTER

1

IT WAS THE day Raish decided to leave them, the day they all started to live. But Mary Ann knew nothing of that yet as she studied the growing cluster of out-of-work miners from her shop window. Some squatted, playing jacks in the dust. Others lolled against the wall of the outdoor beer licence, scuffing their toes as they hurled good-natured insults at their mates crouching on the ground.

Not often did Mary Ann take time off to stare at the jack players, poor devils, trying to be jocular while agonizing over whether the pits would be open or closed to them tomorrow. She could always tell the ones who had been laid off the longest, stripped of their dignity, on the defensive, a touching mixture of arrogance and humility. She sighed. Nineteen-hundred-and-eight and this still going on!

What a contrast were the pitmen, in their collarless flannel shirts, black cloth caps and worn moleskins, to her Raish, in his immaculate suit, shining shoes, bowler set at a rakish angle. The skins of the pitmen were roughened by engrimed coal dust that nothing would shift. Raish's skin was as smooth as a baby's bottom; he often boasted of it. Lily-white skin, he called it.

Nineteen-hundred-and-eight and they were still here, in this Midland village of Heath End, or Cod End, as it was nicknamed; a place where most folk could not pay their way, a place where she never stopped working, from when she arose at four to bake her bread in stone jars until she bolted the shop door at ten before making her way to bed, to lie listening for her husband, wondering how the drink had served him and if he would be boasting of his latest female conquest.

Cod End! The village that was to have been a stepping stone to a bigger shop in a bustling town. Twenty years they had been here. It had taken its toll on her looks, she knew that, whereas Raish never appeared any older. No matter how drunk he was at night each morning saw him sallying forth to the early markets, more handsome than ever, his blond moustache well groomed, his blue eyes still as saucy, his buttonhole dewy fresh. He still walked with that characteristic jaunty gait, head high, shoulders thrown well back, the walk that set him apart from the village chaps. His cock o' the north walk, Cod Enders called it.

Raish's shoulders had not rounded from crawling through suffocating pit tunnels; her lads must crawl and stoop but not her husband. Mary Ann moved impatiently, filled with a sense of injustice for her lads: timid Edwin, married too soon to get away from his father; Paul, shouldering manhood already at fifteen and far too anxious about her, for when all was said and done, she could fend for herself; and Ben, her youngest, just thirteen and starting work at Paul's pit today. Moody, aggressive Ben, bitterly resentful and hating his father.

Raish, dictatorial and contemptuous of them all, was responsible for their varying attitudes to life. Even Katy, who had never shown any fear of him, was so mindful of

Mary Ann's difficulties that she was opting for a safe marriage to a man as dull as a disused coal shaft. Fifteen sovereigns Walter had put down on the table last night, more money than Mary Ann had ever seen at one go.

'Do you think you can furnish our home with that?' he had asked quietly.

'With fifteen sovereigns! Just you watch me,' Katy had chuckled.

True, Walter would bring his money home each week; no doubt he would help to bring up the children Katy had set her heart on 'in an atmosphere of security', the thing she wanted most in the world. But was he right for Katy? She wished she could be sure.

One of the younger miners looked up from the game of jacks, disturbed by the intensity of gaze from the shop window. It was unheard of for Mary Ann Brook to be standing doing nothing. A fine figure of a woman she was, her thick brown hair always clean and shining, her eyes bright and sharp, her full-busted figure held regally. 'Look at the mother, my lad, before you choose a wife', his old grandad had told him. If Katy Brook turned out like Mary Ann she'd do. In her early forties he guessed, although appearing older now with that impatience on her face. Yet when she smiled the years would slide away. God knows she hadn't much to smile about, with that Brookie to contend with.

He made an excuse to the others and sprinted across the road. The tinkling door-bell caused Mary Ann to start as if she did not hear it dozens of times a day. 'Made you jump, did I? You must have been miles away.'

'I was.'

'Anything up?'

'Nothing. What can I do for you, Ted?'

'Give us a pair of bootlaces.'

She stretched to reach two long laces from an assortment tied together, hanging high above the counter.

'I'd better 'ave a collar stud an' all. Mine's missin' again. Can't put a thing down in our house.' He grinned. 'Not with nine of us.'

'How are things, Ted?' Ted's father had been badly injured a month back. 'Nothing from the pit, I suppose?'

He shook his head. 'It was me Dad's fault. Or so they say.'

'Thanks for the groceries you sent,' he added shortly, slightly resentful at having to accept charity. 'How much do I owe for these?'

'That will be a penny.'

'I saw Katy setting off up the road at a great pace this morning.'

Ted Willis had been sweet on Katy for years, ever since she played hop-scotch and tip-cat with him and his mates. A right merry dance she had led him too. He would be curious about Katy being dressed in her Sunday best on a Friday.

'She looked nice,' he continued.

'Yes, didn't she?'

'That's more like it. You look more like your pretty daughter when you smile.'

There was nothing shy about this lad. He was just the opposite to Walter, Katy's intended. She knew that if Ted had a regular job he would have asked Katy to marry him long ago. In nice clothes he would cut quite a dash, with his thick curly mop and those deep dark eyes, half hidden by double rows of thick lashes. He just missed being handsome by the arrogant square of his chin. Nevertheless they would have made a pretty picture, walking up the aisle, confident Ted and tiny practical Katy, with her sparkling eyes and Raish's proud cock o' the north walk.

'Where was she off to, then, our Katy?'

Mary Ann wished she could have softened her next remark. 'She was off to Lawson's Sale to buy things for her home. She is going to marry Walter.'

14

'You can't mean that chap who came down from Derby?'

'I do.'

Ted laughed shortly, the thick lashes immediately veiling the shock in his startled eyes, but not before Mary Ann had noticed.

'Katy! And him?' His fist came down heavily on the counter. 'You can't mean it! Why, he'd never have more'n a dozen words to say to her.'

'She can make up for him, can't she?' Mary Ann replied calmly.

'He's too old for her.'

'Walter has had time to save, Ted. They'll have a start.'

'A start! A start to what? I don't believe it. I can't believe it. Not Katy.'

'Please yourself, lad. But it's true.' She was not unsympathetic, but it had to be said.

Ted's face was a mixture of incredulity and despair. If he couldn't have Katy what was there left for him? No work, no prospects, no Katy. Damn, damn, damn not having a job. He might as well clear out of this God-damned hole. What had he to offer her? More than that Derby wet, surely? But not what she wanted. A start! That's what she wanted. He felt like jumping over the counter to shake Mary Ann out of what he assumed was complacency. 'I won't let her marry him. It can't be true,' he shouted angrily as he banged the door on his way out. 'It can't be.'

How Mary Ann wished that it wasn't. Walter had paid two weeks' rent in advance for the house next door to hers, though. And then there were the fifteen sovereigns. It was true all right!

Mary Ann had a few sovereigns tucked away herself, safe in a bank book Raish must never see: if he knew he would squander the lot. She often dreamed of investing it in something worthwhile for her children, when she had enough saved. She had an idea or two.

Early that morning she had stood in the dark back yard to

15

see her two youngest off. It was Ben's first day. The lads had five miles to trudge to Conduit Colliery before the day's shift. Seeing Ben's downcast face it had been tempting to say 'You needn't go, lad.' But all she said was 'You will have to hurry, you two.'

'Don't worry about him.' Paul, sturdy and strong, with muscles like a man, squared his shoulders. 'I'll keep an eye on him,' he promised from the heights of two extra years.

'See you tonight, Mam.' Ben's voice was sulky as he trailed reluctantly behind his brother. Their heavy pit boots echoed on the grey yard as they disappeared into the gloom. Poor Ben, only thirteen and no choice but the pit. But he had Paul, she consoled herself. Paul would look after him, in spite of their frequent heated arguments. Their tall figures merged into one, the blond head exactly level with the younger darker one.

She switched her mind to Lawson's Sale. How she wished she could be there with Katy, pitting her wits against the other bidders.

Everything about the imposing house facing Pelsall Common was four-square, its red brick walls, its wide windows and solid oak doors, the wood-block floor of the hall which Katy stepped into with such lively interest.

The house breathed Josiah Lawson. A big four-square man he had been, whose great bulk had dwarfed her mother's shop when he came to buy his thick winter underwear. Somewhere there must be mounds of unworn flannel ganzies and long woollen underpants, Katy reflected with a grin. He had not lived nearly long enough to wear out all those Mary Ann had insisted he needed. He had had a soft spot for Mary Ann, while she admired the man who had started with nothing and finished up with a couple of prosperous iron foundries.

Now Josiah Lawson was dead, his only son in London

16

wanted none of this, and other well-fed industrialists from surrounding towns assessed the heavy silverware, the dumpy leather armchairs and the huge, highly polished dining table. Katy had an impish vision of Josiah seated all alone at the enormous square table eating thick square beefsteaks from thick square plates, a fantasy immediately suppressed as she caught sight of exquisitely dainty china displayed on a wedge-shaped sideboard, the more priceless pieces safely behind the bevelled glass of a magnificent cabinet.

The dining room was packed with men, some of them gazing critically at the pictures in which Josiah Lawson had invested a considerable amount of his money.

Ugly pictures, thought Katy, standing well back to study them, stags, battles and ruined monasteries. Only one appealed to her: giant seas pounding against craggy rocks. What must it be like, she wondered, to gaze on such a sea, to taste the spray, to hear the thunder of the waves as they surged on to ancient granite.

'No use, Katy,' she admonished herself wryly. 'You will have to settle for Billy Button's Brook.'

The curiosity in her bright eyes, the firm chin, the dimples deepening as she smiled, made more than one connoisseur pause to appraise the tiny figure, dressed in cornflower blue from head to toe, the only woman in the room.

What fun it was to be here, decked out in the Sunday best outfit she had made, its long skirt slightly swirling at the hem, the nipped-in jacket with tiny covered buttons showing off her slim waist, her golden curls accentuated by the blue velvet creation she had produced from a scrap of material from one of her mother's bundles fetched from the rag market in Birmingham. How her mother would have loved to be here in her place with fifteen sovereigns to spend.

'The monied folk will be bidding for the silver and the pictures, my girl,' she had advised last night. 'They won't

17

be after the things you need, so you should get some bargains. A nice table and chairs, some bedsteads and bed linen. Look out for the curtains: Josiah Lawson only bought the best. One pair will cut up to curtain your whole house.' Mary Ann had produced four half-crowns from the depths of the pocket stitched inside her skirt. 'Any pillows or towels you don't need for yourself, will you bring for the shop?' How proud she would be to tell her customers they came from Lawson's.

Well, there was nothing in this room that would fit into the little house Katy had to furnish next door to her mother's. Just one of Josiah's leather armchairs would swamp it.

She consulted the catalogue she had exchanged for a penny at the door as she crossed the hall into a rectangular drawing room, big enough to house the Wesleyan school-room with some to spare. The auctioneer's rostrum had been set up at the far end of the room and it was here that most of the furniture from the rest of the house was assembled.

Velvet curtains in rich shades of gold, red and green were piled high on one of the trestle tables together with linen of all descriptions. Katy fingered the lustrous material, appreciating its superb quality. Mary Ann was right; one pair would curtain the whole house, with some to spare for cushions.

Tiny enough to squeeze through the rows of tightly packed furniture, she began to mark her catalogue in the way of more experienced bidders: armchairs, bedroom drawers, kitchen chairs, table, wash-stand, bedsteads, rugs; all from the maids' rooms; plus a pair of velvet curtains. She would bid for the dark red ones. Walter's fifteen sovereigns should stretch to all of that.

It was hot inside and the auction did not begin until noon. There was time to slip out through the gate that led on to the common. She breathed deeply of the cool air before reaching into her blue bag where Mary Ann had packed some refreshments.

As she ate she reflected on the women she had seen standing just inside the drawing room, people whose dresses she made, mainly waiting about for their husbands. One or two had called hello in a friendly manner, but most had given her a haughty, barely perceptible nod. It would not do to be seen to be too familiar with a little dressmaker, as neat and pretty as she was. You could not be too careful when your husband was a successful factory owner or pit manager, or an up-and-coming councillor.

Why was it they put on airs just because they had made a bit of money, Katy wondered, as she sank her small teeth into delicious bread and dripping. Her best friend, Sally Dilkes, could buy out the lot of them, yet she didn't put on airs and graces. Outspoken and headstrong she might be, but not stuck-up. How daft they were.

There was still some time to spare when, having drunk some of Mary Ann's home-made dandelion pop and wiped her hands on a piece of clean linen, she wandered back into the big square house.

Most of the valuables were in the dining room and that is where the first part of the sale was to be conducted. Her mother would have loved to have watched and listened and learned, but for Katy it was an opportunity to explore the rest of the house. You had to take the day, and she would never have a chance to do this again.

Another door off the hall led into a quiet, oak-panelled room with lots of bookshelves. It was smaller and cosier than the other rooms with a welcoming feel to it despite the fact that it was completely empty save for a piano in the far corner. Its highly polished walnut gleamed like a mirror, boasting brass candlesticks that shone like gold. It was lovely.

Katy had seen some big ugly pianos in houses she had visited to measure customers. She had also seen some pretty ones, but never one like this. She touched it gently as if it might break like the delicate porcelain in the dining-room cabinet. It was warm and glossy beneath her fingers.

'Like it, do you, m'dear?'

Katy hardly glanced up at the elderly gent with the goatee beard who had bustled into the room, although she instantly recognized him as one of the auctioneers.

'It's beautiful,' she breathed, totally engrossed.

The man spoke rapidly. 'I knew Josiah had a piano some-where. I wondered where it was.' He sighed. 'Not even in the catalogue! You can't trust these youngsters nowadays.'

'It's going to be auctioned? This piano?'

He nodded.

Katy prickled with excitement as she imagined the piano lying against the wall of her living room, dancing firelight reflected in its shining brass candlesticks. She pictured one of her children perched on the tapestry-covered music stool, fingers flying expertly over the keys while the rest of the family sat enrapt, enchanted with the young genius in their midst. Maybe there would be other times when they all gathered round the piano singing lustily.

'How much do you think it will fetch?'

'Twenty five, thirty . . . '

'*Pounds?*'

''Fraid so. A Steinway – a bargain at that.'

Katy smiled appealingly at the auctioneer. 'Will you play for me? Please?' She was certain that he could.

The old man seated himself comfortably before running his fingers melodiously over the buttermilk keys. 'A bit of Chopin I am fond of,' he explained. He was soon lost in the music while Katy watched and listened, hardly daring to breathe, her eyes aglow with admiration, as the lovely music brought the room to life.

'That was wonderful. Thank you,' she said when the auctioneer finally stood up, shutting the piano as he did so.

'Do you play?'

20

She shook her head.

'Then . . . why?'

'One day I shall have children who will play.'

'Oh, you are sure about that, are you?'

'I am sure.'

'Psychic, are you?'

'You have to think positively.'

Such an impish smile. The man sighed. Oh to be young and as sure about life as this.

Katy was thinking rapidly. She realized she may end up with nothing if she did not get the piano. She hesitated only for a moment. She must think positively. 'What time will it be auctioned?' she asked.

'Right at the end, I would think,' replied the auctioneer, business-like again. 'I had better find someone to move it into the auction room.'

The choice items in the dining room were being auctioned now. After that the well-to-do people would gradually drift away, leaving folk like herself looking for bargains, plus maybe the odd dealer who had to sell again. Perhaps, right at the end, she just *might* . . .

'I have fifteen pounds,' she said frankly.

The auctioneer shook his head. 'Not a chance, my dear.'

'Couldn't you leave it here for a while longer?' she pleaded. 'It doesn't have to be moved immediately, does it? If people don't see it they will spend their money on something else.'

'We're in this for the commission, young lady.'

'Oh please! Just for an hour or so? It's the loveliest thing I am ever likely to own – in my whole life.'

He studied her flushed, eager face quietly. You did not have to be a sentimentalist in this game. But, oh well, he would be packing it in soon anyway, leaving it to those young fools who could not even produce an accurate catalogue.

'Very well. For an hour or so.'

She had to set her face against the rich velvet curtains, of course, against the tables, the sets of drawers, the rugs and the bedsteads, all of which proved to be bargains, as Mary Ann had forecast.

She did so want that piano.

If she got it what would they say. Mary Ann? And Walter, how about him? She almost faltered. Then chin up, squaring her small shoulders in true Brookie fashion, she began to think positively again.

After leaving Mary Ann, Ben continued to drag his feet, scowling heavily into the morning blackness. He relapsed into his broadest Cod-End slang, as always when bad tempered. 'Wish we 'adn't gotta goo. Wish ah'd never gotta see down a bloody pit.'

'Oh, hark at you! I've been nearly three years down. It's not so bad.'

'That ain't what ah've heard. When yoh think o' them Dilkes's and Lawsons, and the like, how they live, while Cod-Enders 'ave to sweat their guts out to scratch a livin', it meks yer sick. Apart from me Dad, o' course. He don't sweat, does he?'

'You don't know how lucky you are to have a job to go to. It wasn't easy to get it for you.'

'Couldn't it 'ave bin a bit nearer? What's wrong with The Grove, or Little Wyrley, or Stubbers Green? There's pits all round us. Why did you 'ave to pick on Conduit?'

'Because there's always work at Conduit, that's why. The others are shut half the time. Come on, I'll race you to the school gate.'

Paul knew that his brother, with his long athletic body, would win, and it would put him in a better frame of mind. They raced over the common, nearly eighty acres of which separated Heath End from its rival Pelsall, their snap bags bouncing on their shoulders, passing the vicarage and the station to their right.

After a mile Ben threw himself triumphantly against the locked iron gates of the Wesleyan school playground, pausing for a minute to draw breath, his face pressed to the railings. Little could be seen in the early morning gloom except the rectangular shape of the dark school building.

'Wish you were goin' there today instead, do you, Ben?'

'Oh, gerroff. Yoh know I doh. If yer a Cod-Ender yer a nuthin' in theer. Furthest away from the fire in winter, that's all. I got the cane the day I started. Fancy canin' a little kid 'cus 'is 'ands are dirty! The next day the cane for bein' a minute late. Ar, an' nearly every day after that. If I dain't do anythin' they'd find summat.'

'They didn't have far to look neither,' grinned Paul.

Ben gave the gate a good kick before they continued, passed the Pelsall shops and the neat Pelsall houses standing back from the road, where people still slept. Further on, Willenas Common, which led to the canal along which they would walk nearly all the way to Conduit Colliery.

'There was always a bit of fun on Friday nights, after school though, eh, Ben?'

'Oo, ar! Them fights with the Churchie Bulldogs! We Wesley Spiders gid 'em wot for.'

It was a source of irritation to the Wesleyans that Church of England pupils were allowed to play on the green grass of the common at dinner times, while they had to make do with a playground no bigger than a fowl pen, so after the teachers had hurried home for their weekends, war was declared.

Memories of Friday victories perked Ben up no end. They shouted cheery greetings to the bargemen who were making slow treks along the canal, their long boats loaded with coal or timber. Sometimes the lads caught the appetising smell of frying bacon as they passed, almost too much to bear, after their own hurried breakfast of milk sop. They broke into a run, hurdling the arms of the lock gates at full speed, a

23

startling pastime in the gloom of early morning, which had once landed Paul into the canal.

Paul voiced the niggling anxiety he felt every morning. 'Wouldn't it be awful to turn up to see the last cage going down without us? It would mean the sack.'

'Before I'd even started? No such luck!'

'You'll be all right, our kid. It's interesting work, down the pit, and you'll meet some grand mates.' Paul understood how his brother was feeling. He had started the day after leaving school, a day indelibly printed on his mind for ever. He remembered the first time in the cage when his stomach jerked upwards as the rest of his body shot down; he remembered the bump at the bottom, the thump of his heart as he fearfully stepped out of the cage into the all-enveloping blackness. He could feel now the excitement as he received his lamp. The fireman lit it and then blew it to make sure it was safe; Paul had thought he was blowing it out again. He was directed along the rails with a man called a dogey. Sometimes he stumbled; it was hard to see with such a small light, but he soon got used to it.

He had to couple up the tubs as the drivers brought them up filled with coal. Every six tubs he had to put a rope on them, ring them up as they went to what they called the bottom, to await their journey to the pit head. He also had to return empty tubs to the men working in the back, as it was known. It was warm work. When snap time came he had already drunk all his water and the mice had eaten his snap, but his new mates shared theirs with him: they were a grand lot. That first day his arms and shoulders had ached as they never had, before or since, his hands bled, his lips cracked with dryness.

It was all worth while when he received his first pay packet, five shillings and ninepence, the same as Ben would get at the end of next week. He could not get home quickly enough to present it proudly to his mother. The ninepence she gave him back jingled in his pocket like a fortune.

'You will be five and ninepence better off next week,' he reminded Ben now.

'How do you make that out? Ninepence it'll be, won't it? Me Mother'll keep five bob.'

'Why shouldn't she? She works harder than any of us,' Paul bristled. 'She's the one who has kept you for thirteen years. Don't ever forget it, our Ben.'

'S'pose so,' agreed Ben grudgingly. 'Never 'ad as much as a Saturday penny off 'im, though, 'ave we? He's chucked it about to other kids. Playin' the Dutch Uncle. He was in a right mood again last night. Rantin' at me Mam 'cos 'e said 'is dinner was scalding.'

'That was before he winged it at the wall, and she had to cook him another one,' commented Paul drily.

'I 'ate the sight of 'im. I wouldn't even go to 'is funeral.'

'Don't talk like that. He is your Dad after all.'

'Me Dad? Me *Dad*?' Ben spat out the words bitterly. 'Wish he was somebody else's.' He picked up half a brick and flung it as far as he could before continuing. 'Do you remember, before our Edwin got married, me Dad put that red-hot poker in the fire? He said 'e was goin' to run it right through Edwin.'

'Shall I ever forget it! All because Mother had lent Edwin his white muffler.'

''E would 'ave done it an' all, if it 'adn't been for our Katy. Do you remember how she was pretending to sweep the floor?'

'Yes, and as Edwin came through the door she knocked the poker out of the old chap's hand with her broom. I think, just seeing her there, brandishing it over his head brought him to his senses.'

'What senses?' They both laughed as they recalled the tiny figure of their sister advancing fearlessly toward the father who towered above her.

'She's got pluck, our Katy.'

'What shall you do with your ninepence?' Paul asked, changing the subject.

'Well, I'm thinkin' of gettin' meself a pigeon or two.'

'Pigeons! Where would you keep them?'

'I thought I could use some of the fruit boxes that are lyin' about the yard, to make a pen.'

'We have to pay on those boxes. We get a credit on them.'

'Me Mam would let me have some, I know her would. Anyway, I could beg a bit of wood here and there. It would do for a start.'

'Pigeons need feeding.'

'Me Mam'll give me a bit o' the fowl's corn.'

'Relying a lot on your mother again, I see. It's doubtful if you'll buy one decent pigeon with ninepence.'

It was getting light and Paul could now see his brother's crestfallen face. 'Tell you what. I've always wanted a pigeon or two myself. I'll see what I've got and I might come in with you.'

Ben brightened up considerably. 'Probably get our money back in prizes, you know.'

'Hang on. Don't run before you can walk. Anyway we'll see what Mother says first. We don't want to give her any more expense, do we? She's got enough on her plate.'

They fell silent, Ben thinking of his pigeons, Paul pondering how he could earn more money to take to his mother. He wasn't getting much more than when he started, over two years ago. He had learned coupling and trimming and batting. At present he was pumping water out, a job nobody liked, getting his feet and legs wet through, on a promise that there would be a bit extra for him, but so far it had not materialized. How enviously he had watched the men on the coal face, longing for the day he could work the coal, as they did.

On the coal face they were paid so much a ton; a keen miner could take home as much as three pounds a week. But he needed a lot more experience before they would let him anywhere near it. It was true what he had told Ben. He liked the pit, and did not mind how hard he worked in order to get extra money. Rises came with birthdays and they did not come often enough.

Anyway, he was not learning much, pumping water out, was he? It was the bit of extra money they had promised him which had been the incentive.

They had reached Norton village and could let up a bit. Until now they had no means of knowing if they were early or late, as the only people they had met were the bargees, apart from a scruffy old tramp with a dog. Now familiar figures emerged from rows of blackened back-to-back houses which bordered both sides of the road leading to the colliery. None of the miners were hurrying, so Paul knew they were in good time.

'What a miserable 'ole this is,' remarked Ben. 'The folk all look the same. Not as lively as Cod Enders, are they?'

'Well, we get the fresh air from the common. Makes all the difference. We are in plenty of time, so I'm goin' in to the office to ask about that extra money they promised me. I've seen the fireman enough times about it.'

'They won't like that, will they, our kid?'

'They will have to lump it then. If I don't go now I can't hope to have it in my pay packet tomorrow. Nothin' lost for want o' tryin'. I'll see if Daddy Dale is in the office.'

Lawrence Dale, preacher and Heath End chapel superintendent, held quite an important post at the colliery. Nicknamed Daddy Dale for his fatherly interest in the young, he was always sympathetic to the needs of his flock. He held regular glasses in the chapel vestry for aspiring missionaries, not totally unaware that most of his young students were motivated by opportunities to travel, rather than a calling to spread the gospel.

Yes, Daddy Dale was Paul's best bet.

Wouldn't it be grand he thought, to be able to give his

mother extra cash tomorrow? To see her face light up as she counted it out. To surprise her. To hear her say 'Well done, my lad.' Yes, definitely worth making a stand for.

'You wait here for me, Ben.'

'I bet yer don't gerrit.'

Ben was right. Paul did not reach the office, for noticing a group of miners huddled dejectedly round a black board roughly hammered to a post, he joined them. As he read the message bouncing back from the board in thick white chalk his stomach tilted sickeningly like an unbalanced coal tub. There was no mistaking what the notice said: NO WORK TODAY.

The boot was on the opposite foot on the return journey from Conduit, Ben elated at his reprieve, Paul bitterly indignant and worried. The injustice of the notice rankled him. 'One day *I* shall be the one who decides whether a pit will be open or closed.'

'Oh, ar? When you're the pit manager, I reckon?'

'When I'm the owner.'

'What about them grand mates you was on about?'

'What about them?'

'Well, you'd be desertin' 'em, wouldn't yer? If yoh owned a pit they wouldn't be mates any more, would they?'

'Of course they would. They could come and work for me if they wanted.'

'But then they wouldn't be your *mates.*'

'Oh, stop arguing, and let's think how we can get a day's pay. We could try Bill Brown's coal wharf, just up the road here.'

'Do we 'ave to? We could get a good game 'o football on the common today.'

'And how much do you think that would bring in?' exploded Paul irritably. None of them realized how much their mother needed help. Edwin hardly ever came to see her these days, Katy's head was full of wedding bells, and Ben, well you couldn't exactly blame him; he was only a kid. It was up to himself to look after her.

There was a pile of coal to be bagged up at the coal wharf. They loaded the lorries, weighed up for the wheelbarrows standing in rows, hundredweights, halves and quarters, and sorted out some slack, a good half day for which they were paid sixpence each. Not bad.

They sat on the bank to eat their snap before calling at Five Ways Farm. There they earned only threepence apiece for a variety of jobs, but it was much more to Ben's liking, and the farmer's wife gave them each a big mug of cold milk with a piece of home-made seed cake.

'That's what I'd like to do regular,' said Ben as they rejoined the towpath. 'Farmin'.'

'Farming! You'd never be able to make enough to live on.'

'Money don't bother me.'

'Not until your belly's rumbling.'

'It wouldn't rumble if I owned the farm, would it?'

'*If* you owned it.'

'Well, I'll dream about ownin' a farm while you dream about ownin' a pit.'

Paul had to laugh at that. They jogged along, chiding each other, teasing, arguing, until suddenly Paul stood stock still. 'Do you see what I see?'

'Where?'

'There. Our old man's cart, up there on the bridge, parked outside The Colliers' Arms.'

They scrambled up the steep bank from the towpath to the road above. Sure enough, there was Raish's cart, filled with the morning's greengroceries, rabbits and fish rotting from exposure to the warmth of the day. They walked slowly round the cart.

'Why, he's hardly sold a thing!'

'He'll be after some money from our mother tonight, I reckon.'

Through the window of the public house they could see their father amongst other seasoned drinkers, his handsome face reddened with drink, his waistcoat and jacket lying upon the bar counter. With much ado he was unbuttoning his shirt.

'He's doin' 'is lily-white-skin act again.'

'I'm going in to fetch him,' Paul announced.

'Fetch 'im! He'll kill yer! He'll skin yer like a rabbit.'

'Chance would be a fine thing,' his brother replied drily.

Paul squared his strong shoulders. Today had made him just about as militant as it was possible for him to be. He felt he could tackle anything, today's easy jobs having taken no toll of his energy at all. He swung through the door of the public house, Ben hot on his heels.

Raish did not notice them immediately, so engrossed was he in boasting to the new barmaid leaning across the counter toward him. The lads recognized her immediately as Rose, the grand-daughter of Sarah, their mother's friend, with whom the girl had lived until going into service at thirteen. Their father's voice rang out clearly to the amusement of the other drinkers, although they had probably heard the patter often enough before.

'Run your hand down that, darling,' he was saying to Rose, baring his chest. 'How's that for lily-white skin? Not a blemish. You don't often have a chance to see that round here, do you?'

He whispered something in her ear which set her off giggling. About twenty she was, rich auburn hair framing a round saucy face. Her hands caressed his soft white shoulders and smooth wide chest, before running her fingers through his thick blond hair.

'Not bad,' she murmured. 'Not bad at all.'

'Like to see more? The pick o' the market?'

She giggled again. He was as handsome as they came, Horatio Brook; she had always thought so since living a few doors from him, as a schoolgirl. You wouldn't credit that

30

he was in his late forties, probably getting on for fifty. It was through him she had got this job. He had been good to her.

She was the first to notice the lads advancing. 'Well! Just look what the wind's blown in! Are you two old enough . . . ' Something in Paul's face silenced her.

He could feel the bile in his mouth as he watched the girl fingering the glass of port his father had bought her. He thought of how much it had cost his mother to equip the cart outside with the fish and the rabbits going bad.

Raish, following the girl's eyes, turned round. 'What the hell are you doing here? Get out.'

'We have come to take you home, Dad.'

Raish stood open mouthed and speechless for a few seconds before bellowing 'You have *what*?'

'Come to take you home,' Paul repeated quietly.

He was aware of the complete silence that descended on the room.

His father turned back to pick up his whiskey from the bar counter. 'You had better clear off while you still can,' he threatened, his back toward them.

'You've got enough whiskies inside you already, Dad.'

'Oh, I have, have I? Well, open your mouth. Here is one for you.' Raish turned quickly and threw the drink into Paul's face, the fiery liquid splashing his eyes and trickling down his cheeks. The silence in the bar was terminated by loud guffaws.

'Good shot, Brookie.'

'What a bloody waste of good whiskey.'

'Now clear off, Mother's darling,' Raish sneered. 'Go and ask her to wipe your face for you. And your bum.'

'We are taking the horse and cart. Do you want a lift, or don't you?'

'You as much as touch that cart and I shall thrash you within one inch of your life.' Raish's face was twisted with rage, as he swayed toward them.

31

Ben quiet until now, but wildly excited, lifted his fists. 'There's two of us to reckon with.'

'Two of *you*! Another of her little darlings. Two of *you*!' He spat in cold contempt.

'Are you coming, Dad?'

'Bugger off.'

'Put your fists down, Ben and come on.'

A click of the reins to the surprised horse and they were away. The last they saw as they drove off was their father, his white skin gleaming through the open shirt, shaking his fists and bawling after them, while they laughed aloud with pent-up excitement. At last they had stood up to him and it did not matter what happened next. They were elated for different reasons, Paul because he felt he had scored one for his mother, Ben because they had scored against the father he hated so much.

The out-of-work miners had begun to drift homewards, heads down, hands deep in their pockets, their bellies calling. Wonder what they will get tonight, Mary Ann thought with a sigh. A bit of scrag end if they were lucky. More likely to be bread in cold tea.

She bustled into the living room at the back of the shop which they called the kitchen. There was just enough space for the scrubbed table, chairs tucked beneath it, a wooden armchair and Katy's treadle machine, with the box of sewing on the floor at its side. It was a dark tiny room. A dispute between two rival landowners had resulted in a wall as high as the houses being built less than two feet from the window.

Four doors led out of it. One into the shop, one directly to the yard outside, a narrow one to the stairs, and an even narrower one in the corner, by the black-lead grate. This opened into what they called 'the bogey hole', a triangular storeroom about five feet long, which, at the other end, led into a one-up-one-down cottage, Little Cott, sublet at two shillings a week to a young couple with a baby. Mary Ann had hoped Edwin would have it when he married, but he said it was too near to his Dad. They never used the door from the bogey hole to Little Cott, of course. If they wanted to see Jane and Joe they went to their front door, in the street.

From the oven of the gleaming black grate she lifted a pot bulging with rabbit and vegetables, pushing the huge iron kettle nearer to the fire, to make room on the hob for the stew. How the lads would relish it after their footslog from Conduit; Katy, too, if she were not too excited with her purchases.

Next she hurried along the grey slated yard to fetch coal. On her way to the brewhouse, or 'brewus', as Cod-Enders termed it, she could not resist a peep inside the house next door where Katy and Walter would live after they were married.

She stepped into a room larger than her own kitchen, and lighter due to the extra side window overlooking the generous strip of land which went with the houses, the rough vegetable patch, a couple of empty pig sties beyond and, in the far corner, an old stable where they kept the horse.

How homely this room would look curtained with Lawson's luxurious velvet, a comfortable armchair each side of the fireplace, maybe a gleaming mahogany table and chairs, with sideboard to match, and Katy's treadle fitting snugly beneath the window.

She was aroused from reverie by the voice of her old friend. 'Ah, there y'are, Mary Ann. Ah've bin knockin' and shoutin'. Your geese are marchin' down the road like a regiment of soldiers.'

'They'll find their way, Sarah.' Each morning Mary Ann drove them to the pool on the common but they brought themselves home. Folk said you could always tell Brookie's geese; they walked so high and mighty, like he did.

Sarah's enquiring gaze swept round the empty room, noting the recently-scrubbed quarry floor, the glistening windows, the shiny grate. 'It's right what I've heard then? Katy's havin' this house?'

Mary Ann smiled at the woman who had been so kind to her, befriending her when she first came to Heath End. A bit untidy in dress, sometimes too outspoken, she was also warm hearted and amiable; lonely since her Jacob died and her grand-daughter Rose had left home. 'You go and sit by the fire while I fetch some coal, Sarah.'

There was a pile of allowance coal in the corner of the brewhouse, opposite a brick boiler with fire basket beneath and a wooden dolly tub and mangle. At a time when most Cod-Enders had to share an outside tap, sometimes with as many as a dozen neighbours, they regarded their own cold tap over an iron sink as a luxury.

Sarah was toasting her toes in the hearth. She returned at once to the subject of the house. 'Four shillings a week I hear they're askin' for next door.'

'Four-and-sixpence. The extra because I am setting up a little shop for her in the front room.'

'Two shops next door to one another!'

'Why not? I am a bit stuck for space, Sarah. Katy will take over the sweets; it will give me more room to breathe.'

Sarah put her head to one side and tutted. 'That's your story, Mary Ann. Setting up your Katy in business, an' you havin' a job to meet your bills, what with folk that won't pay up, and that husband of your'n!' She paused. 'I hope she appreciates it.'

'She does. She's a good girl.'

'Well, give me two ounce o' tea, duck, and I'll be off.' She sniffed appreciatively. Mary Ann kept a good table. 'That stew smells good.'

'You must take some, Sarah.' Mary Ann filled a jug, wrapping it up in a cloth to keep it warm.

'I could a' sworn I heard your Ben's voice.'

'Too early for my lads.'

'These are somebody else's then, are they?' Sarah called from the yard. 'Yer wouldn't think you pair had walked from Conduit, by the look on yer.'

'Perhaps that's because we haven't. Tell them, Ben, while I see to the horse and bury the rotten fish.'

'The horse!' Their mother ran out into the yard, startled. 'Your dad, then? He's here?'

'Me Dad? What 'ave you done with me Dad, our Paul?'

'Was that him floating down the cut?'

'Float! 'E wouldn't float, with all that booze inside 'im.'

'I'm sure this tale is worth 'earin'. But later on, ducks. Ta ra.' Sarah shuffled away, clutching her jug of rabbit stew and the two ounces of tea.

Mary Ann followed Ben into the kitchen. Never had she heard him laugh so unrestrainedly. Ben was the one who laughed the least. He bore Raish a grudge so big that somehow it seemed to envelop the whole world. Yet he laughed now until tears left narrow streaks on his dusty cheeks.

'Mother, you should 'ave seen his face when we clip-clopped off! There he was, with 'is shirt 'anging out of 'is trousers, 'is mouth wide open. He'll kill the bloody lot of us.'

Choked with apprehension she whispered, 'What have you done?'

Ben was still rolling about laughing when Paul returned. 'You tell 'er, our kid.'

Paul's face was filled with concern for her. He was remembering they had not done their shift at the same moment that she realized the dust on their faces was not pit grime, the black grime that clogged pores and darkened Paul's blond mop.

'There was no work?'

Paul shook his head miserably.

'Tell me what happened.'

They told their story, leaving out the bit about the fuss Rose made of Raish.

'I asked him to come home, Mother. He said "Bugger off." '

'So that's what we did. Buggered off,' hooted Ben, still insensitive to the fear in her eyes. 'Bellowin' like a bull, worn't he, our kid? And that 'orse! 'E stopped at every single pub on the way home.'

'I wonder how he will be tonight,' Mary Ann murmured apprehensively, more to herself than to them.

'He'll be sobered up, never you fear, by the time he's walked from The Colliers' Arms,' Paul reassured her. 'Now don't worry. Katy and me, we'll handle him. By the way, where is she?'

'Auctioned off at Lawson's Sale by now, I shouldn't wonder,' replied Mary Ann drily, just as the door opened.

'Not me. I was too expensive for them.' Katy bustled in with two parcels. 'What are you all in the dark for? Let's have some light on the scene.'

She reached to the high mantelshelf for a paper spill from the cocoa tin she had covered in brown chenille. The lamps, on table and window-ledge, flickered light into the room, highlighting Katy's pert face, her bright eyes dancing, the dimples deep in her cheeks. Mary Ann felt better just by looking at her.

'Bed linen for the shop, Mother,' she said, handing over the larger parcel, and slipping the other into the bogey hole.

Brisk and business-like she bundled the lads off to the brewhouse, armed with a jug of hot water and hessian towels. 'Hurry up, the pair of you. The stew smells good, and I'm hungry.' She hummed as she swiftly laid the cloth and cutlery for their meal, before tripping upstairs to change the best blue outfit for her brown week-day dress.

Mary Ann ached to know what she had bought from the auction but there was a rush of customers, as was usual at this time of day. Mothers ran about for sons going courting, or for husbands off to public houses. They wanted new stiff collars, studs, cuff links, mufflers, darning-wool, shoe polish. They bought paraffin to light up the oil lamps and penny packets of cocoa as a treat for themselves and the children after the men had gone out for the night.

Katy served the meal from the stewpot, sitting down to eat hers with her brothers. She chuckled as they retold their story, embellishing it more dramatically this time, Paul baring his chest, declaring 'How's this for lily-white skin. I'm the pick of the market and I challenge the trade.' It was Raish's catch-phrase and Katy laughed as much as the lads.

'Now, Mother, see the funny side of it,' she coaxed, as Mary Ann returned to the kitchen with a worried look. 'Wouldn't you have loved to behold his face when they rode off? I bet it's the longest walk he's had for some time. He will visit every pub on the way home, of course.'

'I know that. It's tonight I'm worried about, my girl.'

'Don't worry. The lads are bigger now. He can't knock them about like he's done in the past.'

'That's right, Mother. You go and sleep at Sarah's. Leave Dad to us.'

'To you? I can't leave him to you.'

'Why not?' demanded Katy. 'Do him the world of good to find you gone. We'll handle him between us.'

She was such a tiny girl and Raish such a big man, yet as she squared her shoulders and lifted her chin she looked more like him than she knew. Katy had never been scared of him like the others had. So maybe she *could* handle him.

Mary Ann voiced the question she had been asking herself all day. 'What did you buy, Katy?'

Katy tried to suppress the excitement in her face as she replied calmly, 'I bought a piano.'

'A piano! But you can't play.'

'I can learn if I want to. Anyway, I'll have children who will play. Wait until you see it, Mother.'

'I don't know what Walter will say, my girl.'

'Well, let's find out. Here he is.'

Walter, pale and slight, his sandy hair already starting to recede, had come in so quietly that Mary Ann, her back to the outside door, had not known. She could barely hear his whispered 'Evenin', Mrs Brook,' as he sat down, screwing down his shoulders as if he wanted to disappear.

'You'll never guess what our Katy 'as got from the sale, Walter, for settin' up 'ome.'

'I know what she's bought, Ben.'

'Gerroff. Yer doh.'

Walter studied the cloth cap on his knee, as if to extract from it strength to make a speech.

'I was cycling behind a couple of chaps and I heard one of them say: "That Katy Brook had the best bargain at Lawson's today. Bit o' good bidding that was. Right at the end o' the sale when everybody else had spent out." He said you bought a piano, Katy?'

'I did. You'll love it, Walter.'

Walter was so proud of Katy. She was the prettiest girl he had ever seen. He could not believe his luck when she said she would marry him. He would trust her with every penny he possessed. 'If you like it,' he stated quietly, 'I shall like it.'

After a pause for reflection, and perhaps prompted by the incredulous expressions on the faces of Katy's brothers and her mother, he said, 'What else did you buy, Katy?'

'Nothing worth mentioning.'

'Oh, Katy! You spent the lot on a piano?' Mary Ann gasped.

'The lot.'

They all gazed at Walter, waiting for the explosion that never came. They were so used to Raish's tempestuous ravings if they wasted a penny, although *he* could waste as much as he liked. Walter merely paled a little paler and pushed himself further down into the hard chair.

'Fifteen pounds! What are you going to eat off, my girl?

The piano? Are you sleeping on it as well?'

'We shall need table and chairs and bedroom furniture, Katy,' ventured Walter hesitantly.

Katy broke into peals of laughter. 'Just look at your faces! Whatever is the matter with you all? Every house in Cod End has a bed, a table and chairs. Only ours will have a piano. Lawson's piano at that! I was lucky to get it.'

'To think I've wasted the day dreaming of velvet curtains and mahogany furniture! Katy, what have you done?'

'Mother, you said I could have the bed I'm sleeping on. Walter, your Annie has an old table in her brewhouse she wants out of the way; scrubbed and painted it will do fine. A couple of chairs from Dickinson's second-hand corner won't break us, will it? We'll make it nice, you'll see.'

She looked so joyful and young, the lamplight rippling the gold in her hair and she had such an infectious chuckle. What could they do but laugh with her?

'Walk up. Walk up. This way to see the Cod End piano. The only one of its kind,' intoned Paul. 'The *only* place to keep your rent book, your pipe and the fish that our old chap declines to sell. Easier than burying it.'

'Doubles up as a mirror,' put in Ben.

'Can be hired out for weddings and christenings.'

'Oh, I forgot,' said Katy. 'They threw in six rolls of very posh wallpaper that were unsold. I've brought it with me. I thought you two could fetch the piano for me tomorrow.' She laughed. 'You can take the cart, seeing that it's yours now. Finders keepers, they say, don't they?' The wallpaper, brought out from the bogey hold to be admired, was very grand, dark red, flecked with velvet, exactly as Mary Ann had imagined the curtains might be. 'We'll go and paste it on now, Walter, if you like.' Katy gathered up the rolls of wallpaper, thrusting them into Walter's arms as she reached for the scissors. He followed her meekly from the room. In a second she was back, putting her head round the door. 'Now, remember, mother,' she emphasized, 'do

39

not worry. Go to Sarah's. I'll be back before the pick o' the market comes home.'

Mary Ann sighed. A piano! So out of character with her practical daughter.

'What a wet rag that Walter is,' Ben burst out. 'I know what I'd have said if Katy 'ad spent all my savings on a piano.'

Mary Ann did not reprimand him; she was thinking much the same herself. That Walter! However would he cope?

CHAPTER

2

THEY HEARD HIM from half a mile up the road, the occupants of the red brick, back-to-back houses, unimaginatively called Double Row, that snaked interminably from the end of the common to Heath End Square, separated from the outdoor beer licence by one square, distinguished-looking detached house, incongruously out of place among the smaller dwellings. Brookie was on the warpath again. Those on early shift cursed him for the noise he was making.

Others, not yet abed, parted their curtains to watch him weaving along, his bowler hat set unusually square, his cock o' the north gait much in evidence, in spite of his drunkenness. They thought the moonlight was playing tricks with them. Not that his drunkenness was anything of a surprise - they had often seen him worse - but tonight there was something missing.

'Where's your 'oss, Brookie?' shouted one wit from his bedroom window. 'In clink for being drunk and disorderly?'

41

'Mary Ann, where are you?' Raish was proclaiming in his town crier voice, not to be diverted. It was a cultured voice, even in the thickness of drink, definitely not Cod End vintage. 'Be ready for me, Mary Ann. I'm going to kill those sons of yours tonight. Have the door open for me m'lady. I've a lesson to teach them without delay. Open the door ready for me.'

He was still bellowing 'Open the door!' as he swerved along the grey slate yard. But the door was shut. Shut, not locked. No one would dare lock him out. But the door was shut, and the house as still as a grave, not a light to aid him.

He entered with a great clatter and cursing, heaving himself to the bottom of the stairs, banging the stair door noisily.

Peering through the gloom he let out a thunderous yell. 'Polly!' She was Mary Ann when he spoke of her outside but here she was Polly. 'Polly!'

Nothing stirred.

He swayed for a moment on the bottom stair. 'Where are the buggers? I want to see *you* first, Polly. You have some explaining to do. Why didn't you send them back for me, my lady? It's *you* I want to see first, Polly. And then,' emphasizing each word separately, '*them young buggers*. I'm fetching me strap off. They're for it tonight.'

Two bedrooms led off either side of the narrow landing, the room he shared with Mary Ann, and the room for the lads. The moonlight showed them both empty. That just left Katy's room. He crossed to the far corner of the lads' room, to where narrow steps led to the attic.

'Polly! Come down here. I know you're there, with Katy. I want you here!'

No sound. Just an expectant stillness.

'Right! If you are not coming down then I am coming up.'

That produced an instant scuffling. A light from a flickering candle showed him his daughter, a tiny figure in a long

42

white nightgown, standing on top of the narrow steps, the moonlight glinting through the attic roof behind her. 'My mother's not here,' Katy said calmly, holding the candle aloft.

Raish reduced his voice to a dramatic whisper, gradually increasing it to a powerful crescendo. 'Not there, eh, my beauty? Not there, eh? Well, I know *she is*. Those other buggers of hers are there, too. I know you are there, Polly. I am coming up to get you. Move over, girl.'

Two shadows materialized behind Katy.

'Don't you touch our Katy.'

'Is that Paulie in the little short shirt?' Raish sneered. 'Just the man I am after.'

'You put one foot on those steps, Dad, and you'll get the contents of this.' Paul's heart was lurching like a weather-cock in a strong wind, but he held aloft the water jug from his sister's bedroom, continuing quietly, 'It's full. And it's cold.'

'An' ah've gorra kettle full of hot.'

'*Ah've! Gorra!* You common little Cod End kid, Benjamin.'

'*I have* a chamber pot, Dad,' put in Katy. 'It's not tap water in it, either.'

'Why, you dirty little . . . '

He lurched toward them.

Paul ran down a couple of steps; he did not want to miss. 'I warned you, Dad. Here it comes.' A cascade of icy water fell with full force on Raish's hot angry face, soaking his shoulders through his jacket and shirt. The contents of the kettle followed. Raish flinched himself against what he thought would be hot water, but that too was icy cold. It took his breath away. This was ridiculous. His own kids. Who did they think they were playing with. He lurched toward them again, incensed and threatening.

'Throw the jerry, Katy.'

In astonishment he saw Katy advancing with the chamber

43

pot. He backed away so suddenly that he tripped and fell. Hoots of boyish laughter above him sobered and incensed him at the same time. He picked himself up, roaring like a bull, only to meet the chamber pot full in the face. Not only the contents this time, but the pot as well. It crashed around him in a thousand pieces. He felt a trickle of warm blood ooze down his face.

Enraged, he heaved himself up the first two steps, only to be halted by Paul shouting, 'Get to the window, Ben. Quick.'

And Katy, ice cool, with the voice of a stranger, warned, 'I wouldn't come any further if I were you, Dad. Policeman Millard is just below the window, waiting for Ben to wave a signal and he'll be up.'

'You would do that, would you, girl?'

'I would, Dad. You are not touching us.'

'And you're not touching our Mother, ever again,' Paul added.

'Oh, it's the mother's bloody favourite, is it? The horse stealer. Paulie. Well, just you wait, my lad.'

But Raish, kicking through broken pottery, backed slowly downstairs into the kitchen. Very wet. Very sober.

He poked wildly at the raker in the firegrate and wild sparks shot out, throwing arrows of light. He lit the lamp on the table.

'I wonder if Bobby Millard is out there,' he muttered, 'or if our Katy just made that up.'

He peered through the front window of the shop to where the lamp glowed in the village square. Sure enough, there stood Policeman Millard watching the attic window. They had really prepared themselves tonight, hadn't they? He did not want Millard in on this.

Returning to the kitchen he reached for the mirror which Katy kept beside her sewing machine for her customers' use, anxious to see if they had marked him. Just a nick on the cheek. He had fine healing skin; it would soon be gone.

Could have been nasty, though. Fancy, Katy of all people!

He stripped off his clothes, filled an enamel bowl from the bogey hole with hot water from the black kettle, and sponged all over with a soapy flannel. As he rubbed himself down with the warm length of clean hessian draped over the line beneath the mantelshelf he admired his lily-white skin, as always. As smooth as a baby's it was. Not a blemish. Putting on his trousers he sat in front of the fire, now spitting angrily from its disturbance.

Those kids! They were growing up. They were ganging up. And Polly was not there. He knew now that Polly was not there because she would not have allowed them to do what they did. Where was she, he wondered? Unlike her not to be here to face the music.

His own kids! Not that he had ever cared a fig about the lads. But Katy, she was different.

He gazed into the fire, thinking back. Smart and successful he had been, a counter skipper in a big Birmingham store, before he had come to Heath End with Polly. She had been maid to the owners, earning good money and all found. She had saved some and he had an urge to set up business on his own.

She was different then, tiny waisted, full busted, teasing and seductive. Pretty Polly, he had called her. She had loved him madly. Often were the times as the shop bell tinkled they were rolling about naked on the bed.

'Let it ring,' he would command if she made a move. He would pull the pins from her thick hair, letting it cascade round her shoulders. Sometimes he would gently tie her to him with it, knotting the thick long strands beneath his shoulders. He would order her to sit on her hair in front of the mirror while he admired her firm young body. His own, too, of course.

He cut a fine figure. She would not have found anyone more handsome, he told himself. She certainly would not have found anyone who could make love as expertly as he did. Or as often. Ah, but that was a different Polly, who lived only to indulge him. Pretty Polly.

Too soon there was a puny lad snivelling in corners, hiding away from him because he was scared. Needing his mother when Raish needed her. Calling for her when he took her upstairs. Edwin, of the wet nose and even wetter bum. Raish despised him from the start. He wondered how he had managed to spawn such a chit, with milksop mouth and weepy eyes. No wonder Cod End kids soon named him Jelly-belly. For a jelly he was and no mistake. He shook like one.

Then Polly was expecting again. This time it was a girl. A girl about as different from Jelly-belly as chalk is from cheese. A girl with frank, fearless eyes, deeply blue, edged with grey. A girl with skin as flawless as his own, who would climb into his lap, snuggle into his shoulder, entwining her arms round his neck. A girl who did not cry for her mother. She took Jelly-belly in hand and saw to it that he did not cry either. A proper little mother to him she was. Eleven months younger than Edwin, she wiped his nose, fed him, helped him to dress, entertained him by dancing on the table.

Even as a tiny child she tripped into the shop to answer the ever-tinkling bell when Raish and Polly were otherwise engaged. She stood on a stool to reach things from the shelves, or charmed the customers into reaching them for her. She knew how many shillings made five, and how many pennies in a shilling, that child. He had taught her himself before she could read, and she could do that at four years old. If only all his children had been as sharp! But the lads were only good for the pits, the fools. None of them sober could add up as fast as he could drunk.

Yes, Katy had fussed him, humoured him, even loved him. And tonight, a tiny figure in a white nightgown, she had winged a jerry at his head. She was the best man among

46

them; the only one with any spunk. Neither of the lads could have done it without her.

Yet they had taken the horse and cart today, he reminded himself, his inside writhing as he remembered the guffaws and sarcasm he had suffered at the inn. Despite the taunts he had thrown at Paul he knew he was no mother's baby. He was a tough nut. Ben was growing fast too. Yes, they were ganging up on him.

What with the humiliation at the inn and now this! It would be all round Cod End tomorrow, Brookie getting soaked in a unique way. There was nothing for him here now. Polly had turned against him, that was for sure. How she had changed since the early days. She had hardened. He tried to remember how it had happened.

She had never been quite the same since that affair with the Lady Violet at The Hall. Yet look at the business it had brought in! Fruit, flowers, groceries, he supplied them for all the social occasions, big and small. It was not his fault, was it, that Lady Violet demanded something more than provisions, between her scented sheets, or in secluded corners of the Estate on summery afternoons.

There were a lot of twittering Cod-Enders, with too little excitement in their dull lives, ever ready to put Polly in the picture. In a way Raish was glad when she knew, for he did like to boast about it. No mean achievement, was it, to bed the flower of Pelsall Hall?

At first it seemed to add spark to Polly's ardour. There was nothing she would not do for him. But her jealousy knew no bounds as the affair stretched on through a year, and then two. Often she shook her head, firmly closed her lips and withheld herself from him. It annoyed him when he could not win her over. So it was Polly's fault that the affair stretched on, he reckoned.

She forgave him when the affair at The Hall ended. How gratefully she crept back into his arms, spreading her glorious hair around him, promising he would never need to

47

look at another woman again.

But of course he did. He appreciated variety in his women, as in his drink. Why should he not give them a little pleasure, and himself too? He earned it, didn't he, hulking great cases of cold rabbits and fish from the early markets. He could turn them into guineas faster than anybody when he had a mind to.

Not that there had ever been any money over for Polly. She didn't need it, did she? She had the shop and Katy was trained as a seamstress. She always used to share the money she made, he remembered, but lately there had been less and less in the till when he had gone to it. He suspected she was moving some before he got there; damn spiteful thing to do.

Yes, Polly had changed. Wonder where she was tonight? Ah, no matter. He would not be here himself in the morning. He would not wait to be the laughing-stock of Cod End; he had suffered enough at The Colliers' Arms.

He began to contemplate his best option. There were one or two married ladies obliging him at present, but they were no good if he was planning a permanent move, were they? Husbands tended to get in the way. And young Rose had nothing saved.

How about Dora, who helped her father in The Pig and Dog? Far enough away, at Maldon, to be comfortable until all this died down. Dora had been widowed when her Bert died a couple of years ago from pneumoconiosis, the miners' disease. Fool, that Bert, he had stayed on at the pit, even after he knew he had it.

Dora as good as lived with her father at The Pig and Dog these days, but she had sensibly kept her own cottage, just round the corner from the inn. He was sure he could persuade her to move back into it; for sleeping anyway. The Pig and Dog would suit him fine during the day. He got on well with Dora's old man. There would be a good little business going there one day. Yes, Dora was his best bet, for sure. So that was settled.

How about the horse and cart? Should he take that? Did he really want to carry on as a greengrocer, handling rabbits and fish? Would he not rather sit in the cosy snug of The Pig and Dog, or even help Dora and her old man behind the bar? Get his hand in? Raish considered this carefully as he continued to stare into the fire.

The horse and cart provided freedom from any woman. There was room for it at the back of the inn. Anyway, why should he leave it to benefit them here? He grinned. It would be useful for meeting young Rose on the quiet. What would Polly say if she knew he was carrying on with Sarah's grand-daughter?

He stretched his arms wide as he stood up, rubbed down his handsome chest again, gently tracing the cut on his cheek that would soon heal.

He would creep upstairs, sort himself out some clothes, search the room to see if Polly had any money tucked away, and be off before light in the morning. But first he would finish off the remains of the rabbit stew, now thickly coagulating at the bottom of the stewpot, still piping hot and smelling good. He scraped it out on to his plate.

He hoped that Dora could cook as well as Polly.

Mary Ann had not slept all night. Now a familiar clip-clop drew her from the narrow iron bedsteads where Sarah's grand-daughter used to sleep, to the tiny window overlooking the main street. The lamp in the square still burned, but even without it she would have recognized the arrogant shoulders, the proud head. Raish sat high in the cart, tugging at the reins. She could see their old leather case and several bulging bags. She did not need to see his face to know the excitement it would reflect, the puckish grin, the impish delight in stealing away before Cod End was awake.

Pressing her hot forehead to the cold dampness of the window she permitted herself the luxury of one moment of self-pity before her heart lurched sickeningly in concern for

49

her children. Did she do right to let them persuade her to leave them? 'Let's try it,' Katy had pleaded. 'Another shock to his system won't come amiss on top of his enforced walk from the inn.' Not until they had arranged with Bobby Millard to keep watch did she agree. Now she felt guilty and anxious.

She dressed swiftly, careful not to wake Sarah. It was all right, she could manage without him. Then why did her heart feel like a stone?

At home the clothes he had discarded littered the kitchen floor, the empty stewpot and bowl were on the table. She deftly tidied up before fetching fresh coals for the fire, shovelling the ashes into the empty bucket and finding her way by instinct to the ash pit in a corner of the dark garden. Then pouring the remaining hot water into the enamel bowl she stripped off her clothes, as Raish had done in the same spot last night, and washed herself down.

Moving about her jobs automatically, her mind racing on other lines, she refilled the kettles from the brewhouse tap, reached for flour and yeast, rubbed up the bread and put it to rise. She unbolted the door of the shop. Often she caught early morning trade before the pitmen went to work; today was no exception.

Wives, anxious to please their men, came for a penn'orth of sweets to put in the snap boxes, a threepenny twist of tobacco, matches, a fourpenny pair of socks, or a tuppenny packet of tea.

She was tying up the second snap bag for her lads when Katy appeared. 'Has he gone? We thought we heard him packing up.'

Mary Ann nodded.

'He hasn't taken the horse and cart, I hope?'

'He has.'

'Oh, he would! I was hoping the lads would take it to fetch the piano for me.'

Mary Ann permitted herself a smile. It did not matter that

her father had gone, but Katy would miss the horse and cart.

'What happened last night?'

'Nothing much,' replied Katy, chuckling at the memory. 'He will be back tonight, perhaps.'

'No. He's gone.'

Yes, he had gone. She was on her own. Now to pull herself together and fill that bank book.

CHAPTER

3

THE SAME STARK message leaped from the ragged sheet of tin: NO WORK TODAY. The miners huddled in groups voluble in their condemnation of the uncommunicative colliery managers. Some shouted threateningly, others discussed it quietly, but all were angry, an emotion Ben could identify with. Why they had not been consulted he could not understand.

Yet to his everlasting amazement the men shuffled into a meek and orderly queue as soon as the pay hatch shot open at eight o'clock. Whether it was because the Norton policeman stepped out of the office at that precise moment, to stare stonily at the men before moving down the line as if inspecting his troops, or whether it was fear of the sack, Ben could not make up his mind, but to witness the awed meekness of these strong men made him feel like charging into the office with his fists raised.

One or two brave souls, his brother among them, who

dared to enquire if there would be work on Monday, were curtly ordered to wait and see.

Paul had convinced himself and Ben that yesterday had been a temporary lay-off, probably due to some technical fault. They had been so elated on their journey here, congratulating themselves on Raish's hurried departure, for which they felt personally responsible, while acknowledging Kate to be 'a good 'un'. The prospect of life without their father had given wings to their feet as they scaled the arms of the lock gates at double speed.

The journey home was painful; no jobs for them at Bill Brown's coal wharf nor at the farm today. Paul was mortified at the thought of giving his mother less money instead of more. The closure was probably due to the early spring weather; how he wished it would freeze. The heavy pit boots became heavier as they reached Double Row, the big square house, and then the outdoor beer licence, where they joined some more youths scuffing their toes, on the corner, facing their shop. Paul felt sick with anxiety.

He was the man of the house now. Next week there might be no money to pick up at all. How would his mother manage? While these thoughts nagged at Paul, Ben was considering for the first time what it would be like to be permanently unemployed. The weeks ahead stretched out emptily as his role as a pigeon fancier receded into the unforeseeable future. A job at the dreaded colliery would have been better than no job at all. The ninepence pocket money he had turned his nose up at yesterday now seemed very acceptable. Yet that meek queue! It had nauseated him.

They stood watching Cod End bustle with Saturday activity. No groups of gossiping women today. Those with workers scurried purposefully, choosing Sunday joints with elaborate care. For most of them it would be the only meat of the week, and many would share with those who had none. Wives hurried to the cobblers with pit boots needed for Monday, bought 'fourpennies' of ale from the Outdoor, collected a newspaper so that their men could study form; they would be back later to hand in betting slips to the same shop. Policeman Millard knew what was going on. He also knew when to shut his eyes and when to keep them wide open. Most of the shoppers finished up at Mary Ann's shop across the road. They knew some would be settling up before 'starting off again', while others would ask for more time to pay and more strap.

Children pressed eager noses to Mary Ann's big square shop window that bulged out halfway across the footpath, contemplating the serious business of how to spend the Saturday penny when it came. Should it be a kite or a fishing net, a kali sucker or twenty marbles? Or should the precious fortune be split down the middle on a halfpenny top and a halfpenny stick of spanish, that stick of hard liquorice that gave hours of exotic pleasure and lingered on their teeth for days?

Those who knew that no pennies would be forthcoming torturously scrutinized Mary Ann's window display, lost in wild hopeless dreams. Underwear of all types and sizes hung on lines stretched from one side of the window to another, together with mufflers, socks, towels, baby linen, shirts, blouses and aprons. The base of the window, opposite the sweets corner, sported a fascinating variety of smaller articles, hair ribbons, combs, fancy satin garters, elastic, knitting needles: a hundred and one things constantly needing tidying, for discerning customers invariably preferred to choose from the window rather than from the shelves.

Cod End dwellings hunched together in small cramped streets which branched off, at varying intervals, from the circle they called The Square. A street lamp stood in the centre, a prop for the male voice choir which turned out of The Red Cow on Saturday nights. The circle formed by the buildings was sliced into two semi-circles by the main road running through from Pelsall to Rushall, about a mile away,

54

with the town of Walsall and the city of Birmingham beyond. Most Cod-Enders did not venture beyond Rushall: there were no pits in that direction.

The Red Cow Inn was in the street immediately behind the Outdoor, where the lads stood. Opposite the lamp was Dickinsons store which sold new and second-hand furniture, an imposingly large shop for such a small village. Mr Dickinson handled a lot of good class trade from Pelsall and surrounding districts, travelling miles to get orders; Heath-Enders would never make him rich. Today the large double doors were propped invitingly open and many fine pieces of furniture could be seen, along with rolls of linoleum and colourful rugs. One corner of the store was devoted to second-hand, from which a Cod-Ender could be seen occasionally trundling out a dilapidated cupboard or an off-cut of lino, while more affluent customers from other parts tried out the chesterfields and tub chairs.

The cobbler operated from a front room in a little street which snaked between Dickinson's and the paper shop that took the bets. Next door was a post office. Lastly there was Heath End chapel, tiny but important, fronted with iron railing and a wrought-iron gate. Approaching from Rushall, after the long Rushall Lane, it was the first building you saw on reaching Heath End, sternly presiding over them all.

Opposite the chapel was the barber's. The lads could picture the scene in there. A man in the barber's chair would have his face well lathered, while several more sat on the bench lining the wall, picking out today's winners. There was bound to be at least one lucky lad smacking his mouth round a thick chunk of bread and home-made blackberry jam, supplied by the barber's mother to keep lads occupied while they waited.

It was a treat that Paul and Ben had often enjoyed, although they needed no bribery to wait long after their rightful turn. It was sheer heaven to sit listening to the men talking, about horse racing, pigeon flying, football, the domino league, the clay pipe smoke-ring competitions, and, inevitably, the pits. Ben had gleaned precious information about pigeon flying, while Paul eagerly soaked up talk about the mines, sparking his ambition to advance to more difficult jobs and to earn more money. If only he could earn pots of money to provide his mother with everything she could wish for, visits to the oyster bar and Her Majesty's Theatre in Walsall, bedecked in expensive jewellery; that would be grand, to be able to buy jewellery for her. Some day, when he owned a pit, he would do that.

The butcher's, with its noisy slaughter-house at the back, came next. Then, closer still, Queens Row, built when Victoria came to the throne: six houses huddled together, facing the lamp, opposite Dickinson's. Sarah, where their mother had spent the night, lived in one. Sarah carried milk from the farm early mornings, and re-sold it in penn'-orths.

The wide entrance to the gulley came as a surprise after the squashed houses in Queens Row. It led to a long row of houses that stood side-on to Mary Ann's kitchen, with the high wall between. Beyond them lay the stepping bridge over the railway line and fields stretching all the way to Shelfield where Walter, Katy's chap, lived.

Their own little group of buildings completed the semi-circle. First Little Cott which their mother sublet, then her shop with its Aladdin's Cave window, followed by the house next door which was to be Katy's, with the shared brewhouse and lavatory tacked on untidily. The Cott and the outhouse roofs were very low, emphasizing the height of the two houses between. Beside these stood their patch of land fringed by a rough hedge, and after that there was nothing between them and Pelsall except The Bush Inn facing the common, the inn being in a sort of no-man's-land between the two villages.

Every now and then the lads could see Katy hopping nimbly in and out of the shop window, stretching for something from the furthest corner. Inevitably she noticed them before long and beckoned them over.

'What's the matter with you two? You look as if you have found a farthing and lost a sovereign.'

'No work today.'

'Our kid was gunna ask for more money an' all,' Ben added.

'Was he! Bad luck, Paul.'

'And I was gunna fix up about 'avin' some pigeons with my money next week. Only ninepence apiece.'

'I told you not to mention that.'

'To me mother, ar. Not to Katy. Anyway, I'll please meself.'

'Would they be any good for ninepence?' Katy asked doubtfully.

'They'd be all right for breeding off. We could train the young 'uns.'

'Forget it,' Paul ordered curtly.

They lapsed into brooding silence as Katy went to serve.

'Listen, you two,' she said, as she returned to the kitchen and their crestfallen faces. 'Why don't you *take the day*? Enjoy your freedom. You don't have to worry about the old chap any more, do you?'

'Has he really gone?'

'Well, he's taken too many clothes for a day out. Even for him.'

'Me Mother'll 'ave 'im back if he wants to come. I know 'er will.'

Paul's eyes met Katy's in silent affirmation.

'Where is she?'

'She went to Walsall, in Ginny's trap, first thing this morning. Since then that bell has never stopped tinkling. I have a pile of sewing promised for today. How about looking after the shop, Paul, and Ben, you can scrub this floor. Cheer up, it's easier than mining.'

They thought of how she had helped them last night and

grinned at her. She was a good 'un.

'We'll give you a hand.'

'That's more like it,' Katy laughed.

Inwardly she felt sick with apprehension. She hoped Conduit was not going to make a habit of stoppages. Her mother would miss the cash she contributed from her sewing after she was married, and the growing list of customers owing money was scary. Most Cod-Enders were well intentioned, but men lost their jobs without warning. Sometimes a death in the family would take all they had, or the rent man would refuse to wait any longer. They seemed to think Mary Ann could re-stock her shop for their needs without their money.

Now there was something else. Jane, their sub-tenant in Little Cott, had been round to say they were leaving. Joe had been out of work for months, so they were accepting an offer to live in Worcester with Jane's parents, where Joe could help with their farm. Upset at not being able to give proper notice she explained that a letter had arrived only that morning saying that an uncle going to Lichfield cattle market would be able to give them a lift on the way back.

That would be another two shillings a week less coming in. It would not be easy to find another tenant who paid as regularly as Jane; there were lots of houses in Heath End standing empty, better houses than Little Cott. Mary Ann would be in trouble if the lads had no work. Yet, come to think of it, had there ever been a time when their mother could not cope?

She settled to her sewing, keeping one ·eye on Ben slopping water over the floor. 'Do the corners,' she chided. 'Anybody can clean the middle.' He pulled a face at her, carrying on stubbornly in the same way until they heard the trap arrive, when they all rushed out to greet Mary Ann. Smart in her best black coat and hat she was chatting with Ginny, who was looking incongruous as usual, in a tweed cap and navy serge jacket many sizes too big, and long trousers turned up several times over thick boots. She ran a service into Walsall twice a week, her buggy holding six passengers. Today the only passenger was Mary Ann, her purchases taking up the remaining space.

Mary Ann beamed at the lads as if it was nothing unusual to see them in the middle of the morning. 'It's good to see you two. Come and give us a hand with this.' She indicated a round, deep, heavy iron pan, which they lifted from the buggy between them.

'Put it in the brewhouse. I will bring the other,' she said, indicating a large long-handled wicker basket on three good-sized wheels. And turning to Katy, 'I have arranged for Ginny to pick up the lads to fetch your piano.' She trundled the three-wheeler through the shop. 'How about this, then?'

'Hm. It will do to ferry those great bundles from the station each week.'

Mary Ann's weekly 'bundles' from Birmingham rag market were famous. The shop bell would be tinkling like Christmas before she had her bonnet off.

'Are yer back from Brum, Mrs Brook?'

'What 'ave yer got for we this wik, Mary Ann?'

After Katy had taken her pick to make skirts, aprons, children's garments and men's trousers, to sell in the shop, the rest would be piled on the counter: cast-off clothing, second-hand boots, linen for embroidery, bits of leather and feathers for trimming Sunday hats. It was well worth catching the six o'clock train: the penny a mile fare would soon be re-couped. Bargaining in the rag market, the mental arithmetic in the homeward train, the response from her customers, Mary Ann loved it all.

'Yes, it will do for the bundles,' she conceded now. 'I've something else in mind for it, though.' She accepted a cup of tea from Katy with a smile, outwardly calm and controlled, as if trying to suppress the excitement in her eyes. You would not think her husband had left her today,

59

Katy mused. She wondered what she was planning; she was always like this when buzzing with ideas.

There was a twittering from the basket as the lads returned. 'Chickens!' Ben removed a cloth from the top of the basket and gently lifted out a box containing a couple of dozen day-old chicks.

'Careful. They will have to stay in the kitchen for a day or two. By then I'm hoping you lads will have made a chicken coop. When they start laying we can sell the eggs.'

They each took a chick, a soft downy handful, yellow as a buttercup, at one day old already inquisitive and noisy, jostling for space.

'See if you can find another box, Paul, so that we can spread them out.'

'Mother, what's all the fish in that great pot for?' Paul asked when he returned.

'They're to fry tonight. The pot will fit the brewhouse boiler exactly; I measured it before I went out. You can take them round to the public houses in the new basket. Wrapped in linen they will keep warm in there.'

'Will they allow the lads in the pubs?' asked Katy, surprised.

'To sell the fish, yes. Plenty of salt and vinegar, which we will supply, will make the drinkers even more thirsty. The publicans won't object to that.'

'Well, I suppose we might as well get something back. The public houses have taken enough out of this house.'

Mary Ann ignored this reference to Raish.

'But what about the shop, Mother? You know how busy we are on Saturday nights. I promised to help Walter with the house next door.'

'Never fret,' replied Mary Ann airily. 'The lads can look after the shop while I am frying, and I can come in while they're delivering.'

She has it all worked out, thought Katy; it seemed the planning department had been working overtime. Typical

Mary Ann philosophy, to fill her mind and hands to erase Raish's exit from her thoughts. She realized, of course, why the lads were back home early. 'Do them good, a bit of fresh air,' was all she said. Nothing was ruffling her today, it seemed. Not even when she heard that Jane and Joe were moving out. Later she went round to see them.

Inside the cottage the tiny black-leaded grate with its miniature hobs and small oven gleamed, vying for attention with the bright brass kettle hanging from a shiny hook over the fire. Two armchairs on either side of the fire were covered in bright red and cream flower print, matching the curtains at the tiny window. Walls and ceiling had been painted white, the thick beam varnished a rich brown, and the red quarried floor shone with elbow grease. In front of the window which looked out on to The Square was a round table, four chairs neatly tucked beneath it, and on the opposite wall a chest of drawers, all smelling of recent polishing.

Mary Ann bent to speak to the baby lying on a white pillow in the laundry basket. She stroked his cheek, as round and rosy as a Worcester permain. 'It all looks lovely, Jane.'

The girl blushed with pleasure. 'It's Joe. He's ever so handy. He's upstairs, fastening the trunk. Would you like to see upstairs, Mrs Brook?' It was obvious that she wanted to show off her young husband's handiwork, so Mary Ann followed her up the narrow stairs that curved from the room they were in directly into the bedroom. The ceiling was so low it touched Mary Ann's head and Joe had to bend his. Big brass bedsteads, now devoid of bedclothes, dwarfed the room. A table, tiny wooden chair and a little set of drawers were all painted shell pink. The floor boards, in a bad state of repair when the couple took the cottage, had been repaired and scrubbed white.

They linked hands and smiled at her, waiting for her approval. Mary Ann remembered the day Joe's Dad was killed in a pit accident when he was five years old, leaving

61

his mother with a big family to rear. He had always been a quiet lad, thin and rather pale, but since his marriage to Jane he had blossomed. 'Well! A little one-up-and-down and you have made it like a palace. You are a clever lad, Joe.'

The girl's eyes shone with pride, squeezing his arm reassuringly as he said, 'I'm going over to Dickinson's now to see if they will buy the furniture back.'

Mary Ann noted the disappointment in his voice at having to part with the fruits of his handiwork. 'You are not taking it with you?'

'My uncle won't have room for it in the cart. Anyway, my mam has so much stuff already,' explained Jane. 'We bought everything second-hand from Mr Dickinson. I doubt if he'll give us much back, although Joe has improved it all no end.'

'Then don't go to Mr Dickinson. I will buy it from you.'

They were overjoyed. They wanted to sell everything, they said. Mary Ann paid the price they asked; it just about cleared her out. She had spent a lot today, but was confident she would be solvent again once she had put all her ideas into action. They were too relieved to be curious. 'It has made things so much easier,' Jane confessed. 'I was dreading seeing this place looking bare and empty. We have loved it here.' Joe's arm went round her shoulders as he saw her lip tremble. It had been a sudden decision they had had to make, and it was obvious they were a bit overwhelmed by it. But they would love it anywhere as long as they were together, Mary Ann knew, seeing them standing so close, thinking the same thoughts. How she wished she could see Katy and Walter looking at each other in that way.

Downstairs Mary Ann again leaned over the laundry basket where the fat baby was playing with his toes. 'How much for this?' she teased, to lighten the situation. 'He's priceless,' the girl chuckled.

Mary Ann wished them luck as she took her leave. She

was sorry to see them go, yet it had given her another idea, putting an added sparkle in her eye.

The kitchen was stifling. A roaring fire had been needed to prepare the big black oven for the pastry she had made; now Mary Ann was damping the fire down with wet slack, the oven door open, so that it would cool sufficiently to receive a fruit cake. Katy had gone to deliver her sewing, and Ben despatched to Rushall Brewery for barm. Together with the nettles and dandelion leaves he would collect on the way back, from Rushall Lane, she would be able to make some pop for sale in the shop, as soon as she had cleaned all the fish. He was also going to call on Edwin, to ask him to come up. Her eldest son would not set foot in the house if there was the slightest chance of meeting his father, but Mary Ann knew that, without any prompting from her, Ben would be only too happy to pass on the news of Raish's departure.

Paul, armed with little slips of paper, had been sent debt collecting. 'Leave the bills and tell them you will call again. That way it will remind them to put a bit by when they have their wages this afternoon. And don't worry, my lad. There's not a bill for anybody who can't afford to pay.'

He was so eager to tell his news when he returned he could hardly wait to get inside before explaining, 'I've got three and tuppence in bits and drabs, and a lot o' promises. And what do you think, Mother? At the last house they settled their bill! Twelve bob! The man had won more than that yesterday with his prize pigeons. They said they'd been waiting for summat like that to happen so that they could pay off their debts. Twelve bob all at one go!'

'Well done, my lad.'

Ben had walked in during their conversation, his arms filled with nettles and dandelion leaves. 'I told you we could make some money with pigeons,' he said, immediately receiving a silencing kick on the shins, returning it in good measure.

Their next task was to move the double bed, sideboard and bedroom drawers from Little Cott into Katy's house next door. A small table from their mother's bedroom joined the two already in the cottage vacated by Jane and Joe.

'It looks like a coffee shop in there,' commented Paul, 'with all those tables.'

'You've guessed!'

'A coffee shop! In Cod End? Nobody will come, Mother. Cod-Enders don't go into coffee shops!'

'Maybe not. But when I was in Walsall this morning I noticed how many people were in the coffee shops there; they didn't live in Walsall I'll be bound. No, it's folks that travel in from other parts that use them, and we have a lot of those.'

'We do?' Paul's brow wrinkled doubtfully; he hoped his mother was not in for a big disappointment. Ben, fed up with furniture removing, escaped, saying he wanted to check that the chicken pen they were making was still safe.

'Dickinson's customers come from all over the place,' Mary Ann went on. 'People come to look at his furniture, then they come to buy. Then they come to pay, quite regularly, about once a month I'd say. There are Katy's customers as well, some from as far away as Sutton Cold-field. Often they have to wait while she does some adjusting, or else they want something doing on the spot, a bonnet trimming perhaps. It's not much of a place for them to wait, in here. What do you think, lad?'

'That they'd be more comfortable sitting in Little Cott, I suppose,' conceded Paul.

'Yes, and while they wait they would perhaps buy a cup of coffee with a tart or a cake.'

So that was the reason for the stifling kitchen at this time of day. Maybe the idea was not so crazy after all. All sorts of folk came when his mother brought her bundles; monied folk sometimes, everybody loved a bargain.

Another thing occurred to him. 'It would be cash on the nail, wouldn't it? No strap?'

Mary Ann laughed. 'No strap,' she agreed.

Ginny had taken the lads off in the trap before Edwin arrived. 'Our pit's off as well,' were his first words.

'So you're in no hurry.' Mary Ann studied her eldest son as she went on mixing her cake, one ear listening for the shop. She thought of Joe, who had gone off to start a new life today. Like Joe, Edwin had been the sickly one, pale and timid. Like Joe, marriage – or getting away from Raish, she wasn't sure which – had worked wonders for him. He was not yet twenty-two and had been married for three years to a girl six or seven years older, a serious and bookish girl. She played the organ at Rushall Chapel, where they had met, and she gave piano lessons. They seemed contented together in their own way. She wished she knew her daughter-in-law better, but she never came to visit.

'How is Charlotte?'

'She is quite well. I wanted to see you, as a matter of fact, Mother, to tell you that Charlotte is pregnant.'

'Well!' Mary Ann paused in her task for a moment. 'There was I, looking at a little lad today, wishing I had a grandchild, and today I get the news. How long has she gone?'

'Three months.'

'You will let me know if there is anything I can do for her, won't you, Edwin?'

'I will. But we're right next door to her own mother, as you know. She will be well cared for.'

Edwin spoke quietly, with little trace of the Cod End accent. 'She is pregnant,' he had said. Most Cod-Enders would have said, ''Ers gunna 'ave a babby' or, 'There's a bun in the oven.' He had always been a bit of a loner, Mary Ann reflected, never willingly mixing with Cod End kids in the way of his brothers and sister. Now he had married a girl who, as Raish would say, talked *properly*. Katy could talk either way, the Cod End she had grown up with, or in the manner Raish had taught her. Even when Raish swore it sounded posh. Ben and Paul drove him mad with their slang; Ben did it deliberately in order to annoy him. Mary Ann realized that she herself sounded like Cod-Enders now, living here for so long. What did it matter? She had a great fondness for them in spite of the frustration she often felt at being stuck here still.

As she studied Edwin now, still pale and quiet, yet more composed than he used to be, she felt a twinge of guilt. She supposed she had neglected her first two children in the days when she was so preoccupied with Raish. It had not mattered to Katy; she was independent from the start. But Edwin? He could have done with a bit more loving. By the time she was aware of it, it was too late. He was afraid of his father, and had withdrawn so far into himself she could not reach him. She should have done more to stop Raish's bullying.

'Dad's gone, then, has he?'

Mary Ann started. It was as if he had read her thoughts. She nodded.

'I wonder for how long?'

She did not comment on that. 'What I wanted to see you about, lad, is, are you still doing those paintings?'

Edwin appeared surprised and a little embarrassed. One of Charlotte's uncles had died soon after they married. He left Edwin his canvases, an easel and all his paints. Edwin had often watched quietly as he painted, and had been allowed to have a go, under the guidance of the talented old man. He found it was something he really enjoyed. Now he often strolled, with his sketch pad, to various local places, such as the fields at the back of the gulley, leading to Shelfield, or to the two commons. Sometimes he cycled to Cannock Chase or Milford, searching for scenes to sketch and paint.

Once, when his mother called for a brief visit, Charlotte

had proudly shown off some of his efforts.

'I still have a go, yes,' he answered her now.

'Ever sold any?'

'*Sold* any, mother? They're not that good.'

'I thought they were that good.'

'People aren't buying paintings. There's no money about.'

'In my experience, when there's no money about, that's when people want cheering up. Anyway, I am thinking of people who might have a bit of cash to spare. Just pop and look at Little Cott while I make you a drink. You can go through the bogey hole; we've lost our tenants.'

What Edwin saw were two circular tables, one under the window, the other between two armchairs facing the fireplace, topped with pretty lace cloths and tiny vases of crocuses. Another small rectangular table, which he recognized from his mother's bedroom, was placed against the wall, close to the door leading in from 'the hole', with plates ready to receive pastries and cakes.

His mother was busy in the shop when he returned. He sat, thoughtful, drinking the tea she had left for him. Such a tiny room, bursting with industry. Katy's treadle machine beneath the window, a box of sewing beside it, chicks twittering down under the table, the bowl with the barm and herbs in the hearth. The room smelled of baking, and on the scrubbed-top table were fruit, flour, butter and eggs, promising more. Did his mother never stop work?

When she returned she told him briefly of her plans for Little Cott.

'It looks good, Mother.'

'Don't you think it would look even better with some of your paintings round the walls?'

He gave a little embarrassed cough. 'It might. You can have some, certainly.'

'We could put neat price tags in the corners, like I have seen in Birmingham. Some of the people might want to buy. Wouldn't it be a thrill to tell Charlotte if you sold some?'

'If I sold *one* it would be a thrill.'

'Then go and fetch the best, lad, and let's hang them before the shop gets too busy. While you're home ask Charlotte if she'll come and have tea with us tomorrow.'

By the door he hesitated. 'We go to chapel at six, Mother.'

'Oh, yes.' She looked disappointed.

'We'll have a walk up after chapel, if that's all right?'

'Even better. I close a bit earlier on Sundays, about seven. Perhaps Charlotte will play the piano for us.'

'Piano!'

'You'll see.' She listened, her head thrown back. 'That will be them now.'

So Edwin was able to help his brothers unload the heavy piano from Ginny's trap. It was every bit as beautiful as Katy had said; a quality instrument and no mistake.

'Mother, look what we've got.' Ben was staggering behind a huge punchball. 'Lawson's house was all empty, wor it, our kid? The old bloke's died and 'is son wants to stop in London. This must 'ave been 'is.'

'How did you get it?'

'Well, there was one or two things in an old shed, which a man, who we think was a gardener, said 'ad bin overlooked. He said he'd 'ad permission to get rid of 'em. Ginny gid 'im a florin for the lot, and she said we could 'ave this.'

'Where is it going?'

'We thought perhaps it could go upstairs in the bedroom of Little Cott. It's empty now, ain't it? Could we, Mother. We wouldn't want to use it while yer coffee shop's open.'

'I should think not!' She studied Ben, showing enthusiasm about something for once. 'Oh, all right. You can put it up there for now.'

And that was the start of the boxing class.

While her brothers were trundling her piano into place, Katy was lying in the arms of Ted Willis.

She had intended to hurry straight home. The skirts she had delivered were for two old sisters housebound by arthritis. She would have stayed to chat with them, but there were blouses to finish for the vicar's daughters, and she was very conscious that her mother needed a helping hand. Then, of course, there was the piano; she was so looking forward to seeing it again. So it was at a cracking pace that she set out across the fields for home.

But spring was in the air. March, which had come in like a lamb, continued to gambol like one. Banks were boasting primroses and celandine buds, violets were uncurling, grass was lush after winter snows, the sun made her feel overdressed and the lark was in the clear air. As she lingered to listen to him she spotted a tiny wren and a darting chaffinch, bright as a rainbow. Perhaps she could spare a few minutes.

She watched Billy Button's Brook tumbling joyously over smooth clean stones, and could not resist kneeling to run her fingers through the cold water, as she recollected the games she had played here with other Cod End kids. So absorbed was she that she did not hear anyone approaching.

'Hopin' to catch some jackbannocks?'

'Ted! You made me jump!'

He crouched close beside her. 'We had some fun, didn't we? You were a good sport, Kate. Kate-me-mate I used to call you. Remember?'

'Doesn't seem all that long ago.' She spoke her thoughts aloud. 'Went by too quickly, didn't it, Ted?'

'And now you'll soon be a grown-up married lady. Or so they tell me.'

'Well! Married, anyway,' she laughed.

Their hands touched in the cool water.

'It's warm today,' she said as she drew away.

'Yes, and you can't put your skirt in your knickers.'

'I wouldn't if I could.' She sprang lightly to her feet and they strolled quietly to a corner of the field they knew, where the banks were softer. Large trees made a private little haven of the clearing where they sat.

'I should be hurrying home.'

'How long has it been since you wandered over here, Kate?'

'So long I can't remember.'

'How long will it be before you do it again?'

'Too long, I suppose.'

'Then enjoy the day, kid. That's what you always used to tell us, wasn't it? "Enjoy the day," you used to say, "it won't ever come again." '

'I said something like that to the lads this morning.'

'Well then! Relax.'

'My mother could do with some help,' Katy protested feebly.

'Mary Ann can cope whether you're there or not. You know that.'

'S'pose so.' She sighed peacefully as she snuggled into the grass, putting her arms beneath her head. The soft bank folded round her. Ted stretched out also, barely an inch away. The sun was warm and sensuous on their eyelids. It felt easy and natural to be here together, in the meadow where they had often played. They lay quietly listening to the birds rejoicing in the glory of the spring day.

Katy was first to speak. 'Found a job yet, Ted?'

'No. I've been to Stubbers Green pit this mornin'. There's work there, but they're not settin' any more on.'

'Stubbers Green? That's where Walter works.'

'You're not really marrying that Walter chap, are you?'

'Why not?'

'He's too old for you, for a start.'

'He's only thirty.'

'Thirty, or twenty, he'll always be too old for you, Kate. He's not lively enough for you, my love.'

He turned over suddenly, brown eyes gazing deep into her own before thick black lashes caressed her cheeks. Katy pushed hard at the strong shoulders that pinned her to the bank as his lips came crashing on to hers.

She pounded at him ineffectually with the one small fist that was free, which was quickly captured as he continued kissing her. She resisted uselessly, keeping her lips tight shut, until she realized how lovely his kisses felt. 'Enjoy the day,' Ted had reminded her she was always telling people. This day would never come again, that was for sure. His kisses stirred her in a way she had never anticipated. Walter had not progressed beyond a shy goodnight kiss on her cheek.

Was this really the Ted she had played Tip-Cat with? Yes, it was, they were still children; only the game was different. He flipped off her hat, burying his face in the golden crown of hair, whispering how lovely it was. He cradled her in his arms like a baby, pressing soft sweet kisses all over her face and neck, while she longed for him to kiss her lips again. When he did it was a long, slow, gentle kiss, yet it left her breathless. All thoughts of the piano, sewing and the shop soared away with the lark as she responded with an ardency she had not known she possessed. No, no, this wasn't the same Ted. It wasn't the same Katy. They had both grown up.

At last they lay quietly in each other's arms, their burning cheeks barely touching, though his body felt young and vital against hers. He took her hand, pressing each finger gently to his lips.

'You don't love this Walter,' he said, deliberating each word between kisses so sensuous she ached to sink her fingers into his thick curly hair and once again feel his lips on hers. Instead she moved away from him.

She stood up slowly. The heat was going out of the sun, yet she was glowing all over. She smoothed her dress and put on her hat. 'I must go now,' she said, ignoring his last

71

remark. This place would soon be filled with excited children, on their way home from the afternoon football match.

They held hands as far as the stepping bridge. Katy's heart doing uncomfortable somersaults, but as they passed the long row of houses in the gulley they instinctively drew apart, feeling, rather than seeing, the knowing glances from the windows. At the wide entrance to the gulley they turned to face each other. Ted's hands went out to touch her but Katy moved swiftly away. 'Go now, Ted,' she whispered.

'Katy!' His voice was urgent and pleading. 'You should be in love with the bloke you marry.'

Something in his searching eyes made her drop hers, but a moment later she raised her chin with a defiant little gesture. Looking straight back at him she replied, 'I know somebody who tried that, Ted. It did not work.'

She turned sharply and walked quickly away. All she could think of was Mary Ann in tears because of some scathing tirade from Raish, or because he was having an affair with someone else. If that was being in love she did not want any of it. Ted, like her father, was too handsome by half, she reminded herself reprovingly. She did not want the highs and the lows of her mother's life. She wanted some one reliable, a father for her children who would always be there.

At the wide open door of the brewhouse she stopped suddenly. She was surprised to see Edwin there, putting the finishing touches to a sign he had made. White letters, painted in his best calligraphy, bounced from a black background. Little Cott Coffee Shop.

'What on earth . . . ?'

'Don't tell me you know nothing about it!'

Katy ran swiftly to Little Cott, staring in amazement at a couple of strangers enjoying tea and jam tarts. She darted back to her brother. 'A coffee shop! We serve tea as well, I see. I don't know how she is going to manage. What with the fish frying, the shop and . . . '

'Fish frying!'

'*Don't tell me you know nothing about it.*'

Their laughter released some of the tension locking Katy's chest since walking away from Ted. 'It's good to see you, Edwin,' she said warmly. They had been very close as children; she wished they saw more of him now. 'Are those your pictures hanging in there?'

'Mother has a strange idea she may sell some of them.'

'Well, if anybody can sell them she can. She is even more activated than usual today. Dad going seems to have charged up the batteries. She always seems to find more strength when things go wrong.'

It was true. Mary Ann was a mixture of sentimentality when Raish was being loving, and practicality when he was not.

'By the way, Katy, the lads fetched your piano.'

'Oh? Oh, good.' She had forgotten the piano.

'It's a lovely instrument. Don't you want to see how it looks?'

After the magical afternoon the piano no longer seemed of much importance. 'Later will do. When Walter comes.'

She said the same when the lads urged her to go and look; the same to her mother too. They had so wanted to share in her delight when she saw the furniture from Little Cott. It was as well they were all occupied with fish when that moment came, for they would have been disappointed.

The old table which Walter had lovingly painted looked out of place in the same room as Jane's highly-polished sideboard and the ornate piano, but he loyally enthused about them, in spite of Katy being strangely unresponsive.

Walter could not understand it. She showed no enthusiasm for the jobs they had planned to do. He could not know that she was still lying in a sunlit meadow with the bird sounds in her ear and thick eyelashes soft against her cheek. She fidgeted as she held the lamp while he patiently trimmed wallpaper edges, concentrating hard to get them level. He felt weary tonight, understandably, considering he had been up before five, done a shift, spent the afternoon preparing and painting the table, painstakingly pushing it this evening on a handcart all the way from Shelfield. He had brought it through High Heath, past the vicarage and down into Cod End via the road, being unable to get a hand-cart over the stepping bridge, the shorter route Katy had taken earlier.

Katy looked down at the pale face, noticing the lines of tiredness etched deep.

'He's not lively enough. He's too old for you.' It was as if Ted's lips were still close to her ear. Trying to push away the memory she said, 'I should be in the shop, Walter, while Mother's doing the frying.'

'Yes, of course,' he agreed patiently. 'But first let us look at the bedroom. You can tell me what you'd like doing up there.'

There was something about the dainty set of drawers and the bed with its huge brass bedsteads that rendered Katy speechless. She knew instinctively that was where Jane and Joe had slept; those two who could not look at each other without touching. For the life of her she could not imagine herself in there with Walter. Walter touching her, loving her like Ted had.

Walter, totally wrong in his assessment of the reason for her silence, said, 'It's ever so kind of your mother, Katy. She'd have the best intentions. You don't mind, do you?'

'Oh, no. No!' She still stared at the enormous bed. All she could see was Ted, his smouldering eyes setting hers on fire as his hands and lips awakened her body.

She was jerked back to earth by Walter hesitantly suggesting, 'Isn't it time we fixed a date, love? How about putting the banns in?' Panic arose in her throat. She looked

74

straight at him now with startled eyes, as if seeing him for the first time.

'Let's wait a while, just until we see how Mother gets on with all these extras she's taken on.'

Walter sighed. He was so looking forward to having Katy for his wife, and to seeing an end to his uncomfortable lodgings. But knowing she was not herself tonight he left it. When they went together to thank Mary Ann for the furniture they found her elated at the success of her venture. It seemed that every drinker was fancying a fish tonight. She was just despatching Paul and Ben with the basket on wheels for the third time, and gratefully accepted Katy's offer to help with the shop.

The lads paused only for a moment in The Square to watch a stealthy game of Tin-Can-Eye-Erkie. A big circle had been drawn in chalk round the lamp-post, where a minder had to guard the tin can in the centre, while all the others went to hide in shadows and alleyways. Occasionally one of them would sing out or whisper 'Tin-Can-Eye-Erkie'. If the minder could find one of them before another kicked the can out of the ring his 'find' had to become the new minder.

They were a happy-go-lucky bunch, Cod End kids. Growing up in close proximity, sharing the same backyard, often the same wash-house or yard tap, they were like members of the same family. Fights were many but feuds were few, the only real antagonists being those who did not reside in the confines of Cod End.

In the lights from The Bush Inn others hooted noisily, playing a game of four-a-side Tip-Cat, in which the lads would have loved to join. The tip-cat was a six inch piece of wood, sharpened at both ends. Woe betide anybody who might be in the path of it as it hurtled across the road on to the comparative darkness of the common on its flight after being struck smartly with a strong stick. 'Do it in ten!' the striker was shrieking challengingly to his opponent in the opposite team. The young fish merchants could not linger to see if he would manage it in ten strides, or if the score of ten would be chalked up on the side wall of The Bush for the striker. The fish must not be allowed to go cold for one thing; for another Ben felt a bit shamefaced about the three-wheeler trolley his brother was pushing. Paul did not mind a bit as long as he was helping with finances.

Back down in The Square a vigorous game of leap frog had started in the pool of light from their shop window, but all were home and in bed before The Red Cow turned out its male voice choir for its Saturday night performance round the lamp-post, some of the choristers having to hold on to it, while others were supported by good mates, in order to serenade Saturday out in appropriate style. Mary Ann could hear them as she climbed the stairs for bed, exhausted in body, although her mind still raced. She had not slept at all the previous night at Sarah's, and today had been non-stop. She must remember to do something for Ginny. Fancy giving that punchball to the lads when she could have sold it in her own scrapyard.

She was a strange one, was Ginny, she reflected, as she undressed. Quick tempered with a sharp tongue. Folk were a bit wary of her. Once, having a disagreement with a passenger, she had turned them all off half way, leaving them to walk the rest of the way in to Walsall, but she was waiting to bring them home at the appointed time. A silent journey back that was.

Yet she had always had a soft spot for Mary Ann's lads, perhaps identifying them with the three she had lost in childbirth. Mary Ann sympathized deeply, for she had known the heartache of losing a baby. It was a child she had badly wanted, conceived immediately after Raish's Lady Violet affair ended. Maybe that was why Paul, when he came, was doubly precious.

Poor Ginny. Not only was she childless, but she had lost her Will in a pit accident. Ever since that day she had worn his clothes, as if to bring him closer. As Ginny got thinner by the hour, so did Will's clothes appear more voluminous.

Mary Ann lay thinking how lucky she was to have her children. She would save hard for them. Hadn't Paul been delighted to bring her the debts he had collected? And how proud Ben had been of the chicken pen. The chicks were healthy; she would be able to sell the eggs when they were reared. The fish frying had gone well and publicans were asking for more; maybe she could take on one or two more inns. She was glad she had been able to have the piano fetched and get a bit of furniture for Katy. And oh yes, she had opened a coffee shop. No grass had grown under her feet since she had watched Raish making his exodus this morning. Not a bad day, considering. Best of all, she was in touch with her eldest son again and she was going to be a grandmother.

'And you, Raish, will be a grandad,' she whispered into the darkness.

Before she settled to sleep she reached out to his pillow, letting her hand linger for a moment where his head should be. She wondered where he was and whom he was with.

CHAPTER
4

THERE WAS NO work at Conduit for the next three weeks.
Paul, with Ben trailing reluctantly in his wake, tried for jobs
at every pit he knew. Not that they had many moments to
spare. Everything at home was booming. There were two
pigs in the previously empty sties and the stable was
occupied again. Mary Ann had invested her fish profit in a
donkey and cart she had bought from Ginny. The donkey
was dark brown, a nice looking little thing with an agree-
able face. They called her Dandy. She had nuzzled her head
into the shoulders of the lads the first time they met, eager
to be friends with them.

'What's she for, Mother?'

'We can use her to fetch grain and potatoes. If I buy grain
in quantity I can get a load from the brewery for half a
crown; pig potatoes at two shillings a hundredweight. You
two can work yourself up a little log selling business.
Brookes & Orton, the timber merchants, will sell you some
very cheaply.'

'*Logs*, this time o' year, Mother?'

'Yes, logs. A lot of pits are off, aren't they? So there'll be no allowance coal. The women have to keep the fires goin' if they're going to cook any meals. Logs will be cheaper than coal.'

So the lads started to take Dandy into Walsall for logs. But as pretty as she was, and as friendly as she was, it was not long before the men at Brookes & Orton were heartily fed up with her, for after they had loaded the cart she would refuse to budge. It took three or four of them to push her into the road. No other customers could get in or out while she parked herself stubbornly across the entrance.

'I know you can't help it,' the boss said to them one day, 'but she is a damn nuisance. Don't bring her here again.'

'Just give her one more chance. She'll get used to it.'

'Well, *we* never shall,' declared the exasperated man. Then, seeing their disappointment, 'Oh, go on, then. But *only* one more chance.'

Once out of the timber yard Dandy trotted from Walsall to Cod End like a Derby winner. They swore she had understood every word, for, although she often staged sit-down strikes elsewhere, from then on her behaviour at Brookes & Orton was impeccable. There was a fair bit of profit from logs; it was cash on the nail as well, which was more than could be said for the shop.

Mary Ann also had a cash-on-the-nail order from four publicans for fish twice weekly; on another night she supplied home-made faggots with peas. When the pigs were fattened they would show a decent profit and Paul had started to earn a few coppers from cycle repairs: to him it all seemed too good to be true. Yet still he hankered to be down the pit, earning a regular wage. The fear that Raish would turn up and spoil all this was always there.

The coffee shop got off to a slow start. Mary Ann could have counted her customers on one hand that first day, but she was not discouraged, for she had no doubt that she would more than cover the two shillings a week rent. Two hikers on their way to Malvern Hills were her first customers; they were the ones whom Katy saw when she dashed in to inspect Little Cott on that first Saturday. The hikers took away bags of pastries, two bottles of dandelion pop and packets of home-made treacle toffee. Better still, they spread the word and other hikers had appeared from time to time.

An elderly gent in plus-fours called at the shop one day to buy a cycle repair outfit. 'Do you know of anyone who would mend a puncture?' he boomed. 'I don't know a thing about the damn machine.' He was delighted to sit with a pot of coffee, a sandwich and his newspaper while Paul put his bicycle in order, rewarding him handsomely with two silver sixpences. He said he was often with a 'bicycle party', and promised to tell them about 'the coffee shop with a repair service'.

Then there was the exciting day when the first picture was sold. The vicar's spinster daughters called, too early, for their blouses.

They were quite happy to wait in Little Cott, exclaiming chirpily at its prettiness. Mary Ann felt she could not charge them for two cups of tea, which was all they asked for. But before they left they had bought a picture. It was of Pelsall Church, in stark black and white, depicting the first of the winter snows. They asked if Edwin would paint the same scene for them again, as it was now, in the spring; they planned to give the pair to their father as an Easter gift.

So as Mary Ann closed the doors of the coffee shop that day she was able to put more money in the tin marked 'Edwin' than the one marked 'Little Cott'. She could hardly wait for Edwin to come so that she could give him the good news.

It was developing into a regular routine for him to bring Charlotte after Sunday evening chapel. The first time had been the day after Raish had gone. They had all looked forward to it, and were not disappointed.

'Might as well let them come next door,' Katy had suggested, 'where we can't hear if anybody comes pounding on your shop door.' So they carried chairs round, and Mary Ann's best baize tablecloth disguised the offending table. It was a cosy scene which greeted Edwin and his wife when they arrived, the dancing flames from the fire mirrored in the brass kettle and in the piano, lighted lamps showing up the richness of the red walls, a white crocheted runner on the gleaming sideboard, with cups at the ready and a newly-pegged rug, hurriedly completed by Mary Ann the previous night. They had invited Sarah, who would otherwise have been alone.

It was she who called out, 'Come on in. We're all sat in the music room tonight.'

Charlotte's brown coat and hat and the mousy hair pulled tightly back into a bun made her look older than she was, but her plain face was softened in anticipation of the child she was carrying, and in no time at all they were all eating out of her hand.

She radiated a sort of inner glow. There was a soothing stillness about her body, in contrast to the Brooks, who all, with the exception of Edwin, were constantly mobile. She did not say much but had a way of listening carefully with such genuine interest they found they wanted to talk with her. Ben confided about the pigeons he hoped to acquire and Paul about the bicycle he planned to build as soon as he could get the parts together. After listening patiently to the history of Sarah's arthritis she promised some magical liniment her mother made. You knew instinctively she would not forget.

'I suppose Edwin spends a lot of time painting?' quizzed Katy.

'He does. He becomes totally absorbed.'

'What do you do while he paints?'

'I read a lot.'

'You don't mind him not talking?'

'Goodness, no!' she replied in her soft attractive voice. 'No more than he minds if I play the piano while he is painting.'

'I like it,' Edwin chipped in. 'A bit of background music does wonders for me.'

'We are hoping you will play for us, Charlotte.'

Charlotte walked over to Katy's piano and ran her fingers gently over the keys. 'A lovely tone,' she murmured appreciatively.

She played hymns, at which the lads grimaced. Choosing well-known ones she sang, totally unembarrassed, in a soft contralto voice, not asking them to join in, yet it seemed the natural thing to do. Mary Ann was the first to add her clear voice, then Sarah, a bit shakily, in 'O for a thousand songs to sing'. Soon Katy, Paul and Ben were lustily bawling 'Onward Christian Soldiers'. When they came to 'Crown Him Lord of All' they nearly lifted off the roof. The family who had never sung together before felt all the closer for doing so now. Walter and Edwin were less inclined to let themselves go. Charlotte gave them one of her rare slow smiles, which assured them it did not matter at all.

'I did enjoy that, love,' remarked Mary Ann enthusiastically. 'We must do this again.' It touched a tender chord within her when the girl replied simply, 'I would like that, Mother,' using the name for the first time.

There was no doubt in her mind, after seeing them together, that Edwin was happy with Charlotte. She was tranquil and soothing and Edwin more relaxed than Mary Ann would have thought possible. Charlotte's faith in him had given him faith in himself. It was almost as if he had replaced Katy with another well-loved older sister, although the two girls were so different.

Paul and Ben pronounced Edwin's wife a 'good 'un'. They joked about the 'Brookie Choral Society' that would be meeting again at Katy's house tomorrow, Sunday, as they made their way one Saturday, to Ginny's, carrying a square basket which Mary Ann had packed with potato pie, a bread pudding and a fruit cake; she was convinced Ginny did not feed herself properly.

'Dunno when our wench is gunna get married and move into that 'ouse, do you? The wedding plans seem to have gone dead.'

Paul admitted that Katy did seem to have gone off the idea, not that he blamed her. He had thought at one time there might be something going between Katy and Ted Willis, who was much more her type, in his opinion. But Ted seemed to have vanished from the village as suddenly and as completely as Raish.

'She'll get married soon enough, I daresay,' he answered Ben now.

His voice was drowned by the sounds of chanting girls with their skipping ropes in the lane ahead and raucous shouts from lads kicking old stockings rolled up tightly to resemble footballs, while on the common, the ones with a real ball seemed constantly to be yelling 'Goal'. They would have loved to have joined the ball game but there were jobs to be done first.

Further along the lane marbles were being rolled into a circle etched into the earth with a piece of slate. The same slate had been used to draw the squares for a hop-scotch game nearby, where girls screamed and argued far louder than their brothers.

Almost opposite the brickyard were several rows of houses, each with a communal yard where men and boys could be heard clucking to their pigeons 'C'm on. C'm on.' Ben would have lingered if Paul had not edged him on. They had almost passed the final row of houses when, lounging against the side wall away from the general hub-bub they could see three youths.

'Hi up. 'Ere's Boney and 'is mates,' warned Ben.

83

Eric Bone and Conker, so-called because of his double ration of nose, together with Tony Hales, known as Toenails, detached themselves from the wall and swaggered toward them. 'Doin' errands for yer Mam again, are yer?' Boney shouted, while the other two hooted in derision.

'Give 'im one, our kid,' urged Ben. 'Or I will.'

'Oh, come on. We haven't the time to bother with him today. Put your fists down, Ben.'

The three youths formed themselves into a threatening semi-circle, Boney well to the fore. 'Got a different sort o' basket today, 'ave yer? I 'ear yoh was doin' a bit o' runnin' about for yer Mam last night, yoh two.'

'What of it?'

'Pushin' a basket trolley, I 'eard. Like a couple o' wenches.'

'Looking for trouble, are you?'

'An' what if I am? I doubt if you can gie me any, girlie.'

Boney was a big threatening hulk of a lad, but, having been out of work for a twelvemonth, he was flabby and far from fit, in contrast with Paul, whose square shoulders and chest rippled with muscles well-oiled from trundling tubs and pumping water. He knew he could take Boney on, but they had a basket to deliver to Ginny, there was a load of coal at the wharf to be bagged up, payments to collect this afternoon. He had planned to have an hour cleaning and re-spoking a couple of bicycle wheels he had picked up, to say nothing of watching some football at The Bush field before taking the fish round. Every minute of his day was spoken for. He could deal with Boney another time, so he just said, 'Move out o' the road, the lot of you.'

But Boney hadn't any jobs to do. He was bored. He had been bored for months, and today he felt like showing off his single talent. 'Yer Dad's gone again, I 'ear.'

'You hear a lot. What's it to do with you?'

'My Mam says it's yer mother's fault. Her don't know what to do fer 'im. 'Er's that took up with mekkin' money,

84

'er don't know what to do fer a bloke. An 'usband needs more'n food on the table, yer know. That's why yer old man 'as gone. He 'as to look elsewhere, 'cos 'e can't get it at 'ome, I reckon.'

The other two started giggling. 'Yer've 'it it on the nail, Boney. 'E can't get it at home,' they chanted in unison.

'Let's get at 'em, our kid,' shouted Ben, enraged.

By now his brother needed no persuading. Incensed at such disrespect for Mary Ann, the blood rushed to Paul's face. He placed the basket on the ground, and took off his jacket.

'Watch that,' he ordered Ben. 'And you keep out o' this.' Then he turned to his opponent. 'Get your hands up, Boney.'

Before the words left his mouth the breath was knocked out of him by a thumping blow to the stomach, followed by a kick on the shins and a hefty blow to the face. Boney's mates shouted in glee. Ben clenched his fists, hopping first on one foot and then on the other, hoping one of them would make a move, so that he could justifiably join in. But Conker and Toenails had seen the Brook brothers fight before and had no wish to be actively involved. To be on the sidelines shouting for their hero was enough for them.

Winded and caught unawares by another kick, Paul landed on the floor, pain cramping his stomach.

'Come on, our kid. Get up. What did 'e say about our mother?' yelled Ben.

Paul did not need reminding. He uncurled deceptively slowly. The next time Boney flailed out with his elbow he dodged, coming straight back with a punch to Boney's jaw that sent him reeling, followed by another to his face which made his nose bleed, and yet another which shut his eye. Thoughts of his hard-working mother whom this thug dared to insult gave extra power to his punches.

The crowd, which had collected as rapidly as sparrows round a few crumbs, were shouting 'C'm on, Brookie. Give 'im what fer.' It was left to Conker and Toenails to shout weakly for Boney.

Ben would have rather it had been himself doling out the thrashing. He was a more aggressive fighter than his brother and felt he could do better. It should have been his Dad, though, feeling the force of those punches, for subjecting their mother to such insults. He flailed imaginary blows to his father's head while he shouted encouragement to Paul.

Boney was rolling about painfully on the floor. Following every move, Paul saw the jagged piece of broken bottle in his hand as he got up. He went for Boney's wrist, grasping it in a vice-like grip until he dropped the glass.

'You'd do that, would you, you coward!' He shook him again. 'What did you say about my mother?' He took hold of Boney's shoulders, shaking him like a rabbit until his teeth chattered and his eyes were popping out of his head. 'What did you say about my mother?' he yelled again.

'Nuthin'. I daih say nuthin',' panted Boney, his flushed face suddenly whitening to a sickly pallor, as he saw the threat in Paul's blazing eyes and felt the steely strength in his hands as he lifted him off the floor. One more punch for Mary Ann and Paul knew that Boney had had enough.

'Don't ever speak of her again. Do you hear me? She's worth a hundred of you lot.'

'Yeah. Yeah. I know.'

Paul looked down at the now pitiful heap on the floor. He picked him up, thrusting the dusty cap that had been kicked around as they had struggled into his hands. 'Don't ever forget it, Boney. My mother's worth a hundred of anybody else's.' He shoved him toward his mates. 'Take him home and get him cleaned up.'

'Let that be a lesson to you,' screamed Ben, angrier than his brother, and frustrated at being left out of the fight. 'You showed 'im,' he acknowledged as they left houses and spectators behind, kicking an old tin to one another with unnecessary force as they sprinted down the stony lane that led to Ginny's yard.

'He asked for it,' Paul muttered grimly.

'Ar, he did an' all. I'd 'ave given 'im a bit more. Serve him right.'

'If he hadn't mentioned our Mother I wouldn't have touched him. After all, kids that are out o' work; I feel sorry for them. They don't know what to do with themselves.'

'We're out o' work an' all,' replied Ben forcibly. 'Don't feel sorry for 'im. You'll 'ave to face his old man when you go to their 'ouse collectin' this afternoon.'

'I'll worry about that when it comes.'

But Paul did not relish the prospect. Dicky Bone was a hefty, red-faced man, twice the size of his son. He knew there was nothing for it but to face him. He would have to call on him, and on every other house in that yard. This morning he had been with Mary Ann when some bills arrived that his Dad had run up at the public houses. Word had got around that Raish, had hopped it and they had addressed the accounts to his mother.

'Do you have to pay his bills, Mother?'

'These are from people I'm hoping to continue business with. They're allowing me to sell my fish on their premises,' she reminded him. 'But not to worry, lad. We'll cope.'

Her resilience was amazing. She bounced back from every knock like a rubber ball. This morning Paul had hated Raish almost as much as Ben did.

There were no more buildings after the brickyard until Ginny's; only Gipsy Gert, perched on her caravan steps smoking her clay pipe, a scary figure, with wild grey hair to her shoulders and wrinkles deep as furrows in a face nearly as grey as her hair. Occasionally she tugged at the black shawl draped round her narrow shoulders.

They called 'Hello Gertie' as they passed. A wicked grin showed two brown stumps of teeth like sawn-off pit stumps in an otherwise toothless mouth.

'Some say she's a hundred and two,' stage-whispered Ben as soon as they were out of earshot.

'They also say she was a good-looker once. She used to come round the villages selling pegs, artificial flowers and bits of lace. Wonder how she manages to live now?'

'Oh, folk give 'er bits o' this an' that. She probably gets more food than them that's workin'.'

They had reached the five-barred gate to Ginny's yard that was always propped open with a large stone. Ginny's scruffy cottage had a forlorn, forgotten look, almost as if it were part of its surrounding scrap. They banged at the front door and at the back before they lifted the latch of the kitchen door that was never locked, leaving their offerings on the table. The scrapyard was a treasure trove. There were garden tools, old wheelbarrows without wheels, oddments of wood, prams, buckets and bowls, iron bedsteads, nuts and bolts and a variety of old lamps. It was an exchange market, filled with a jumble of things useless to the folk who had parted with them yet useful to others.

They wandered round, fascinated with it, as always, until they paused near a pile of old metal. For some time Paul had been trying to collect enough parts to build a bike. He rummaged around until he found a few bent spokes; the wheels he had acquired were short of a few. He could straighten these. He picked out a couple of worn pedals, and was bent over still searching when suddenly a terrifying screech jerked him upright.

Ginny appeared from the back of the tumbledown shed, her trousers, or rather Will's trousers, tucked into enormous wellingtons which caused her to stamp rather than walk. She looked rougher than ever. As she stomped angrily toward them she was shaking her hard brown fist. 'What are you doin'? Put them things down this minute.'

'I'd like to buy them from you, Ginny.'

'What did I tell yer? Put 'em down!' Paul dropped the things he had collected as if they were hot cakes. Ginny, in this mood, her small beady eyes about to pop out of her head, was more frightening than ten Boneys. 'What's that great bruise on the side of yer face? Bin fightin', 'ave yer?'

He nodded, watching her warily, in case she landed him another on the opposite cheek.

'Go and bathe it under the yard tap. Go on!' she screamed. 'And when you've done come back 'ere. You,' she said, indicating Ben, 'come with me.'

As Paul returned, Ben was just about to open a rectangular pigeon basket. It was an ancient one, but the lid had a good fastener.

'Go on, then. Lift the lid. But bang it down again quick.'

Ben did just that and in a split second he saw two of the finest-looking grey and white pigeons he had ever imagined. It couldn't be, could it? He must have dreamed it. He gingerly lifted the lid a second time to make sure. His face was radiant; it held a joy such as Paul had not imagined his brother could feel, let alone show.

'Ginny! You must be a witch. How did yer know? Ginny, yer me best mate.'

'Oh, get away with yer.' Turning to Paul she yelled, 'And what was you ferreting about after, eh?'

'Just some bike things, Ginny. I've got the money to pay for them.'

'Well, keep it in yer pocket. I told you I'd look out for some things, didn't I?' she tutted sharply. Round the back of the stable she removed a couple of sacks; underneath, neatly lined up, were a pair of pedals, a decent saddle, a bent set of handlebars which could easily be straightened, a couple of old inner tubes, some brake blocks and six spokes, almost new. This must be the tidiest corner of the scrapyard. Paul was speechless for once. ''Ow's that to be goin' on with, then lad?'

'Thanks, Ginny,' Paul breathed. 'It's nearly enough to build a bike.'

89

'Here's an old sack to put 'em in.' She ushered them toward the gate. 'Get off then now, the pair o' yer, and no more fightin'.'

She watched them go, both with that proud tilt to their heads: sturdy, square-backed Paul, carrying the sack as if it were feather, and the one like a bean pole reaching for the sky, handling the pigeon basket as if it contained the crown jewels. She could take to that one.

'Had a surprise, did yer?' cackled Gipsy Gert, as they hurried by.

Mary Ann said that Ben could share her corn. The pigeons could have one end of the stable, providing he separated them from Dandy with a good substantial divider, so that was a job to keep him busy all afternoon. Paul earned sixpence from the coalman, and later went round the houses collecting. He left Boney's until last; he had already had one or two scares. One woman had screamed at him, 'Does she think I'll run off? Where 'ave I got the money from? Bugger off.'

And once a man had staggered to the door, already the worse for drink. 'We ain't got the stuff any more,' he said, swaying, 'and if yoh want it, get to Rushall pawn shop.'

He had collected quite a sum from folk genuinely trying to pay their way. He squared his shoulders now as he went into the backyard of the row of houses where Boney lived. Some of his neighbours paid up; others who had seen him coming locked their doors. Boney's Dad was a big powerfully-built man with a large red face. His braces were dangling untidily, his shirt was off as if he had been washing, showing the holes in his flannel ganzie. 'Do you want to pay anything off your bill today, Mr Bone?'

'Come in,' the big man ordered curtly. Paul followed, knees knocking. There was no sign of Boney, just his little sister playing on the floor. Dick Bone reached down a shilling which his wife had left on the mantelshelf, and Paul marked it off the bill.

'Thank you very much,' he said, relieved that it looked as if he might get through the door in one piece.

'Are you the kid that gid my lad a pasting this morning?'

'Yes, I am.'

To his surprise the big man, who worked across the road at the brickyard, laughed loudly. 'Did 'im the world 'o good, an' all. You wouldn't like to teach 'im a bit o' boxin', would yer? He could do with a lesson or two.'

'I'll think about it,' replied Paul and went on his way whistling. He thought about it, realizing there must be a few lads in Cod End with time on their hands who wouldn't mind doing a bit of boxing. He didn't fancy teaching Boney, though; not after he'd said that about his mother.

But a practice booth, in the little bedroom over the coffee shop, after his mother had closed, might pay its way. They had the punchball to fitten people up. The out-of-work lads would not be able to pay more than a copper, but it would keep them occupied and would be bound to bring in a bob a week. He felt reasonably certain Mary Ann would agree with him.

CHAPTER
5

IT WAS A mixture of Sunday School Anniversary and Charlotte that decided Katy. Anniversary Day began earlier than most Sundays, with Mary Ann doing a roaring trade in white socks and pinafores, bootlaces and stiff white collars, peppermints and cough sweets.

Every pew in the little chapel was packed with a congregation breathing as one, while others perched on chairs in the schoolroom, craning their necks to see through the big double doors into the chapel proper, where boards had been hammered into tiered seating for the youthful singers, the boards covered with miles of white crepe paper. A sudden ripple of excitement preceded a sedate procession of demure little angels advancing in single file toward the platform. Parents and grannies oohed and ahed at the miracles that had been wrought with bits of silk and crepe de chine, mainly from Mary Ann's bundles, or older sisters' garments which had been taken up, down, out or in. Katy felt she had personally sewn for every child on the platform. Were these white-robed innocents the same boisterous girls who had giggled and shoved around her sewing machine every day these past two weeks, after school? Their chapel superintendent, resplendent in morning suit and silk topper, welcomed the visiting minister with due reverence and smiled encouragingly at the tableau of whiteness.

One day, Katy promised herself, I shall have girls of my own to sew for and, as the newly-installed organ thundered out rapturously, she vowed that at least one of her children would learn to play her piano. But first there had to be a husband. She knew she must somehow come to terms with the see-sawing waves of indecision that plagued her about that. That night, at the weekly family get-together, she watched Edwin and Charlotte closely, Charlotte ever patient, not minding if Edwin, quietly content, did not want to sing or talk, yet somehow managing to include him. They seemed so close there was no need for words between them.

'I think our Edwin could have chosen far worse,' remarked Mary Ann when they had gone.

'He seems happy enough.'

'He *is* happy. Because no-one is trying to change him any more,' conceded Mary Ann thoughtfully. 'Charlotte accepts him for what he is. We were always trying to push him into things he did not want to do, weren't we?'

'I suppose we did try to change him, yes.'

It had seemed necessary if he was to survive in Cod End, thought Katy, remembering how she used to drag him across the fields to play when all he really wanted was to sit quietly out of sight behind the stable, reading or drawing. Remembering too how Edwin's timidity seemed to fan the flame of anger in their father, resulting in him lashing out physically with his strap, or verbally with demoralizing sarcasm.

No wonder Edwin was happy with Charlotte. He had at

last found the tranquillity that had eluded him all his young life.

Mary Ann, reading her thoughts, said, 'His peace of mind comes from being accepted for what he is.'

The remark stuck in Katy's mind. 'Accepted for what he is.' Could she accept Walter in that way?

She had suffered nightmarish dreams these past three weeks since she last saw Ted. There had been nights when she was running in terror across the fields, two men chasing, gaining ground, striking terror into her heart. When she reached the haven of trees there was nowhere else to run. Slowly and fearfully she forced herself to turn, only to find no-one there. Nothing but an empty meadow, an ominous frightening silence and a little jenny wren. It was not in Katy's nature to be afraid or to have nightmares and she hated the experience.

Walter appeared at the door of the brewhouse just as they finished washing up. How comfortable their house had looked again tonight, he thought enviously. He wished Katy would hurry up and make up her mind; she had appeared to avoid him again all evening.

'I'll be off now, then,' he said diffidently.

'I'll walk to the end of the gulley with you.'

At the stepping bridge he took her hand and planted the usual shy kiss on her cheek. Light as a feather it was, like his voice. 'Goodnight, Katy love. Sleep well.'

She made as if to walk away, then turning, smiled at him impishly. 'You did say you would like to put the banns in, Walter?'

He gaped in astonishment. 'You mean it?'

'There's not much point in saying it if I don't, is there?' she laughed.

'I shall never let you regret it, love.' It seemed too good to be true. Katy as his wife and that comfortable little house for a home. He could hardly believe it; she had been so distant lately. He travelled back to his digs as if on wings.

94

That night Katy closed the door of her mind on Ted Willis so that she could sleep comfortably. Her last thought before closing her eyes was, 'If Charlotte can make a go of it, I can. And I shall have lots of children dotted about on that Anniversary platform. All of them happy.'

She did not want the ups and downs of Mary Ann's life, she told herself; just the calm and certainty of Charlotte's.

In spite of her doubts Mary Ann received the news from Katy calmly enough. Home from Birmingham rag market, with her bundles, she said, 'Look, Katy. I thought this might do for your wedding dress.'

'Oh, Mother! I don't have to have a dress from a reject out of a *bundle*, do I?' Katy exclaimed.

'Look at it first, my girl.' She handed her a length of material. It was a beautiful piece of tussore silk, the colour of rich dairy cream. The only fault seemed to be a small hole burned in the extreme corner. Katy examined it carefully before looking up with a smile.

'Right again, Mary Ann,' she chuckled.

She reached into the bottom of her sewing box where she had been saving a piece of lace once rescued from the same source. It matched the silk exactly.

So, the day after her twenty-first birthday, Katy wore a wedding dress of rich cream silk, with a tight bodice of real lace and a tiny stand-up pleated collar. The sleeves were gathered into the lace that capped her shoulders and ruched all the way down to her wrist, while the skirt, fitting snugly into her tiny waist, was cut in panels, each panel ruched from top to bottom. Her hat was a wide brimmed cream straw, trimmed with posies made from the odd snippings of silk and lace. She wore a brooch from Walter at her neck and his heart in her hands. As she walked down the aisle toward him on Edwin's arm he felt the luckiest man in the whole world.

All Cod End had turned out to give her a send-off. Only a

handful were in church. If they went anywhere it was to chapel. The women had no choice but to be churched after the births of their babies before they could decently present themselves in public. It was enough to have to do that and attend their own weddings and funerals without going to anyone else's, they said.

But they crowded into the road outside the shop to wave off Katy seated regally in Ginny's horse and trap, especially cleaned up for the occasion, with Ginny reasonably tidy in Will's best black jacket and bowler, a skirt that fitted and her own shoes.

'There were cries of 'Ooh, yoh look lovely', 'Watch out tonight, gel', and 'Good luck, me wench'.

'Yoh are the pick o' the market today, Katy,' one voice shouted above the rest, reminding her of her father, who should have been taking her down the aisle. Nothing had been heard of him since he left, and his children were enjoying the most peaceful period of their lives. Sometimes Katy missed the stimulation of pitting her wits against his. She missed his colourful personality when he was sober, and the excitement when he was drunk, but she wouldn't have dared say so, and felt guilty about even thinking it.

Six of them squashed into the trap for the return journey: bride and groom; Edwin, earnestly attending to Charlotte, now expanding daily under the voluminous brown coat; Sarah, proud to be part of the family on such an occasion; and Mary Ann, looking beautiful in the rose-coloured wool skirt and jacket, with velvet hat to match, all made from bundle pieces. She looked years younger since Raish left and all the recent organizing and planning had resulted in her face becoming even more animated than before.

Paul and Ben, hot in Sunday suits, with high-buttoned waistcoats, knickerbockers, new shirts and tweed caps, walked home across the common with Walter's sister Annie and her four children, three dopey lads and a girl, all with bright red hair like Annie herself. Only the girl, Lucilla,

96

seemed to have any life in her. If this was an indication of the family, what was Katy in for, the lads wondered.

'Ah, well, what has to be will be,' remarked Annie inconsequently. 'At least our Walter will be out o' them lodgings. That woman didn't give him enough to eat half the time. I would have had him with me. But how could I? Six of we, and only one bedroom. Ah well, what has to be will be.' She paused long enough to reprimand Lucilla, showing off her stick-thin black-stockinged legs and red flannel knickers as she performed cart wheels on the common.

Charlotte, now so much a part of the family, played light classical music softly in the background while people ate and talked. Even Ginny chatted away sociably with Sarah, before being taken to look at the pigeons. The photographer, whom Walter had booked, forgot to come until the guests had disappeared. They were able to muster the family, but the lads took a bit of persuading to change back into their uncomfortable outfits while the man fitted up his equipment. They all posed stiffly for the picture in the garden, surrounded by chickens, donkey, pigs, pigeons and squawking geese, the photographer assuring them that none of these would be seen. He was wrong about that too.

When they were alone Katy and Walter went into the front room to gaze appreciatively at their little shop. Every kind of sweet and chocolate filled the shelves Walter had fitted. He had made a counter with a glass case containing tuppenny and fourpenny woodbines, tobacco, twist and matches.

'Isn't it good of your mother to provide us with all this, Katy? We must pay her back as soon as we can.'

There was a card propped in the window stating 'Opening Tomorrow'.

'Shall we open now?' Katy suggested impulsively.

'If that's what you want, love.'

97

How often she was to hear him say that in the future. And when they climbed into the big double bed that night and she wanted to go straight to sleep he said it again. In the days that followed he never argued with her. In fact he did not say much at all. Katy was used to arguing with her brothers, her father, even her mother. Always she reminded herself of Charlotte's patient example. But Katy was not Charlotte and Walter's pliability often exasperated her. And Charlotte was in love with Edwin. It would be better when the babies started arriving, she told herself.

She couldn't be bored living close by her family. Something was always happening there. Conduit had opened up again, much to Paul's relief, but its three shifts a week was hardly conducive to asking for a rise. Ben hated it from the first day. It wasn't the work that bothered him; he was a tough lad. He hated the humiliation of being bossed about by the fireman. It was worse than school, he said, and often he would answer back cheekily. One day he would have been sacked but for Paul's pleading. 'He's only a kid. Give him another chance. He'll settle down.'

'Well, get him to button up his mouth, will yer; otherwise he's out on 'is arse.'

'I ain't gonner bow and scrape to 'im,' he protested when Paul reminded him on the way home that they were both dependent on the fireman for a job. 'Who does he think he is?'

'There's got to be somebody in charge, you fool. And just remember how hard our Mother works before you open your mouth again, and how she needs the money.'

But at home the summer was bowling along swiftly and happily. The coffee shop was a great success, mainly due to Edwin's paintings. It became known as 'The Little Gallery that serves coffee' by people who considered it fun to gather in the quaint little room. Sometimes they would ask Edwin to meet them there and they would wander round, coffee in hand, discussing his work. Word had spread like wildfire to the people who could afford to buy once the vicar had displayed his paintings of Pelsall Church at one or two church events. Edwin had as many orders as he could cope with, sometimes working far into the night. His pit had been on three shifts a week for some time. Charlotte suggested that he give it up altogether, but with a baby on the way he was not yet bold enough to risk it. It was difficult for him to believe the extent of his success.

Buyers preferred paintings with which they could identify. The miller came after hearing that the painting 'Stepping Bridge and Fields' showed his mill in the background. Daddy Dale chose one of the chapel and donated it to the schoolroom. 'Willenas Common', with its canals and bridges, was bought by the family from the Toll House, and Mr Dickinson from the furniture shop requested a view of the common which would also show his house. People from as far away as Sutton Coldfield commissioned Edwin to paint scenes from Sutton Park, while publicans wanted impressions of their inns. One gentleman who said that Edwin had remarkable talent offered to set him up in bigger premises in Edgbaston, but Edwin refused.

'You should never look a gift horse in the face, my lad,' Mary Ann said, but he was quite firm, and remembering the mistakes she had made when he was a child, she said no more.

The fried fish business was booming, the lads had no trouble selling their logs on their days off, the boxing booth was open three nights a week and Paul was servicing machines for the Pelsall Cycling Club. Mary Ann's bank balance was growing rapidly. She still worked feverishly throughout the day, nipping from shop to shop when necessary and never appeared tired. Charlotte helped out regularly; they had become very close.

'You are a good girl,' Mary Ann remarked one day. 'I don't know how I shall manage without you when you've had that babby.'

99

'You won't have to. I shall bring Mark Edwin with me. He might as well start learning the business early.'

'Oh, it's going to be a lad, is it?'

'Definitely.'

Mary Ann had just returned from Birmingham with her bundles. Already customers were popping in enquiring, ''Ave yer got anythin' for we today, duck? Any bargains?'

Charlotte hummed softly as she carried the bundles next door, where Katy sorted through them rapidly, quipping as she did so.

'Look at this great piece of calico. It will do for a tent I suppose. Oh, a bit of leather; Mother may have plans to start a shoe factory. How about this?' She draped a length of bright red satin tightly round herself. 'Do you think we could open a music hall? We could hire the schoolroom from Daddy Dale. Imagine, Charlotte, a notice in the *Walsall Observer*, ''The Red Satin Music Hall, the only one of its kind out of London.'' Have you ever been to London, Charlotte?'

'Once, with my parents. We went to see Queen Victoria's Jubilee.'

'Did you *see* the Queen?' asked Katy, entranced.

'We did. She was an old lady by then and very frail. It was such a thrill. But, oh, the crowds! I didn't like that part of it.'

'Did you often go out with your parents, all together, like that?'

Charlotte caught the envy in her voice. 'Quite often. But I was the only one they had to think about, Katy.'

'*I* am going to London on Saturday.'

'With Walter?'

'Goodness, no. It would be agony for Walter. With Sally Dilkes.'

'Mrs Dilkes, the landlady? I thought she was always abroad.'

'No,' Katy laughed. 'Sally's her daughter. We are going

to ''Women's Sunday'' in Hyde Park, to support Mrs Pankhurst and the suffragettes. They need all the support they can get. Don't you agree?'

Charlotte hesitated. 'You may be right. I haven't thought enough about it.' She patted her bulge. 'I suppose my mind has been on other things.'

'Wish I had the same distraction,' Katy murmured enviously. 'I was hoping I would be expecting by now. A little cousin for yours.'

'It's early days yet. Look how long it took us.'

'Hm.' Not many Cod End women failed to have a baby within the year. Katy had expected to become pregnant straight away. 'You didn't mind, though, did you? I am eager to make a start.'

'It will come.'

'And when it does you are going to teach *it* to play the piano, aren't you?'

'Of course. Meanwhile you can share Mark Edwin.' Charlotte gathered up the items Katy had discarded. 'I had better get back to Mother. She will be waiting for these.' She paused at the doorway. 'We are all so fortunate, aren't we, Katy? We shall remember nineteen hundred and eight as the happy year.'

'I'll say! You with a baby on the way and Edwin becoming a famous painter.'

'You with your little sweet shop and Walter on a full week.'

'Mother and the lads with the shops, fish frying, pigs and pigeons, chickens and cycle repairing . . . '

'Logs and boxing booth.'

They both laughed happily.

'And now you are going to get us the Vote. Good luck on Sunday, Katy.'

Katy and Sally Dilkes were the only passengers to board the early train on Sunday morning. Sally yawned as they put their bags on the rack and settled down. 'We must be mad, getting up at this hour of the morning. Thank heaven we only have to change once, at Birmingham.'

'I was awake in plenty of time. Too excited to sleep.'

All Cod End had been agog when they heard that Katy Brook, as they still called her, was off to London. Some criticized her for her friendship with Sally. 'Hobnobbin' with the nobs', they called it. Others took the view that Sally was 'a nice enough wench' and that was all that mattered.

The girls had first met when Sally used to come to the Big House at Pelsall to stay with her grandmother in school holidays. Old Mrs Dilkes was as eccentric as they come. She wore a fur coat and shabby down-at-heel shoes, winter and summer alike. She collected her own rents in those days. Every week she would walk round Cod End exclaiming at any rubbish on the ground, commanding the first person in sight to pick it up. Like Old Lawson she bought all her clothes from Mary Ann. Sometimes she went with her to the warehouses for a day out, paying her expenses and compensating her for her loss of takings in the shop. When she died she left her house to Sally who, to everyone's surprise, although she travelled abroad and to London a great deal, continued to live in it for much of the time. Katy did her sewing. The expensive materials she could afford were a joy to work with and Sally assured her that the garments were better than any she could buy in London.

Extreme antagonism toward each other when they were children had somehow developed into firm friendship. They shared the same frank outspokenness and found it easy to talk together. Sally was more than surprised when Katy married the colourless Walter.

'Did your husband object to you coming?' she asked now.

Katy laughed. 'Walter? He just said, "If that's what you want, love." '

'Why didn't you bring your mother along? She would have enjoyed it.'

'What! The place would fall down if Mother wasn't there.'

'Proof of just how necessary a woman is. Yet most of the girls at boarding school left with just one ambition. To be married before anyone else. I can't understand it. Husbands! I can manage without one.'

'Really? They tell me they're useful if you want to start a family.'

'Do you?'

'Yes, I do, while I am still young enough to enjoy them.'

Sally raised her eyes in mock horror. 'You can't mean it.'

'I do. My children will have the sort of happy settled childhood we never had. Perhaps that's not quite fair. We *were* fairly happy, thanks to my mother. But settled? Never. We shall go out and about as a family,' she added. 'Like Charlotte did.'

'Charlotte?'

'My sister-in-law. I've thought a lot about Charlotte, and I have come to the conclusion that what gives her such tranquillity is that every morning of her life she was woken up knowing that everything that day would be all right.'

'I know what you mean,' mused Sally. 'I was neither happy nor settled when I was a child.'

'*You?*' Katy was astonished.

'Yes. Me. The parents were always abroad. I hated being separated from my brothers, boarding school was awful, and during school holidays we were packed off to other people. On the odd occasion that we did see our parents they argued the whole of the time. My father always presumed he was right. Like all men. Like Asquith. That man has said that Votes for Women would do more harm than good! Perhaps after today's meeting he will see that we mean business. The country would be a better place if women were in charge.' Sally's black eyes flashed with fervent conviction.

103

Katy could only judge by the women she knew: her mother, Ginny, Sarah, Charlotte, Sally, Ted Willis's mother and other Cod End women managing to feed large families on a pittance, yet still able to provide their men with a twist of tobacco at the end of the week. As she considered the men she knew, Walter, Edwin and Raish, she decided on balance that her friend may be right.

Sally suddenly tossed her hat on to the seat, put her head back and closed her eyes. With her perfect oval face, olive skin, a mass of blue-black hair the colour of a gipsy's, and long silky lashes she looked very beautiful. Katy had imagined that children of the well-to-do had everything they desired. Now she knew different. Poor Sally. Everyone had their problems.

At Birmingham they found a special train had been laid on. It was so full they had difficulty in finding two seats together. Sally could have travelled First Class, of course, but preferred to be expounding her theories to other women sharing the carriage. Katy decided to 'take the day' without getting too serious about the reason for it. It was exciting to get away from Cod End and be on her way to London.

Crowds of women poured from the trains pulling in at Euston from all over the country. Organized groups held their embroidered banners aloft, while a noise resembling Five Ways Colliery Band pounded in the distance.

The girls joined the masses surging through the stone archway into a pretty square fringed with summer flowers where hundreds of women, tingling with infectious enthusiasm, assembled behind the band which was to lead them to Hyde Park. As they stepped out briskly to the music Katy craned her neck to peep inside high perambulators being pushed by uniformed nurses in the opposite direction. 'It will be Regents Park today for the little darlings,' commented Sally drily, 'Hyde Park will be too noisy.'

They had to wait for traffic at Marble Arch. Although Mary Ann often told her how the number of motor cars in

Birmingham was growing, Katy, who had only ever seen one go through the village, was fascinated with the assortment of horse-buses, open-topped motor buses, taxi-cabs, horse carriages and motor cars.

The sun was intense in a cloudless blue sky. Perspiring policemen lined the railings of the park, and some women, tightly corseted and clad in serge suits, looked fit to drop. Sally, conversant with the suffragette colours, wore a pretty green and white muslin dress with a straw hat trimmed with purple ribbon; Katy a cool white cotton patterned with tiny primroses, and her wedding hat. They made a pretty picture, the dark gypsy-like beauty and her diminutive golden-haired friend.

For a while they watched the punters on the Serpentine, young men in boaters and striped jackets, their female companions more intent on impressing the men than getting the Vote.

The noise in Hyde Park was deafening as women of every age, size and class bustled and pushed, shouting to make themselves heard. Every now and then a cheer would go up as some famous man, sympathetic to the Cause, was recognized.

'There's George Bernard Shaw,' Sally pointed out, and a few minutes later, 'Thomas Hardy is over there.'

'That will be something to tell Walter,' commented Katy, craning her neck to see. Since they were married Walter often read to her at night while she sat hand sewing, excerpts from Hardy novels which Charlotte had lent him.

In the centre of the stands erected for speech-making was a large furniture van whence the general proceedings were directed by the blowing of bugles. They joined a tightly-wedged crowd round one of the stands to hear Helen Fraser speaking about the progress already made in social services for women, and emphasizing that before they could do more, women must work together for the Vote. The meeting closed on a note of high resolve as the loud-speaker van announced that the resolution was carried: 'That this meeting calls for the Government to grant Votes to Women without delay.'

After discussing their experiences and showing off the souvenirs they had bought, most of the women dropped off to sleep on the journey home. Katy had the impression that many had come out of simple curiosity or for a day out; very few were as inspired as Sally.

It was a relief to get a carriage to themselves at Walsall for the last lap of the journey, but, just as the train was pulling out, a young man ran and jumped on. He flopped, breathless, in front of them.

It was Ted. A different Ted, looking very smart and prosperous. Katy felt her colour rising and her heart beating a strange tattoo as disturbing as the drums she had heard earlier today.

'Well! I couldn't have dropped in at a better place, could I?'

As she introduced him to Sally, Katy noticed that he talked differently and his hands were softer.

'Where have you ladies been?' he asked in his direct manner.

'We have been to London to see the Queen,' replied Sally tartly before Katy could answer.

'Took tea with her did you?'

'Actually we have been to a W.S.P.U. meeting in Hyde Park. But I don't suppose you know what that means. Not many men do,' returned Sally icily.

'You have found one at last then. Aren't you lucky? Been to support the Votes for Ladies, have you? I'm all for it. I would like to see women in Parliament; even a woman Prime Minister one day.'

'I don't suppose you mean a word of it.'

'But I do, Miss Dilkes. I do,' he said, inclining toward her in mock deference. 'And what about you, Katy? Do you agree with all this?' He studied her quizzically. 'You have been a long way from home. A long way from Walter,' he added cheekily.

With his brown eyes stripping her naked, Katy felt she must change the subject. 'What have you been doing with yourself, Ted? I heard you were working away.'

'Only as far as Birmingham. I started off by chauffeuring a chap who is making motor cars, and now I am helping him to sell them. Very interesting job. Pays well too,' he added significantly.

'Well, here's a coincidence. I have been thinking of buying a motor car,' announced Sally coolly.

'Aren't you a lucky girl, then, to have met me! I can arrange a demonstration at any time to suit yourself.'

'Would it be possible, do you think, for me to learn to drive in time for the Olympic Games at the White City?'

'Hm! Third of July. Doesn't give us much time, does it?' He grinned. 'But we would do our best.'

'How do you feel about coming to the Olympic Games by motor car, Katy?'

'I think this outing will have to last me a while, Sally.'

'Very staid married woman, our Katy,' put in Ted, much to Katy's annoyance which she demonstrated by kicking his ankle.

Sally, not noticing, again launched into her favourite topic. 'Did you know we are not even allowed to enter women in the Olympic Games? Only Denmark will have women gymnasts there, and they will have no medals or points awarded to them.'

'Is that so! Yet still you would like to go?'

'Yes. If I witness it for myself perhaps I can do something about it.'

Katy was remembering the traffic she had seen earlier today. 'It would be a long way to drive in a new motor car, Sally. Especially as we have such a good rail service; you said so yourself.'

'But it would be so much more intoxicating.'

Ted was at his most charming. 'If you are not quite ready for it when the time comes, Miss Dilkes, I shall be happy to chauffeur you myself.'

'We will have to see about that,' replied Sally rather haughtily. 'Why is it you are travelling by train now?'

'A Cod End kid doesn't need a car for a weekend in Cod End, Miss Dilkes. And when I do drive into Cod End it will be in a car I have bought, not one I've borrowed.'

Katy could only sit wide-eyed and unusually tongue-tied, listening to the fast repartee between Sally and this new Ted, as they discussed cars and politics knowledgeably for the rest of the short journey. As the train pulled in at Pelsall station they could see Walter by the lighted lamp, patiently waiting. Ted immediately offered to escort Sally home.

Walter had prepared a hot supper and Katy tackled it gratefully, hungrier than she realized. She found she was relieved to be sitting with Walter, kind thoughtful Walter, telling him about her day out. She thought of Sally going home to no-one but servants. Unless, of course, she invited Ted in? Seeing Ted again had disturbed her more than she liked to admit.

Walter interrupted her thoughts. 'You didn't tell me Ted Willis was going to London.'

'Ted? He boarded the train at Birmingham. He is working there. Something to do with cars; he might sell Sally one.'

The relief in his eyes surprised her, as did his lovemaking that night.

Next day Ted came into her shop to buy a fancy box of sugared almonds. 'For Miss Sally Dilkes,' he said, a twinkle in his eye.

'Did you get an order for a motor car?'

'Now give me time, Katy. I am meeting the lucky girl again tomorrow. You know she would want to try the goods before committing herself.' He deliberately gave his words a double meaning.

'She doesn't like men, Ted.'

'Oh, I see. She just takes us like castor oil for her health, does she?'

She stared at him, not wishing to comprehend. His hand closed over hers for a second. He patted it lightly as if she were a child. 'You're out of your depth, love. Believe me, it's just *marriage* your friend doesn't like.' He grinned as he reached for the doorlatch on his way out. 'And I don't go much on that, either.' Why should her heart lurch so sickeningly? It couldn't be jealousy, could it? Oh, damn Ted Willis. Damn his cheek. And damn Walter's lack of it.

While Katy was in London Ben was running in a race. He had been sprinting round the common regularly and one day a fellow who had often stood watching approached him.

'Fancy yourself a good runner, do yer?'

'No. I only do it to keep fit.'

''Cos if yer do I'd like to run yer for thirty bob.'

'I couldn't afford that.'

'Think you'd lose then, do yer?' The man grinned.

Ben flushed. 'No. I doh.'

'Well, think about it, and let me know. I'm always around.' And off he went.

'Have a go, Ben,' urged Percy, his mate who had been practising with him. 'That's Toby Poxton from Walsall Wood. I've seen him run; you can beat him.'

'And if I don't? How about the thirty bob?'

'Tell you what. We'll all have bets on you. If you lose, which you won't, we'll lose our money. If you win, our money will be doubled.'

'I've got ten bob saved. I'll put that on you for a start,' Paul offered. He felt confident he would get a pound back. Ben was good.

'And I'll risk five,' put in Percy, who was on a full week at Stubbers Green. 'We've already got half. Got any yourself?'

'I might rustle up half-a-crown.'

'That's seventeen and six,' said Paul. 'I bet Katy would have a bob on.'

'We're nearly there, then, mate.' Percy rubbed his hands. 'What do you say? I'll hold the money. It'll be a bit of sport.'

So that was how it came about that in spite of the usual Sunday hush in Heath End Square, the common came to life on Women's Sunday, as an excited crowd of men and boys gathered round to watch the race.

Percy had raised the rest of the money in shillings, sixpences and threepenny bits. It was safe in his pocket, with a list of punters' names.

Toby Poxton turned up in a flashy jersey, black shorts and real running pumps, flanked by his mates.

The race agreed was once round the common, starting and finishing at The Red Cow Inn, the publican being the starter. Ben was used to sprinting round the common several times at one go. At first he was well in front, but as they came back, toward The Bush, Toby put on a terrific spurt and charged past him, the crowd yelling wildly. 'Come on Toby!' 'Gerra move on, Brookie!'

'I'm gonna lose all me mates' money,' flashed through Ben's mind, as he heard Paul yelling, 'Think o' that pigeon you're gonna buy, our kid.'

It was enough to rescue his flagging spirits and draw him level with his opponent. It was neck and neck for the next few yards, and just before The Red Cow came into sight Ben sprinted ahead to loud cheers from the crowd.

Ben and Toby collapsed on the floor for a second or two before rolling over, grinning to one another as they shook hands.

Percy, like a well-seasoned bookie, was paying out the winnings. Paul's ten shillings was now a pound. He ran home as fast as Ben had run round the common, to place it on the kitchen table in front of Mary Ann.

'Twenty shillings for you, Mother. Ten bob turned into twenty.'

'You haven't been gambling, have you, lad?'

'I have. And it's great. Oh, Mother, you should have seen our kid.'

'I am glad he won. But I don't like you gambling, Paul.'

'It's for you, Mother.'

'Pick up your money, lad. I'm all right.'

Ben appeared, flushed and triumphant.

'Well done, my lad,' Mary Ann congratulated him as she poured them each a mug of tea.

'What do you think? Percy's fixed me up for a return run with Toby at Walsall Wood in a fortnight's time. It's for fifty bob this time.'

'That's a lot of money.'

'Percy says he can raise it. He had to refuse bets today.'

Paul glanced at the money still lying on the table. 'Mother, can I put that pound on? I'll be able to give you two pounds after the race.'

'It's yours, lad, to do as you like. But remember this, both of you, the best money is the money you earn for yourself.'

'Ben will be earning it. You'll have it returned double, Mother, you'll see.'

Ben immediately went into serious training. He sprinted on the journey to Conduit. He ran up and down the stepping bridge, across the fields, past the mill and along the road to Shelfield. He had nightly sessions with the punchball and exercised every morning.

Even with Paul's pound to start him off Percy discovered it was a different kettle of fish to try to raise fifty shillings, but on the day of the race he had it all in his pocket, and a fair number of supporters were at Walsall Wood football ground by noon. There was an air of rivalry between the Cod-Enders and Walsall-Wooders as they argued the merits of their runners.

Heavy rain in the night, still spotting, made the ground sticky, but Ben, extremely fit, was cockily confident.

'How's that brother o' your'n goin' to do, kid?' one Cod-Ender enquired. 'Ah've got some money on 'im.'

'You have never had your money on a greater certainty, mister,' Paul replied convincingly.

The competition was four times round the football field, and during the first two laps the runners were almost touching, Toby Poxton keeping immediately behind Ben. It was soon obvious that he had not wasted this last fortnight either. About halfway round the third lap Ben, glancing behind to see if Toby was still there, slipped in the mud and twisted his ankle; the pain was excruciating, but he carried on, encouraged by the yells of his supporters.

The end of the third lap saw him two yards behind Toby, who had reserved his best skills for the last quarter of the race. Ben's swelling ankle was throbbing unmercifully. He carried on doggedly, but Toby was at the winning post when he was only halfway round. Paul and Percy were soon at his side.

One or two Cod-Enders were grumbling at him. 'Last time we put money on *you*, Brookie. What did yer look round for yer, daft ha'porth?' But most of them accepted their losses philosophically, shouting 'Bad luck, kid,' before making their way to The Jolly Collier to watch the cock-fighting taking place at the back of the inn, hoping to recoup the money they had lost.

The Walsall Wood football trainer bound up Ben's ankle. 'You will have to keep off this, at least for a couple of weeks, lad.'

Toby Poxton came over, grinning. 'Sorry it had to be like that, kid. But it could happen to anybody.' This time Ben did not grin at him or shake hands. He hated losing.

Ben was bitterly resentful at what he termed his bad luck, but deep down he knew that Toby would have been a tough opponent to beat, mud or no. It was a bitter pill to swallow, and Percy hated handing over the fifty shillings.

Paul was full of remorse. Why hadn't he left the pound lying on his mother's table for her to pick up? Not only had he lost it for her, but she would be short of Ben's money for a couple of weeks. He fretted more than Mary Ann. She was sorry Ben was in pain, of course, but comfrey leaves and vinegar would work wonders. And they were learning that nothing in life is a certainty.

CHAPTER

6

It WAS A long hot summer which meant that the fish trade fell off and the log business came to a halt; miners were selling their allowance loads for three and sixpence. Little Gallery continued to do well but most of that money went to Edwin. Now that Charlotte was getting too big to help much, Mary Ann seemed to be continuously poised for flight, almost running from one shop to another.

Three days a week down the mine was more than enough for Ben. He was able to give time to his pigeons and the poultry, practise his running round the common and spend long hours with the punchball; his only concern being that his Dad would stay away.

But every day that Conduit was off, Paul was at some other pit, trying to get work. Sometimes he went 'catching', which meant going to the pit on the off chance that someone might not turn up, but when that did happen it was the more experienced colliers who were asked to step in. The one cloud on his horizon in this glorious summer without his father was not being able to further himself at the pit.

One day Katy glanced up from her sewing machine to find him looking down at her anxiously.

'Will you do me a favour, Katy?'

'Something in his face made her reply, 'If I don't land in gaol for it, yes.'

'I've heard that Tack-a-Rue, a new pit in Hednesford, is setting on seventeen-year-olds and over. They've no short working there, and they want lads with a bit of experience.'

'Seventeen-year-olds, you said? Stop me if I'm wrong, Paul. You were *sixteen* yesterday?'

'They don't know that, though, do they?'

'I thought you had to show a certificate to prove your age before a pit sets you on these days?'

'You do. Will you alter mine for me, Katy?'

'*Alter it!* Me? No fear.'

'Listen, Katy,' he pleaded, 'I'm getting nowhere at Conduit. Not only would I be on a full week, I'd be earning seventeen-year-old's wages. There's our mother to think about.'

'Mother? I've never heard her grumble about your money.'

'That's just it; she doesn't grumble, does she? But you know she works herself to the bone from morning to night. I want to *learn* more about the pits, Katy, and I want to *earn* more.'

'You have your bicycle repairing.'

'Fat lot that brings in! You never know how long it will go on, do you? Or when the jobs are comin'. There's nothin' regular.'

He brought out a crumpled piece of paper from his pocket, smoothing it out on the table. It was headed: Certified Copy of an Entry of Birth, issued for the purpose of Factory and Workshop Act, 1901. 'It just means altering that 1892 to 1891; it's not a very good figure two to start with. Just go over it and make it a thick figure one, will you?'

'Why me? Why not you?'

'You're a dab hand with a pen, Katy. Far neater than I am. I can't do it round home, can I? Mother would never let me risk it. If they do find out, Katy, I wouldn't let on it was you; you know I wouldn't do that.'

'Well, I don't know, Paul. It might mean trouble for you.'

'All right,' he stated suddenly. 'Lend me your pen and ink and I'll do it meself.'

'I hope you know what you're doing.'

Katy reached pen, ink and blotting paper from her sideboard drawer. Paul took the pen determinedly. As Katy saw the stubby fingers, hardened and callused from all the work he did, she felt a lump in her throat. They were hard times for Cod-Enders in general, but some lads lolled about and never looked for anything, and here was her brother, as keen a worker as Mary Ann herself, desperate to make his way and to see his mother more comfortable.

'Give it to me,' she said resignedly, 'and God help us if we're found out. Get some writing paper out of the drawer.' She settled herself firmly at the table to test the colour of the ink on the writing paper. 'It's too blue. Don't let's be in too big a hurry.' She got up. 'I have some black in the shop.' Carefully she changed the rather vague figure two into a one.

'And again, Katy, where it says "date of registration".'

This time too much ink on the nib smudged. She tried to mop it up with the blotting paper. 'Oh dear! It doesn't look too convincing to me, Paul. What if they can tell?'

'They won't. It'll be all right. I'm going over now, this minute. Thanks, and don't tell Mother, will you?'

'You know I won't.'

Once it was done Katy did not regret it. She had not felt so excited since her father was around making all their

116

hearts race. What would Walter say if he knew? And Mary Ann? They would be sure to point out that Paul would be getting extra wages by false pretences. But if he was willing to do the work of an older lad, why not?

She could tell by his face when he returned that it had worked. He was jubilant. 'They looked me up and down and asked me what jobs I had done,' he told her excitedly. 'The manager said to the fireman, "Can you fix him up?" "I can do with one at the bottom for tramming," the fireman said, "Have you any proof of your date of birth with you?" I was almost afraid to give it to him. Anyway I handed it over and the fireman passed it to Mr Fletcher, the under-manager. Fletcher squinted at it through his glasses. "This looks as if it's been altered," he said, passing it on to the manager.

'My heart was in my mouth, I can tell you. It's a wonder they couldn't hear it ticking. The manager looked me up and down again and then studied the certificate. Then he said "Oh no, Fletcher. It's just a smudge." '

Katy chuckled. 'He should have borrowed Fletcher's glasses. Oh, Paul! Just a smudge!' She started to laugh; and it was such a joy to hear him joining in, that worried look gone.

'Katy you're a good 'un. Three-and-nine a day it will be and three-quarters on a Saturday! I'll be able to give Mother above a pound.'

It was hard work at Tack-a-Rue; he was put on to a job that a nineteen-year-old had been doing. He did not mind that, for when the pitmen saw that he was willing to tackle anything they gave him a variety of jobs, including 'running-on', which was getting the full tubs to the cage, and 'pulling-off', getting the empty tubs back. It wasn't long before he was made a driver, responsible for his own horse.

'What does that involve?' quizzed Katy.

'It means I have to fasten the tubs to the back of the horse and get them from the coal face to a place they call the meeting where the runners-on send them up to the cage.'

'With the tubs bouncing about at the back of the poor old horse?'

Paul laughed. 'Oh no. You're thinking a tub is a tub. A tub is a *truck* on four wheels. And a stall is not like one in the market. It's like a room where they're workin' on the coal face. The stallmen have been grumbling at me today. "What the devil are you playin' at?" they've been saying. "Gerra move on." I'm not as quick as the others yet. You see the coal I get up there makes a difference to the stallmen's wages; they're paid on the coal they manage to get to the top, and they have to pay me out of their money. If I'm late with the tubs the others get there first and I have to wait. But I'll be as good as any of 'em in a couple of days.'

He was as good as his word and it wasn't long before he was telling his mother, 'The stallmen were a bit put out today, because the fireman took me away from 'em. When they've got a good driver they like to keep him.'

'Then why were you moved?'

'The dogey was away and I said I'd do it, 'cos it's a chance to learn. The dogey has to tackle any job if men are away. I've been putting new props in today. But I nipped back and helped the stallmen when I could. They've been good to me. It's exciting when they do the shot firing. I'll be glad when I'm on the coal face.'

'Don't try to run before you can walk, my lad. There's plenty of time.'

'But I want to earn more. I want to give you more.'

He was filled with enthusiasm and delight at being back at work. 'Arthur and me, we're going to stay on the shift to clear the sump out, that will get us a bit more. Arthur's a good mate. He's comin' to Bloxwich Wakes with me on Saturday.'

Wakes week was the third week in August every year,

when Pat Collin's Funfair came to Bloxwich, a couple of miles further on than Ginny's. There was a long procession in the afternoon; anybody could dress up and join in, followed by street dancing and singing, with everyone finishing up at the fair at night. There was nothing doing in Cod End on Wakes night, so they closed the shops. Mary Ann had a lift with Ginny, the others strolled leisurely in twos, Katy with Walter, Paul with Arthur, and Ben with his pal Percy.

Percy was now playing football for Pelsall Panthers, and Ben was going for a trial next week. 'They're glad o' blokes what can move fast,' Percy assured him.

'Pelsall Panthers, they call themselves,' Ben scoffed. 'They're nearly all Cod-Enders wot are in the team.'

Arthur, a couple of years older than Paul, was talking about the opportunities in Canada. He was keen to go, and Paul could not wonder at it, in Arthur's case. He lived in Double Row, a squashed row of a dozen dwellings that housed twenty-four families, back to back, toward The Bush, on the opposite side. They all shared a communal yard at the back, with two brewhouses, two lavatories and one outside tap to serve the lot.

Arthur's home consisted of one room up and one down. Facing the road, as they did, they had to walk all the way round to the backyard to fetch water, go to the lavatory, or for Arthur's mother to do her washing. His mother and dad slept downstairs where they all lived and ate, while Arthur, his brother and two sisters slept in one small bedroom. His dad spent most of his time at The Bush. Unlike Mary Ann, his mother had no spark, her spirits having sunk beyond repair.

'I think it would ease things for me Mam,' Arthur was saying now, 'if I went to Canada.'

'Wouldn't she miss your money?'

'I would be able to send her as much as I give her now, and she wouldn't have me to keep. And when I come back

119

to Cod End I'll be able to bring her a nice little nest-egg. How about comin' with me?'

'Not me. No fear!' For Paul was riding the crest of a wave, at last earning a bit more about the pits and getting paid for it. Anyway he could not consider leaving Mary Ann.

The oil lamps were just being lit as they reached the entrance to the fair, where ear-splitting music and screams from the ghost train vied for attention with the loud hailer reminding them not to miss the jump, never before attempted, into a barrel of fire. Smells of hot potatoes, ginger bread and the sweet gooeyness of hot toffee apples mingled with putrid odour from the hot Wakes' engines.

Giggling revellers were trying to decide whether to succumb to the wiles of a fortune teller, the performing bears, the jugglers, or the Fattest-Lady-in-the-World, for not many could afford more than one treat of that sort.

The four lads opted for the Boxing tent, where three spindly youths were prancing around on the platform outside the tent, challenging all-comers to a three-round contest. A sovereign would be paid for the attempt if the volunteer managed to stay on his feet, and five sovereigns if anyone could put 'one of us' down within three rounds.

Five sovereigns! Weighing up the opposition, Paul and Ben decided it would be a piece of cake and handed in their names on the way in. Once inside it soon became apparent that the 'one of us' was not one of the spindly characters persuading customers in, but tough, experienced, well-muscled men with biceps like Hercules. Too late they realized they had been roped in as cheap entertainment. One by one they saw volunteers felled to the ground while the audience yelled, jeering or shouting encouragement, depending on the performance of the victims. Their spirits sank as they accepted they were in for a hiding.

It said much for them that neither hit the canvas, but it

was a pair of battered and bruised brothers, Ben with rapidly swelling eyes, Paul with a cut lip, who emerged from the tent, clutching their well-earned sovereigns. Paul wondered whether he was suffering from a softening of the brain due to the effect of the blows, for straight ahead he thought he could see two familiar figures.

'Ben! Look!'

'Me Dad. Me bloody Dad.' Then in horror, 'Me Mother an' all.'

There was no mistaking them. There was their mother, the flickering lights from the stalls giving a rosy glow to the pink outfit she had worn for Katy's wedding, and Raish, resplendent as always, in a well-fitting suit, his buttonhole a red carnation, his bowler tilted at a familiar angle. No mistaking the cocky walk as they turned away from the main crowds, Raish guiding Mary Ann, his arm beneath her elbow, deep in conversation.

If they had felt hard done by in the Boxing tent it was nothing to how they felt now; the bottom fell out of their world.

'He's after her. She'll take him back. I know she will.'

'I'll bloody kill 'im,' threatened Ben, his fists raised, his blood already boiling from the ignominy he had suffered in the tent.

'And I shall help you.'

They were about to dash forward when they were each restrained by a hand and their sister's urgent voice. 'Don't. Don't do it. She won't thank you, either of you.'

'Want 'im back, do yer, Katy?' screamed Ben, panic-stricken.

'No, I don't,' replied Katy defiantly, suddenly regretting she had ever thought she might. Anxiety was back in Paul's face; the old truculence in Ben's. Freedom, that was what they had all enjoyed, these past months. Peace. She had dared to imagine it was worth sacrificing that for a bit of excitement; she felt ashamed.

'Leave it to your mother, Ben,' counselled Walter quietly. 'It has to be her decision.

Ben turned on his brother-in-law angrily. 'What do you know about it? Her decision! It'll be *his* decision. He always talks her round. Always. He's got a voice as smooth as a baby's arse.'

'Calm down, our kid. We can't do anything here. It would only upset her. But if he comes back he won't do as he likes with her. Or us. Ever again. We shall see to that.'

'I expect he's heard we're doin' all right.'

'And his latest woman has had enough of him.'

'All our mother's hard work will be for nothing. He'll have the lot.'

Their night was ruined. They discussed what might happen as they walked home together, their stomachs knotted with fear. Katy had to admit the truth; their mother could easily be swayed by Raish.

But to their amazement Mary Ann was home before them. And alone.

One word, 'Polly', the name of endearment he used only in the house, was enough to put her on her guard. She had often rehearsed the part she had to play when this moment came.

'Polly! You look beautiful, my love.'

He was stone sober, suave and debonair, those insolent eyes stripping the clothes from her as only he could.

'Raish! All alone?'

'I am with you, dear.'

She looked round ostentatiously, as if searching for someone. 'No other lady?'

'There has never been any other *lady* in my life, Polly. Only you.' He took her arm and propelled her away from the crowds. 'I guessed I might find you here. Can we talk?'

She was very composed. 'Why not?'

'Polly, I have missed you so much.'

'We have missed you too, Raish.'

He looked gratified but not surprised. 'What have I always told you, Polly? We can't live without each other for long. Missed me, have you m'dear?'

'Very much, Raish. We have missed your drunken ravings. We have missed our sleepless nights. The lads have missed being struck for nothing, and I have missed the money disappearing from the till.'

'Come, now! That's not my Polly! That sarcasm! It does not suit you, you are too much of a woman. You need me to soften you up, my love.'

'I don't want you back, Raish.'

He smiled, unperturbed. Women always liked to play hard to get. 'But I want you, Polly. Very much. What's wrong with us doing a spot of courting with a view to getting together again?'

'I want contentment and a peaceful life for my children. I have discovered how much they mean to me these last months. If you came back I would lose Edwin and Charlotte again.'

'Forget the children, Polly. How about you? And me?'

'Please go, Raish.' She moved away, dismissing him coolly.

He stared, flabbergasted, at her calm face. Could she be turning him down?

'You don't mean that, Polly. I am the only man in the world for you, you know that. Just as you're the only woman who has ever meant anything to me.'

It was as if she had not heard him. 'I see Ginny over there. She is ready to leave,' she said as she moved off.

A couple of long strides and he had caught her up. He reached out roughly, jerking her round to face him, in a grip of steel. Don't walk away from me, woman. You are my wife, remember.'

'I am not *your* anything, Raish. *You* walked away from *me*. Take your hands away before I call for help.'

Surprised by the previously suppressed anger in her face

and voice his arms fell away. Her voice was very quiet, very steady. 'Remember, Raish. Stay away from us. We do not need you.' She did not bother to glance back as she walked quickly away.

Well! Fancy that! Little Polly. He had heard she was prospering too. Pity. He sighed. Women! God, that one had changed. Dora too; she had started nagging. She seemed to think he should pay his way. He shrugged. Ah well, there would be another day. Meanwhile there were other women who would be glad to have him.

As Mary Ann gave a brief account of what had happened she saw the four worried faces change to incredulity. As bad as he had been they had never known her to refuse him anything. It felt too good to be true, like the tappings of a rescuer after a pit fall. Paul could laugh about the Boxing tent now; he could even give a funny account of what had happened, although Ben was still suffering from hurt pride.

'Come on, our kid, what's a couple of black eyes and a few bruises? I'd go through it all again to hear news like this.'

'He'll 'ave summat up his sleeve,' muttered Ben darkly, but was unable to hide the relief in his face. Katy's face shone too, and when she and Walter announced they were going for a walk at that time of night everyone guessed they were going to Rushall to tell Edwin the good news.

CHAPTER
7

THE DAY AFTER Bloxwich Wakes Edwin awoke early. The promise of a perfect summer day enticed him to the window. A bright orange band decorated the tree tops in the distance, an almost imperceptible mist arching it gently. The dawn was creeping softly and shyly. Only a moth fluttering against the window disturbed the Sunday stillness.

He stayed until the roses in their little backyard focussed, flame red against dark green leaves. He would pick some later for Charlotte. The orange ribbon suddenly widened and spread its glorious glow across the sky, the sun refusing to contain its energy any longer.

With the explosion of sun Edwin felt an explosion of happiness, a new sense of freedom. His father's reign of terror haunted him less these days, but always at the back of his mind had remained the apprehension that Raish would come home and spoil everything. Until last night, when Walter and Katy had told them how Mary Ann had refused him, insisting that her children were most important to her. With that news the one cloud on his horizon had vanished like the mist that had now disappeared.

He enjoyed being in touch with his family again; he and his mother had never been so close. As for Charlotte, they had accepted her as their own and she had responded wonderfully.

He had not been in love with Charlotte when they married; to him she was like an older sister he could lean on. Suddenly he wanted to tell her for the first time how much she meant to him.

It had been a magical summer. Soon he would be finished with the pit. The paintings were selling well; to be paid for what he enjoyed doing most of all was still unbelievable. He had regained his family and he suspected he was falling in love with his wife.

He walked back to the bed and looked down fondly at Charlotte's contented face. He took her hand gently. She opened her eyes and smiled at him, that long slow smile. He wanted so much to tell her he loved her, but, although he could put his feelings on to canvas, he had never been much good with words, so he just said, 'I have been watching the dawn.'

She cottoned on to his thoughts immediately, like she always did. 'You were very happy with what they told us last night.'

He nodded. 'I never thought she could refuse him, Charlotte. Always before she has seemed so relieved to have him back, in spite of everything. We are all better off without him.'

She stretched, and sighed happily. 'Life is marvellous, isn't it, Edwin. Whatever happens we have each other. Even if your father does come back eventually, I feel we shall always be in touch with them now.'

She knew what had bothered him.

He squeezed her hand. 'How's baby Mark today?'

'He is very active.'

'Never mind. Only a couple of weeks to go. I'll go down and make us some tea. Perhaps that will quieten him.'

The Singing Sundays, as Katy called their get-togethers, had become a ritual enjoyed by all. As they sipped their tea Charlotte said, 'I'm getting very big and awkward. Do you think your mother would mind if we didn't go tonight?'

'Of course not. She will understand. Shall we invite your parents round here instead? Having them next door it's something we don't do often enough.'

'Edwin, why don't you go up to Heath End? Have a whole morning with the lads and your mother. They would like that. You could tell them not to expect us tonight.'

They had an early breakfast and he picked the roses. It was such a tiny backyard, yet Charlotte had made the most of every inch. Along the pathway she had planted pansies, lupins and dahlias, while sunflowers and the rose bush camouflaged the wall. They were all in luxurious bloom.

She stood beside him now, clasping the roses.

'It's going to be a beautiful day.'

She looked suddenly drawn and old.

'Charlotte, are you all right?'

'Yes, of course.'

'You're not? It isn't . . . ? I'll stay with you.'

'What! It's two weeks away, Edwin. And first babies are often late. Go on. Away with you. Enjoy your walk, and give them my love.'

But as soon as he had gone she fetched her mother.

Edwin met no-one along the mile of Rushall Lane. Hedges were heavy with fat ripe blackberries. The butterflies were busy among red poppies and purple hearts-ease lining the banks. Sometimes he sketched briefly in a pad he always kept in his pocket, pausing to study the wide variety of wild flowers. He was hoping to paint some tiny miniature flower studies one day.

It was a slow, meandering, peaceful journey.

By the time he reached Heath End one or two people were stirring and the paper boy was whistling as he went his round.

Edwin often thought how unusual it was to have a mining village placed in such a pretty position, between Rushall Lane and the lovely common, with its majestic trees lining the road to Pelsall. A mining village far enough away from the many pits in the area not to have sight of them, yet near enough for its men to work them.

What a contrast to Norton and Hednesford, where the pits on their doorsteps polluted the atmosphere, blackened their walls and caused houses to subside. Yes, Cod-Enders were well placed.

He breathed deeply; what a marvellous day. Even the black iron railings fronting the chapel gleamed in the sun like black boot polish.

Owners reverently bearing pigeon baskets were emerging from side streets into the square, heading toward The Red Cow. He saw Ben with his basket, and joined him.

'What's happening today, Ben?'

'It's a five-miler. I'm enterin' two o' mine. White Wing stands a good chance.'

What a good day it had been when Ginny started Ben off with the pigeons, thought Edwin: he had been so much more approachable since.

Two officials were seated in the centre of the inn yard, each with a large mug of beer on an old table; one of them collecting the entrance fees.

'We pay two shillings per pigeon and threepence each to a bloke to tek 'em on 'is bike,' explained Ben. 'The other chap stamps the inside wing of each pigeon. We have to bring 'em back to this point when they come home.' Ben talked quietly to his two pigeons as he transferred them from one basket to another. They waited until the cyclist set off with them before strolling home together.

Paul was busily repairing a bicycle in the yard near the

sign which said: Bicycles Repaired Here. He was fitting new brake blocks and putting in a couple of new chain links. It looked as if the handlebars would also need straightening; the spokes too.

'What happened to that?'

'Somebody had an argument with a brick wall,' Paul grinned. 'Funny thing, those blokes in the bicycle parties that call in the coffee shop and buy your paintings have not the slightest idea what goes into a bike. And yet they travel for miles.'

'Getting plenty of jobs?'

'As many as I can manage, now I'm on full time at Tack-a-Rue.'

Edwin sat on the ground, his back against the wall warmed by the sun, feeling very relaxed as he watched and listened to his brothers.

Paul turned to Ben, now busily cleaning out the pigeon loft, while his birds exercised in the sun. 'Got them away all right?'

'Ar. I think I stand a chance with White Wing, our kid.'

'It will be 'ticing that White Wing to come down that will be the trouble,' said Paul, addressing Edwin. 'He's always the first to arrive and the last to come down. He sits preening himself on the top of the stable. We can't get hold of him.'

'He must be a good pigeon to be always fust, though,' boasted Ben.

'Fat lot of use that is, if you can't persuade him to come to The Cow to prove it.'

'He'll be all right today. I've been training him to recognize my call.'

'That White Wing's got to learn English first,' teased Paul, winking at Edwin. 'I reckon he's a foreigner.' Ben could even take a teasing these days.

Walter came out and quietly set about tidying and

weeding the vegetable patch, side by side with the few flowers he was trying to grow.

'I think you are fighting a losing battle in this farmyard, Walter.'

'Can but try,' he replied as he patiently shooed away chickens pecking at his lettuces.

Edwin shut his eyes. It was pleasant hearing the lads' voices, amidst the other sounds of bees and birds, chicken and goslings, an occasional coo of a pigeon and grunt from the pigsties at the extreme end of the garden. They had Kitty the donkey on the end of a long rope, in the shade of the stable, and she made herself heard. They were such happy peaceful sounds; life had never been so good. He was aroused from his reverie by Ben. 'Are you still on three-a-week, Edwin?'

'Yes. But I'm finishing altogether in a week's time.'

'Ooh. I wish that was me. Why can't we do summat like paintin', so we don't have to go down that dark 'ole? Blimey, don't them goslings mek a row? They're enough to frighten my pigeons to death. Talk about Walter fighting a losin' battle!'

'They will be going soon,' Paul assured him. 'Mother's had orders for them all. Five shillings each. Not bad, is it? And the chickens will soon be laying; we'll have eggs to sell. Everything's picking up. Have you heard about the old chap being turned down, Edwin?'

'Yes.' Edwin sighed contentedly, stretching his arms to the satin blue sky. 'Isn't it marvellous?' He unwound himself slowly as he stood up; they had never seen him so relaxed. 'I'm off to see Mother.'

'I could 'ave killed me Dad last night,' spat out Ben as their brother left them. 'With his hand under her arm he was, as if he owned her.'

'She put him right on that score, though, didn't she?' Paul reminded him.

''Ow long for, I wonder?' Ben muttered bitterly, his

recent equilibrium disappearing as he remembered his parents together. 'All this can't last. We ain't that lucky.'

'Enjoy it while it's here, then,' Katy counselled as she joined them.

There were the usual baking smells in Mary Ann's kitchen. Pastries and scones lined the table ready for Little Gallery tomorrow.

'We won't be up tonight, Mother,' Edwin explained. 'Charlotte's getting a bit uncomfortable.'

'We can't expect her. Here, take this pie for pudding, save Charlotte bothering. The blackberries are as big as plums this year. So early too.'

'It's a regular hive of industry here, isn't it? Inside and out. You're all making me feel useless.'

'Can't have that. You make the tea for us, my lad. I expect we're all ready for a cup,' his mother suggested as she tripped lightly into the shop in answer to the bell.

He called her when tea and cups were on a tray he had found in Little Gallery. 'Drop everything, Mother. We will drink it outside in the fresh air. Customers will shout.' He felt so light-hearted. The knowledge that she had refused his father put a new face on his world.

He carried out chairs for Mary Ann and Katy, and the whole family sat together in the sunshine for the first time ever, an air of peace over them all.

'You're a good tea-maker, big brother.'

Edwin smiled at Katy, pretty in her lavender and white printed dress and hat.

'You're a good dressmaker, little sister. May I escort you as far as the chapel? Then I must be on my way.'

They laughed together as she rested her hand lightly on his arm.

Mary Ann watched them down the road until Katy entered chapel and Edwin was out of sight. Like the other two, just the way they walked reminded her of Raish. She was happy that Edwin was so carefree today. He looked such a boy, not much older than Paul. Certainly not old enough to be a father, she thought, as she returned to her baking.

In an hour he was back. Ashen-faced, wild-eyed, an old man. She steadied him into a chair as he staggered through the shop into the kitchen.

'*What is it*, my son?'

He choked on unintelligible sounds. She ran to lock the shop door, the kitchen door also in case the lads should burst in. She put her arms around his shaking body. Burying his face into her shoulder as he had never done before he sobbed in heartbreak.

Mary Ann stroked his hair gently, holding him tightly to her, trying to stop the shaking. When the sobs finally subsided an awful stillness came over him as he pulled away. Not the stillness of calm, but of despair. His shoulders sagged forward. He seemed drained of all life.

'My dear lad. What is it?'

At last, with great difficulty, the words jerking out one at a time, he told her. She did not want to believe what he was saying. It must be a mistake.

'Charlotte . . . is . . . dead.'

She sank into the chair opposite. A dreadful thing had happened, she knew that, as soon as she saw him. But not Charlotte. No! She had thought it was the child. 'But don't let it be Charlotte' her mind screamed. Not the Charlotte they were all learning to love and trust.

If she felt so bereft what of the son who sat facing her? The son who had swung off down the lane so jauntily but one hour ago, and who now sat like a ghost, his lips deathly pale, staring ahead as if he would never move again.

She found a little bottle of brandy and poured some into a glass. He indicated his refusal by the slightest shake of his head.

'Was Charlotte . . . ?'

Through parched lips he answered slowly. 'No. She was

132

alive when I arrived. The baby was born. It was as if she had waited for me. She wanted to tell me something . . . ' His voice trailed away.

There was a long pause as Mary Ann tried to absorb the awful truth.

At last she stood up. 'We must go.'

Then words came tumbling out, panic making his voice plaintive. 'No! It's nothing without her. I don't want to go back there, ever again!'

'But we must, Edwin. It's your home. Your baby is there. Come on, my lad.'

She left word with Walter to send Katy, after chapel. Edwin accompanied her without a word, his face set, like a child being forced into something supposed to be for his own good. They were halfway along Rushall Lane before she realized she had done it again. She had pushed him into something he did not want to do.

Charlotte would have left him and he would have come round to it himself in his own good time. Wouldn't it have been better if she had waited for the lads to come in; for a degree of normality to return? Gradually Edwin would have realized there was somewhere else he ought to be. The baby would be with Charlotte's parents; it would be quite safe, she should have remembered that. His mind was not ready for the child; he had not even told her what it was.

She glanced at his white stricken face, chiding herself silently. 'Oh, Charlotte, my girl! I didn't learn from you, did I? Oh, Charlotte!'

It would do no good to turn back now. As they neared his home he said, 'I left the midwife in.' But all was still when they pushed open the front door.

They stepped into a comfortable, airy room. Shelves by the fireplace were crammed with books. Music was open on the piano. There was a vase of red roses and a half-knitted white garment on the table. They lived and ate in here, as Charlotte had turned over the kitchen entirely to Edwin.

That was filled with canvasses and easels, palettes, sketch pads and paints. There was a working surface he had made along one wall, containing pencils, tubes of paint, paper. Among them lay the blackberry pie where he had dropped it.

The only other furniture was a single armchair in the corner of the kitchen, Charlotte's book still open upon it. Edwin dropped to his knees, flinging his arms round the chair. His head dropped forward as if on to Charlotte's lap. There were no more tears left in him, but a long moan of despair escaped from somewhere deep inside. This time Mary Ann left him alone until he was ready to leave. They found Charlotte's parents calm and composed. Mary Ann clasped their hands silently, feeling the tears welling up in her throat.

The frail little mother in a voice so like Charlotte's murmured, 'She was sent to us when we had almost given up hope. We had her for nigh on thirty years. We must be thankful for that.'

The old man nodded in agreement, although his eyes were filling with tears.

'The doctor came. He said she should never have had a child. But they told me that too. Come and see the baby.'

As Mary Ann bent over the cradle to look at her grandchild for the first time she was conscious of Katy appearing at her side; she must have run every inch of the way.

Charlotte's mother lifted the child gently, placing it in Katy's arms. 'She kept saying she wanted you to have him, Katy. She hung on to tell Edwin. She so wanted to tell him herself.'

'What do you say, Edwin? He is your son,' Katy whispered.

Edwin shook his head. 'Just before she died she said, "Let Katy have the baby. If she wants him." '

Katy's arms folded round the soft body of the tiny child, cuddling him to her breast. 'If I want him,' she murmured.

Tears dropped silently on to his little face. 'Oh, Charlotte! If I want him! You know I do.'

She kissed his eyes, screwed tightly shut. She kissed his sweet chin. The baby's eyes fluttered open. They were as blue as today's skies, as blue as her brothers' eyes. As blue as her father's.

'Hello, Mark Edwin.'

He seemed to know who she was.

CHAPTER

8

IT WAS THE best time of the year for Cod-Enders. When the weather turned cold more miners were in work, and they intended having a good Christmas. Conduit Colliery was now on a full week. Ben had mixed feelings about that for he still detested the pit and all that the pit owners stood for.

At Mary Ann's shop the thirteen-week Christmas club was well on the way. Members paid a shilling a week. Sarah had been lucky enough to draw number one, which meant she could have spent the whole thirteen shillings at the end of week one, but she had swapped with a young mother who had been so dismayed when she drew number thirteen because her offsprings were desperate for winter boots.

Children were shouting up chimneys for impossible things, for the most a Cod End kid could hope for was a sock with a giant potato in the toe complete with various-size buttons to make a potato man, and in the leg of the sock, a banana, an orange and some nuts. A banana and an orange that they did not have to share! If they were extra lucky there might be an apple with a threepenny bit pushed deep inside, or a bag of sweets. On days that Paul was cajoled into wearing the old Santa Claus outfit many a sly coin was prized from precious money boxes by the use of a flat knife for the joy of dipping into Father Christmas's bag. A penny dip might contain a mouth organ, a trumpet, a doll, a hair ribbon or two wooden soldiers. For a halfpenny there was a top or a dice, a toy watch or a kali sucker.

Mary Ann had baked cakes and puddings, putting one each aside for Sarah, Ginny and Gipsy Gert. Others were displayed for sale in Little Gallery, as it was still called, although now almost pictureless and patronized mainly by Katy's customers from surrounding villages, pleased to take a bowl of warming soup and a home-made bap when attending for fittings.

Edwin had tried very hard to carry on with his painting, but his heart had gone out of it. He missed Charlotte being near as he worked, relaxed and trustful, giving him confidence. Now that she had gone the newly-won confidence evaporated as if it had never been. He finished the paintings already commissioned, but they were mechanical and uninspired. Once they were done he wandered aimlessly, dreading the moment when he had to return to his empty house each night. It made it worse having no job. He had immediately attempted to withdraw his notice when Charlotte died, but was told that his job had already been promised to another.

At last it was decided that he should move into the attic room vacated by Katy, where Mary Ann hoped that the constant activity of the family would bring him back to life. Her heart ached as she watched him daily draw further into his shell, reverting to the timidity he had shown before he had met Charlotte. If it were not for the baby it would have seemed that her daughter-in-law and Edwin's contentment had been but a dream.

Walter had accepted without question that they would take the baby as their own. So did Cod End. In 1908 it was common enough for a mother to die in childbirth. If the child lived there was always someone willing to bring it up. When large families were left, neighbours kept a proprietory eye on older children, while the younger ones were accepted into their homes, growing up alongside their own, without favour being given on either side. Sometimes brothers and sisters had to be split up, but no child from Cod End ever went to Barnardo's, just as none of their old folk ever went to the workhouse. Death was no stranger to any of them. They sympathized about Charlotte, but there was no time in their lives for over-sentimentality. Life must go on, they said; you had to take what came.

Katy tried to interest Edwin in the baby. 'He's yours, too, Edwin,' she would say.

So to please his sister he would sit in her kitchen watching the chubby, contented child, but just as his home meant nothing without Charlotte, the baby, without Charlotte to hold him in her arms, meant nothing to him either.

One day Katy found him with his head in his hands, a picture of despair. She placed her hand on his shoulder sympathetically.

'Why did I never tell her I loved her, Katy?' he murmured.

'She knew, though, Edwin.'

'How could she?'

'The same way I know that Walter loves me, although he never puts it into words. Charlotte knew you so well, didn't she?'

He nodded. Charlotte did know so much about him without being told, so perhaps she had known that too. He supposed she would have also understood how indifferent he felt toward his son. She had made the right decision in giving him to Katy. He was so very much loved. Walter would hurry in to see him before he had washed off his pit dust, the baby responding with loving signs of recognition and baby talk. Paul, too, could hardly wait before rushing in to his nephew, carrying him off at the first opportunity to see his grandmother next door.

Walter was so quiet and kind; he reminded Edwin of Charlotte and they were becoming firm friends. Knowing that Edwin could no longer concentrate to read, Walter would read out to him and Katy in the evenings, but the blue eyes would quickly haze over and they knew he was somewhere else entirely.

They tried to involve him in preparations for Christmas, in making lanterns or paper streamers, or covering steel rings from old barrels to hang from the ceiling, but everything he did was done listlessly, a set white vacant expression on his face.

Afterwards they all said it was Paul's accident that started the cure.

Edwin was absently brushing down Dandy when Paul appeared in the yard, painfully trying to prop his bike against the wall, his right arm hanging grotesquely from a jutting shoulder.

'What's the matter?'

'Just a bit of an accident. My own fault.' His arm did not look part of his body any more.

'We must get you to the colliery doctor at Walsall Wood.'

Edwin quickly prepared Dandy and the cart, taking his first decision for weeks. 'How did it happen?' he enquired as they jogged along.

Paul explained painfully, through gritted teeth. 'I was dogeying, standing between the rails, trying to get a bloke to do some running-on, when the tubs suddenly shot along the lines and knocked me hell-for-leather. My own fault entirely; shouldn't have been there between the lines. And now, I reckon, I'll be on the box.' That possibility upset him more than the pain.'

When he came out of the doctor's his shoulder was bound back in place, his arm in a sling, his wrist tied close to his neck. 'It's a broken collar bone. The doctor asked me if they let me walk home, and when I said they did, he said they think more of their horses than they do of their men. He reckons I won't be able to go back until well after Christmas. Just as everyin' was goin' right. That'll mean less money for Mother.'

'Never mind. You have already bought the port and sherry.'

It was Edwin's turn to offer comfort. His brother's misfortune took his mind off himself, and in the days ahead Paul was determined to keep him talking, refusing to let him lapse into mournfulness. Those days formed a bond of understanding between them, making them closer than they had ever been.

One day they took the donkey and cart to Cannock Chase where Edwin dug up some Christmas trees for themselves and their neighbours; any surplus their mother could sell.

Paul chatted away the whole of the time. 'Mother's having the pig killed for Christmas. There will be a couple of joints for Katy and ourselves; she's got orders for the rest. We shall be able to sell some of the bacon an' all. The lard will come in handy for her frying. They'll all be glad to get back to fried fish after Christmas. Hasn't she done well without the old chap?'

'She has. She makes me feel ashamed,' Edwin agreed, lapsing into silence.

Paul battled on. Couldn't have him mopsing. He must keep talking. 'We had a lot of carol singers last night, didn't we?'

Edwin nodded.

'They're chuffed if they can get a penny in their tin.'

'Yes.'

'I remember when our Ben and me went carol singing in

Pelsall. I was about ten at the time; he'd be eight. We thought we'd try some of the posher houses; they could spare more, or so we thought. After we'd sung our hearts out we knocked. Two blokes came to the door. The one said, "Who's having it then?" We had agreed that I would collect the money, so I said "Me". The other chap had a mouthful of beer, and he let it fly all over me. They thought it was hilarious. It was the last time we went round there singing. We decided to stick to Cod End after that. Smellin' the beer on our old chap was enough, without having it spat at us.'

It wasn't easy to keep his brother's mind on what he was saying, but he tried.

On Christmas Day white frost lay over everything, crunching beneath the feet of the three brothers as they walked between the towering trees skirting each side of the path which split the common in two. Children were gingerly testing the thin layer of ice on the pool, while others blew their trumpets, tin whistles and mouth organs, all from Mary Ann's lucky dips. Proud little girls risked frozen wrists and ears to show off toy watches and hair ribbons. The one side of the vicarage roof, where the sun slanted, was coal black against the whiteness of the rest.

'It looks like that first picture you sold,' said Paul.

Edwin nodded. It seemed like a lifetime away.

The smells of Christmas cooking assailed them as soon as they entered the yard. A small table from Little Gallery had been brought in. By propping open the door leading into the shop ten people, including four neighbours, were able to sit down for Christmas dinner in the hot, tiny kitchen.

Mary Ann put aside some thick slices of pork and cold pork pie for Ginny to take to Gipsy Gert on her way home. Gert would not have entertained the idea of entering a house, not even on Christmas Day, and as far as anyone knew no-one had been inside her caravan, although in summer, when the door was open, they had all seen the

141

gleaming copper and brass, everything neat as a new pin, despite Gert's own unkempt appearance.

Mrs Willis, who was never short of money these days, with Ted doing so well, and who lived as close as anyone to the caravan, was taking Gert her Christmas dinner. It was rumoured that Gert had forecast Ted's success; indeed she had prophesied that all the Willis children would prosper. It looked like coming true. So far not one of the lads had gone down the pits. Two of them were working at Ted's motor factory and Reggie, the brainiest of all, had secured a good job at the ticket office of Walsall railway station. He would be a station master one day, according to Gert; while Ted was destined to marry a rich wife. 'That'll be Sally Dilkes,' said Sarah. 'He seems to be goin' great guns there.'

Katy had to bend low over the baby to hide her burning cheeks. Why did gossip about Ted and Sally always sting like an open wound? After all, they were both free. It was none of her concern. But she had to admit that she did mind, very much.

After they had all eaten their fill, Paul's one-and-ninepenny bottle of port was opened and it loosened their tongues no end.

Mary Ann was grateful to have all her children together, although her thoughts were never far away from the daughter-in-law who had been like a daughter. Between them they were gradually helping Edwin back to normality, but she longed for the Edwin they had known for such a short time.

Later they went round next door, to Katy's. An uneasy silence settled upon them as soon as they were through the door; it was the piano standing there untouched that did it.

Suddenly Sarah blurted out, 'Charlotte wouldn't a-wanted us to be sittin' 'ere, mopsin' like this at Christmas. Give us a lead, Edwin.' They all held their breath. Edwin quietly crossed over to the piano, hesitating for only a moment before playing 'Away in a Manger' with one finger. He held his son close to him while the rest of them sang, the tears never far away.

Early in the New Year he surprised them all by announcing he was going to India. Daddy Dale was arranging it for him. Not to preach, he could not do that, he said, but to help in a medical mission for the blind.

From that day they no longer had to rack their brains to think of something to occupy him. He worked feverishly to leave everything in order before he went, seeing to all the repair jobs, tightening loose latches and locks, replacing a cracked window pane, repairing the stable roof. He read everything he could lay his hand on about India and studied the lantern slides provided by Mr Dale.

The night before he set off on his journey he visited his sister. Katy was just taking Mark to bed. With his fair hair, bright blue eyes and rosy cheeks, he was so like the Brooks he could have easily been Katy's own child.

'It's Mark I want to talk to you about,' said Edwin when she came downstairs. 'You know, I regard you two as Mark's parents, and I want him to grow up calling you Mother and Father. Let him call me Edwin. He's your child, Katy, for ever.'

'Oh we have already talked this out, haven't we, Walter? We're Mom and Dad, yes. But you shall be his father also, Edwin. As soon as he is old enough we shall tell him about Charlotte and the fact that he had another mother too.'

'I would like that. Thank you, Katy. Thank you both,' he replied huskily.

They all missed him, especially Mary Ann, yet she was relieved that a sense of purpose had returned to his life. She was ready for something new herself.

So engrossed was Katy in the baby that she had less time to make up the materials from the bundles these days, and Mary Ann had found a supplier of ready-mades at reasonable prices in Birmingham market. She felt that she could run a successful clothes club all the year round, but space was her problem. She suggested Katy take over the foodstuffs but was not surprised when Katy, determined to keep enough time for Mark, refused.

So Mary Ann went to see Sarah. Sarah was ageing too fast; she was bored, she decided.

'Have you ever thought of opening a shop in your front room, Sarah?'

'Not me, Mary Ann,' she stated emphatically. 'It would worry me to death. I'm not like you. I wouldn't know how to buy in or when. Wouldn't risk me money neither. If I 'ad any.'

'Would you like to work in one?'

'Ah, now you're talkin'. Are yer offerin' me a job?'

'I might be. How about letting me rent your front room? I would put my groceries in and you could look after it for me.'

'Just the grocery? Hm. Well, I'd consider that. As long as I didn't 'ave to pay for the stock or anythin' like that.'

Mary Ann reassured her on that and promised she would pop round each day when the lads came home from work.

There were a couple of nice tub chairs in Sarah's front room, a pot stand in the window, and an ancient sofa; that was all.

'That sofa! I should 'ave chucked it out years ago. I'll gie it to the rag-and-bone man. I could get one chair into my kitchen; the other could go upstairs. I've always fancied an easy chair in my bedroom. Like the toffs that would be, wouldn't it?'

Mary Ann smiled. 'You think about it, then.'

'I've thought about it already. Suit me fine that would. Funnily enough, the farmer's talkin' about bringin' me the milk; I've needed more'n I could carry lately. And when folk call for their milk, Mary Ann, they'll buy summat.'

She was plainly excited now at the thought of running a shop without any of the risks. So it was agreed that Mary Ann would pay two shillings a week for the front room, plus any extra the landlord might put on the rent, and ten shillings a week wages.

The lads transferred most of the shelves from their shop to Sarah's, leaving the top shelf for underclothing and shoes, beneath which they fixed rails for the ready-mades.

'I say, our kid,' Ben pointed out as they pushed the full trolley round for the tenth time. 'We've got four shops now, countin' our Katy's. Four businesses! Sarah was gettin' bored, me Mam said.'

'One thing's for certain,' laughed Paul. 'Our mother won't ever be bored, will she?' He was delighted she was doing so well.

It was about this time that Katy twice heard news of Raish. First from the man who sharpened her knives and scissors and parked his machine outside her shop.

'I seen Brookie at a pub in Maldon. He 'ad got 'is feet under the table there all right. But 'e'll be 'avin' to shift 'em soon, if wot I heard is truth.'

Soon after that the organ grinder, a tiny man with little eyes as black as his monkey's, brought her more news. He was a great favourite in Cod End. The girls loved to dance round the lamp to the tunes of 'The Blue Danube' and 'After the Ball', while their brothers fed the monkey with nuts. The old man had known Katy since the days when as a lively little girl she had danced lightly round the lamp herself. He always found her out for a chat.

'Want news of your Dad?'

'If you like.'

'He's running a greengrocery shop for a certain party in Barr.'

'Female?'

The old man nodded. ''Fraid so.'

'He's nothing if not versatile, my Dad. If he should ask, tell him we are all doing well without him.'

So, after so long without a word, she heard of Raish's feet

being moved from underneath one table to another.

Sally Dilkes came quite often. As she was being measured or fitted she would tell of her latest activities with the W.S.P.U. She was one of the women who had stoned Mr Asquith as he left a public meeting in Birmingham and related the incident with some relish.

Whenever she came, Cod End kids would gaze in awe at the motor car she had bought from Ted, forming a circle round it at a respectful distance. Folk still gossiped about the time Ted chauffeured her to the Olympic games in the summer, for it was rumoured that they had put up at the same 'lodgings', which ranged from a small inn to the biggest hotel in London, depending upon who was telling the tale.

Ted, looking increasingly prosperous, still visited his family regularly. He invariably went to see Sally, too, if she was at Pelsall. Katy, ashamed to admit to herself feelings of jealousy, teased her friend about his visits. Sally laughed light-heartedly, remarking that Ted was 'good fun, as men go'.

Sometimes Ted came to buy sweets or chocolates.

'What do you think Miss Sally Dilkes would like today?'

'You should know by now.'

'Women are such changeable creatures, though, aren't they, Katy, love?'

He flirted with her outrageously, leaning over the counter to kiss her lightly on the nose or the chin. He would momentarily caress her hair or stroke the back of her hand. It was all so light and casual it would have seemed ridiculous to take offence. Yet it was sensuous enough to trigger off conflicting emotions. Sometimes, as he leaned tantalizingly across the counter, stopping just short of her mouth, Katy longed for him to kiss her as he had on that day in the sunlit meadow.

'Poor little married lady,' he would taunt, as he drew back, searching her brightened eyes with his own deep dark ones, half-hidden by the plethora of thick black lashes. 'I come only to check whether you are happy, Kate-me-mate.'

'Well, you can rest your mind on that score,' she would reply tartly. 'Because I am.'

And she was, wasn't she? Then why did her face in the mirror with its heightened colour remind her of a long-ago Mary Ann? She had what she wanted, a kind and reliable husband, and she had Mark. Then why was it that Ted could make her heart skip a beat? Oh, *why* did Charlotte have to die? She would have helped her keep her feet on the ground. Yet hot on that thought came another. Charlotte's death had given her the baby. Waves of shame immediately washed over her. Oh how wicked she was to think that. But Charlotte would understand. Mark was such a sweet and precious child.

CHAPTER

9

Edwin had been gone for over two years and they had
not heard from him for some time. On the rare occasions
they received letters Mary Ann read them aloud to the
whole family. His life was so different from theirs; the
England they wrote to him about must seem almost foreign
to him.

His bed was a mat on the floor, his food rice on a banana
leaf. He occasionally mentioned the extreme, almost unbear-
able, heat, yet he also wrote about India with fondness. He
told them of plains that stretched yellow and flat, of forests
that spread for hundreds of miles and of beautiful rust-
coloured bison. He described how he had journeyed up into
the hills one day, during some rare time off, from where he
could see miles of tea plantations stretching into the
distance, formed into mosaics by the paths of the pickers.

But mostly he wrote about the extreme poverty he had
come across, unlike anything he had dreamed possible. 'You

are all so rich in Heath End,' he wrote. Most of the time he spent in the sweltering mission compound, trying to lighten the lot of the blind children there. He mentioned them fondly by name, and was working hard to master their language.

'We are so busy,' he wrote. 'You may not hear for some time. Please do not worry.'

Mary Ann sent lively entertaining letters, whether he replied or not. He was reminded of the stories she used to tell them as children, and of the poems she used to write; half-forgotten memories of another of her talents.

She described to him how, every Sunday afternoon, Katy and Walter set off on their second-hand bicycles, Mark perched expectantly in a little seat in front of Walter, of how they took picnics to Sutton Park, Cannock Chase or The Wrekin, staying out quite late if the weather was fine. At other times they took Mark to see his grandparents at Rushall. Walter's job was secure; he was a good worker who never made any trouble, and Katy was a good manager. They considered it worth losing Sunday trade to be able to go out as a family.

The innkeepers were ordering a certain number of fish for a fixed time, sending someone to collect them. This meant that the lads were free on Saturday nights. They rode in to Walsall on the new trams which were now running hourly from Rushall for tuppence each way.

At The Grand Theatre, for tuppence in the gallery, they were able to see 'Trick Cycling Extraordinary', 'Witty Watty Walton', and 'Johnny Fuller, the Great Little Cat on Wire'. Once they saw 'The Merry Widow' at Her Majesty's, which, being newer and more luxurious, was well worth the extra penny. After the show they strode along Park Street feeling prosperous, gazing in at the windows of the big stores. Taylor's music shop was demonstrating the new-fangled gramophones and they allowed themselves wild dreams of saving for one between them.

Across The Bridge in the centre of the town, past the statue of Sister Dora, and they were in Market Street, where Dance's cookshop lured them with the aroma of succulent roast beef or pork, carved in the window, in full view of passers-by, by a corpulent chef in a tall, white hat, wielding a vicious knife. As he carved, the juices ran out of the meat into the gravy below. They would each buy a bap, sliced into two halves and dipped generously into the fatty gravy, for a penny. It would be hot and juicy to sink their teeth into, and would last them for the rest of Market Street, up past the Woolpack, to where St Matthew's Church stood, keeping an eye on the town from the top of the steep hill, elevated to even greater importance by its sixty steps.

Sometimes they spent Saturday afternoons playing billiards in the room over The Arcade, filled with the thick fog of young amateur smokers. The lads tried choking over one packet of Wills Woodbines, which cost them tuppence, but decided that the baps from the cookshop were better value.

On summer evenings there was Walsall Arboretum. Paul was walking out with Edna Willis, Ted's sister, for a time, and she would bring a friend for Ben. Occasionally Arthur, Paul's mate, would join them. They would hire a boat, threepence for half an hour, and row round the lake. After their row they would watch the tennis without understanding it, listen to the band, or wait for ages for the strutting peacocks to open their tails.

The lads would treat the girls to a penny ice cream wafer, or a tuppenny block of chocolate if they felt rich. And they often felt rich. Coronation Day on June 11th meant that their mother had lots of souvenirs for sale, so they bought the girls a red-white-and-blue silk scarf each. The girls immediately presumed that that meant they were practically engaged, so they stuck to ice creams after that; it was safer.

By now Ben had moved from Conduit to The Grove,

their nearest pit, being just beyond Pelsall village. Paul was learning a lot at Tack-a-Rue from the experienced miners; they liked him for being so keen, and taught him all they could.

New industries springing up at Birmingham meant more orders for local coal, and both lads had been on full time throughout the summer. Paul often stayed over to do necessary jobs after the shift had finished, for which he earned overtime. He was able to give Mary Ann thirty shillings, sometimes two pounds a week, and hear her say 'Well done'.

So all was well, until a new manager came to Tack-a-Rue. Determined to make bigger profits for the company, he said the miners were earning too much, and asked if they would take less. When they refused he decreed that savings had to be made somewhere, and started by cutting down on safety.

Paul and Arthur discussed it as they rode home together.

'That timber we're propping up the roof with has been used so many times it's rotten.'

'I'll say. The damn props get so short we have to make concrete trees, and they weigh a hundredweight.'

'And they don't last do they? They crumble and bend in the middle.'

'Nobody seems to care,' said Arthur glumly.

'Our blokes in the stall are working in coal only three feet thick. On their backsides all day. Ten tubs a day, that's as much as they can send.'

'And what happens when they get to the checkmen weighing up? They tip tubs over to see if there's slack in. If they say there is, whether there is or not, the blokes don't get paid for it.'

'Yet we all pay for one of the checkmen to see fair do's.'

'Ar, but the company man's the boss, ain't he? What he says, goes. Our man don't have a chance. He's frit.'

Paul nodded in agreement as Arthur continued.

'Then there's that ripping we're doing, to extend the roadway. We were all promised more money in our pay packets for that, but there's been no sign.'

'That's true.'

'So why don't we pack up and try our luck in Canada? I've got relations out there we could make for. There's a lot more dough to be made there, Paul. We could send some home and in a year or two's time we could bring back a nice little nest-egg. How about it?'

It was an old argument of Arthur's which up to now had not tempted Paul, but lately the injustices at the colliery against men who were working their guts out had sickened him. For the first time Canada sounded attractive.

But he shook his head. 'I couldn't go. Not with Edwin away.'

'Yer Mam'd still have Ben at home.'

'She can't have two of us away at the same time. Count me out,' Paul emphasized. But he looked disappointed as he said it.

Mary Ann knew nothing about how he felt. She was nearing the goal for which she had long been working and saving. How she wished Edwin could be there, with the others, so she could tell them all together.

Then suddenly he was. They had not received a letter for three months when Mr Dale called one Sunday morning, to tell them Edwin was on his way home because of a breakdown in health. It was the climate, he said. A bad attack of fever had left him weak and exhausted.

'They're going to miss him so much at that Mission. Their letters have been full of praise for him. But you will soon nurse him back to health, Mrs Brook. And when he is well enough, if I can help him find a job I will.'

'You don't think he will want to go back, then?'

'After the sort of attack he has had,' said Daddy Dale, 'It would be wiser if he didn't.'

So Mary Ann prepared for her eldest son.

Two of the tables were moved out of Little Gallery, and Katy's old bed from the attic was moved in. The lads could have the attic for their boxing, and Little Gallery would do fine for Edwin. Trade had dropped off there since Katy had reduced the amount of sewing she took in, and anyway, Edwin's needs were greater.

A newly-pegged rug was put down on the hearth, a new kettle on the hob, food in the cupboard and Little Gallery reverted to Little Cott again.

Edwin was touched and grateful when he saw it; it looked so homely and welcoming.

He looked far worse than they had imagined. India had played havoc with his health, leaving him hollow-eyed and bony. But it had given him an inner strength, an air of determination, that was not there before. After witnessing so much poverty and deprivation, death and deformity, he had long ago ceased to brood on his own loss. Seeing pregnant mothers who knew, before their childrn were born, that they would have no milk to feed them and starvation or disease would kill off their babies within weeks or days, had swept away all self-pity. The sight of pinch-faced, pot-bellied, homeless youngsters, permanently hungry, searching for mothers who no longer existed, was indelibly etched on his mind.

He was overwhelmed with gratitude when he saw his own happy well-loved child.

Caring for the blind had made him more aware than ever of the beauty all around him. England was so green and lovely. He had feasted his eyes on her every minute of the train journey home, and, although part of him was still in India, he was glad to be back.

Little Cott felt like a palace. It proved perfect for his needs. He could be alone, yet he was within minutes of his mother's industry or the bantering chatter of his brothers. They were both now taller than he and twice as broad. Ben was seventeen, while Paul, at nineteen, was older than he had been when he married Charlotte. The age gap had closed. It was good to see them.

Mark, three years old, spent a lot of time in Mary Ann's kitchen, sometimes standing on a chair beside her, rolling out sticky bits of pastry, scrubbing a corner of the table, or being allowed to help lay it for a meal. A huge fire-guard protected him from the hot kitchen range. One day he looked up from the pegs his grandmother was teaching him to count as Edwin walked in.

'You're my other Daddy, aren't you? Mom says you're my Daddy-Edwin and you're coming to my party.'

'A party? Why?'

'Because I am three.'

'Oh yes,' laughed Mary Ann. 'Katy says, since you missed Mark's birthday, she will have a tea party on Sunday, for the family.'

Birthdays were not usually observed in Heath End. There were far too many in each family. But Katy was determined that her children should enjoy what Sally described as 'highlights'.

So they were all together on Sunday to share the first birthday party they had known. After the jelly, gingerbread men and birthday cake they played a noisy game of hide-and-seek, blew soap bubbles from a clay pipe, and Mark sang the nursery rhymes he knew, Walter painfully picking out the tunes on the piano with one finger. Later Mark proudly carried to bed the little musical box Edwin had brought back from India, 'to sing me to sleep', he said.

There were pigeons, pigs, poultry and a donkey to attend to before they all settled down round the fire. Mary Ann was plainly excited about something. Suddenly she announced 'Now that we are all together I've something to tell you.'

They exchanged tolerant smiles, expecting her to say 'I've an idea.'

Instead she startled them all by stating, 'I have bought

four houses.' There was a stunned silence before Katy spoke.

'Only four, Mother?' she asked with a little laugh.

'Yes, Katy.' She went on to explain, slightly breathless, 'I've four children, haven't I? I thought the rents would keep me independent as long as I live, and, after I'm gone, there will be a house for each of you.'

'Good heavens! Where are they?'

'They are at Pelsall, not far from the church.'

'Well, go on. Tell us all about them.'

'They're good houses, well built, in a nice spot. Three bedrooms, front parlour, kitchen and scullery, that's what they call the wash-house. The staircase is in between the parlour and kitchen. There's a good strip of garden to each one, at the back.'

'However did you get all that money?'

But they knew the answer to that before Ben asked. She had done it by careful planning and budgeting, by working every minute of every day for the last three and a half years, since Raish went, and because he wasn't there to take it away from her. She had done it by single-minded striving toward this goal.

Four houses! It felt strange and uncomfortable to be so rich. Almost indecent.

She sat patiently, watching the mixed reactions flit across the faces of her children, her workworn hands for once resting uncomfortably in her lap. Something about those hands filled Edwin with an overwhelming sense of love and protection and he crossed over and put his arm along her shoulders.

She had done it all for them, he knew. Like the rest of them, she had to admit to the possibility of Raish returning one day. She knew her weaknesses better than they did. If she had the cash he would wheedle it out of her, and lose no time in spending it. This way the money was invested for their future and meanwhile there would be an income for

155

her, so she would not be a drag on anyone in her old age.

'I think it is wonderful what you have achieved, Mother. All by yourself.'

'Not by myself, Edwin. You have all played a part. I couldn't have done it without each one of you.' But they all knew for certain that she could.

'Well! I am still in a state of shock,' gasped Katy. 'I must say it's a marvellous feeling. Like being handed an insurance policy already paid up. Just to think! We might all be living next door to one another some day.'

'Heaven forbid!' groaned Paul in mock horror, nudging Ben. 'Do you mean to say I'm never going to be rid of this one? How about that, Ben? Property owners! At the posh end of the common. Your kids will be Churchie Bulldogs, do you realize that?'

Ben groaned inwardly. Property owners! That would not go down very well with the Union mates he met at the meetings held in a back room at The Bush Inn where he regularly gave vent to his antipathy toward pit bosses and property owners. Apart from Mr Dickinson, their mother would be the only property owner in Cod End. He did not like the idea. 'Keep at it, Mother,' he commented drily. 'If you buy up a few more we can extend Cod End as far as the church.'

Edwin took his mother's rough hands gently between his own. 'You are a marvel, our Mary Ann, and we are grateful. But remember, we would rather have you than all the houses in England. Ease off now.'

Once over the shock they all, with the exception of Ben, discussed the surprising news, joking and happy, until bedtime, filled with admiration for the woman who had made it possible.

That night Mary Ann was too excited to sleep. The houses were let out at five shillings each per week. She made up her mind to bank that pound a week for little Mark. Whatever happened now they were all taken care of.

CHAPTER

10

A WEEK OR two of his mother's food and of sleeping without fear of being called in the night improved Edwin's health rapidly. The hollows of his cheeks began to fill out. His clothes did not hang quite so loosely on his spare frame.

Cod-Enders were genuinely interested in his experiences and he, who had imagined he could never make an impact in private, let alone in public, found himself talking on Poverty in India in the chapel schoolroom. His audience gave as generously as they could to the mission funds, and, surprised at the impact of Edwin's sincerity, Daddy Dale invited him to give another talk at Pelsall Central Hall.

Best of all, he found he could paint again. He saw every colour, every shape, every sunset, with greater clarity than ever before. His easel was set up in the small living room of Little Cott, where he had fixed a wide shelf along one wall for his bits and pieces, as he had done in his own home. He started work on the miniature flower studies, which Mary Ann promised to display in both shops, still not having the strength to walk far enough to sketch landscapes. Any money he might make above his immediate needs he resolved to send to India.

One day, as he concentrated on the tiny brush strokes of purple heather, he was aware of Sally Dilkes at his side. She had let herself in quietly through the door from the street. She stood watching him for several seconds before wandering restlessly round the room.

'What patience,' she commented lightly. 'May I look at these?'

She crossed over to the shelf where his two latest miniatures lay. One was a bright red poppy on a black background, and the other a sprig of Golden Rod.

'These are lovely. May I buy them?'

'I'd be happy to give them to you, if you like them.'

'Come on, Edwin. Let me pay. You know you are hoping to send something out to India with the proceeds.'

'How do you know that?'

'I can guess, can't I? I saw the posters. You are going to speak at Pelsall Central Hall?'

He nodded.

She sat down. 'Well, I won't be there. So tell me about it,' she commanded.

Seated so regally, against the bright covers of the chair, she reminded him of a gypsy queen, her mass of black wavy hair tied back with red ribbon at her neck, her black eyes flashing. She wore a dark cotton dress, a riot of red looped braid round the hem, waist and wrists. One tiny black-patented foot crossed the other.

'I would love to try to paint you.'

The words came of their own volition. He was as surprised as she.

'Well!' Her mouth curved. 'Have you ever? Painted a portrait, I mean?'

158

'Never.'

'Mmm. I don't know whether I have the time to let you practice on me. Meanwhile . . . India?'

She looked so spoiled, tapping her foot imperiously. Her peremptory tone decided him to spare her nothing. So he told of the lepers, young men with no arms or legs, propelling themselves along the street. He told of the old men, deformed, past caring, sitting cross-legged, their loin cloths all they possessed. He told of the children too far beyond hope to beg, of festering sores on young bodies, of feet callused and cracked. He spoke emotionally of the blind children, abandoned or lost.

He saw the dark eyes quickly give way to compassion, so he softened his story by explaining how loving care and proper food could transform these same children into mischievous youngsters with wide grins.

'How can you bear to remember it all?'

'How can I bear to forget?'

She stood up quietly. 'I won't forget, either, Edwin. Thank you for telling me.'

He handed her the flower studies she had admired. 'Please take them. As a present.' He was surprised by tears lingering like diamonds on the edge of the long black lashes.

Sally made her way along the front footpath to Katy's, where a group of Cod End children gazed inquisitively at her motor car, keeping a respectful distance, as always.

Walter was playing with Mark as Katy led Sally upstairs to fit on a completed garment and to discuss the next order. She slipped the tape measure round her friend, unnecessarily she thought. Her voice registered disbelief. 'What's this? Been attending a lot of parties? An inch on your waist, and nearly two inches on your tummy!'

'Only to be expected, dear, isn't it?' replied Sally flippantly, 'considering I am *with child*, as they say.'

Katy's heart missed a beat as she flopped on to the bed.

'Oh, Sally!' She hesitated before asking quietly, 'Is it Ted's?' A little bird fluttered in her throat as she waited for the answer.

'Very perceptive of you, dear.'

'Does he know?'

'Of course.'

'Are you going to be married?'

Sally laughed shortly as she continued dressing. 'Katy! Don't be ridiculous. You *know* how I feel about that. Ted feels the same. Neither of us wants marriage.'

'But what about the *baby*?'

Sally let out an exaggerated sigh. 'Oh, yes! The baby! Well neither of us is very interested in that either. I suppose we shall have to think about adoption.'

'Sally! You wouldn't give your own baby away?'

Sally opened her wide eyes even wider. 'You are the one who always says that a child needs a stable home and two loving parents. Remember? It wouldn't have either of those with either of us, now, would it?'

Katy could hardly breathe. *It wasn't fair.* She and Walter longed for a sister or brother for Mark, with never a sign of their dearest wish being granted. Yet here was Sally talking about giving an unwanted child away. How could she! A preposterous thought flitted across her mind for a second, so preposterous she pushed it away as soon as it surfaced. For it was one thing for Walter to take her brother Edwin's child as his own, and quite another for him to accept the child of Sally and Ted Willis. Even Cod End would not accept that he should do that.

Ted's child. Ted and Sally. She thought her heart would choke her.

'Do consider this very carefully, Sally.'

'Of course!' Sally dismissed the subject curtly. 'Have you an envelope, dear?'

In amazement Katy watched as she wrote out a cheque for fifty pounds and slipped it into the envelope. On the flap she

160

wrote 'For the India Fund'. 'Please give this to Edwin, from me.'

A week later she was back for another fitting. Again she called first at Little Cott. Edwin, concentrating on his work, acknowledged her presence with a little nod. Sally sat perfectly still, watching him intently. No foot tapping this time. In one way it was like having Charlotte sitting beside him, Edwin felt, while admitting that Sally excited him in a way Charlotte never had.

After a few minutes she closed her eyes with a sigh, resting her head back. As his sister had done on the train journey he studied her dark luscious beauty; the perfect oval face, the sensuous lips, the soft sweeping lashes that curved away as soon as they touched her smooth olive skin. Today she wore a plain wine-coloured suit. She had wound her hair into demure rolls on either side of her face, the style emphasizing her classically-chiselled chin and long smooth neck. A few silken strands escaped on to her cheeks. Edwin felt an almost irresistible urge to release the rest of the imprisoned locks. He pictured them falling in gay abandon on to her shoulders.

Her eyes opened suddenly as if aware of his scrutiny.

'I wasn't being awkward about the portrait. I am going away soon.'

'I doubt if I could ever portray you on canvas anyway. Your face changes every second.' He smiled. 'Thank you for the cheque. It is already on its way to the Mission.'

She handed him a card. 'The address of an art shop in Edgbaston who are willing to take some of your flower studies.'

Hildred Antiques, it said. Edwin knew the name; he remembered thinking how unusual it was when Gareth Hildred offered to set him up in bigger premises.

'He saw the flower studies you gave to me. He says he thinks he can find a good market for them.'

'Thank you, Sally. I will get in touch with him later.

When are you going away?'

'Within a few weeks. I will see you before then, I hope. In fact, I am expecting you will come to a garden party I am giving next week.'

'A garden party? Me?'

'It's for the India fund. There will be wives of colliery owners, factory owners, landowners. None of them know what to spend their money on. I thought perhaps you would come to help to persuade them.'

Edwin hesitated. 'They're hardly the sort of people I am used to, Sally.'

'They're hardly the sort of people *I* am used to, Edwin. But, for this cause, I will put up with that. I rather thought you might, too? If you come and talk to them you will make a lot more money than at the Central Hall, I assure you.'

He smiled again. 'I see. All right, I'll be there. Thank you.'

'Three o'clock then. A week today.'

Carriages and several motor cars were parked in the long drive which led to Sally's home. Edwin followed the sounds of laughter and conversation which brought him to large lawns at the back of the important looking house, second in prominence only to Lady Violet's at The Hall.

Garden chairs and tables were set out in corners, shaded by high flowering shrubs, where many well-dressed people were mingling and chatting. Busy maids in black dresses and white aprons carried out plates of tiny sandwiches and wheeled trolleys loaded with silver teapots, milk jugs and china cups.

He stood near the house, away from the rest, looking for Sally. It wasn't long before he caught sight of her, moving among her guests, introducing people to one another. Today she looked more gipsy-like than ever, in a long swirling black skirt, edged with red, and a frilly white blouse with red embroidery, wide sleeves gathered into tight cuffs. Her hair hung down in thick dark plaits. As soon as she could she came toward him, walking with languid, unhurried grace.

'Looks a bit ominous, doesn't it?' she commented, indicating the cloudy sky.

Sure enough, before long, raindrops began to fall, sending guests scurrying into the house, while servants swiftly and unobtrusively transferred the food to the huge dining room. It was here that Edwin made his appeal.

Introducing him, Sally said, 'I am sure, Mr Brook, that you will discover that I have invited here today some of the most generous people in the county.'

Edwin was able to begin by saying, 'You were able to shelter from the weather just now. But many people have no shelter . . . '

At the end of the afternoon Sally helped him tot up cheques and cash totalling nearly three hundred pounds. Edwin was astounded. Never in his wildest dreams had he expected so much. How many working days would that be for a miner, he wondered. How long would it take his mother to save such a sum? It was almost as if they had tried to outdo one another in their generosity in order to prove how affluent they were. But for whatever reasons they gave, Edwin was full of gratitude.

'Thank you, Sally, for suggesting this,' he exclaimed fervently when they later walked out into the garden, where the late afternoon sun slanted across the damp grass. 'This money will help a lot of people.'

'Your talk made all the difference. I didn't realize you could be so persuasive.'

'Didn't realize it myself,' admitted Edwin, feeling a little embarrassed. 'Sheer desperation, I suppose, knowing this is the only way I can help now. I would only be an encumbrance if I tried to go back yet. But, perhaps, one day.'

163

She strolled alongside him to the end of the long drive. There was a strange air of loneliness and uncertainty about her as they said goodbye. She looked so small and young, standing there, dwarfed by the tall cypress trees, despite her graceful height. Acting on impulse he kissed her, very gently, on her cheek. 'Thank you, Sally dear.' His action surprised himself; he immediately felt he had been presumptuous.

She turned and walked slowly, almost reluctantly, away from him, toward the house. He thought he heard her say 'It's too late', but could not imagine what she meant.

She called on Katy once more before she left. 'I am going to lose myself in London for a few weeks.' She patted her tummy. 'Until this is over.'

'Oh, Sally, you're going to be so lonely.'

'Not me. I have friends there, and I expect Ted will come to see me. Far better this way. My parents need never know; nor anyone else.

'Take that worried frown off your face, Katy. I am not going to do anything foolish. There is good medical care and a life of luxury laid on. The adoption will be arranged by my consultant.'

'You will write?'

'I promise.' She paused at the door. 'And thank you for caring.'

Edwin felt strangely bereft when he knew she had visited Katy without calling on him. He had puzzled over why she had looked so sad when he left her, after such a successful afternoon.

He pinned the card she had given him on a small notice board he had made. As soon as he had a fair selection of his work he would go and see Gareth Hildred.

Meanwhile, apart from the excruciating headaches he sometimes suffered, his recovery continued steadily. Remembering the example of Charlotte, Mary Ann left him alone for as long as he wished, taking his meals into Little Cott; welcoming him warmly when he cared to join them. He still tired easily, looking far older than his twenty-five years. His boyish features had gone. There was a maturity that had not been there before. Edwin had grown up at last.

Ben, now seventeen, grumbled constantly about the pit, but with his Saturdays in Walsall and his Sundays pigeon flying, Mary Ann guessed he was as content as he ever would be. It was Paul, the one who never grumbled, who puzzled her. Lately there had been an air of unrest about him, over and above his usual anxiousness.

Her own life was as full as ever, her ready-mades selling well during the week, while on Sundays she looked after the grocery shop so that Sarah could visit her relations and take her weekly flowers to the cemetery.

Christmas was approaching again. It was not necessary to tackle it with the fevered haste of the last few years. Her main goal was achieved, her money safely invested in the houses for her children. She even left Edwin in charge occasionally while she visited Sarah, or Ginny. She often took Mark with her. He liked to go when she collected the rents from the four good, solid houses near the church, when he could gambol on the common or chase the geese.

Sometimes, like today, they would go over the stepping bridge, where Mark played jumping up and down the steps, as they watched the 'Puffing Billies' shunting beneath the bridge amid clouds of steam.

He was a handsome little lad, with his corn-coloured hair and bright blue eyes, unspoiled, despite all the attention lavished on him. Far too much for one child, Mary Ann thought. Katy and Walter regularly took him out for Sunday treats and occasionally he went off with Edwin, scouring the fields for unusual wild flowers or leaves. He liked nothing better than to pass the necessary tools to Paul for his cycle repairing; Ben, with unaccustomed patience,

165

taught him how to gently handle a pigeon without frightening it; Walter helped him with the tiny patch of garden he had set aside for him to tend, and she herself always called him to feed the fowls and pigs.

Yes, far too much attention. She was glad that Katy had arranged to visit the specialist in Birmingham, to see if there was any reason why the baby they longed for had not arrived. She had insisted upon giving her the consultation fee.

'Come along, Mark,' she called now. 'It will soon be dark. Your Dad will be home.'

'And Daddy Edwin is there already.'

'Yes.'

He sang happily, holding her hand, as they walked past the long row of houses in the gulley, and one or two Cod-Enders, going in or out, laughed, and paused to say, ''E's a little sharp 'un, 'e is.'

Suddenly he asked, 'Where is my Mom's Dad?'

'I don't know.'

'Well you are her Mom, aren't you, Gran'ma? You should know where her Dad is.'

I should indeed, my little lad, she thought. Aloud she said, 'If we hurry we may just have time to pop in to see Sarah.'

Sarah looked heaps better and tidier since she took the grocery shop over; it had given her a sense of purpose. She broke some toffee into a dish for Mark, seating him at her kitchen table with pencil and paper, while they talked in the shop. Sarah loved to pass on snippets of gossip and today was no exception.

'Did you know that Arthur, your Paul's mate, is planning to go to work in Canada? He's been trying to get your Paul to go with him.' She eyed Mary Ann keenly. 'Ain't he said nuthin' about it?'

So this was it. This was why she often caught him studying her doubtfully, as if about to say something, then changing his mind abruptly if the shop bell tinkled or one of the others walked in.

'There's bin a lot of shinaniggin' goin' on at Tack-a-Rue lately,' Sarah was saying. 'It's not the safe pit to work in that it was when it first opened.'

'They have a new manager, who is not fair. Paul did tell me that.'

'Ar. He's bin doin' the colliers out o' some o' their money.'

That night Mary Ann closed the shop earlier than usual. With Edwin at a meeting and Ben playing snooker with Percy she planned a quiet chat with Paul. She sat opposite him across the table, not even her knitting in her hands.

'What's this about Tack-a-Rue, lad? Sarah tells me things aren't all they should be.'

'True enough.'

'She also tells me that Arthur is off to Canada.'

'She's right.'

'He has been wanting you to go with him, has he?'

'I shan't leave you, Mother.'

'Paul! Why ever not? I have two more sons and a daughter round me. If you want to go, my lad, now is the time. While you are still free to do it.'

She had to make an extreme effort to prevent her voice from shaking as she watched relief flood the face of her dear son. He could not hide the sudden enthusiasm in his eyes. How had she been so blind?

'Are you sure you would be all right, Mother?'

'Now, what do you think you could do that the others couldn't?'

'S'pose you're right there. I think I'm more important than I am, don't I?'

She reached out and placed her hand over his. 'You are important, my lad. You will always be important to me. That's why I want you to do with your life whatever is best for you. If the time's come for you to leave Heath End, then

167

you must do it. Edwin went when he wanted to go.'

'They're doing well out there, Mother. I shall be able to send you more than I'm earning now, and bring you a nice little sum back. We wouldn't be leaving Heath End for good, you know. I couldn't leave you for good.'

She smiled. 'You go. And don't worry about sending money, lad. We've got houses in the bank now you know.'

As Paul and Arthur prepared to board the *Lusitania* at Liverpool Ben felt as if his right arm was about to be amputated. 'I'm the one who hates the pit, and you two are the ones who're supposed to love it. So tell me, our kid, why ain't it me that's goin' and you that's stoppin'?'

'Now how would Pelsall Panthers survive without its star player? And who else would the pigeons win prizes for?

'Any pit's all right, Ben, if the management is good. You're all right at The Grove. I hope I find one as good where I'm going.' As he gripped his brother's hand tightly he said, 'Look after our mother. And don't forget, let me know the minute it happens, if the old chap turns up. Goodbye, me old boxin' pal.'

Ben was too choked to answer. He stood with the crowd and watched the other passengers go aboard. It was like watching a crowd of Wolves supporters arriving. There seemed as many folk waving goodbye as were boarding. Most of them were going looking for work, and their relatives wondered if they would ever see them again. All around there were women crying, and set-faced men, who looked as if they wished they could. All the passengers leaning over the rail seemed to be waving to somebody, except for a sad group of Barnardo children he had watched go aboard, accompanied by four adults. They each had a little case and marched silently, in twos. He gave them a special wave as the *Lusitania* pulled away.

Suddenly he found his voice and yelled, 'Don't worry about me Mother, our kid. She'll be all right.' But his voice was lost in the noise of ships' hooters and the general commotion of the docks. As they sailed from sight he muttered, 'If I'd had the thirteen pounds for the fare I'd 'ave gone meself.'

The *Lusitania* was a fine ship with a thousand passengers on board. For the first few days they were able to enjoy the food and activities, until the roll of the ship got the better of them. Numbers in the dining room became noticeably less as the week went on.

'Wonder 'ow them poor little kids are?'

'God help them if they feel anything like I do.'

'They say there's a new Home bein' set up for 'em in Canada. I expect they'll end up as proper Canadians. Wonder if we shall an' all?'

'Not me,' stated Paul emphatically. 'I shall be back as soon as I've saved enough.'

'Ar. Me an' all.'

Standing on top deck as they sailed into the St Lawrence, they absorbed their first views of mighty Canada. The rectangular farms, each with a frontage to the river, were covered with snow. The ship had to manoeuvre slowly to avoid the ice that was just breaking up. In spite of bright sunshine, cold seared bitingly into their lungs, right down as far as their toes. They had never known such cold.

After answering questions at Quebec as to where they were going and declaring the fifteen pounds each they had brought, they deposited their cases at the station and climbed from the lower town, through the old walls, into the upper city. They found a suitable lodging house run by a French family where they could sleep for a dollar. They must remember that a dollar was worth four shillings and fourpence.

As they boarded the seven o'clock train next morning for the five-hundred-odd mile journey to Toronto it was mid-day in London. Katy was just getting into a taxi-cab with Sally, who had met her off the Birmingham train.

'When your letter said the name of your gynaecologist I couldn't believe it. It's the man who is looking after me. His place is only round the corner from where I live.' They stepped out of the taxi at the imposing door of a grey building where a brass plate announced Mr D.T. Spence.

Sally indicated the direction she should take to her flat. 'The next square, first to your right. Up one flight of stairs. Good luck.'

'Thank you, Sally. I shall find you.'

It was Mary Ann who had suggested Katy stay the night with Sally. She hated leaving Mark, but with Walter and Edwin assuring her that between the three of them they would manage, she had been persuaded.

She was the only patient in the comfortable waiting-room. The specialist at Birmingham had said that if Mr Spence was not able to recommend anything Katy might as well give up her quest for a baby. When she knew the consulting fee was twenty pounds she had considered selling the piano, but Mary Ann had insisted she let her pay. Now here she was. Full of hope. Surely this clever man would find a way.

But it was a dispirited Katy who came out of the consulting room later, her heart as heavy as a ton of coal.

She found Sally's apartment in a tall building facing on to a neat square park. The long drawing room was richly furnished with soft pink sofas and armchairs on a thick rose carpet. Elegant crystal chandeliers hung from ornate ceilings, heavy velvet curtains stroked the floor, while beautiful gilded mirrors reflected the pale pink of the walls.

What a lot of money somewhere like this must cost. She knew that Sally's father owned several iron and steel works in the midlands, and that her mother had come from a monied family, but it was still difficult to come to terms with the fact that the down-to-earth friend who loved to sit and chat with her in her own tiny house, and who wore the clothes she made, could afford such opulence.

'How did you get on?' asked Sally, although the pale face told all.

Katy sank despondently on to one of the pink armchairs. 'No child of my own. Ever.' Sally had to bent her head to hear the whispered voice. 'Thank God for Mark. Although he's Edwin's really, and there is always the chance that he might get married again. He said that Mark is ours for ever. But...'

'Do you think it's likely that he will marry again?'

'No.'

'And if he did, he would never take Mark away from you. You know he wouldn't.'

'Oh, Sally, if he did! I couldn't bear it.'

She put her hand to her lip to stop it trembling. She must not cry. Her head fell on to her small tightly-clenched fist for a moment, the knuckles opaque. Why did this have to happen to her? She had wanted a family more than anything in the world. Not romance. Not riches. Just a happy family. She mentally shook herself and raised her head.

'Here I am, spoiling our day together. What a lovely room this is, Sally.'

'I told you I intended being comfortable, didn't I?' she replied lightly. 'Come and see the rest of it.'

Sally's bedroom was decorated in the same pink as the drawing room. The guest room, smelling of lavender, was a mixture of lavender and white. Purple towels had been placed ready for Katy, on a rail near the window.

The kitchen, painted white, had a recess at one end, where the table was laid ready for their lunch with a linen tablecloth, edged with lace, and napkins to match. There was a bowl of salad, a large piece of ham to carve from, and a loaf. Sally poured out the coffee which had been bubbling on the new gas stove. 'I enjoy looking after myself here,' she said.

But it was the bathroom, also in lavender and white, which evoked cries of pleasure from Katy. She had never seen one anything like it before. 'A bit different from our old tin bath on the hearth,' she exclaimed.

Every Saturday night, after he had stoked up the fire, Walter fetched the bath from where it hung on the garden wall to their cosy hearth. He filled it with hot water from the brewhouse copper. Katy was the only one to enjoy this luxury. The rest of them bathed in the draughty brewhouse, the only advantage being that the sink was there to pour the water away when they had finished, whereas it meant Katy putting her coat on top of her nightgown and scooping out jugs of water with the big enamel jug, carrying each one outside to the drain, until the bath was sufficiently emptied to be dragged to the door. She always tried to do this quietly, but more often than not Walter would come downstairs and say, 'You go to bed, love. I'll do that.'

And here was this gleaming white porcelain bath, with taps and a plug to let the water out. Lots of thick white towels hung on a portable wooden towel holder; a glass of lavender bath salts sat on the shelf. A little chair, upholstered in purple and white, nestled in the corner.

'What luxury, Sally!'

'You can use it tonight.'

Seated in the clean white kitchen Sally cut bread and ham and served the salad but every mouthful stuck in Katy's throat, unable to get past the lump of tears. Eventually she gave up trying to eat. No brother or sister for Mark. No baby of her own, ever. As she laid down her knife and fork Sally put a hand on her arm. 'I am so sorry, dear.'

Katy's hands clenched and unclenched while she tried to hold back the tears. 'We both wanted a family so badly. Walter never had much family life. Constant difficulties between his parents resulted in him being pushed from pillar to post. We had such plans for our children. Now Mark will be an only child.'

They both sat silently until Sally suddenly burst out, 'Isn't this ridiculous? There you are, eating your heart out for a baby, and here am I, with one to give away.'

'Sally! You're not still thinking of doing that?'

'I thought I had made it quite clear.'

'But you look so . . . '

'Serene? Radiant?'

Katy nodded.

'I have read all the right books and done all the right things, dear. I decided that the least I could do for the poor unwanted little mite was to give it the right start while it's part of me. I am assured by Mr Spence that I shall have a fine healthy child. He will arrange the adoption for me.' She paused. 'If *you* want it, Katy, you can have it.'

'You can't just give a baby away like *that*,' protested Katy angrily. Oh, none of this was fair.

'Like *that*. I would be sure it was going to have the loving attention I never had.'

'Sally, you are the mother of this child inside you.'

'What difference does that make?'

'It makes all the difference. Think of the feelings you have for your own mother and how she must feel about you.'

'None.'

'Sally!'

'Don't "Sally" me like that. It's true. We feel absolutely nothing for each other. Never have done. In fact we antagonize one another. Can't bear to be together for more than five minutes, either of us.'

Katy stared in amazement. She had always felt such closeness with her mother, despite there being little show of open sentiment between them. Her anger dropped away from her.

'Don't you *mind* that?' she whispered, thinking of the richness Mary Ann added to all their lives.

'Why should I mind? Just because you are born to someone, Katy, doesn't mean you own them. Or they you. You are just as likely to be incompatible with your mother as with anyone else.'

173

There was a long silence from them both before Sally asked, 'So what do you say?'

'Sally, it isn't easy to say this. When we took Mark it was different. This time there would be Ted . . . '

'There would not be Ted. He doesn't know a thing about it.'

'But you said . . . '

'I know what I said. It was to stop you fussing over me.'

'Then you haven't seen him? You haven't . . . told him?'

'I have not. Things were over between Ted and me, Katy, before I knew about this. He is away in France. He went over to do some research on motor cars for his Birmingham boss.' She laughed shortly. 'And Ted being Ted, he has allowed himself to be lured away by a French company offering him more money. I had a brief note from him, sent on from Pelsall, telling me how much he is enjoying living over there.'

'Ted need never know anything about this,' she concluded firmly. 'I can keep a secret. And I know you can.'

She watched as the hopes, doubts, fears darted in quick succession across her friend's face, reading them correctly. 'I shan't be popping up and putting in a claim, if that's what you are worrying about. It would all be drawn up legally. Anyway, as soon as I have shed this load I shall be well out of your way. I am off to India.'

'India!'

'Yes, that is something else I have been occupying myself with, arranging a long, long trip to India. You can thank your brother for that. It's Edwin who has embued me with the desire to go and see for myself what needs doing. I had a lot of money settled on me when I was twenty-five, by my maternal grandmother. It may be of more use out there than here.'

'You have to have a Cause, don't you, Sally?' said Katy, remembering the last time she came to London, the day

174

Sally met Ted, the day that led to all this. 'But India! You will have to be pretty tough for that.'

'I'm not thinking of roughing it, like Edwin did. I intend to be reasonably comfortable.' She stood up. 'Let's have some more coffee.'

As she poured she asked, 'Well? There's something else troubling you.'

'Yes. Walter. I haven't told him about you and Ted.'

'Then why do so? Katy, I know you want to accept this child. Tell Walter that the consultant you saw today is going to arrange adoption for you. That's feasible. It would be just a three-way secret; you, me and Mr Spence. No-one else need ever know.'

Katy knew by now that Sally's flippancy often disguised deep feelings. 'When you see this baby you will feel differently about all this.'

'The child plucking at the heart strings, and all that? I have been warned.' She paused thoughtfully. 'If by a miracle that does happen, dear, then of course it will all be off. From your point of view it would be rather like waiting for your own child, for one is never really certain, isn't that so? But I am not ready for a child, if I ever will be. There is so much else I want to do.'

'Like going to India?'

'Like going to India, yes.' She changed the subject abruptly. 'I have started having the recommended rest on the bed in the afternoon. What would you like to do, Katy? Go for a breath of fresh air? Or read?' She smiled. 'Or have a bath?'

Katy felt a sudden overwhelming desire to go home. After the devastating diagnosis at the surgery it was so tempting to take up this wonderful alternative, and here, in Sally's rooms, it all seemed so easy and possible. She needed to get away and consider it from the distance of her own home.

She glanced at the little silver clock on the shelf. 'I could get a train at five o'clock. Would you think me very rude, Sally, if I went?'

"Of course not. I will walk as far as the road with you. I can get you a cab there.' She seemed to understand the sudden decision.

'I've never hailed a cab in my life, but I am sure I can manage it. You have your rest, Sally. I will write soon.' She embraced her friend. 'I shall understand if you change your mind.' But already she was praying desperately she would not.

'Give my love to Edwin,' called Sally from the landing.

Why single Edwin out, Katy wondered? Sally used the word love more lightly than most, so she tucked that question away for the time being.

Journeying home on the train her mind see-sawed back and forth. One moment she was crooning to the new baby; the next she was telling herself that none of this was possible. By the time she reached Pelsall she had decided she could not possibly keep such a secret from Walter. He did not deserve that, did he? How he loved Mark, going to him without hesitation whenever he cried in the night, swiftly and quietly, before Katy was out of bed, helping to nurse him through measles, influenza and ear-aches with never-ending patience.

But this was different. This would be Ted Willis's child. How would Walter react to that? Ted had often flirted brazenly with her in front of him, and although Walter chose to ignore it, she sensed he did not like Ted. Walking home along the path by the vicarage she changed her mind yet again. She would tell him half the story, that the baby was Sally's. No need to mention Ted. She convinced herself that would be the kindest thing to do. For by now she wanted the baby, very, very badly.

Walter showed no surprise at seeing her. 'I thought you might come straight home, love,' he said. 'I put a dinner in the oven for you, just in case.'

176

Katy had eaten little or nothing all day. The overdone sausages and hard potatoes he placed in front of her tasted delicious. It was good to be home.

'I'll lock the shop up so that we can talk,' he said when she had eaten.

Her mind had been so full of Sally's offer she had almost forgotten the bad news from the doctor. Of course, Walter was waiting to hear the result of the examination.

She told him what the consultant had said. 'In his opinion, after examining me and studying the reports of the tests from Birmingham, I shall never be able to conceive a child.'

She watched the disappointment cloud his face, followed by concern for her. She hurried on, her heart bouncing about in her throat, making her voice breathless. 'How would you feel about adopting a baby, Walter?'

Walter gazed quietly at the flushed face of his wife for a few seconds before replying. 'If that's what you want, Katy, then that's what I want.'

She hesitated for a moment. 'It would be Sally's baby.'

He listened carefully as she told him about how Sally felt about the baby, how she would like it to come to them, and how she was going to India after the baby was born.

'She says it could all be drawn up legally. No-one need ever know. I trust her, Walter.'

He considered it all gravely, gazing for a long time into the fire and then back at Katy. It was her turn now to see the regiment of doubts and fears flit across his face. His kind face looked sad; his shoulders slumped with the responsibility of decision.

After what seemed an eternity, he spoke. 'It's Ted's, isn't it?'

Katy's heart did a double somersault right down to the pit of her stomach as she watched the chance of the baby slipping away. She nodded miserably, although she recognized an overwhelming sense of relief that Walter knew the whole of it.

'You will have to give me time, Katy.'

'Yes. I know.'

Next night at the same time, when the shop was closed and Mark asleep, Walter said, 'Come and sit down, love.' All day long she had thought about the situation. Not only about the baby, but about her husband. She could not say she was in love with Walter but she was surprised how much she leaned on him. She wondered now how she would ever manage without his gentle kindness, his thoughtfulness and patience. She remembered Edwin saying, after Charlotte's death. 'Why did I never tell her how I loved her?' And she had replied, 'She knew.'

She knew that Walter loved her. It was in his every action. But did he know how she felt? The nearest she could get to telling him was to say, 'I shall understand, Walter, if the answer is no.'

'Do come and sit down, Katy.' This time she did. 'I have thought of nothing else today, like you, I expect.' She waited while he paused, considering how to put into words what he felt. 'After a lot of thought I realize that this baby won't be Sally's, or Ted's. Or ours, for that matter. Children are only ever lent. They belong to themselves. The home they are brought up in and the love around them does any shaping it is possible to do.' It was a long speech for Walter and he seemed relieved when it was over.

Katy looked at him in surprise and with new admiration.

'Does that mean . . . ?'

'It means that, if Sally's of the same mind when the baby's born, we'll take it. If you're sure that's what you want.'

'Oh yes. I am,' breathed Katy. 'But how about you, Walter?'

Walter looked at her long and seriously. 'We have to face the fact that Sally might want to keep the baby, love. But, if not, yes, I think we could make it work. This time the parents' identity would have to be our secret, for the child's

178

sake. No-one else must know,' he stressed. 'Ever.'

'Yes, I know. We'll tell no-one. No-one.'

'Would you like to leave Heath End?' he asked suddenly. 'It might make things easier.'

'Oh, *no*, Walter. I love it here. The furthest I shall ever want to move is to one of those "good solid houses" by the church, one day, when we are old and the children leave us.'

'We'll look forward to April then.'

'Oh, Walter. Didn't it sound nice, "the children"?'

She crossed the hearth and put her arms round him. 'Won't Mark be pleased?'

Then, after a pause. 'You *both* mean such a lot to me, Walter.'

'I know,' he stated quietly.

Of course, when she thought about it, he could not have agreed to all this otherwise.

She settled down happily to write to Sally.

CHAPTER

11

PAUL LAY STRETCHED out on the stubbly grass, lazily reflecting on the last few months. The scorching Canadian sun seared his bare brown back, while a wide-brimmed hat protected his neck. His hair was fairer than it had been since childhood.

Miles of flat prairie plains, with huge patchworks of green Springing wheat stretched ahead of him, toward the horizon which seemed a million miles away. The only buildings in sight were the McNabs' farmhouse and outhouses to the right of him. Further away, to his left, was the kaboosh, with its ten bunks, where he slept with the other farm workers.

The sky was vast and cloudless, yet he knew that instant storms, from sudden veils of clouds, could drench him through at any moment, but that he would be dried equally as fast by the tremendous power of the sun.

Skies seemed so much smaller in England, but then everything in Canada was vast. Strange to think that this same sun, in a few hours' time, would be shining on Heath End, not a ray of it penetrating into the tiny dark kitchen where his mother would be scurrying through her never-ending tasks. He had thought about her a lot today. Not that he was homesick; there had been no time for that. Perhaps it was because he wondered if there would be a letter today. Mrs Mac sometimes collected mail from Moose Jaw on Saturdays when she went to the bank.

He and Arthur had signed on for six weeks building a school in Toronto, when they first arrived, lodging with Arthur's relations for four dollars a week. It had been easy, compared with work in the mines, and their strength and eagerness to learn had pleased the more experienced builders.

They offered them a permanent job at the end of the agreed period. There was a lot of building going on in Toronto and pay was good, but there were also temptations to spend it; attractive shops, music bars and card games, leaving them with far less than they had counted on.

The biting cold that froze lakes solidly day after day and took their breath away suddenly came to an end, and like the turning on of a gas jet, spring arrived.

News of a special train, put on to transport farm workers to the prairies, enticed them to buy specially reduced tickets to Moose Jaw, seventeen hundred miles and three days' travelling away. It was during that journey that the sheer size of Canada penetrated their consciousness. The scale of everything was so much bigger than anything they had ever dreamed of. Mile after mile of unattractive grey stubble, not yet recovered from winter snows, was relieved by fascinating glimpses of the St Lawrence and hundreds of lakes, great rocks, and acres of fir trees.

Occasionally they caught sight of black squirrels, chipmunks and bears. The train, which had a huge bell on the front to give warning of its approach, was comfortable with clean, well-equipped dining cars. Entranced, they saw great timber rafts floating down the river, white windmills, barns

181

with massive stone foundations, immeasurable forests and scattered villages, each with an impressive church and houses made of poplar logs.

They stopped off at Winnipeg for a few hours, where they watched as ships were loaded with furs, marvelled at the huge grain stores and visited the various markets. All nationalities seemed to be in Winnipeg, including the first pig-tailed Chinamen they had seen, who ran the laundries with great enthusiasm and always seemed to be in a hurry. They were excited with all the new sights and with the sense of adventure of it all.

Photographs and souvenirs of Queen Victoria were on display in the shops, in spite of the fact that a king had come and gone since her death. In a strange way it made them feel at home.

Men were replacing or repairing wooden pavements to minimize the effects of summer dusts which they knew would soon be upon them. There was a sense of pride and purpose about Winnipeg, and they felt they would have liked to have stayed, but their tickets would take them another four hundred miles yet.

Beyond Winnipeg scrubby copses and dark marshes appeared among the grasslands. As the land became flatter it was less interesting to look out of the train's windows apart from watching the great migrations of birds which darkened the skies every now and then. Paul and Arthur slept and talked intermittently.

They discussed the railway itself. The physical and financial difficulties of building such a railway, running from one sea to another, through thousands of miles of Canadian marshes and rock outcrops alike, must have been almost insurmountable. It provided a means of taking wheat to sea ports and bringing men in to work the land to grow it.

The first thing they saw when they pulled in to Moose Jaw station was a group of farmers lining the track. Most of the passengers disembarked there. Others were going on to

Medicine Hat and Calgary. The farmers, big men though they were, were dwarfed by hefty Bill McNab, standing four-square and casting a shrewd and experienced eye over the men stepping off the train.

In no time at all he had rounded up ten of them, including Paul and Arthur, quickly agreeing on terms, directing them to his horse-drawn wagon standing a few yards down the track. His farm was about ten miles from the station. He showed them their sleeping quarters, a kaboosh, which was like a shed on wheels.

'After you've had a wash, lads,' he said, indicating lined up buckets of cold water, 'come and have some tea.'

So after freshening up and throwing their luggage into the kaboosh, they went in to meet the McNab family, Bill McNab, his wife Maisie, and their two lovely daughters, Liddy and Meg. It was a satisfying tea, with plenty of cold lamb, home-made cheeses, pickles and honey cake. They all sat round a great wooden table with the family, Bill McNab explaining to them, in his deep Canadian voice, that, in addition to the normal work, in time they would be taking his thrashing machine out from farm to farm, the men being fed by the farmers they worked for and sleeping in their own horse-drawn kaboosh.

Bill McNab was a bluff likeable man, whose father had emigrated from Scotland in 1863. He had regaled his son with tales of the old country, and Mac, as he liked to be called, was keenly interested in any news from Britain. In the days to follow he often questioned Paul and Arthur about their work in the coal mines. He told them how his father had tried gold mining in British Columbia before settling for a life of farming. Paul thought he might like to have a go at that, although Arthur soon found that he preferred farming to the pits.

Mac was a dedicated farmer who extracted every ounce of co-operation from his men. They worked twelve hours each day and they enjoyed it. Mrs Mac provided plenty of nourishing food, and each morning they were conscious of the energy surging through their veins. It was as if the pure air manufactured it by the minute.

After three o'clock, Saturdays were their own, to do as they liked. The men went into the weekend town of Moose Jaw, where they packed their week's drinking into half a day. They always had a 'skinful', as Arthur termed it, by the time they rolled home in the wagon on Saturday nights, most of them sporting black eyes from fights, but they were good-humouredly ready for work the next day, and equally ready for a repeat performance the following week.

Mac sometimes went along with them, for he liked the occasional drinking session himself. The story went that once, in winter, he was so drunk that he forgot to put his mittens on, and had lost two of his fingers on the left hand from frost-bite.

But, in the main, he could hold his drink, and was always an amiable man. Not like Raish, whose antics had turned Paul off drink for life.

He and Arthur went, out of curiosity, into Moose Jaw on the first Saturday, immediately concluding it would be more profitable to stay around the farm. They came to an arrangement that, apart from the fixed sum Arthur sent to his mother each month, Mac would keep their wages until the end of the season. The way their money had frittered away in Toronto had given them both a bit of a jolt and they were determined to start saving in earnest now.

Arthur had taken to walking alone on his Saturdays off, covering distances that made the trek to Conduit seem like a walk round the garden. He would go for miles before finding a shady spot to rest, returning hours later. So that was how Paul came to be lying by himself, drowsily reminiscing about the last few months.

A shadow covering the sun made him turn over slowly. Mac's younger daughter, Meg, smiled down at him. Her neat little body reminded him of his sister, her rich brown hair of his mother; her laughing eyes were bright hazel.

'Come on, old Sleepy Head.' She sat down beside him companionably and poured home-made peach wine from a jug into two mugs. Paul had not realized until now how thirsty he was. It was cold and delicious.

'Nearly as good as me Mam's pop,' he said, as he drained the last drop. He liked to tease her with Cod End dialect. When he had first arrived they found some difficulty in understanding one another.

'Wouldn't you like to know what I have in my pocket? I went in to Moose Jaw with "me Mam" today.'

'A letter?'

'Two letters and a postcard.'

He knew who the postcard would be from. Ben did not like writing, but regularly there came a few words from him on a postcard. Today it was a view of the arboretum lake at Walsall.

Paul turned the card over and read out, 'Come and see the new babby in the family. Regards from your old boxing pal, Ben.'

He had to read Katy's letter to find out what that was all about.

'Well! Our Katy and Walter have adopted a baby girl. And they have christened her Ann Marie! Our mother is Mary Ann. It's like her name, reversed.'

Meg could tell he was pleased about that.

He read from the letter.

'We have christened your new niece Ann Marie, but from the start, Mark, who is very proud of his little sister, has called her Marie, so we all do. She is a pretty little thing, with dark hair and brown eyes, much more demanding than Mark was. She keeps us all awake at night. But we love her just the same.

Sally Dilkes has gone to India. She hopes to find the medical mission where Edwin used to work.

Ben moons about all the time complaining how much

185

he misses you. Just your luck to land on a farm, he says, while he slaves away at the pit.

I am dropping off to sleep as I write, Paul, so you will understand why my letter is short this time. We are always talking of you, and are pleased you are with a family who sound so nice.

Lots of love from Walter, Katy, Mark and Marie.

'You would like our Katy. She is a dressmaker, like you,' Paul told her as he folded the letter, for Meg did all the sewing for the household and for the family, while Liddy was responsible for the cooking.

'You told Katy we were nice, did you?'

'All except the younger daughter, I said,' he teased.

She smiled at him mischievously. 'You know you like me the best.'

She wanted to know all about Katy and was curious as to how she managed to sell the things she made. He told how she and Walter took Mark when Charlotte died, which meant telling the story of Charlotte and Edwin. When she said, 'And who is the lady named Sally who has gone to India?' he had to think hard, to remember all he could about Sally Dilkes.

Meg sat close beside him, her knees pulled up to her chin, engrossed in his stories, her hazel eyes sparkling with curiosity. It was pleasant sharing his news from home with her like this. He usually shared his letters with Arthur, who never received any mail.

'Aren't you going to open your other letter?'

'Now this one's special. It's from me Mam,' he said with a grin.

'Would you like me to go away?'

'Stay where you are.'

He scanned his mother's letter before reading it all out to her.

'My dear lad,

I expect Katy has already given you news of the baby.

186

They are such a happy little family now; I am glad there is another child in the house.

My main news is about Edwin. He has rooms over an antique shop in Edgbaston where he works. Mr Hildred, his boss, kindly fetched me over one day, in his very spruce motor car. Edwin has a good-sized bed-sitting room, a little scullery and a big airy studio. He is painting landscapes again. I think they are very good; Mr Hildred does too. He sells them in his shop. Now that the weather is improving Edwin can get out more to do some sketching in the evenings and at weekends. Often he is left in charge of the shop while his boss is out buying and he is becoming very knowledgeable about the lovely things he sees and handles. So Little Cott is empty again, Paul, and I shall not be in a hurry to let it, in case Edwin finds he needs it.

Tell Arthur his family send their regards. None of them write letters, but they are very pleased to hear from him. His mother says to thank him for the payments.

Sarah and Ginny send their best wishes to both of you.

'We are always excited when your letters arrive. Enjoy yourself, my dear lad, and don't worry about a thing. Everything is fine here. Your loving mother, Mary Ann.

'She would say that if she was dying,' he remarked as he read her last sentence.

'You love her a lot, don't you?'

'She is the best mother anybody could have.'

'Sorry you came?'

'No fear! I wouldn't have met you if I'd stayed with me mam in Cod End, would I?'

'Do they catch cod in Cod End?'

'Cod? A few tiddlers from Billy Button's Brook is our lot when it comes to fishing,' he laughed.

'Then why . . . ?' she asked, joining in his laughter.

He explained how the nickname given to Heath End by

187

Pelsall had stuck. 'I think they meant it as the end from a cod that you throw away,' he said, laughing again. 'Rubbish.'

'They don't sound very nice people in Pelsall.'

'They're all right. Officially we're all one village,' he replied. 'We all go into the same census figures. There's a sort of friendly rivalry between us. Nothing vicious. We like each other really.'

She seemed genuinely relieved about that.

He found himself telling her about the Churchie Bulldogs and Wesley Spiders; about Ben's races, his football and the boxing booth; about how they used to take the fish to the inns; about pigeons and bicycle repairing. And about the pits. He had never enjoyed talking to anyone as much as this before. She was such an easy girl to talk to.

She asked a lot of questions about the people he knew. He covered just about everybody, except Raish; he did not want to talk about him.

'It must be a very big place, your Cod End. How many people live there?'

The thought of Cod End being a big place struck him as funny and again she joined in with his laughter. He mentally walked round the streets he knew like the back of his hand, assessing the approximate number in each house, before he answered, 'About a thousand, I would say. And between us, we know every one of them.'

'A thousand! Then it *is* a big place!'

'It is what we call a small village, Meg. I suppose there are a couple of thousand in Pelsall.'

'That must be huge!'

'No. Over there we all live much closer together than you do here, don't forget. We practically huddle together. You could get a bundle of Heath End's into your father's acreage.'

'It must be lovely, being huddled together, as you call it. It sounds kind of cosy.'

Paul thought of the bitter fight he had had with Boney. Then he thought of how neighbours unhesitatingly took in any child or old person in need, and how they shared their meat on Sundays, and he replied, 'Yes. It is cosy.'

'In the winter there are only the four of us here.'

'You can only talk to one person at a time,' he pointed out.

'S'pose you're right. But it sure must be grand to have all those folk queuing up for a chat.'

'Especially if they talk as much as me, eh?'

'Who are Ginny and Sarah?' she wanted to know. 'Your sweethearts?' Perhaps that's why he had missed them out, she thought.

The amusement in his eyes told her she was wrong about that, although he replied, 'In a way, yes, I suppose they are. But we shall have to leave the stories of Ginny and Sarah for another time.' He pointed to where the figure of Arthur was appearing in the far distance, and indicated Liddy who had come out into the yard to bang the gong for supper. He sprang up, helping Meg to her feet. 'I'll go and meet Arthur.'

He was stopped in his tracks by Liddy's voice, shrill and sharp.

'Paul Brook! Don't you dare walk away from me when supper is ready. Just cos' that fool of an Arthur is late.

'You sure took enough time to deliver a couple of letters, our Meg,' she added.

Meg chuckled as they paused to wash their hands in the yard buckets. 'Liddy's on the war path. We had better go right in.'

The two sisters were alike in colouring, but there the similarity ended. Liddy, three years older than Meg, was much taller, and her tongue was razor-sharp. She bossed every one in sight, without scaring anybody, for they all knew that beneath that horny exterior she was as soft as candy and would not hurt a fly. To Paul she seemed like a younger edition of Ginny: a neat and tidy edition. Perhaps Ginny had been like that once.

She fussed about mealtimes. Once that gong was sounded she wanted them all in at the double. Like any good cook who spent a lot of time preparing food, she liked the meals to be eaten while they were at their best.

She chivvied her own family as much as she did the hired hands. Mrs Mac, a tall slim woman, still attractive, accepted it with amused tolerance. As with her husband, you sensed Mrs Mac was no fool; she didn't miss a thing. She kept the accounts, dealt with the wages, and, if need be, could tackle any job on the farm. All of it she approached as casually as if she had time to spare.

A schoolteacher in Montreal when Mac met her, she had educated both her daughters at home, fitting in all the other jobs as well. They had learned, in addition to the academic subjects, cooking, dressmaking, how to play the piano and the flute, how to feather a chicken and plough a field. The McNabs were a happy family, as close as peas in a pod, openly showing their affections in a way that the Brooks found difficult; neither Arthur nor Paul had ever seen such open affection before.

There were only the family tonight, the other hands having gone in to town. Liddy had cooked a delicious boned chicken in pastry, with lots of vegetables and gravy, and for afters she had made a thick rich ice cream, topped with maple syrup.

'Take no notice of Liddy,' said Mac. 'She's all bark and no bite.'

Arthur, when he came in halfway through the meal, was red faced from the sun or embarrassment, or both. 'I went to sleep,' he confessed. 'Sorry, Liddy.'

He had to endure a long ticking-off despite his apology. 'Seven o'clock's supper time in this house,' she concluded. As they all sat on the porch later, she asked, 'Why do you do all that tramping about, Arthur, when there are horses?'

'Maybe because we're not too clever at riding those horses o' your'n, Liddy.'

'That's right,' agreed Paul. 'Pit horses we've handled, yes, and we used to own a horse and cart, but that's slightly different. Now Dandy, the donkey, she's a bit like a race horse when she's in the mood, which isn't often.' He amused them with tales of how often Dandy had caused them embarrassment by her tantrums. 'They're highly bred, your horses, aren't they? How about you girls giving us a bit of tuition.'

'As if I ain't got somethin' better to do with my time!' exclaimed Liddy.

Mac winked at the younger men. 'You are free now, Liddy.'

She nattered about how tired she was, but the four of them went as far as the lake. The girls had ridden since they were two years old. The men did not do too badly, helped by expert tuition, interspersed with Liddy's banter. It turned out to be an enjoyable evening, all four of them comfortable together.

'Of course,' said Paul as they dismounted on their return, 'One lesson is useless. We shall need lots of follow-ups before we are any good.' He was grinning widely as he walked off jauntily toward the kaboosh, where he could re-read the letters to Arthur and they could talk about home before the loud snores of the black-eyed monsters from Moose Jaw prevented them hearing themselves speak.

After that the two men regularly rode off on Saturday afternoons to discover the joys of fishing when you are always certain to return with a good catch. Sometimes the girls would come along too. Paul and Meg would leave Liddy to instruct Arthur on what not to do while they wandered off until they found a shady spot where they could sit and talk; they were never lost for words, either of them.

When Paul's birthday came round Meg made him a shirt. Katy, in her birthday letter, had written: 'I know your birth

certificate says you are twenty-one, but I don't believe it.'
So the story of the alterations to his birth certificate was
told, a secret he had shared only with Katy until now.
Meg's birthday followed close on, in August, when he rode
into Moose Jaw and bought her a little gold brooch.

The sweltering days of summer ripened into autumn;
peaches, grapes and apples were ready for picking. Miles of
golden summer grain were replaced by patterns of black soil
alternating with yellow stubble. The men were away for
days on end, thrashing for other farmers. Paul and Arthur
never ceased to be surprised at the angularity of the fields
compared with the higgledy-piggledy ones they had been
used to at home.

By now Meg was regarded by the others as Paul's girl. He
did find that he missed her more than he cared to admit.
There was something very comforting in knowing he would
find her eagerly waiting to welcome him when they
returned from other farms.

The men liked to be back at the McNabs by Friday night,
ready for their Saturdays in town. By now two of them had
regular girl friends in Moose Jaw and some belonged to a card
school; the rest went for the beer and the skirmishes that
followed. Paul liked to be back for a different reason.

Often Saturdays brought letters from home. Meg was
never happier than when Paul was reading them out to her
and she was learning more about the village in England with
two names. Oddly enough, it was Ben's brief postcards that
provoked the longest discussions. One card, which stated:
'Wish you had been at Bloxwich Wakes with us, to get
your lip cut again', led to a funny account of what happened
to them in the boxing tent. Once again Paul omitted to tell
her of the meeting between Mary Ann and Raish that night
because he did not want to talk about his father.

She wanted to hear all about Bloxwich and the other
neighbouring villages, Rushall, Pelsall, Shelfield, Norton.
He described the many collieries in the area, although not

192

one could be seen from Heath End: Stubbers Green, where Walter had been for years; The Grove, where Ben worked; Littleton, Five Ways, Dry Bread, Conduit and Tack-a-Rue. Meg pealed with laughter at some of their names. They could always find something to laugh about.

His mother wrote of how she was starting her thirteen-week Christmas club again. Paul told Meg about the year they set Edwin on to wrap the lucky dips, the same year he broke his collar bone, and he and Edwin fetched Christmas trees from Cannock Chase. Meg was tickled pink to hear about the lucky dips and how it was Paul who donned the Father Christmas outfit which Katy had made.

Meg's name cropped up more and more in his letters home. He found he was writing about their outings together, as well as telling them about her insatiable curiosity regarding Heath End. One day a letter from Edwin enclosed a black and white sketch of their mother's shop, with its big display window, flanked by Katy's front-room sweet shop on the one side, and the low-roofed Little Cott on the other. On the back of the sketch he had written in his beautiful sculptured writing, 'For Meg, from Paul's family'.

Meg was delighted. She hung it on her bedroom wall and wrote a neat little note of thank-you for Paul to enclose with his next letter.

So the busy days slipped happily by and they tried to ignore the fact that their stay with the McNabs was drawing to its close. One by one, as the weather became colder, the men packed up and moved on, some to try their luck in British Columbia, some going back to Toronto, where they knew they would find building jobs, until there were only Arthur and Paul left.

Mac had become quite attached to these two, and he was well aware of the feeling between Meg and Paul. There was still a lot of clearing up to do around the farm, maintenance work to attend to before the winter set in, animals to care for, some tree felling and logs to chop for winter fuel. All the grain had been sent off by rail; they missed the rippling gold of it.

The winter hit them as suddenly as summer had done. One morning they awoke to find the orange-yellow of the willow branches catapulted into their consciousness by the white layer of snow behind them.

They had to crack the ice on the top of the water holes which had supplied them until a few days before. They were grateful for the thick woolly hats, socks and mitts which the girls had knit for them. The kaboosh became as chill as a cheese cave, so they moved into a bedroom of the McNabs' house. One night, after supper, Liddy played the flute, accompanied by Meg at the piano. As the rest of them sat round the fire Mac put a surprising proposition to them.

'How about you two staying on and taking a parcel of my land? You can buy it cheap or you can rent it from me. I'll set you up in equipment and you needn't pay me anything back until you have made enough. In the spring we could build you a nice little place to live.'

Arthur had not one moment's doubt. He had not cared much for Toronto, but out here it was different. The wide expanses of space, the generosity of the McNabs, an opportunity of being his own boss, and the thought of all the elbow-room he would have, after sharing a cramped little one-up-one-down at Cod End with five others, were all instrumental in his eager acceptance without hesitation.

Paul, although grateful, felt differently. 'I couldn't make up my mind that quickly,' he said.

'You don't have to decide now,' said Mac reasonably. 'Discuss it between the two of you. But I'd like to know soon. 'Cos if you are not staying,' he grinned, 'then I shall have to be shunting you off.'

'We would like to have you as neighbours,' put in Mrs Mac, and the pleading in Meg's eyes as she looked across at Paul was difficult to resist.

Later that night Arthur tried to persuade him. 'I know I

said I would go back to Cod End, Paul. But this is too good an opportunity to miss; something we never dreamed of.'

'It is a generous offer, I know that. But if we start a place of our own we shall be so busy working it up we shall never get home for years and years. Not even for a visit. Perhaps never.'

'I wouldn't mind. This is the reality for me now. The other, well, a bit like a bad dream.'

'What about your mother?'

'One less in the house makes it easier for her. When I left she said she would be able to share the bedroom with the girls now, and me brother and our Dad could have the downstairs room. As long as I send her some money each month she won't mind.'

At that moment Paul realized how the exchange of letters had kept Heath End alive for him, while the lack of communication from Arthur's family had brought about this estrangement. He felt grateful for the mail he had received, sustaining the link with home. To make some money and be able to present a nest-egg to Mary Ann upon his return, that had been the extent of his dream. No, he could not give up Heath End and all that it meant: not even for Meg. Yet he did not want to leave Meg.

He allowed himself flights of fancy which took him to England to fetch his mother here, out of Raish's clutches for ever. When he touched down again he had to admit that even if it were possible Mary Ann would not like it. There was not enough human diversity here for his mother, she would not have enough problems to solve, and the rest of her family would be too far away. She would not leave Ben, and Edwin, and Katy with a baby he had not even seen yet. He would like to see the new member of the family; he must see Cod End again before he settled down.

Anyway there was some unfinished business he had to do in England. To work on the coal face, to do every job in the pit it was possible to do, that ambition was unrealized.

The workers they had shared the kaboosh with were all right in their own way, nice easy-going mates, but they weren't miners. No lasting relationships had been formed. Next year they would be working on another farm near another town. There could never be the close companionship he had come to expect among his workmates. Of course there were mines in British Columbia. That wouldn't solve the present problem, though; it was still a long way away, and he might get too involved. No, a temporary building job would be best if he stayed longer in Canada; he would not mind leaving that.

Immediately he thought he had come to a decision he would think of Meg again, and her pleading eyes when Mac made his suggestion last night. He had never met a girl quite like her. She had the natural frankness of his sister, the kindliness of his mother, and her own special brand of gentle humour and understanding. Yes, the thought of spending the rest of his life with Meg was very pleasant. In the end he decided on a compromise.

'I shall get a winter job in Toronto,' he told her. 'I shall be back here in the spring. That's a promise.' That would give him another year in which to think things out, by which time he might have saved enough to go to England and come back again.

'If that's what you want, Paul,' said Meg, turning away from him so that he should not see the disappointment in her face. But it was there in her voice. It was obvious she wanted him to stay. He did not want to lose her, but neither did he want to tie himself up here for ever. The problem seemed insoluble.

CHAPTER

12

NEWS CAME FROM England that decided everything. It was a postcard from Ben, containing just two words, 'He's back.'

Paul showed the postcard to Arthur. 'Remember what I said to him in Liverpool? "Let me know the minute it happens if he turns up".'

'That seems like a million years ago to me.'

'And like yesterday to me. I shall go back straight away.'

Once again Katy's letter, by the same post, explained the situation more fully. He read it out to Meg.

'Mother heard from the Sister Dora Hospital in Walsall that they had Dad in there. They were drying him out. He has had a bad scare, Paul. The drink nearly finished him off. He has been warned to stay away from it if he wants to live. Mother is nursing him back to health. It was like pneumonia, but worse.

There was a big scene with Ben. He refused to stay in the same house with Dad; said he would rather sleep in the stable. Poor Mother! Finally they came to an agreement that he would live in Little Cott. Mother cooks for him and he eats his meals alone. He only goes into the house when Dad's out, like Edwin used to.

Edwin, on the other hand, comes over to see Mother regularly, the same as before. He is quite indifferent to Dad now.

Mother says you are not to concern yourself, Paul. She certainly has taken it all very calmly, and seems all right. So do not worry. We are well and the children are lovely.

'She seems all right!' Paul repeated as he folded the letter. 'How do they know? What with Edwin living in Edgbaston, Ben sulking in Little Cott, and Katy engrossed with her two little kids! I have to go back and find out for myself how she is, Meg. You do see that, don't you?'

He tried to explain what life had been like with his father, but how could she possibly know that all fathers were not like her own, especially as he had avoided talking about Raish before. Yet she nodded, her eyes awash with tears. He tried to imagine what it would be like leaving her. He wanted to go, but he wanted Meg too.

He took her gently into his arms. 'Do you like me a little bit?'

'You know I love you, Paul,' she answered with characteristic frankness. Suddenly the solution seemed so easy.

'Then come with me, Meg. We'll be married.' How wonderful it would be to take her home to England. Did she really love him enough to leave all this? 'Do you love me enough for that?' he asked.

'If Dad says I can,' she replied without hesitation.

It was difficult to explain about his father to a family who had known only love and kindness, but Paul did his best to make them understand the necessity for him to go home. When he asked if Meg could go too they could not contain their emotion at the thought of losing her.

'You will have to give us time to talk this over,' Mac

said. 'Like I gave you time to think about my offer, Paul. I know you are in a hurry to go home. We won't keep you waiting too long.'

Next night Meg was very quiet at supper, and afterwards Mac and his wife called him into the parlour.

'We like you a hell of a lot, Paul,' said Mac in his direct way. 'But we love our daughter and want what is best for her. England is a long way off.'

'I know how you must feel. I love her too, and will take good care of her.' It wasn't going to be easy. He must fight for her.

'There's no guarantee, is there, that you will get a job once you're back?'

'I shall get a job, never fear. I'll find a pit that will take me.'

'There are often times when the pits are off, aren't there, Paul?' put in Maisie. 'You said so yourself.'

'I can always turn my hand to something. I shall never let Meg go short. I promise you that.'

'I know you would keep that promise if you could,' Meg's mother murmured. 'Yet you have known each other such a short time.'

'Long enough to know how we feel about each other.'

'We are not saying it's too short a courtship,' said Mac, putting an affectionate arm round his wife's shoulder. 'I had known Maisie for only four months when I married her. But I wasn't whisking her off to another continent.'

He did not need to add that the thought of conflict within the Brook family on their father's return was repugnant to them. He went on to say 'You will be twenty-one in July, Paul, and Meg will be of age in August. We would like you to wait until then. That will give you time to sort things out over there. If you are both of the same mind then Meg can go to England with our blessings. Don't you think, Paul, that is a reasonable request from a doting father?'

Paul's heart sank. Eight months without seeing her! Yet

he had to admit that if he had a daughter like Meg he would feel the same. But he tried once more. 'We could wait that same time before marrying if she came with me now.'

'Leave it there, son,' said Mac firmly. 'A few months' separation won't hurt either of you.'

They had only three precious days before the Saturday train to Toronto. They gathered in armfuls of greens and Paul helped decorate the house for Christmas, laughing and teasing one another as they did so. 'Don't let's spoil these three days by wishing for what we can't have,' Meg said.

Together they went into town where he bought a gold ring with a blue stone for her and a long gold necklace for his mother.

'You are promised to me now,' he said as he put the ring on to Meg's finger.'

She flung her arms round his neck. 'For ever and ever,' she said, 'no matter how long we have to wait.'

Paul was entrusted with twenty pounds for Arthur's mother after Mrs Mac paid them their wages for the summer. He had over a hundred pounds of his own, which he decided to give to Mary Ann. He would save hard between now and August for Meg.

The days rolled by all too quickly. They all came to the station to see him off, Arthur looking part of the McNab family as he stood among them, waving. As the train pulled away. Meg held up her hand so that he could see the new ring he had bought. 'Don't forget. For ever and ever.' She ran alongside the train until the end of the platform. 'Tell them all about me in Cod End,' she called, smiling as he disappeared from view when she could let her tears fall freely. Mac hugged her to him closely. 'Don't be in such a hurry to leave us, sweetheart,' he said huskily. 'It will come, all too soon.'

Passengers were few at this time of year. During the long train journey and on the boat Paul's mind constantly see-sawed between Canada and Cod End, longing for Meg, anxious for Mary Ann. The thing they had all dreaded had happened: she had taken Raish back. He wondered how he was treating her. The worried frown was back between his brows by the time he arrived in a Toronto shrouded in snow and ice. An office in Yonge Street booked him to sail on the *Virginia* in five days' time. After arranging to stay with Arthur's accommodating relations he went in search of a pendant to add to the gold chain for his mother; he wanted the finest he could find.

The bells of St Michael's Church were pealing across Pelsall Common as he walked down the moonlit path from the station just before midnight on New Year's Eve. Grass crunched like tinkling glass beneath his feet and he could see his breath on the air, yet, after Toronto, the weather here seemed mild.

Paul knew now what Arthur meant when he talked of time seeming like a million years. It was a million years since he last saw Meg waving him off at the station. The five days he had spent in Toronto had been endless agony, the longest he had ever known. He had been torn in two, and was relieved when he could walk on to the *Virginia*, knowing he could no longer be tempted to return to Moose Jaw. He must keep his promise to Ben.

Singing rang out from The Bush Inn, where glasses were hurriedly being re-filled for the toast to the New Year. Just ahead Cod End moved toward him, like the *Virginia* all lit up after dark. Gas lights or oil lamps flickered and glowed from every house.

First-footers were about, each clutching a lump of coal and a loaf of bread, symbolizing the hope that the household they serenaded would not be without fuel or food throughout the coming year. One or two of them shouted to him as if he had never been away before hurrying to their tasks. 'Adieu, Paul. Happy New Year, mate.'

201

At Double Row he put down his trunk and paused to listen as one particularly resonant voice, from somewhere round the backs, sang out lustily.

> Ah've cum to loose the new 'ear in,
> The old 'ear out and the new 'ear in.
> A pocketful of money, a barrel-full of beer,
> A big fat pig to last you all the year.

> My shoes are very dirty, my hands are very clean,
> Ah've gorra little pocket to put a penny in,
> If you 'aven't gorra penny an 'aipenny will do,
> If you 'aven't gorra 'aipenny,
> God bless you.

Double Row, shabby and grim in the moonlight, had not attracted any first-footers. It was traditional to go in at one door and out through the other, and there was only one door to each dwelling in Double Row. Some of the occupants came to their doorsteps to listen to the knocking-off buzzers now vying with the church bells for attention. Every one of them called out to him. It gave him a warm feeling of home.

'Why, it's Paul, ain't it?'

'Glad to see yer back, mate.'

'Yer Dad's back an' all.'

'Are yer back 'um for good?'

'Nice to see yer, Paul. Happy New Year, our kid.'

After returning their greetings he realized he was immediately outside the door of Arthur's old home. On an impulse he knocked. He could just make out a faint 'Come in.' Paul pushed open the door that led directly into the only living room. 'Happy New Year, everybody. I know I am not tall, dark or handsome, and I can't sing. But I'll have to do.'

There was just space enough for him to stand. As he

entered he was slapped across the face by the wet washing which hung on several lines strung across the room. The tiny lamp kept the room dimmer than the moonlit street.

Arthur's mother gasped in horrified surprise. 'Paul Brook! Is Arthur with you?'

He would not have liked Arthur to have seen the relief in his mother's face as he shook his head, or to have heard the disinterested voice that said, 'Come in if you can get in.'

Arthur's two pasty-faced sisters were huddled on the sofa in front of the fire, which was not giving off much heat, having been rakered for the night. The girls had curling rags in their hair and coats over their nightgowns, obviously ready for the off as soon as their Dad returned home to sleep on the sofa. Their seventeen-year-old brother lay on the narrow bed pushed against the wall, close behind them.

The only other furniture was a tiny wooden table near the stairs door, not big enough to seat them all. It held a loaf and a jug of milk, with some mugs and dishes ready for breakfast. There was a bucket of water and a tablet of carbolic in a small bowl beneath it.

Arthur's mother had borne several children between Arthur and his brother, all of whom had died in infancy. Paul could see why Arthur had often remarked bitterly, 'Thank God it finished up with only the four of us.'

'I expect you are off to bed,' he said kindly. 'I'll pop in again.'

'Ar. We just waited to see the new 'ear in.'

The younger girl piped up shrilly, as if afraid he might disappear as swiftly as he had come. ''As our Arthur sent us any money?'

'He has.' Paul dug deep into his pocket for the envelope containing the money he had changed into sterling while in Toronto. He handed it to Arthur's mother. 'He will be sending you some more, he says.'

'Ar.'

'Now don't let me Dad get 'is 'ands on this, Mam.' It

was the younger girl again, the only one who seemed to have any spirit left in her. She pointed accusingly at her mother. 'She lets me Dad 'ave the money our Arthur sends. Don't know what Arthur'd say.'

The mother looked embarrassed. Although only the same age as Mary Ann she seemed an old woman. The grey skin stretched taut over her bony face, her lifeless eyes were like pale pools sunk deep into her skull, her hands shook uncontrollably as she folded the envelope and put it into her apron pocket.

'I'll not stop now, then.'

'Ar. Thanks, lad.'

Outside he realized she had followed him. She stood on the step, twisting her rough apron nervously. 'Our Essie, me youngest, her's startin' in service tomorrow mornin'. I 'ave to get 'er things dried and ironed by then.' He knew this was by way of apology for the wet washing.

'Of course you have. I hope she likes her new job.'

The thin voice floated after him as he turned to go. 'Paul!' She gave a little nervous cough. 'Is he all right?' she asked breathlessly. 'Our Arthur?'

'Arthur's fine. He will be sending you all his news in a letter soon, I expect.' He hesitated for a moment. 'He sent you his love.'

She had long ago forgotten how to smile, but a little light appeared in her eyes, making the fib he had just told worthwhile. 'Ar. He's a good lad, our Arthur.' She shuffled inside and shut the door.

Is he all right, she had asked! He pictured how Arthur would celebrate New Year, in the warmth and comfort of the McNabs long low parlour decked with the seasonal greenery and berries he and Meg had gathered. Arthur was probably seated in front of the log fire, a glass in his hand, listening to the girls' music. That would be a few hours hence, he reminded himself. Meg was still in 1912, while he had reached 1913. 'Oh Arthur!' he said to the cold clear night, as he approached The Square, 'You made the right decision, mate.'

The Red Cow revellers had encircled the lamp-post, arms entwined, singing Auld Lang Syne, every now and then breaking off to slap each other on the back.

He halted at his mother's gate, grinning and watching them for a minute, before turning into the yard. Moonlight showed up Walter's cabbages, the pigeon loft and fowl pens, and way back the pig sties and stable. He wondered if the horse and cart were back in place, and if so what had happened to the donkey.

He lifted the latch of Katy's door quietly. Seated round a roaring fire were Katy and Walter, Edwin and his mother, and Raish. Katy's furniture glowed brightly in the firelight. Holly, mistletoe and Christmas streamers decorated walls and ceiling. A Christmas tree stood near the sewing machine beneath the side window, a few toys piled neatly beneath it. Their first-footer, just on his way out, was his old adversary, Eric Bone, now grown tall, with hefty shoulders like his father. Boney, with his mop of dark hair, was very suitable as a first-footer.

'How are you, Eric?' They shook hands and wished each other a happy new year at the door.

The overwhelming joy on Mary Ann's face made every mile of the five-thousand-odd mile journey worth while. 'My lad!' she whispered as he went straight to her, her voice filled with emotion. 'My lad.'

Edwin gripped him firmly by the hand, Walter said, 'Welcome home', Katy flung herself at him. There was pandemonium for a few minutes, as he lifted her off the floor to kiss her. He could not help comparing the welcome here with the one Arthur would have received if he had arrived home tonight.

'Your Dad's here,' said Mary Ann, her face filled with unspoken requests.

Father and son faced each other squarely across the table.

They had not met since the episode of the horse and cart at The Colliers' Arms. Unless you could call that a meeting, when the stairs were between them and Raish was soaked to the skin.

They eyed each other steadily, both with the same proud set to their shoulders. Not one ounce of the old arrogance had departed from Raish's face. He offered his hand. Paul took it because his mother's eyes were pleading with him. Is this why he had travelled all these miles, to shake hands with his father? The moment was swallowed up with questions from them all.

Here, like this, among his family, it was as if he had never been away: except for Raish's presence, of course. Paul studied him during a lull in the conversation. He was thinner, slightly paler, but just as debonair as ever, if not more so, without the drink that sometimes had blotted out his good looks. His suit and shirt were immaculate, and even now, in the middle of winter, he sported a buttonhole, a red rose which looked as if it had just been plucked. He appeared to be younger than Walter, on whom the pit was rapidly taking its toll. Paul watched as his brother-in-law poured out glasses of port, spilling it as his hand shook: Walter was not built for a pitman. How long could he carry on? In those fleeting moments he worried about Katy and her two little children.

Raish was on his feet, a glass of water in his hand. In his well-modulated voice he pronounced, 'Although I have the water and you have the port I would like to propose a toast. To Polly. My Queen. May we have many happy new years together. And a happy new year to all our family.'

Paul felt slightly sick. Part of him ached to say, 'If she is your queen why did you go off and leave her to manage all these years on her own?' But the calm look of content and trust on her face stopped him. He raised his glass to her, as he would any day, without a toast from his father.

Ben was overjoyed to see him when he went round to Little Cott later.

'I knew you would come, our kid.'

'Thank your postcard for that.'

'The others didn't do a fat lot o' good, did they? Thought the last one might.'

He poked at the fire as they settled down to talk well into the night. There was so much they had to say, about Canada, Cod End, Meg, the pits, about their mother and about Raish.

'Shall you stay here with me?'

'No, I want to be there. I want to see for myself how she is, Ben; to see if he's behaving himself.'

'I would have murdered him if I'd had to live there. To think, after all this time, he expected her to nurse him. None of his fancy women wanted him, I notice, after he was ill. He's settled in as if it's his right. Putting on his airs and graces, as if butter wouldn't melt in his mouth! *Why* did she take him back?'

'I suspect she didn't have much choice if the hospital requested it.'

'He's like a cat playing with a mouse before he pounces on it. She's waiting on him hand and foot. And to think how he used to treat her. As if she was dirt! I wish he'd have died. I'd have helped him on his way if I could. How I wish he'd have died.'

Paul sighed. 'Well, he didn't. Anyway, we had no idea we'd have such a long reprieve when we pinched his horse and cart, did we? Has he brought it back with him?'

'Need you ask? He sold it for booze, didn't he? It wasn't his to sell either. Our mother paid for that.'

Ben kicked viciously at a piece of coal in the grate, which promptly fell into the hearth where he stamped on it impatiently to put out the flame, causing acrid smoke to rise.

'I shall never forgive him for the sort of lives we had as

207

kids. Never! Jealous as hell he was. Many's the time I've had a clout just because Mother's been nice to me.'

Paul nodded. 'Me too. He had always got his strap off, whaling us across our backsides.'

'And we 'adn't got much backside in our trousers any road! Me mam was always patching and darning to keep our bums from hanging out.'

'There wouldn't be any money for clothes by the time she had fed us all.'

'And why? Because he had it all, that's why. Always got his hand in the till. As fast as she put some in he fetched it out. Remember how he always insisted on his cooked breakfasts? And meat for his dinner? Milk sop 'ad to do for us.'

'We never went hungry, though, did we?' Paul reminded him.

'Only because our mother did without. Remember how the four of us would huddle on the landing, listening to him venting his spite on her?'

Paul remembered only too well. That was what had brought him across the world to see that it did not happen again. It had brought him in spite of having to leave Meg behind; his lovely Meg. He wondered what she was doing tonight; if she was thinking of him. How he wished she was here by his side.

Ben's voice became more bitter as he ranted on about his father. 'I think Edwin was the worst off. God, the taunting he had to suffer. I can remember when I was a little 'un, and he was quite big, he'd run behind the stable. He'd hide for hours on end, trembling like a leaf. Frightened to death he was.'

'Yes, Edwin had the worst of it,' Paul agreed.

'Remember when the old chap was gonna run him through with the poker? How he put it in the fire and made it red hot, ready for when he came in? Just because me mother had lent Edwin me Dad's white silk scarf.'

'He would have done it as well if it hadn't been for Katy

knocking it out of his hand with the broom. Pretending to sweep up she was. What pluck! Remember that?'

'Shall I ever forget? I was scared that night. Yet our Edwin comes now as if nothing ever happened. Talks to me Dad quite civil, Katy says. I'll never talk to him! I shall never forgive him.' Ben's voice was hoarse with anger by now. 'He never had a good word for any of us. It can't all be wiped away. How our Edwin can put that time behind him I don't know.'

Paul thought he knew the answer to that, but doubted if he could explain to Ben. Edwin's time in India had put it all into perspective. He had seen far greater cruelties and injustices by the minute out there. His own childhood traumas must seem as nothing now, by comparison. He was able to look back on a good mother, food and shelter, and a family.

Paul knew that the time he had spent in Canada had been a therapy too, although an entirely different experience from Edwin's. There was no poverty in Canada to draw a comparison with, yet there had been something about the liberating environment of the prairies that had breezed away any acrimonious reflections. Out there, telling Meg about Heath End, there had been so many happy days to remember and relate.

The free and easy relationships of the spontaneous McNabs had shown him the difference that a loving father could make. Yet Paul felt no antipathy toward his childhood days, like Ben did. Mary Ann had more than made up for Raish, and his only anxiety now was that she might be hurt again.

Yes, he and Edwin had been fortunate. Ben had not yet been able to stand back and assess it all from a distance.

'Any jobs going at your pit?' he asked, changing the subject.

'No. But I heard today that Conduit are after one or two experienced blokes.'

'I'll be there tomorrow.'

Next day Paul was signed on at Conduit to start the following week. It gave him a few days in which to visit Ginny, as vigorous and outspoken as ever; to spend a few hours with Sarah, becoming more arthritic and having to resort to a stick; to get to know Katy's baby, who flirted outrageously with all the men; to take a box of groceries to Arthur's mother; to observe Raish and Mary Ann together.

It was strange having his father in the house so much, something they had never known; it was even stranger to see him sober for so long a time. Katy had stressed how ill he had been when they first saw him in hospital, and how it had frightened him.

It was difficult to assess how Mary Ann really felt. Ben was right; she did wait on her husband. She was different, though, from when Raish had come back to her before, when everything she had worked for in his absence had been allowed to slide. This time she seemed calmly determined to hang on to what she had gained, particularly the relationships with her children. Outwardly she accepted Raish quite amiably in his imaginary role of boss, while continuing to do as she liked.

In spite of Raish's protests that it was 'not fitting' for a wife of his to be doing 'such a menial task' as fish frying she carried on doggedly, answering him calmly, no longer afraid of him. 'Now is not the time to give it up, Raish, while I have you to watch the shop.' He was pleased they had the trap as a form of transport, but suggested she get rid of 'that bloody bad-tempered donkey', and buy 'a decent pony', at which she merely laughed. 'I know she is a bit unpredictable, but Dandy will do for me.' He referred to Ben's pigeons as time wasting, to which she replied, 'Maybe we all need a bit of that.'

She always had his cooked breakfast ready for him when he came down at nine o'clock. He would leisurely read his newspaper, comment knowledgeably on its contents, then

210

go for a steady walk, as he called it, reminding her that he could not do anything too strenuous.

'This was the time when Paul could talk freely with his mother. 'I can't believe he's off the booze for good.'

'When he was ill he realized how much he wanted to live, even if it did mean giving up the drink.'

'Do you think he can keep it up?'

'Of course he can, if he really wants to.'

'Are you all right, Mother?'

'Of course I am all right.' She chatted on happily about how she was attracting a better class trade for her ready-mades, 'like Mr Dickinson with his quality furniture'.

'I still cater for my old customers, of course, with my second-hand rail,' she added. She suddenly became aware of Paul's intent scrutiny, and paused in her task of ironing. 'You didn't come home because of me, I hope, Paul?'

'In a way, yes. I came back to give you this.' He placed the hundred pounds of accumulated wages on the table.

'All that money! I would not take it from you, lad. You've had to work hard for that.'

'And the times I have imagined you saying, "Well done, my lad", like you used to say when I brought home my five-and-ninepence. Say it, Mother, and pick the money up. Because that's what I have dreamed about while I've been out there.'

Placing the black iron she was using in front of the fire to re-heat she put her arms round him in an unusual show of affection.

'My dear lad. Well done. Oh, it's good to have you back, Paul. I have missed you; we all have.

'And now. Tell me about Meg.'

Paul was only too ready to talk of Meg. He told of his hopes that she would be coming to England to be his bride in August; how, between now and then, he would be saving for that day.

'Then I *will* pick up your money, my lad. I shall put it

into something for you both.' She smiled in the old way. 'I've an idea or two.'

The middle of January was her fiftieth birthday. Katy was planning a family get-together.

'You will come, won't you, Ben?' she pleaded with her brother.

'Not if me Dad's there I won't.'

'Not even for Mother's sake? We have never had a celebration for her before. It won't be complete for her if you're missing.'

'Oh, all right, then,' he agreed grudgingly. 'But only for tea. I don't want to 'ave to sit with 'im afterwards. And only as long as you don't expect me to speak to 'im.'

At the tea table Mark proudly presented his present, a picture he had drawn. 'That's the pigeon loft, Grandma. And that's Dandy. And there you can see the geese. It's from me and Marie, although she can't draw yet.'

'What a lucky girl she is, to have you to draw for her.'

Paul had given her Meg's present earlier, a pair of sheepskin slippers she had made herself. 'Why, they fit perfectly! How did she know my size?'

'I remembered of course. Size tens, aren't they?' he teased her. Tears came into her eyes when he gave her the gold locket and chain. She turned it over and over, hardly able to believe such a gift was hers.

'Fancy buying this for me, lad,' she murmured. 'I never imagined I would own anything so beautiful. All the way from Canada!' It hung low on the royal blue silk dress which Katy had made as a birthday gift. She did look like a queen today, so proud of the lovely link chain, with its heavy gold pendant. 'If anything happens to me I want Paul to have this back,' Mary Ann informed everyone.

'Now what is going to happen to you, Mother?' chided Katy. 'Talking like this at fifty! Why say that?'

'Because it's a suitable time to say it, while we are all together. Remember what I have said. And remember, also, there are four good houses at Pelsall, one for each of my children.' She looked directly at Raish as she spoke, demanding confirmation.

'Of course. They are an insurance for the children, as you say, Polly,' said Raish in his silkiest tones. 'You did very well to buy those, my dear.' He was dangling his watch chain for the baby on his knee, who gurgled at him in adoration. Girls are the thing, he told himself. This one must have had a good-looking mother. He had to admit, though, that Mark was a handsome little chap. Not a bit like Edwin. More like himself.

CHAPTER
13

Paul was back at the colliery where he had started at thirteen, happily working with mates he had known years ago, who were all pleased to see him. Working on the farm in Canada had quickly become a preferable way of life to Arthur, but to Paul it resembled an extended holiday. This was real work again.

Conduit had acquired a new-fangled coal-cutter. Paul's job was to clear the dirt away that the cutter left after slicing along the bottom of the coal face, before fitting wooden sprags to prevent the coal dropping down. There were six stalls in all, a hundred-and-fifty yards of coal face. At the end of that distance the coal-cutter had to be fitted with chains, a tricky job, and manoeuvred back to the start again.

Within a few weeks he was earning seven-and-six a day operating the machine himself. There was overtime to be had, too, for the cutter had to be shifted and serviced after the other men had gone home. He was grateful for the opportunity of learning how the cutter worked, but still he hankered after a stall of his own. He despaired whether there would ever be one available, for all the stallmen were well-satisfied colliers who had worked at Conduit for years.

Then one day he was unexpectedly offered a stall as a result of a tragedy he would never forget. That was the day he saw a man killed, right at the start of the shift.

There were turn-offs along the road to the coal face where empty tubs were turned over, off the rails, so that full tubs could get by. The last full tub had gone up to the top the night before; the empty tub was still in the turn-off.

One of the stallmen, after examining the coal face, walked back the ten or twelve yards to fetch it himself, as the loader who usually fetched it had not arrived. As he leaned over toward the truck down came a huge piece of rock from the roof, dropping on his back and killing him instantly.

Paul, with the man's stallmate, Jackie Lee, ran to him. All that was visible was the man's head and hands, as he lay, frog-like, flattened by a rock it was impossible to move, for it must have been about three ton in weight.

It had been all over in seconds; the man had not even cried out. No groaning of timber had warned him to jump.

With shocked, muttered instructions to one another they fetched the sylvester, normally used to draw the timber props out, fastened the chain round the rock, slowly winching it up sufficiently to enable them to pull out the man's mutilated body. All his mates stood around in stunned silence as the first aid men lifted his body on to a stretcher that had been sent down in response to a signal to the top. It seemed only minutes before that they had heard him cursing the loader for not turning up. Now there was not a breath of life left in him. Paul felt there was little in himself either. He had always maintained that accidents were usually the fault of carelessness; now he had witnessed one that was the fault of no-one.

He knew who the dead man was, Sammy Gunn, who lived opposite the brickworks, but he was out of date with his circumstances since being away and was further shocked when the man's stallmate, Jackie Lee, told him, 'His missus was taken into the San last week with TB and there are four kids.'

So the moment that should have been such a joyful occasion, when the fireman told him to join Jackie in the stall, was spoiled by having to step into a dead man's shoes. His heart was heavy as he returned home at the end of the shift. Was it fair to ask Meg to face the possibility of becoming a widow as suddenly as Sammy Gunn's wife had today?

Heath End was already in mourning for Sammy. Mary Ann had visited Mrs Gunn at the sanatorium to try to persuade her to stay where she was. She was able to reassure her about the children. Neighbours had taken in the two little lads; the girls, aged twelve and thirteen, were with Sarah. Everyone rallied round to help, accepting resignedly that in the midst of life they were in death, according to the teachings of Daddy Dale.

Paul, at twenty, was the youngest stallman in the pit. He and Jackie worked well together. Each day when they arrived one of them would fetch the powder and candle and the other would collect the sharpened tools from the blacksmith. Jackie, although ten years older, was also saving to get married, so their combined incentives meant that they always managed to send up more tubs in a day than anyone else. They were each taking home seven pounds a week after they had paid their driver; luckily they had a good one. Paul could now sympathize with the miners who used to grumble at him to 'get a move on' when he first started driving, for their money depended on how many tubs the driver was able to get to the top.

The bicycle repair business was booming; there was always plenty of work for Paul after he arrived home from the pit. There seemed twice as many bikes on the road as there had been before he left for Canada.

In reply to his letter explaining how he felt about the risks she was taking in marrying a collier, Meg wrote back saying that he was not getting rid of her as easily as that, and if there were risks, it made sense to spend as much time together while they could. He read extracts from her letters to Katy and his mother; this way they were able to get to know Meg in the way she had learned about them.

One day he read out: 'Arthur's bungalow is ready. He still eats here with us, of course. Liddy is often over there, fitting curtains and covers. They argue a lot, but that doesn't hide her love for him.'

So it was no surprise when he heard that Arthur and Liddy were getting married on the last day of July. Meg wrote: 'Dad says this is one wedding he will not be done out of. He is inviting everyone for miles around. There will be a big feast in the town hall at Moose Jaw, with a band for dancing.'

'There will not be anything as grand as that here,' Paul wrote back. 'Do you want to change your mind?'

The next communication was a postcard, like Ben used to send. 'I will sue you for breach of promise,' was all it said.

'I like the sound of your Meg,' laughed Mary Ann, when Paul showed it to her. 'By the way, where are you thinking of living when you are married?'

'Don't you want us here?' Paul teased.

'Meg would find that great wall a bit inhibiting, after the wide open spaces she's been used to. Every young couple should start on their own anyway.'

'Right again, Mary Ann. What have you got in mind? Because I can see there is something.'

'That square house on the opposite side of the road, between the start of Double Row and the Outdoor.'

'The double-fronted one, where old Mrs Mason lives?'

'Where she did live, you mean. She has just moved, to share a house in Sutton with her sister.'

'It is rather big. How much is it?'

'Ten shillings a week.'

Paul gave a low whistle. 'A bit steep! There won't be many takers at that price.'

'But it's worth it, lad. It is the only four-bedroomed house in Heath End, and there is a yard big enough for a coal wharf at the back, a high brick wall all round it. In addition to the two front rooms, there is a large kitchen and a scullery.

'How about starting a bicycle shop in one of the front rooms?' she went on eagerly. 'One of the bedrooms would answer as a stock room. That would leave a room at the front for a nice parlour.'

It was worth consideration, Paul had to admit, for it was obvious there was scope for a bicycle shop in the area. 'It would be some time before we could stock bikes,' he mused. 'But we could start with accessories. I will write and ask Meg how she feels about it.'

'You would need to know how to ride a bike,' he wrote teasingly. 'Demonstrations will be necessary, and as I would be down the pit for most of the time it would be up to you.'

Meg replied that she reckoned if he could learn to ride a horse she could manage a bike. She went on to say that as a wedding present for them her father was paying for Liddy and Arthur to accompany her to England. 'He says it will be a chance for Arthur to see his folk, and that he and Mom will be able to have a second honeymoon while we are all out of the way. We all think it is very generous of them both, for, as you know, it will be the busiest time of the year here. We shall arrive in Heath End three weeks before the wedding so that the banns can be read. Arthur and Liddy will have to return home soon afterwards.'

'Do you think Arthur's mother will be pleased to see them?' queried Katy doubtfully.

'No, I don't.' Paul's spirits sank for Arthur as he thought of the squashed little room. How would he feel about taking Liddy there? What on earth would Liddy say?

For the first time he worried how Meg would feel about Heath End when she saw it.

The double-fronted house across the road was easily acquired, nobody else in Heath End being willing to pay ten shillings a week.

By the time Meg arrived Mary Ann had used Paul's hundred pounds to stock the bicycle shop for them. One of the four bedrooms was equipped as a stock room with tyres and inner tubes of every conceivable size, while the shelves in the shop bulged with all the paraphernalia of spare parts which go into a bicycle, in addition to the fancier items such as saddle bags, bicycle bells, cleaning and repair outfits. Six sparkling bicycles stood on the small forecourt.

Enough money was left over to put a new double bed into two of the bedrooms, so Arthur, Liddy and Meg had somewhere to sleep for the period before the wedding. Ginny had lent kitchen table and chairs. The rest they had left for Meg to choose for herself.

Cod-Enders, who had been agog with curiosity about the Canadian sisters, were soon won over by the chatterbox girl with the laughing face and funny accent who seemed to know so much about them already and had a wonderful memory for names. She stopped to speak to everyone she met, young or old. Ben declared that Paul had all the luck and it was a good job for his brother he hadn't seen her first. 'Your Meg could sell a repair outfit to folk who ain't even got a bike,' he said.

Meg loved Heath End on sight, which was more than could be said for Liddy, who provided the best entertainment the village had had for years. She felt constricted by the buildings all around her and what she called its 'huge' and 'nosey' population. Every morning 'in order to breathe' she would stride off round the common, like a caged creature looking for escape, belittling the seventy-nine acres which separated Heath End from Pelsall and a further fifty

219

acres to the north by calling it 'that strip of lawn'.

She was horrified when she saw the conditions that Arthur's family were living in, reprimanding Arthur soundly for allowing it to happen. She decided that something had to be done immediately and started by tramping round every inch of Heath End inspecting empty houses.

Two days after her arrival she saw men at work re-roofing and re-flooring a tumble-down cottage near the stepping bridge. Another group were building a corridor to join the outside wash-house to the main building. When they had finished, they told her, there would be two bedrooms, a front parlour and a kitchen, in addition to the scullery, with water laid on.

'By the time we've done it'll be too damned dear for any Cod-Ender,' they forecast gloomily.

Liddy searched out the owner and came to terms. After that the poor workmen hardly dare pause for a drink, so often was she on their heels, querying how long this would take, or wouldn't it make more sense to do that a different way.

She and Ginny, kindred spirits, hit it off together from the moment they met. Ginny found a presentable set of pots and pans, buckets and bowls, from her collection, to equip the renovated cottage, together with some decent crockery. Mary Ann gave enough food from her grocery shop to stock the pantry, while Katy hurriedly machined curtains, cushions and towels from material Liddy bought from Mary Ann.

Within a fortnight of them landing in England Arthur's family were installed, the new plaster hardly dry on the walls, a talking point in Heath End for years afterwards.

Arthur's mother, by now much in awe of her bossy daughter-in-law, wandered about in a daze, wondering if it was all a dream from which one day she would awaken to drown in her own tears. Arthur was to undertake to pay the rent for as long as his mother lived, Liddy insisted, arranging for it to be paid directly into the bank for the landlady, so that Arthur's father could not get his hands on it.

That done they were free to go to Scotland for a few days. Tucked in a quiet valley in the Trossachs they found three of Mac's cousins, where their family had dwelt for generations. Mac, having kept the addresses from old correspondence of his father's, would be delighted to know they had found some kin.

The Trossachs were much more to Liddy's liking, and she came back, refreshed, for the wedding. In spite of her outward toughness her heart was heavy at the thought of leaving her sister in England. She must love Paul an awful lot to be willing to stay here, in this detestable little village, she felt. She knew if it meant choosing between Arthur or Canada she would have had to let him go.

Never before had so many Cod-Enders been in church for a wedding on the day that Arthur stood in for Mac when Meg walked down the aisle in the white dress she had made, pink carnations framing her shiny brown hair. Ben was Paul's best man, envying his brother his good fortune. At this wedding there was no hitch with the photographer, Liddy having made the arrangements. No-one would dare be late for Liddy.

Raish provided the flowers. He was at his most charming with the Canadian sisters and they could be forgiven for wondering if he was as bad as Paul and Ben made out.

The newly-weds went to Liverpool to see Liddy and Arthur off. As they watched from the quayside Paul was reminded of Ben, in this same place, gradually becoming a tiny spot in the distance, just over a year and a half ago. He could hardly believe all that had happened in so short a time. Now Arthur was leaving his birthplace for good with hardly a backward glance, and Meg was beside him as his wife. As he looked down at her, smiling and waving vigorously, he resolved to make her so happy she would never regret it. He would work every minute for her, if need be.

While her sister had been occupied preparing the cottage for Arthur's family, Meg had been getting better acquainted with Edwin, visiting him several times at the antique shop. She had enlisted his help in choosing some lovely old pieces of furniture with the money her father had given as a wedding present. She also bought three of his pictures.

Edwin, who called her his Merry Meg, was enchanted by her frankness and sincerity. He found it easy to talk to her about Sally, who had arrived at the medical mission in India where he had worked. To his delight she regularly sent him news of the children he knew and remembered. Not only was she helping out with money, but to Edwin's amazement was working among them himself, as he used to. Knowing the conditions he was overwhelmed with admiration for her. It seemed that Sally had at last found a cause that claimed her wholehearted dedication.

Meg settled down to enjoy Heath End. She was so genuinely interested in its people that they loved dropping into the bicycle shop for a chat with the effervescent girl, whether they wanted to buy anything or not. Mary Ann looked forward eagerly to her daily calls after Paul had come home from the pit and Katy felt she had again gained a sister. She gave Mark his first piano lessons, making them such fun that he never minded practising. She could even entice a chuckle from his temperamental little sister.

Her happiness was infectious. She sang as she did her housework, as she pegged out her washing in the walled yard, as she sewed covers and cushions for their home, or as she cooked the afternoon dinner for Paul, perching on his knee after he had eaten while they exchanged news of the hours they had spent apart.

Mary Ann introduced her to Birmingham; to its huge outdoor markets, to the warehouses, to Marshall & Snel-grove's. Like Mary Ann, Meg loved the crowds and bustle of the milling city. Their shared interests shortened the train journey and added new delights for Mary Ann. She encouraged Meg to talk of the farm and of her parents, for she knew she must miss them, although she never once heard her complain. Meg learned fast by watching and listening as her mother-in-law bargained and argued about prices and quality, usually getting her way in the end.

Salesmen at the warehouse were soon won over by the young Mrs Brook, letting her coax them into allowing her to have goods such as tents, camping equipment, collapsible chairs and pigeon baskets 'on appro' – 'Because I am not quite sure whether they will sell in our village.' Sale-or-return was a phrase Mary Ann had not come across until now. In introducing her to it, Meg won her unstinted admiration. No doubt the wholesalers realized, like Ben, that here was a girl who could sell a tent to someone who had never even given camping a thought before.

She learned to ride a bicycle, with Ben or Paul running alongside, holding the saddle. The great day came when their first bicycle-made-for-two was bought for stock. 'To prove to everyone how easy it is to ride we shall have to demonstrate,' Paul declared.

So Meg put out the word that they would be giving the tandem its trial run on Saturday afternoon. A jovial crowd had gathered outside the shop by three o'clock, including the reporter and photographer from the *Walsall Observer*.

Ben had heard Meg insisting that she claimed the privilege of being at the front of the machine. He had also heard his brother's reply. 'Oh, all right, then.' But Paul had no intention of being a back seat rider. He hopped on to the front saddle, and there was nothing for it but for Meg to sit behind. Immediately he called out, 'Ready to go?'

'Ready to go, partner.' Meg gripped the handlebars determinedly just as Ben shouted, 'No! Don't! Wait.'

Too late. The handlebars he had loosened earlier as a joke had already pulled out in Meg's hands.

223

'Whoa, Neddy,' she shouted, holding the handlebars aloft, but Paul took no heed of that, nor of the laughter of the Cod-Enders until after a few turns of the pedals he heard a thud. He turned to see Meg seated in the road, her long skirt ruffled above her knees, her arms outstretched, the handlebars still held tightly in her hands.

'I thought you were just fooling about . . . '

Ben raced over.

'Sorry Meg. You said it was our kid that was riding on the back. Have you hurt yourself?'

'You damn fool, Ben. You could have killed her.'

Meg just sat there, her knees up to her chin, and laughed and laughed. She laughed until the tears ran down her cheeks, and all the spectators joined in. After that anyone in Cod End would have eaten out of her hand.

Paul re-tightened the handlebars and away they went, Meg still hooting with laughter, but not before the *Walsall Observer* photographer took a lovely picture. The day after the publication the tandem was bought by the Editor and his wife, and Meg said the bruises she could not show to anyone but Paul were well worthwhile.

''Er's a good sport, Paul's missus,' was the general verdict from Cod End. They were proud of their little piece of Canada; that was something Pelsall had not got. They had never realized marriage could be such fun.

CHAPTER
14

MR DICKINSON, OF the furniture store, had died suddenly, leaving the business and all he possessed to his only daughter, Maud, who kept house for him. Raish decided that he was the man to put Maud, forty and unmarried, on the right track. To everyone's amazement he had stayed off the drink: the fact that Maud Dickinson was a teetotaller may have had something to do with that, for he did like to please her. 'The accounts are in a dreadful mess,' he explained to Mary Ann. 'I am sorting them out for her. The poor girl needs a bit of guidance, especially while she is so upset over her father. It is the least we can do.'

He spent long hours at the furniture store. Maud made him manager, and sometimes it was 'absolutely necessary' to visit her home at weekends. Ben swore he would kill Raish if the gossip in Heath End proved to be true, and Paul said he would speak to him. Mary Ann begged her sons not to interfere. 'It's only business,' she insisted. But her period of content was over. He had needed her; only her.

Now that was finished. Once again she plunged herself into feverish preparations for Christmas.

Ted Willis called on Katy one cold December day to buy fancy boxes of sweets as presents for his family. Little Marie was perched on the counter. Her eyes, with the double rows of thick lashes, were so like Ted's, that Katy held her breath, convinced he must notice, but Ted hardly glanced at the child. He was preoccupied with the fact that his mother refused to move into a better house he was anxious to buy for her in Pelsall.

'I'm a Cod-Ender,' she had stated flatly. 'And Cod End is where I stay.' So Ted was trying to negotiate with her landlord to let him buy the house, so that it could be improved. Trouble was, he said, he could not afford much time. He was anxious to return to France where he intended to settle.

He left the shop without so much as a smile. Katy clasped the baby tightly to her, burying her face into the child's soft shoulders, feeling strangely lost. What did she, a married woman, expect? 'Whatever is the matter with me, Marie?' she murmured. As she lifted her head she was startled to see Ted leaning toward her, very close. She was ashamed that he had found her off guard, that he must be aware of the disappointment in her face.

'You didn't think I had forgotten, did you?' he teased softly before kissing her tenderly full on the lips. Her hand shot up toward his face, but he caught it tightly as he had once before. His lips became more demanding, forcing her own apart, kindling an answering yearning within herself. She hung on to Marie with one arm and found his there too. Their arms entwining around the child caused tingles along her neck and spine as sensuous as those evoked by his kisses. When she determinedly pulled apart he let her go quite suddenly, leaving her with a feeling of humiliation, as if it were she who had provoked his behaviour.

'What are you up to, Ted?' she whispered breathlessly.

'Just a goodbye kiss, Katy.'

'We have said goodbye before.'

'But this time it is for real, my love. A rich little French lady is willing to take me on as a husband. You will be rid of me for good.' Katy tried to ignore the banging in her chest, the tightness in her throat, as Marie's soft little hand curled round his thumb and he gently smoothed the child's cheek. 'Perhaps we may start one of these . . . '

'Are you sure you have not done that already?'

The bitterness in her voice surprised herself, but Ted merely raised his eyebrows and smiled. 'Jealous?' Katy bit her lip, horrified at her outburst, her heart pounding in her ears. She wished she could push the awful accusation back down her throat.

'Jealous, Katy?' he repeated softly.

'Of course not!'

'Pity.' Leaning across the counter he enveloped herself and the baby loosely in his arms for a moment. ''Cos I'll take you, penniless, any day, in preference to a rich French lady, Kate-me-mate.'

She tried to laugh casually. 'Ted Willis! You are impossible.' Treat the whole thing as a silly flirtation; that was best.

But his voice was pleading and deadly serious. 'I have plenty of money for us both, Katy. I've bought a nice little house in France, not far from the coast. You would love it.

'I even talk posh now,' he added more lightly.

'Like my father,' commented Katy drily.

'No. Not like your father.' He seemed annoyed at that. He glanced round the shop. Spreading out his hands he said, 'You need something more exciting than a sweet shop in Cod End, Katy; admit it, love. You are missing so much. So much that I would like to give you.' He grasped her shoulders firmly, forcing her to look at him. 'You know I love you, Katy. Come with me. We'll have fun, I promise you. *Fun.* I bet that's something you haven't had much of since marrying Walter.'

'Go away, Ted. I mean it!'

'*I* mean it,' he whispered urgently in her ear.

A customer came in as his hands dropped away. Ted immediately strode to the door. 'Let me know if you change your mind,' he said, brazenly blowing her a kiss over the woman's head. 'I shall be here for a few more days.'

'Tryin' to sell you summat, is he?' the customer sniffed disapprovingly.

'He is.'

'Gettin' a bit above 'imself, that Ted Willis! Tryin' to shift his mam now. Ain't 'avin' much luck, though, is he?'

'No.' Frustrating tears stung the back of Katy's eyes as she lifted Marie from the counter, studying her as she had done so many times. She had Sally's oval face; in complete contrast to Ted's square chin. The give-away was the brown eyes, Ted's eyes, weighed down too heavily with lashes for the wide-open expression that had been Sally's. Perhaps she was so much a mixture of both parents that she did not look like either. She was a demanding child. Katy blessed Mark's placidity on days when she tried to cope with Marie constantly screaming for attention.

Yes, Ann Marie was a mixture of both her parents. Katy faced for the first time her jealousy of their union. What had possessed her? 'Are you sure you haven't started one already?' she had asked. How easily that could have led to questioning, to a moment when she could have blurted out their secret; hers and Walter's.

'Oh, Marie! Oh baby! What did I nearly do to you?'

An awful doubt chilled her spine. Did she love the children for who they were, or whose they were? Charlotte's Mark Edwin and Ted's Ann Marie? Did she tolerate Walter just for the security he gave to her and her children? She sobbed in frustration for the man the pit was making old and tired before his time. She sobbed because *she*

228

wanted to go. Damn that Ted Willis! She convinced herself she was glad when he left for France.

A few days after Ted's visit, news reached Mary Ann that Ginny was ill. In spite of the vicious rain lashing at her windows she packed some things into a basket, covered it with an old mackintosh, and set off for Ginny's. Outside the gypsy caravan the lane was flooded, soaking through her boots. No sign of Gert today; the caravan door was tightly shut. By the time she reached the gate to the scrapyard she was drenched and shivering.

Ginny had influenza. Mary Ann warmed up the soup she had brought, persuading her to take some. She found extra blankets, plumped up the pillows and made a bread poultice for Ginny's wheezy chest. She ventured into the wet wind-swept yard to find sticks and coal to make a fire in the little bedroom grate. Finally, she fed the pony.

'You shouldn't have come on a day like this,' croaked Ginny. 'Whatever possessed you? You're wet through already and you've all that way to walk back yet. If you had to come why didn't you bring the trap? T'would have been quicker.'

'In this weather? You know Dandy. She'd have sat down and refused to budge. Anyway, it's you we must think about. Try to sleep now, Ginny. There's a jug of hot lemon by the side of your bed. I am leaving a milk pudding, in case you feel like eating. I'll be back tomorrow.'

But next day Mary Ann was far worse than Ginny. She was hot and shivery at the same time. Katy, who had never known Mary Ann stay in bed in her life before, fetched the doctor. By then her mother was complaining of a violent headache and had developed a hacking cough. The doctor said it was pneumonia.

Sarah came with advice and remedies. 'Plenty of fluids is what's needed,' she said. The strong beef tea and lemon barley she prepared gave Mary Ann some relief, but Katy was less happy about the bread poultices slapped on while they were steaming hot, causing her mother to cry out. She knew Mary Ann did not cry for nothing.

But what with having to attend to both shops and care for Walter, who had one of his regular bronchitis attacks, with Marie protesting noisily every time she turned her back, she was grateful for Sarah, who cooked meals, kept the bedroom fire going, and dealt with the many visitors who called to see the patient.

Her brothers, devastated by the unfamiliar sight of their mother ill, did all they could. They would have sat with her for ever if it had not been for Sarah turfing them out; she said Mary Ann tried to talk too much when they were there. They took it in turns to sit through the nights, their eyes never leaving her face.

Raish appeared for his meals, but otherwise kept well out of the way.

Neighbours popped into the shop every morning to enquire how she was, and dole out advice. 'Sweat it out of 'er'; 'A drop o' brandy's the best medicine'; and 'Once she's over the crisis on the seventh day she'll go all one way.'

Children bought gifts with their Saturday pennies: a penn'orth of cocoa, 'Cos me Mam says it does yer good'; a long stick of barley sugar, 'To stop her thirstin''; a new hair slide 'For Mary Ann's nice hair'. The messages made Mary Ann smile; she whispered she would soon be out and about to thank them herself.

She was the one topic of conversation among her customers. Mary Ann was an institution; she shouldn't be ill. It didn't seem right to find Katy darting from one shop to another. She was always in a rush. Not like Mary Ann, ever ready to listen to their woes. They missed her understanding, her good sound common sense, her help when money was short.

Each day she seemed to get worse. It hurt her to breathe,

the pain in her chest and shoulders increased. Katy could not look at her without feeling anxious and afraid.

Ginny, when she heard, forced herself out of bed and came running. She cried; Ginny, the hard little nut who had not shed a tear when she lost her man, or when her babies died, cried like a baby herself. She wound her thin arms round her friend, tears spilling over her crusty old face. 'Don't die! Don't leave me. Not you, Mary Ann. Not you! Get better. *Please*, God, let her get better.'

Mary Ann stroked the rough hair soothingly. 'I will, Ginny. Don't worry. Don't worry.'

The day after, she became delirious and mumbled about the houses. She asked for Raish and did not know him when he came. She constantly repeated that she hoped Katy would be all right.

'Delirium is followed by the crisis,' Sarah said. 'She'll be better tomorrow.'

But she was proved wrong. That night, with only Paul beside her, Mary Ann died. Only minutes before she had whispered haltingly, 'I am so glad you have Meg, my lad.' Then, trembling and agitated, 'Come out of the pits. Please, Paul. For Meg's sake . . . I have an idea . . . '

'Tell me, my dearest Mam.' He loved her so much. He would promise anything; anything to give her some peace.

Even bending close to her he could barely hear what she was saying. It was so painful for her to breathe. 'You could . . . sell the coal. For . . . Meg's sake. Come out, lad.'

Her voice faded away; it was too much of an effort. But the last word she uttered was quite clear. A word of indescribable longing. 'Raish!'

Paul sat with her for a long time afterwards, remembering all the things she had planned and worked for, her resilience, her energy, her concern for them all. He could not believe his mother would never chat or laugh with him again; that he would never again be able to watch her baking or pegging a rug. Never to hear her say 'I have an idea,' or 'Well done, my lad.'

At last he wept.

All Heath End wept for Mary Ann. There was hardly a family she had not helped in some way or another.

Meg was devastated. She had taken all Paul's family to her heart, but it was to Mary Ann she turned to fill the place of her own mother so far away. Only her mother-in-law had known just how jumpy she was if Paul was so much as half an hour late home. Even without the mutual love they shared for Paul there would have been an affinity between them. Mary Ann's funeral was the first time the people of Heath End had seen Meg without a smile. That night she and Paul cried in each other's arms.

Raish had no time for tears. He was too busy, frantically searching for the bank book he knew she had. He accused each one of them in turn of stealing it. Katy searched high and low without success until one day she came across it between sheets of newspaper her mother kept beneath the counter for wrapping. A piece of writing paper, neatly folded, fell out of the bank book. She looked at it incredulously for a moment.

'He shan't see this,' she said, as she pushed the paper into her pocket just as Raish walked in.

'Is this what you are looking for?' she asked, handing him the book. He snatched at it without a word.

Cod-Enders were shocked to the core when Raish married Maud Dickinson a fortnight later at a Birmingham registry office. He could have waited a decent interval, they said.

'God help the woman,' was Ben's only comment. 'It's a good job he's found somebody who will take him on, as none of us would want him.'

Soon Cod End was buzzing with the news that Brookie had given Maud four houses as a wedding present.

'He won't get away with this,' protested Ben. 'Not after her slaving like she did. He can't!'

'If there is no will he can,' Edwin pointed out.

It was almost unheard of in 1913 for ordinary folk like Mary Ann to leave wills. Bequests were usually made by word of mouth beforehand, and the wishes of the deceased honoured and respected.

'It's not just that we're losing the houses she wanted us to have. But it's everything she worked for, all the years she was on her own.' Paul felt sick at heart.

'It may be only a rumour,' said Katy. 'I can't believe he would do *this*. I shall go to see him.'

She went on Thursday afternoon, when Dickinson's store was closed, leaving the baby with Meg. Maud Dickinson's house was the only one that stood on Willenas Common, looking down on the canals where the lads used to walk to Conduit. Maud herself answered the door, a tall business-like woman, looking older than her forty years, yet not unattractive.

'Is my father in?'

As Katy stepped into the wide hall a glint of gold caught her eye, and there, in the folds of Maud's dress, was the pendant that Paul had given to his mother.

'Your father's in there.'

Maud indicated a heavy door before disappearing through another. Raish was relaxing in a deep leather armchair pulled up to the fire. He was smoking a cigar. Katy knew that now he had married Maud he would resume the role of pampered invalid, quickly losing his enthusiasm for the business.

He rose as she entered the room. 'Katy! What a pleasure. Do sit down, my dear girl. A glass of port?'

'I'll not, thank you. What I have come about won't take long.'

He settled her in the chair opposite. 'Why so serious?' he queried lightly.

'I have come to ask you about the houses, Dad.'

'What of them?'

'You know what Mother wanted. One for each of her children she said.'

'Did she say that?'

'You know she did! You were there, on her birthday.'

Raish looked directly into his daughter's eyes while shaking his head. 'No, Katy. I never heard that.'

Katy stared at her father disbelievingly. 'Is it true that you have given them as a wedding present to your new wife?'

He laughed shortly. 'You could say that. But a wife's property is her husband's. Isn't that so, my dear?'

She gazed hopelessly into the blue eyes that could be so attractive, now like miniature ice rinks, and realized there was nothing in him she could appeal to. But, for her mother, she tried once more. 'What about the gold chain and pendant, Dad? The one that Paul gave Mother for her birthday.'

'He's not asking for it back, is he?'

'No. But I am. For Mother. You know what she said.'

'Come girl,' he replied impatiently. 'It was a birthday gift. You are not asking for the dress you gave to her, are you? Or the child for his picture?'

'This is different, Dad. You know how much she wanted Paul to have it.'

'Did he give it, Katy? Or did he lend it? Anyway,' he added spitefully, 'he can buy another from the business she set him up in.'

'That was Paul's own money that he brought back from Canada. Mother told me.'

'If it was his money why was it in her possession? Once again, did he give it, or merely lend it?'

'So you are not even going to honour that request?'

He shrugged his shoulders. 'It all belongs to me now.' He walked her to the door. 'Do come again, my dear. Any time. Maud and I will be more than pleased to see you.'

Katy turned. She took a long hard look at him as he stood by the door, dapper in his expensive suit, a white carnation in his buttonhole, a cigar in his smooth white hand. She thought of her mother's roughened hands that were never still and in that moment she hated him. She walked away without a backward glance.

The four of them met that night in the house where they had spent their childhood. It was completely empty. Raish had arranged with an auctioneer to take everything, lock, stock and barrel, including the donkey and cart. Even the pigeons had gone, resulting in a furious argument between Ben and his father. They were on his property, Raish said, therefore he could do what he liked with them. He had settled on a price with Sarah for the goodwill and stock of the grocery shop. He let her have it cheap: he wanted to be shot of it.

He gave notice to the landlady and told Ben to clear out. This was the last time they would be able to meet in the little kitchen.

Edwin wandered into what had been, in turn, The Coffee Shop, The Little Gallery, and Little Cott, his home, where Mary Ann had given him time to find himself again.

Paul and Ben took a last look at the little upstairs room where the boxing booth had been, while Katy stood in her mother's shop, now cold and empty, picturing it as it had been in the days before her wedding. However had it held everything without bulging at the seams? Of course, half the stock had been in the window. She smiled sadly as she recalled how she used to sit on her heels inside it, watching Cod End go by.

Later the four of them stood with their backs to the fireless grate, gazing at the tall grey building that blotted out the light. It was the first time they had been aware of it: there had been so much life in this little room. They huddled close together, as they used to, on the landing, years ago, listening to their father's ravings, hoping they would not hear their mother cry.

They were each remembering something: Katy the

colourful contents of the bundles spilling on to the kitchen table, how they would chat together and laugh as they sorted them out; Edwin his mother's encouraging words about his paintings as he sat in this kitchen among the smells of baking, after staying away so long. Ben could feel the soft down of a chicken in his hand on the day he should have started work at Conduit. Paul was hearing his mother's voice before he sailed to Canada, 'Don't worry. We've got houses in the bank now.'

Katy was the first to speak. 'I have been to see Dad. What we heard, about the houses, is true.'

'I shall kill him!' threatened Ben wildly. 'He can't do this.' He had forgotten the embarrassment he had felt at learning that he was a future property owner, remembering only that Raish had foiled Mary Ann's plan. 'He can't do it.'

'He can, Ben. It's no use.'

'What does it matter,' exclaimed Edwin. 'She left us far more than houses.'

Ben rounded on him angrily. 'I'll tell you why it matters,' he yelled. 'It matters because it's *him* that is getting away with it again. Our father!'

'It matters because she worked damned hard for us every minute he was away,' added Paul.

'She worked because of something else too.' Katy unfolded the paper that had been hidden away in the bank book. It was a poem, written in Mary Ann's generous flowing hand. 'This is dated 21st June, 1908. I shall never forget that date. It was the hot summer's day I went with Sally to London. Women's Sunday.'

'Then that must be the day I was running in a race round the common,' said Ben, calmed at the memory.

'And I won a bet. Mother refused to take my winnings. "Pick up your money, lad", she said. "I'm all right." She was always "all right", to hear her talk. "The best money's that which you earn yourself," she said.'

'It was the time Charlotte said we would always remember because we were all so happy,' Edwin recalled.

'Well, Mary Ann wasn't happy.' Choked with tears Katy handed the poem to Edwin. In his clear quiet voice he read to them their mother's words.

> Must work
> In order to forget.
> No respite all day through,
> No noontide break,
> No moment's pause
> To think of magic that is you.
>
> Too tired
> To dream of what was bliss.
> Thank God that aching limbs
> And weary brain
> Help dim the mem'ry of your kiss.
>
> Day breaks.
> One heavenly breath before
> Recall. Was that my voice?
> Or some bruised bird
> About to spin
> Around the treadmill of the day.
>
> Must work
> In order to forget
> The magic that is you.

Edwin's voice faltered on the last word. She had signed herself Polly. Polly! So tough. Yet so vulnerable.

'It couldn't have been written for *him*,' Ben groaned. 'It could not be for *him*.'

'His name was the last word she said before she died,' Paul admitted.

'And who else called her Polly?' whispered Katy.

There was a long awed silence. To love like that, however

guilty the loved one. Such a love was beyond the personal experience of any of them. Katy wished that she had asked the questions that were in her heart when she could. 'Was it all worth while?' 'Is the loving worth the heartache?' 'Would you do it all again?'

Now she would never know the answers.

CHAPTER

15

'Are you ready, Marie?'

'I am not coming.'

Katy stared at the sulky back of her eleven-year-old daughter, seeing the long black hair flouncing in revolt like the rest of her slim young body. She recognized the familiar stubborn tones that heralded a storm.

'Get your coat, love,' she replied calmly. 'Uncle Edwin will be here for us at any moment. Of course you are coming.'

'There's no *of course* about it. Uncle Edwin! What difference does Uncle Edwin make?'

'I thought you liked him.'

'That doesn't mean I have to come.' Her voice rose to a shrill scream. 'You can't make me!'

'Marie! Why do you have to spoil today, of all days? Mark will be so disappointed.'

'Oh! Mark will be so disappointed, will he,' she

239

mimicked rudely. 'Then all I can say is bloody hurray. Do him good to have a disappointment.

'Mark will be this! Mark will be that! All I ever hear is Mark, Mark, Mark! *You* will be there, won't you? And Uncle Edwin! His *real Dad.* Anyway, I loathe the rubbish he plays.'

As Katy turned to reach gloves from the sideboard her sister-in-law appeared in the doorway, announcing cheerfully, 'Here I am, all dressed up and ready to go. Lucilla's installed in the shop and . . . ' Meg stopped abruptly, interpreting the scene immediately, the angry child not yet ready, and Katy white with the effort of keeping calm.

'I am not coming,' Marie repeated stubbornly, sitting herself down with a bounce.

Meg glanced from one to the other. She knew that Katy would not leave Marie on her own while Walter was out working; she also knew that nothing would induce Marie to change her mind. Meg had been looking forward to going to Manchester to hear Mark play almost as much as Katy, but it was far more important for Katy to be there, so she simply said, 'I'm off to Birmingham. Care to come, Marie?'

'But . . . you have so wanted . . . '

Katy was silenced by Meg shaking her head vigorously. 'No, no. I have changed my mind; there's something I must get.'

Marie hesitated, torn between keeping Katy at home, and the pleasure of a shopping spree with her aunt, who was always generous. Perhaps she could do both.

'How about it, Marie? We could look for those shoes you wanted.'

Marie shrugged, feigning indifference. 'I might think about it. Say in an hour or so's time,' she added impertinently.

'Marie, get your coat this minute. You are going to go to one or another, my girl.'

As Katy's voice rose sharply the child suddenly grinned

like a satisfied cat, noting Katy biting her lip in self-annoyance. She slung her coat carelessly across her shoulders.

'I'll go to Brum. It'll be better than Manchester bloody Free Trade Hall anyway.'

Later, beside her brother in the car lent by his boss, Katy sighed unconsciously.

Edwin glanced across at her, reading her thoughts. 'Pity about Marie not coming.'

'Yes.'

'Another scene?'

''Fraid so. I was on the verge of losing my temper again when Meg turned up, I am ashamed to say.'

'Don't worry. It is a phase she is going through.'

'A phase that is lasting a long time, then. She has always been a difficult child, but since she has known she is adopted it has been ten times worse. Living in Heath End, I suppose it is inevitable she would find out. Oh, Edwin, she is so jealous of Mark knowing about his real parents.'

'It must be difficult for her, Katy.'

'I realize that.'

'Pity you do not know who her parents are. It might be worth telling her about them.'

Katy's heart did a double somersault. She never failed to be amazed that people who had known both Ted and Sally could not recognize them in Marie. With her brother's eye for detail why hadn't he recognized something of Sally? Couldn't he see she was Ted's? But there was no guile in his honest face as she continued, 'I feel I have failed.'

'Nonsense. You are the most wonderful mother a child could have. She will grow out of it, never fear.'

Maybe he was right. She remembered how much she had disliked the selfish Sally when they were children, and how her friend had changed in adulthood. Yet on days like today she despaired of ever succeeding with Marie.

She thought back to when she and Walter had travelled to London to fetch the baby they both longed for. Katy's heart had pitched uncertainly as Sally welcomed them into her apartment. Motherhood appeared to have worked miracles. She looked so radiant, her face considerably softened. An air of unaccustomed serenity seemed to surround her as she offered them tea and sandwiches. Katy could not help but comment. 'You look as if you have come through a marvellous experience.'

Sally smiled. 'It is quite something,' she admitted, 'giving life to another human being. Awe-inspiring somehow.'

Yet she later handed over the month-old baby as unconcernedly as she would a bundle of washing. Katy recalled how she had searched her friend's face anxiously for signs of regret. 'Are you absolutely sure, Sally?'

'I am certain!' she stated emphatically. 'Hope you have better luck with the little minx than I have had. She cries continuously. I could not have survived without a good nurse. Yet I am assured she is healthy enough. Can't imagine why she bawls so.'

As Katy protectively tucked the tiny flailing fists into the warmth of her snowy shawl she kissed the red puckered indignant features of her new daughter, totally convinced that there **was nothing** that loving arms and loving hearts could not cure. **But** Marie had cried all the way home that day and had continued to make her presence felt ever since. She was anti-authority from the word go. Only Walter, patiently accepting her as she was, could exert any influence. What a pity he could not have been with them today, but jobs were so scarce he was convinced that had he taken a day off without a doctor's note he would be instantly sacked. Katy felt he was right; the powers that be would be only too glad to find an excuse to sack a man whose failing health may ultimately lead to a claim for compensation.

She sighed. The rift between herself and Marie seemed to

be widening as time went by and was a daily source of heart-ache. But not today. She must not let it spoil today. Mark's day.

Edwin, echoing her thoughts, said, 'We are not going to let anything spoil today, are we?'

Katy pushed all thoughts of Marie out of her mind and smiled at her brother. 'Hasn't he done well, Edwin? A solo performance and only fifteen!' Katy had thought she would burst with pride when Mark won a coveted scholarship to attend a famous school for music, where he lived in, except for weekends. Now this! A solo performance at Manchester Free Trade Hall. 'Hasn't he done well?' she repeated, excitement taking over.

'Marvellously. And it is all thanks to you and Walter. What a shame he had to work today. You two have kept yourselves poor for Mark's tuition.'

'You as well.'

He laughed shortly. 'I have had little enough to give.'

She patted his knee affectionately. 'Anyway, we are going to "take the day", Edwin.'

He smiled a little sadly. 'That is something you always used to do. Such a long time since I heard you say it.' She looked so pretty and lively today, his sister. Yet she worked so hard and had such a problem with Marie.

Katy settled back and allowed herself to think solely of Mark, the son given to her by Charlotte. He had been worth every minute of every effort, worth every stitch as she sewed well into the night, every extra shift that Walter accepted. What a lot of happiness the kind, loving lad had brought them both.

Four seats had been reserved for them in the centre of the hall. Katy eagerly scanned the programme. There was his name, heading a whole paragraph of praise. It said he showed a greater maturity of approach and style than many more experienced pianists, and that he would be playing a selection of Chopin.

243

There were some orchestral numbers and a contralto singer, but the concert did not start for Katy until the moment she thought she would burst with pride when Mark appeared, a tall figure in a dark suit, smiling gently at the audience before bending his blond head lovingly over the keys and becoming lost in the music. How much like Charlotte he was in temperament, demanding nothing from the audience, yet immediately captivating them. How much like her brothers in looks, with his bright blue eyes and tall figure.

The programme listed Mark's first item as Souvenir de Paganini. She did not glance at it again, lost in the music that stirred memories. With what ease his fingers flew gently but surely over the keys. Never had his quiet confidence been so much in evidence. The peaceful haunting melody carried her back in time to an oak panelled room, she in her best suit, entranced as the elderly gent with the goatee beard played 'a little bit of Chopin I am fond of'. He it was who gave her the chance to spend all of Walter's savings on the piano that started all this. How she wished he could hear the results of his kindness.

The next piece began with the simplicity of a child learning to play. She could see Meg leaning over her young pupil, praising him, humming the music he played, a Meg bubbling over with youth and love of Paul, a love as strong as ever, Katy knew, but now and then tinged with disappointment because he was never there. Embued with the old desire to make money, he was too busy. Too busy to be with Meg; too busy to have children.

After their mother died, Paul had become a coal merchant, and did well out of it, but he was not satisfied until he had acquired a supposedly worked-out pit, which he was adamant had a lot of life left in it. He was proving it now, but it utilized his every minute. Pity; all Meg ever wanted was to be near him. She would have valued that far more than the material things he loved to lavish on her.

How enthusiastic she had always been about Mark's talents, helping him financially whenever she could do so with tact and diplomacy; and today Marie had done her out of this proud moment.

She was aroused from her reverie by a change of mood, rhythmic dancing music, which made her itch to get up and dance in the aisle as she had danced for the organ grinder so many years ago. Edwin smiled as he noticed the tapping foot, the movement of her small firm body.

Fantasie Impromptu followed. How could one so young portray such intensity of feeling? Music of lost dreams; of the children she was unable to give birth to; of the secure family atmosphere destroyed by a wilful little girl who refused to appear on the Anniversary platform in a white dress with the same obstinacy she had displayed today, the obstinacy that came to the fore whenever she realized that Katy wanted something very much.

Mark ended his performance with Waltz in E Flat; she had heard him play it often during his hours of practice at home, music which seemed to signify youth looking forward, eager anticipation.

She was jerked into the present by the ecstatic reaction from the audience, Mark acknowledging it with that lovely slow wondering smile, as if he had not yet come back to earth from wherever his music transported him. The applause seemed to go on for ever. At last they reluctantly allowed him to go, but not before he had played another lively little piece.

As the applause went on and on Katy remembered the day in the little chapel when she vowed that one of her children would learn to play the piano; that dream at least had come true. Thank you, dearest Mark, for that. And thank you, Meg.

They met him briefly during the interval. Tall, handsome in the well-fitting suit which she had made, every stitch sewn with love. He was happy about the performance, more so for them than for himself. He let her reach up and pull his head down to kiss him.

'Mom. Edwin.' He hugged her close before grasping Edwin's outstretched hand. 'Where's Marie? Didn't she come? And Aunt Meg?'

'Marie was not very well,' Katy fibbed. 'Meg stayed with her.'

'Poor Marie! What is wrong?'

'Just a sick headache. She will be all right. She . . . she said good luck.'

Later, at home, Marie said, 'I expect you lied to him? Told him I wasn't well?'

'Yes. I did.'

'I shall tell him you lied. I shall tell him I refused to listen to his rotten music.'

'That won't make him very happy, love, will it?'

'What do I care?'

'Will it make *you* happy?'

'Who cares about that?'

'I do.' A tell-tale quiver of Marie's lips caused Katy to open her arms wide, anxious to comfort her. 'Oh, Marie, love, I care very much.'

'Well, I don't care for *you*. I had a lovely time with Auntie Meg today. Better than I ever have with *you*.' She turned quickly and ran to her room.

Katy's empty leaden arms fell to her sides despondently. Later she crept up to where the child lay pretending to be asleep. Slipping her arms underneath her she held her tenderly, cradling her head on her chest, as Marie sobbed uncontrollably. Walter came from their room where he had been sleeping and stood by the bed. Marie pushed Katy away and went into his arms.

Knowing how eager Meg would be to hear about the concert, Edwin called to see her after he had delivered Katy home. Meg had bathed and wore a cosy pink dressing-gown tightly belted at the waist. She reminded him of a sweetly-smelling rose as she bent forward, listening avidly to his account of the evening. He found himself describing the poetry of the music, the adulation of the audience and Katy's pride.

'She is very grateful she was able to be there, Meg. It was good of you to take Marie as you did.'

'I quite enjoyed it. Marie can be charming when she's a mind to be.' She yawned. 'I am tired, though. She wanted to tour the whole of Birmingham in one day.'

'I'll let you off to bed, then.'

'No. No need. Don't rush off. I have decided to wait up for Paul tonight. He is still working.'

'And Ben?'

'At a Union meeting.'

Edwin leaned back in his chair. 'All right. If you're sure.' He always felt at home here. He had always admired the spontaneity that made his sister-in-law such a comfortable person to be with. She was so genuinely interested in everyone, and had a special affection for Mark.

'Mark reminded me so much of Charlotte tonight,' he mused.

'I wish I had known your Charlotte. Tell me about her.'

'She came and went so quietly it's sometimes difficult to realize I was ever married to her. Odd, isn't it? Yet tonight she came alive again. I could sense that Katy felt it too.'

'Did you love her a lot, Edwin?'

He paused before replying simply, 'Like a sister. I know that now. She was a wonderful experience, Meg. Calm, soothing, tranquil. Yet with such hidden depths. She was able to express them in her music. As Mark did tonight.'

He spread out his hands, searching for the right words. 'Mark, although he holds some firm convictions for himself, like Charlotte did, is able to accept the rest of the world without apportioning an atom of blame. Just like her.

Acceptance. Of both good and bad.' He sighed. 'Such maturity! I shall never be as mature as he is now.'

'His music does show maturity. As do your paintings.'

His eyes strayed to three of his pictures adorning the walls of the room they were in. Whenever Paul gave Meg any money to buy jewellery she persuaded him to let her buy a picture instead. She followed his gaze. 'I look at them a lot.'

'You really like them, don't you?'

'I really like them, Edwin,' she stressed, knowing that his confidence was oozing away because, since he had discovered he could portray people and had decided to depict the way of life all around them, his pictures had not sold. 'What's more, they are brilliant.'

'You are the only one who thinks so.'

'Silly people.'

'Katy thinks I should go back to painting landscapes. She reminded me of what Mother said, that people buy pictures to cheer them up.'

'Your mother would have recognized the skill in what you are doing now, Edwin. She would have said "Keep at it, my lad. They will sell one day." '

He smiled at her fondly. It seemed very remote, the time Meg was not a member of their family. 'In that case I shall leave them with Katy for Mark, to sell when that happy day comes. I am thinking of joining Sally in India.'

'Oh, Edwin. Do you think you should?' Could he stand up to the conditions out there? He looked so thin. Katy had often voiced her amazement that Sally had stuck it for so long, despite her enthusiasm for Causes.

'Do you think you should?' she repeated.

'I have thought so for a long time. I have stayed on because I have been able to make some small contribution to Mark, but it is becoming so small it won't be missed. Gareth Hildred is finding it difficult to make enough for himself in the present depression, without having to pay me. Anyway, I should be doing something more useful than painting pictures no-one wants to buy.' He stood up to go. 'And I would like to see Sally again,' he added simply.

Meg had not known Sally, but she knew of the regular correspondence that passed between them, and she knew from her own experience that strong bonds could be formed and strengthened by an exchange of letters. She guessed that his feelings for Sally were very different from what he had felt for Charlotte.

'I expect she would like to see you too, Edwin,' she said now. She wondered how he would find the money for the fare.

As if she had spoken out loud he said, 'Sally has many times offered to pay my fare, should I want to go. I think it is time to accept. Some day perhaps I shall be able to pay her back.'

'You will pay her back just by being there.' She stood on tiptoe and kissed him lightly on his cheek. He could smell the sweet cleanness of her. 'Good luck, Edwin.'

After he had left she studied the three paintings on her walls, as she often did. 'Morning' showed a dismal street with drunken, blackened houses leaning perilously toward the colliery, cloth-capped men swarming from them, clutching their snap tins, their faces set anxiously toward the brooding pit shaft dwarfing the street, their progress in heavy pit boots slow and reluctant. Such a variety of expressions was cleverly portrayed on their faces, gratitude, truculence, despair, indifference. Over all of them hung a touching humility.

In the second picture, entitled 'Afternoon', a hefty miner with rippling shoulders was stripped to the waist, braces dangling, scrubbing down at an iron sink in an old cluttered brewhouse. Carbolic and pit dust mingled into an oozing grey foam so realistic you felt you could sponge it from the canvas. There was a swagger about this collier, a cock-a-hoop lift to his shoulders, master of his own domain, his day's work done. His face was alert with anticipation for his pigeon flying, the domino league or whatever was his favourite sport.

In 'Evening' a group of men, dressed in clean shabby suits, some with mufflers, linked arms round the lighted lamp in the village square, a warm glow suffusing their contented faces. It was their happy hour of escape and comradeship.

A way of life was accurately and sympathetically portrayed by the paintings. Meg had others. What a pity people could not see their worth. She was so absorbed she did not hear Ben come in until he was standing close behind her. 'God knows what he wants to paint things like that for. Who wants to be reminded of a collier's day?'

'I do.' She smiled at her brother-in-law.

'You wouldn't if you had to live through one.' He looked tired and disgruntled. She made him a cup of tea which he drank silently, slumped despondently in the depths of his chair.

'Didn't the meeting go well?'

He shook his head. 'You know what they want to do now, the bosses? Make the shifts longer and the pay packets shorter.'

'They can't do that, surely?'

'Can't they! With pits closing every day and unemployment rising? Men who fought in the war still out of a job? What chance have miners got? Families living on next to nothing. Filthy, sweaty, primitive conditions down the mine, the risk of pit disasters. Gaffers will always take risks with other people's lives, just like politicians take risks with other folk's lives in wartime. Our Paul takes risks now that he's gaffer.'

'I am sure you are wrong about that,' Meg bristled.

He did not tell her that last night, after she had gone to bed, he had quarrelled bitterly with Paul. He had heard that he was re-using old props and clapped-out machinery that was constantly going wrong, and the men were working in too much water; all the conditions Paul himself had deplored at Tack-a-Rue.

'He is providing means of a living for a dozen men now,' Meg was saying.

'And perhaps means of dying for one or two.'

'Don't say that, Ben. You take more notice of others than of your own brother. There's no more caring person alive than Paul, you know that. If there is anything wrong it is only temporary and will be put right as soon as possible.'

He looked across at her and spread his hands despairingly. 'You'll never hear a word against him, will you?'

'Never. And you shouldn't,' she said sharply.

He sighed and lapsed into silence. After a pause he said, 'I lost my job again today, Meg.'

'Speaking up in the wrong place again, were you?' she chided gently, her indignation receding immediately.

'Somebody has to speak up for 'em.'

'That's true.'

'The married men daren't. I haven't anyone to bother about.'

It wasn't in her nature to speak sharply to anyone, and he looked so dejected sitting there, she bent to kiss him gently on the cheek, a sisterly peck like she had given Edwin, her arm resting lightly on his shoulder. He gave a little moan as he reached out for her, pulling her on to his lap, pushing her arm further round his neck. Pinning her closely to him, his lips bore down, sealing hers for what seemed to be eternity. She could not move nor breathe.

'If you only knew how I've loved you all these years,' he murmured, his lips still close, his arms like steel. 'Meg my little love. My little love. When I see you lonely like this, I . . .'

'But I am not! Ben. Dear Ben. I am not. Please!'

She struggled uselessly to free herself.

'Let me love you, Meg. Just this once.' His lips crashed

251

on to hers again, with an incredible pent-up longing, holding her so tightly she thought she would suffocate. She could feel him tugging at the belt of her robe until it slid to the floor, as his lips became more demanding, more searching. She shut her eyes hopelessly. She felt she was sinking into a deep bottomless pool, as he undid the buttons of her nightdress.

Suddenly rough hands jerked her away from him.

'What the hell do you think you're doing, you two? This is what happens when my back's turned is it?' Paul's eyes were blazing, angrier than she had ever thought it possible for him to be.

'Stand up, you,' he shouted at Ben, 'so that I can knock you down again.'

'It's all my fault.'

'It's you I am going to thrash.'

'Paul! Both of you! Stop this!' Meg was trembling violently yet managed to place herself between the two men, unaware that her robe fell open without its belt. Paul lifted her out of the way as if she were a feather. 'Go and make yourself decent,' he ordered scathingly. 'Now. You! *My brother*!'

Ben did not even raise his hands. He stood while Paul pounded him like a punchbag, making no effort to defend himself, as blows rained all over his body. Meg watched horrified as his lips swelled, as cuts on his face bled, as he doubled up in pain on the floor. It was as if there had been a reversal of roles, with Paul taking on Ben's usual aggressiveness.

'Get your hands up and fight, you coward,' Paul was shouting. 'Fight!' He was like a man demented. His brother! With his wife! 'How dare you touch her?' he breathed when at last the pounding ceased.

'Be good to her.'

'Do I need you to tell me?'

Ben moved toward her, his swollen face covered in blood.

'I'm sorry, Meg. I don't know what came over me. I am very sorry.'

She was sobbing. 'I must bathe your face.'

'Sit down!' Paul thundered, pushing her into a seat.

Meg sat, white and shaken, silent until she heard the outer door open and shut. 'Where will he go?'

'To take a jump in the cut, I hope.'

'Oh, Paul!' She could not stop her body trembling, waves of nausea surging over her, the disgust in his face tearing her body apart.

He was quiet now, distant, out of reach, gazing down at her with contempt. She said nothing, fearing if she described exactly what happened she would land Ben in more trouble. Surely he trusted her? In the morning, when he had had time to think, he would realize how wrong he had been and she would have thought how best to explain. Yes, she would wait until morning.

She stumbled dazedly to their room where she lay waiting for him. After what seemed an age she heard soft footsteps on the stairs. It would be all right when she held him in her arms; it must be. But he went into the next room without a word. It was terribly lonely without him. Although he was often late home it was ten years since she had not had the comfort of his arms in the night. She lay taut and still, numb with shock, seeing first Ben's battered face, then Paul's contemptuous gaze. He had never looked like that before; how hurt he must be.

As dawn approached and her head became more and more blurred with the pain of sleeplessness Paul suddenly appeared at her bedside. It was obvious he had not slept either. He stood silently studying her, as if for the first time. Meg's heart seemed to stop. At last he spoke. 'You seemed to be enjoying it? With *my brother*?'

'No. I was not.'

'You put up a good show, then, your eyes closed, arms round his neck, all open at the front, ready for him.'

253

'Paul! It was nothing like that.'

'What was it like, then? Like this?' He pulled the bed-clothes swiftly aside, tore her nightdress from her, ran his hands insultingly over her naked body. 'Was it like this, you little slut? Or like *this*? Come on, show me. You've more experience than I have. Did you have Edwin as well last night?'

Meg gasped. 'Edwin!'

'I saw him leave. I had to call on a chap up the road. Queuing up, were they, my brothers? What did Edwin do? This? Ben would be a bit rougher, wouldn't he? Like *this*.'

Meg had never imagined that sex with him could be distasteful, never thought he could subject her to the humili-ation that followed. It was a nightmare from which she kept hoping she would wake. As she lay, spent and bruised, wondering if she would find the strength to get up, Paul, shaken and disillusioned, was being violently sick. He did not know who disgusted him most, his wife, his brother or himself. He had adored her. How could she!

By mid-day Cod End was split in two. Everyone knew that the Brook brothers had had a bust-up. Ben had been seen leaving the house, battered and bleeding, carrying a hurriedly-packed bag. They were surprised he had taken such a beating, Ben, the better boxer of the two. It was easy to add up two and two to get the reason for the dispute. They all knew Ben had been up in arms about the conditions operating in Paul's resuscitated mine. They also knew he had now moved in with Ginny, who supported him openly in his bid to bring his brother to his senses. Wanted to run before he could walk, that Paul, she said; he always had. Half of Cod End agreed with her. There were many fierce arguments that day in the pits, in the streets, pubs and shops, with the opposing side led by Sarah. Paul was a worker, if ever there was one, she maintained. He deserved some results from all his labours, and he was providing employment, wasn't he? Ben was jealous, that's what was the matter with him. They were all agreed on one point, their sympathy for Paul's wife; that poor girl was the pig in the middle, trying to keep the peace between those two. No wonder she looked fit to drop today.

Never had there been such bitter disagreement on the rights and wrongs of a quarrel, and never had they been so wrong as to its cause.

Meg did not know how she got through the endless day, with more customers coming into the shop than usual, quizzing her, anxious to get first-hand information. When Paul came home they must talk, however late he was.

Normally when he stepped through the door he could hear her singing, bustling in the kitchen, or calling out a cheery hello to him before she ran to greet him with a kiss, bubbling over to tell him about her day, and wanting to hear about his. It had always been wonderful to come home to her, however late, however tired. Even if she was in bed she would lie awake for their 'chat'.

Tonight as he entered she stood like a tiny ghost, perfectly still, searching his face. All day he had felt sick at heart, ashamed of the mad jealousy that had made him behave so disgustingly. He had degraded her and himself. For one moment he was tempted to open his arms and let her run into them.

Instead he said, 'I apologize for my behaviour last night. It was unforgiveable.' He ignored the rush of colour to her cheeks, the brightening of her eyes. 'I won't bother you again. Ever.'

He watched the colour drain away again. It was almost more than she could bear, the hurt in his eyes, the closed face, the cold unfamiliar voice.

'Paul,' she pleaded, her voice trembling. 'Have I ever lied to you?'

'How do I know?'

'Because you know me.'

'I thought I did, you mean.'

She paused, wondering how best to go on.

'Ben had lost his job.'

'I see. That was his consolation prize, was it?'

He turned away so that he did not have to see her eyes beginning to fill with tears. 'I have to be up early in the morning. Don't bother to get up.'

She tried once more. 'No goodnight kiss?'

He left her without even troubling to reply. She heard him shut his bedroom door, as she faced another lonely night.

She tried again next morning, catching him at dawn, just before he left. 'You must know, Paul, there has never been anything between me and your brothers, apart from sisterly affection. You know that Edwin wouldn't . . . '

'Yes. I do know that *Edwin* wouldn't.'

'Ben was so upset. He was not himself.'

He pushed past her. 'I have to go.'

And on the next day. 'Paul, we have to talk about all this.'

'Talk. Talk. That's all we've ever had. Talk to yourself; I don't want to listen.'

The silences, night and morning, became more prolonged and painful. He could not concentrate at work for thinking of her, and he needed all of his concentration. He wanted to believe her; God, how he wanted to. They could not go on like this; it was murder. He loved her too much, that was his trouble.

Katy was alarmed at Meg's unsmiling face. 'You are not worrying about those two falling out, are you love? They've always argued, you should know that. They love it. They never bear grudges. Ben will soon be back, you'll see; and Paul pleased to see him.'

'It's much more serious than that, Katy. I can't tell you until I have talked to Paul. And he's not speaking.'

Katy resolved to tackle Ben that night.

Next day as Paul rode his bicycle toward the mine a tall

figure stepped out from the gloom of the bushes at the side of the lane. He had to swerve to avoid him. It was Ben.

'Knock me down if you like. But first listen to what I have to say.'

'Be quick about it. I've more important things to see to.'

'Nothing is more important than this. I've kept out of your way to give you time to settle things between you, but Katy tells me you've not spoken to Meg for days.'

'You're sure it's Katy who told you?'

Ben went on rapidly, ignoring the implication. 'She's your life, you know she is. What's more, you're her life, damn you. She sees no wrong in you.'

'Get out of the way, and mind your own business.'

'You're going to listen to me. Even if you knock my head off when I've finished.' He repeated, word for word, the conversation he had had with Meg that night; stressing how she would not hear a word against her husband. He did not spare himself in describing how jealousy had overcome him. He said nothing of how much he loved her; that was part of his bad luck. He finished by saying, 'Ask yourself, what chance would she have against me? You know what jealousy can do.'

Yes, he knew. My God, he knew. What chance had she had against him either. What a night she must have had, with the pair of them.

'Do you believe me?' Ben was asking.

'Yes, I believe you.' His brother had never been chicken enough to lie. 'Now keep away from both of us.'

He left the mine early that afternoon, to find Lucilla, Walter's niece, minding the shop. Lucilla still looked very much as she had at Katy's wedding, flat chested, freckled, with a mass of red hair. The only jobs available for young women with no training were skivvying and she did not want that, so having become adept at helping in Katy's shop, she offered her services to relieve shopkeepers who needed extra help or time off for any reason, whether it was

257

for an hour or a month. Energetic and efficient she had worked up a good little round for herself. Meg had had to go out, she said, 'to try to book a berth for Canada'. She announced it as coolly as if she were saying she had gone for an ice cream.

Paul's heart skipped a beat as he picked up a letter addressed to both of them which lay open on the sideboard. It was from Mac, telling them of the cancerous growth that was slowly killing his Maisie. 'Try to come, Meg,' he pleaded. 'We have kept the news from you for as long as possible. Now she has only a few months left, and she asks after you constantly.' Poor Mac. Poor Mrs Mac. He had not thought of her much these last ten years; now memories of her flooded over him. Meg had no doubt missed her terribly, especially since Mary Ann died, but she had never moaned about it.

'You have read Dad's letter?' Meg had entered quietly.

'Yes.'

'I must go.'

'Of course.'

She had a booking for tomorrow's sailing. 'I have discussed matters with Lucilla. She will come in for as long as you want her, to look after the shop and do some cooking for you.'

There was no time for all the talking he had planned; he had left it too late. Now it was she who was distant, unreachable, worried about her mother, her mind on plans for her departure.

In a business-like way she showed him the outstanding bills, orders, and the account books kept in her neat hand; she told him about delivery days and where he could get his laundry done. Other than that it was impossible to penetrate the wall of silence they had built up between them, what with Lucilla within earshot, last minute jobs and packing.

She went to say goodbye to Katy and they arranged for Edwin to take her to Liverpool early the following morning. It was midnight before, worn out, at last she was done. As she made for the stairs she suddenly stopped, puzzled, remembering something. 'You were early, Paul. Anything wrong?'

'Nothing.' Inwardly he groaned. God, everything was wrong.

'Goodnight then, Paul.'

He watched her climb the stairs, sagging with weariness. He wanted to call after her, 'Us, that's what's wrong. Me, I'm wrong. I came home to put it right.'

'Meg!'

She turned and looked down at him from the landing, a subdued, quiet little figure. Remembering the animated daughter he had let go, what would Mac think when he saw her? 'We must talk, Meg.'

'Not now.'

'When you come home?'

She smiled at him sadly. 'Yes, Paul.'

Afterwards he could never understand why he did not go to her at that moment and take her into his arms. Why did he not tell her how much he loved her, how much he needed her? 'Forgive me' was all he need have said for that generous warm-hearted girl to open her arms to him. Instead he let the events of the last two weeks take over, changing their lives for ever.

CHAPTER

16

Katy felt as if her world were falling apart. It was like playing a game of ten green bottles; she wondered which would be the next to fall.

Walter was repeatedly ill, Meg had been gone almost six months and Edwin was in India. Mark was abroad; a member of the audience in Manchester had offered to pay the necessary fees for extended studies, so impressed was he with the talent of the young pianist. It was thrilling, of course, and he wrote when he had time, but it was not the same as seeing him regularly.

She had seen nothing of her two younger brothers for weeks. She heard news of Paul through Lucilla, who efficiently ran the bicycle shop for him. She usually left his supper in the oven, for he was not often home before she closed, although he made an effort to see her once a fortnight so that they could go through the books together. Lucilla reported that he was quieter than she had ever known him. She also said that never a day went by without a customer asking, 'When is Meg coming back?' The business ticked over by sale of accessories. Only the very favoured few could afford new bikes; the 1930s was not the time for that.

Everyone said that having Ben to care for had given Ginny new life. She prepared and ate regular meals for the first time for years, because he was there to share them. He had put some semblance of order into her scrapyard, mended her leaking roof, decorated the house from top to bottom, and was in process of bringing running water inside. Being without a regular job, he was able to give more time to his Union work and he had joined the Labour Party. He was free to argue with the bosses when men had grievances, which he did frequently. The brothers had not met since the day Ben had stopped Paul in the lane.

Katy missed them both and longed to see Meg again. Her life felt empty and she found herself thinking of Ted much more than was good for her.

What would Mary Ann make of it all, she wondered. She would doubtless have an idea designed to get them all back together again; she wished she could think up such a scheme.

The doctor had attended Walter so often he was an old friend by now, and kept his bills as low as possible, but they had to be paid. They were constantly short of money.

There was not the means to re-stock the shop shelves; not that many could afford to buy sweets these days. There were eight children next door, in Mary Ann's old house. The family spilled over into Little Cott, although they could never pay the rent of either. Mr Mason earned good money at the foundry, but spent it all on fishing tackle. His wife, a round placid woman, fortunately did not let anything worry her, and had perfected a knack of disappearing whenever the rent man appeared. She and Katy shared many a laugh, despite their difficulties. One day, on a sudden impulse, Katy took all the sweets that were left and shared them

261

between the delighted Masons. She was then able to convert the front room that had been the shop into a sitting room for Marie, where she could do her homework and invite friends, without having to hear the whirr of the sewing machine, which nearly drove her crazy. She wished she could make Marie happy.

If I think positively enough something will happen to ease matters, Katy repeatedly told herself. And one day it did.

A letter arrived from Sally. Now in charge of the Mission for the Blind she told of structural and medical improvements she had been able to organize, with Edwin's help. She could not contain her joy that Edwin had joined her. Katy had guessed for some time that Sally was in love at last, in love with Edwin. Her house in Pelsall had been rented to the government during the war and for some time after, but had been unoccupied since, except for the housekeeper and her gardener husband. 'I am ashamed I have left it for so long,' Sally wrote, explaining that she now intended retiring them on a pension. 'I thought I might want to come back some day, but now that Edwin is with me I shall never return.'

She wanted to give Mark the house, she said, to be held in trust for him by Katy until he was twenty-five; in the meantime she would make him an allowance. 'After that he can sell the house if he wants to,' she added. 'Meanwhile, why don't you and Walter live in it, Katy? Edwin has told me how often Walter is ill and would be better out of the pit. How he would enjoy working in that lovely garden! Edwin also says how much poverty there is at home now, and that you have often said that you would like to run a Reception Home for children in need of care. Would you consider the need great enough to make a reception centre of the Pelsall house?'

Oh yes, there was a need for such a scheme, thought Katy. Unemployment was causing so many problems. People were not so willing to take in extra youngsters as they had been ten years ago. If only she could feed some of the children! She could also take some for short or long stays when mothers were ill or in need of a rest. But it would all cost money, more money than she could lay her hands on.

Her eyes widened in astonishment as she read on. Sally was willing to finance such a project. Her parents had both died recently, she said, and left her 'a small fortune'. 'So please do not feel beholden to me, Katy. I have more money than I know what to do with.'

Katy smiled fondly, as she felt the excitement mounting. Another Sally 'Cause'. She re-read the letter carefully, to ensure she had not misunderstood anything. All her positive thinking had not prepared her for this. She took the letter to where Walter was resting on the bed, to ask his opinion.

'If that's what you want, love,' he said.

She wrote letters to both Sally and Edwin that evening. In answer to her question, 'How does Sally seem?' Edwin replied with typical honesty. 'She looks and is very different from the Sally we knew. Her hair has been cut short to save time. As long as the shift she is wearing is clean she no longer bothers about clothes. Everyone relies on her; she is on call day and night. She has mastered the language; just the sound of her voice brings a look of hope to the face of a blind child. There are so many who need hope.'

He went on to relate the many improvements she had already made before he arrived. The Mission was becoming well known owing to its unusually good medical facilities, resulting in more and more patients pouring in daily, some being brought by other social workers, others making their own painful way. Consequently their camp was always over full and under-staffed, yet no-one was turned away.

He wrote of how happy they both were about the plans for Sally's old home and hoped that Walter would feel better there once he had come out of the pit for good. After he had signed the letter it was as if he were afraid he had painted a faulty picture, for he added, 'Sally is still hauntingly beautiful, her lovely eyes burning with the intensity of all she is doing. I am overflowing with admiration for her.'

'And love, you could have said, Edwin,' whispered Katy thoughtfully as she re-folded her brother's letter. But she guessed that now more than ever he did not have the temerity to suppose he could be worthy of Miss Sally Dilkes.

Sally had already written to her solicitor, setting the whole business in motion. Before many weeks they were installed in Sally's former home, just round the corner from the four good, solid houses Mary Ann had bought which faced the common.

Walter left the pit and they had their first needy cases, much to Marie's disgust. She had been excited at the thought of having such an elegant home and showing off to her friends at Queen Mary's High School in Walsall, where she attended by virtue of a scholarship. She had not envisaged having to share it with the four scruffy urchins her mother insisted on housing. Their father had left home in search of work while their mother was in hospital. They tore round the garden, yelped and climbed trees, calling her names when she looked down her nose at them. It was not long before she was complaining that it was worse than Heath End. She did not mean it, though. She shuddered at the thought of ever going back there. Here, with wide windows overlooking the lawns, she had a lovely carpeted bedroom with a big bed, a place where she could shut herself away from the rest of the world whenever she wanted, a place to put the gramophone and wireless set Edwin had given her before he left, safe from prying eyes and dirty interfering fingers. All this would be Mark's one day. It made her feel sick, just thinking of it.

Walter was content, seeing Katy so happy, but he did not get any better. Sometimes when he had been trying to do too much Katy would find him, seated on a bench, gasping for breath, his face drawn and blue. To help him she gardened herself as much as she could, aided by the four

264

willing boys who loved to be with her. Lucilla also helped in the evenings after Paul's shop was closed. Katy found her a little room in the big house where she could sleep, more convenient to Heath End where she spent many devoted hours caring for Paul as enthusiastically as she worked for Katy.

The doctor brought a ten-year-old lad with a crippled leg, an orphan whom nobody wanted since his grannie died. Katy made a great fuss of him, while Marie felt intense irritation whenever she saw him painfully limping around.

The number of children calling for a hot meal on their way home from school increased rapidly, including the Mason brood. At last Katy had all the children she needed. She had less time to worry about Marie's hostility, which she was relieved did not include Walter. Sometimes she would come across them sitting quietly together in the garden, Marie reading her books, or doing her homework on her lap, her books strewn untidily on the lawn.

One day Lucilla brought the news that Meg's mother had died. She said that already Paul looked more like himself. He was sorry that Meg had lost her mother, but he could now start to plan for her return. The brief, infrequent notes to one another had been unnaturally stilted; unlike their former frank correspondence, they did nothing to unite them. When she came home he could take her in his arms and gently and patiently win back her love: he was eagerly making plans.

He was stunned when she wrote again soon after to say that Mac had had a stroke. 'They were so devoted, Paul. It is pathetic. He is lost without her, and needs a lot of care and attention. I can't leave it all to Liddy. She has five little boys now and not a minute to spare.'

Paul, heavy hearted, visited Katy for the first time in weeks. In her little sitting-room, just the two of them, they talked about everything under the sun, as they had done in the old days at Heath End. They talked about Katy's extended family, about Walter, Paul's mine, and about Raish, who had started drinking again, to Maud's horror. Finally about Ben, Meg and himself. He showed her the latest letter from Canada.

'You want to see your Meg very much, don't you, Paul?'

He nodded. 'I've so much to make up to her.'

'You must go to her.'

'*Me* go *there*! It's impossible.'

'Oh no. What is impossible is for her to come to you. You *must* go, Paul, if only to let her know how much you care. You will sort something out, the two of you, you'll see.'

'There's the mine to think about.'

'It's going well, you say.'

'Like a dream. To think they said there was no coal left in there!'

'The new equipment is installed. And you've a good fireman, you just said so. You've patched up the mine, Paul. Now patch up your marriage.'

Put like that it sounded so simple. 'You're right, of course.'

'Will you go?'

'I shall certainly think about it.'

Another green bottle about to topple off the wall, Katy thought, as she watched him walk away. And she had only herself to blame for that.

Paul contemplated the sailing ticket in his hand. Might as well put it on the fire. Tomorrow he would have been off, sailing toward Meg. What had seemed so simple when he talked to Katy had since become impossible. A roof-fall in the mine had seen to that, trapping four of the men for hours. They had managed to dig them out, but they were all still in Sister Dora Hospital in Walsall, from where he had just returned, after visiting them. The fireman was badly injured; the other three would pull through, given time.

The ticket slipped from his fingers back into the drawer. At least he had told no-one except Katy. Not even Meg; he had intended to surprise her. There would not be another chance now for months. The rest of the work force, most of them youngsters, had been badly scared by the fall. Their dads and grandads still talked about the Pelsall Hall Colliery disaster when twenty-two perished because of water breaking out in old workings. It only needed something like this to set off a variety of fears about an old pit. He could not consider leaving them, at least not until the fireman was back, if he ever was.

Oh Meg! Somehow I have to put down on paper how I feel. I will tell you how I had planned to come. I will send you the ticket. Not that you would doubt my word like I doubted yours. My darling, I have to reach you in the old way, despite the miles separating us.

He reached for pen and ink, but before he could start to write there was an urgent knocking on the door. It was Ben. Sweating and breathless, he pushed past Paul into the house. 'I've murdered him, Paul.' Muddy clay was caked to his clothes and hands.

'Are you drunk, or what?'

'I've murdered him. The old chap. I always said I would, didn't I? I never meant it. It was a mistake. I swear I never meant to do it!' He sank, panting, into a chair. 'But I'm glad he's gone,' he groaned. His face was clammy white despite the glistening beads of sweat: his clothes stank like rotten eggs.

Paul handed his brother a large brandy: normally Ben never touched it; now he drained it at one go. 'I had better get off to the police,' he said as he put his glass down.

'Sit still and tell me what happened while it's fresh in your mind.'

Ben related the nightmare he had just lived through. Heading toward Ginny's, after a solitary walk over the common, he was passing the marlhole, a deep basin-like pit half-filled with water. It was a dangerous spot, left over from the old brickworks, before they moved them to Aldridge. The council were always talking about fencing it round, but nothing was ever done. One or two Cod-Enders, fed up with life, had found a means of ending it there. Children were warned to keep well away, for there was no hope for anyone who slipped down into its coppery depths, the murky grave of cats and dogs that had strayed or been thrown in by owners who could not afford to keep them.

Despite the cloudy night he recognized the familiar arrogance of the drunken figure weaving toward him. Raish was dangerously near the edge and Ben remembered thinking at that moment he wished he would slip and fall in. He had not come face to face with his father for years. He could feel the bile rising in his throat, the old anger quickening his pulse, but decided to pass by without a word, until Raish accosted him.

'It's our Ben, isn't it?' His words, slightly slurred by drink, were nevertheless comprehensible and authorative. 'In a hurry, are you, Benjamin?' He lurched toward him, catching at the lapels of Ben's jacket to steady himself, thrusting his face, reeking with whiskey, close to his. 'Don't like to think of Maudie having the houses, do you Benjamin? Four good solid houses they are; bring us in quite a bit of pin-money. Fancy Polly working her guts out for her children and never having the good sense to make a will!'

He started to laugh sarcastically, hysterically. 'Too busy making money to make a will. Typical of her, that was.' He laughed again.

'Stop it, will you, before I stop it for you.'

'You! All by yourself? Had a good hiding from Paulie, I heard. Chucked you out, didn't he? Now you would have had a nice place of your own if your stupid mother had remembered to make a will, wouldn't you?' he goaded. 'After your brother's wife, were you?'

He had not suspected any such thing, believing like everybody else the quarrel had been about the mine, but Ben's startled reaction told him he had hit the jackpot.

'You *were* after her? Well! Fancy! Little Meg! You bloody fool. Couldn't you do it without being found out? Where do you think I've been tonight?'

'How should I know?'

'You should be able to guess, Benjamin. I have been visiting a nice little lady in Bloxwich. Does Maudie know? Of course not. Does she know I have Rosie regularly? You remember Rosie, don't you, Benjamin. You met her in The Colliers' Arms, the day you stole the cart. She is *our cook* now.' He started to laugh again. 'I have her in the same house. Does Maudie suspect? Of course not.'

Ben pushed him out of the way, first loosening the hands grasping at his jacket. 'Oh, get off home. I don't want to hear any more.'

Raish lurched back toward him. 'All in good time. When I am ready, Benjamin. Would you like me to give you a few lessons on how not to get found out?' he sneered. 'Polly didn't know the half. The women I had without Polly, without *your mother* ever knowing . . . '

This was too much for Ben. He had controlled himself up till then by a superhuman effort. 'I still owe you something for that,' he whispered through gritted teeth. He grabbed his father beneath the elbows, holding him a few inches from the ground, watching the eyes bulge from his bloated face. 'I've a good mind to throw you in the marlhole. Except it would be too good for you.'

Ben paused in his story, his head sinking forward on to his hands for a moment before continuing. 'I let him go suddenly, pushing him away in disgust. He lost his balance and somehow started to slide down the inside surface of the pit. I'd forgotten how close we were to the edge. You know how steep and slippery it is. I was horrified, I was horrified. I tried to drag him back and went over myself. It

269

was darker than the blackest coal mine. I was thrashing about wildly, trying to follow his voice. Do you know what he shouted? As he slid down. Do you know?' Paul shook his head. ' "Polly", that's what he shouted.'

It was Paul's turn to feel a trickle of icy sweat slither down his spine. Remembering his mother's anguished cry, he realized they had each called for the other in their last moments. He had to bend to hear what his brother was saying now; his throat seemed constricted and the deathly pallor had reached his lips. Paul handed him another drink.

'Once I felt the posh material of his jacket between my fingers, and I thought I'd got him, but it straightway slipped away. Soon after that I heard a splash. I was half lying, peering down, for ever it seemed, my heels pushed into a piece of jutting clay, expecting to follow him into the murky water any minute, my heart clanging like a knocking-off buzzer. I felt sure I was going to drown with him.

'I don't know how I clambered to the top. I just stood there, for ages, in the dark. It was then I realized I had his carnation. After all that clambering! It was as if it was stitched to the palm of my hand. Then the clouds suddenly cleared, and in the moonlight I could see Gert sitting on her caravan steps. Staring. Still and staring. It was weird, I can tell you. I turned and ran straight here. I couldn't think where else to go.'

'Where is it now?'

'Where's what?'

'The carnation.'

Ben brought it from his pocket, flattened like a pressed flower. Paul quickly dropped it on to the fire.

'It wasn't intentional. I'd have saved him if I could. Do you believe me?'

Paul did not know at that moment whether he believed him or not. He only knew the old protective instinct was working; he had to get him away from those who would be

270

sure to disbelieve him. There was no hope of saving Raish. He had to save Ben. 'A lot of people won't believe you, that's for sure. Just about everybody in Cod End has heard you say you would kill him some day. Did Gert recognize you?'

'I don't know.'

'Was there anybody else about?'

'Not a soul. They're all still in the pubs. But Maud will report him missing. The sooner I get to the police the better.'

'They will hang you. You won't have a chance, Ben.'

A low moan escaped Ben's lips. 'If I'd intended to kill him it wouldn't be so bad. At least I'd have the satisfaction of knowing I'd done what I set out to do. But that's always been my luck.'

'Let us think this out. Maud won't report him missing for a day or two. Neither will Rose. They're not daft; they probably know he is seeing someone else. Maud will want to keep it quiet, hoping he will be back. How about you? You still out of a job?' Ben nodded. 'So nobody is going to miss you there.' Paul crossed over to the sideboard decisively. 'Take this. A ticket for Canada. Boat sails tomorrow, four o'clock. I was going myself. Nobody knew but Katy, and I told her yesterday it's off because of trouble at the mine. Go and find Meg and persuade her to come home. You'd be too conspicuous on Walsall station; you'll have to walk it to Brum.' He uttered his thoughts rapidly as they came into his head.

Ben was staring at him dazedly.

'Wake up, Ben! We have to think fast. Go and clean up. Shave off your moustache. I had already packed a bag; you can take that. Some of your clothes are still here.' He dived into the drawer again. 'Here's some money.'

'What about Ginny?'

'Haven't you ever stayed out all night? No questions asked, I bet? Ginny would cut off her right arm rather than

271

land you in anything. She will know what to say. You had better be off, before the pubs turn out. Don't let anybody see you. Don't talk to anybody. And don't go spillin it all out when you get to Canada.'

The whole thing took less than half an hour. Paul checked if there was anyone about before pushing his brother through the door. '*Don't write,*' was the last thing he said to him.

He could not send the letter he had intended either. Too dangerous now to tell Meg he had arranged to come. The letter might be opened before it reached her; that would enable them to trace the sailing ticket. He realized it would be best not to write at all for a while.

'You knew I would always look after him, didn't you, Mary Ann?' he whispered as he sat down to consider what he had done.

Before he had time to collect his thoughts there was another knock on the door. Good God, were they after him already? He glanced round to see if there were any tell-tale signs of Ben before he went to answer. It was Ted Willis.

Ted had lived in France, except during the war when he had fought with the British Army. He had had a tough war, but came out of it relatively unscathed, and with many useful connections. They shook hands cordially before Paul poured him a drink. 'Good to see you, Ted. It's been a long time.'

'Started already I see,' Ted commented, glancing at Ben's empty glass. 'Didn't think you touched it.' He had an unmistakeable air of prosperity about him.

'I am on my way back from the funeral. It is a bit late for a call, but you know how it is when families get together. Couldn't pass your door.'

Paul remembered hearing that Ted's mother had died. 'Sorry it's such a sad occasion for you, Ted.'

They exchanged news about their families and their businesses. Ted seemed particularly interested to know how

Katy and Walter were. He was still in the car trade, travelling all over the world, looking at new designs and finding new customers for the French company he represented.

'What is Ben doing now?' he asked as he stood up to go. 'You two had a bit of a barny, I hear?'

An infinitesimal pause before Paul replied, ''Fraid so. We don't see much of each other now, but I understand he went off a couple of days ago looking for work.'

Ted had never seen Paul ill-at-ease before. Anxious, yes, usually worrying over money, but never ill-at-ease. He puzzled about it as he drove off. There were a few people about as he went through Walsall, making their way home from pubs and theatres, but Birmingham Lane, as he turned into it, was deserted, except for one figure whom he thought he recognized. He slowed up. 'Ben!'

The man hurried on as if he had not heard.

Ted stuck his head through the window. 'Ben! Want a lift?'

'Oh, it's you, Ted. Going anywhere near New Street station?'

'Yes. I'll drop you off there.' He opened the door for him, but Ben climbed into the back seat and huddled down as if afraid of being seen. Ted indicated his travelling bag. 'Where are you off to?'

'Me? Oh, I'm going looking for a job.'

Well, that part of the story tallied anyway.

'I saw your Paul tonight. He said you went a couple of days ago.'

'He did? Well, I did intend to, but you know how it is. Couldn't make up my mind.'

There was something strange. Ted was annoyed with himself that he could not put his finger on it.

Raish's body was spotted the following day. Fortunately the news reached Ginny before the police did. Ben? 'He said he was going to find work.' When? 'A couple of days ago.'

273

Where? 'Yorkshire was mentioned.' They searched her cottage for his clothes. Not a single item was found. He had taken them all, hadn't he? He'd said he was never coming back.

If Cod End was split in two before, it was nothing to what it was like now. Some maintained Brookie would be so drunk he probably walked into the marlhole himself, while others argued that not even at his drunkest would he do such a thing. No, it would be that Ben who would give him a shove. He had been heard threatening to kill his dad often enough. But the people who had stuck up for him before, in the dispute about the mine, remained loyal. He was just a lad when he was shooting his mouth off, they said. He hadn't been heard talking like that for ages. It was just as likely to be Paul, they maintained; he didn't like his dad any better. Arguments, for and against, were bitter and prolonged.

Bobby Millard, now a sergeant, visited the mine to question Paul.

'My brother? Last time I saw him was months ago. We did not part on the best of terms, as you may have heard.'

Where was Paul last night, Sergeant Millard wanted to know. He seemed satisfied with his alibi. An injured miner's brother was visiting the hospital last night; they walked back together, parting at the door of Paul's home. Half an hour later Ted Willis was with him. His car had been seen by several witnesses.

They managed to contact Mr Willis, who confirmed he had spent some time with Paul last night. No, he did not see Ben; hadn't seen him for years.

They knew what time Brookie left Bloxwich. A lady had come forward with the information, so they could calculate the approximate time he would arrive in the lane in question. The only person who appeared to have been in the proximity of the marlhole at that time was old Gert. Yes, she had seen a man go by, swerving as if he were drunk. She

274

considered the next question very carefully. No, there had been no-one else in the lane at the time.

At Raish's funeral Katy remembered the glow he was able to bring to her mother's face when he was being kind to her, while Paul thought of the day his thirteen-year-old brother had threatened, 'I wouldn't even go to his funeral.'

That night he found a package pushed through his letter box. It contained his mother's gold chain and pendant. After holding it in his hand for a long time he placed it carefully in the brimming jewellery box Meg had left behind. All the pieces he had chosen for her; one day he would place the box in her hands, even if he had to go to Canada to do it.

Following a few fruitless enquiries in Yorkshire the police closed the file on the death of Horatio Brook. But the village never did.

No amount of knocking brought a reply, although every room in the homestead was lit up. As Ben pushed open the door and stepped inside the first thing he heard was a plaintive cry. A minute or two later Liddy, as if it was the most natural thing in the world to see him standing there in the middle of the kitchen, placed the newly-born baby in his arms. 'There!' she said. 'Go to your Uncle Ben.' He gazed wonderingly at the tiny pink scrap. His brother's child. And Meg's. If only it had been his!

Just a little sentence in a short note from Meg told Paul he had a daughter. 'Laura Ann Brook was born on 1st June, 1924,' she wrote. She also said, 'The package you sent arrived safely. It is proving to be very useful.' That told him that not only had Ben arrived but that he had acquainted her with the whole story.

He was stunned. A child! Why hadn't she told him she was carrying? He calculated she could not have known when she left. It must have been *that time*! A wave of overwhelming remorse and nausea assailed him. No wonder she had not written about it sooner.

Even taking into account how the child was conceived he knew that Meg would be delighted at becoming a mother. He imagined the bubbling enthusiastic letter he would have received under different circumstances. She had mentioned several times she would like to start a family, but he had been insistent they wait until the mine was paying its way. 'When we have children,' he had told her, 'I want to be absolutely certain they will be well provided for. Like you and Liddy were.'

Meg had never argued about it. 'As long as I have you,' she would reply, 'I can wait.' How she had loved him. How could he ever have doubted her? If only he could take her in his arms at this moment. If only they could talk.

There was not a chance of him going to Canada in the foreseeable future. He could neither afford the time nor the money. The further they went into the mine the more it protested about being disturbed; the more costly it became to make safe.

And she said nothing about coming home.

A daughter with one of his mother's names! How long would it be before he saw her? He could not even hazard a guess.

CHAPTER

17

'WE WANT TO get married.'

The sewing dropped from Katy's hands into her lap, her fingers, like the rest of her body, suddenly frozen, despite the warmth of the day.

Marie stood at the window, idly gazing out to where a big lad was mowing the lawns while Lucilla weeded the flower beds. Among the shrubs some of the younger children collected rubbish for burning, calling and arguing with each other as if they were all deaf. What a relief it would be to get away from all this for good. This last year, travelling around the world, meeting interesting people, sleeping in luxurious hotels, had given her a taste for more.

Katy sat transfixed trying to convince herself she must have misheard or that she was dreaming.

The silence in the room caused Marie to spin round from the window. 'Good God! Your face! Anyone would think I had said we want to get buried.'

Through stiff lips Katy forced herself to answer, 'Who is

we?', knowing full well what the answer would be.

'Ted and me, of course. Who else?'

Who else! All these years of secrecy. Now this! 'Dear Lord, help me,' she prayed frantically. 'What can I say?' Her mind in a turmoil, Katy could only play for time.

'But you are only eighteen!'

'Only!' Marie laughed shortly. 'I have seen more of life at eighteen than you have at forty-three. Years don't count for a lot, do they, if you have been content to stick around in a dead hole all your life, like you have.'

'Ted is more than twice your age!'

'Oh, God!' Marie flopped into a chair, picked up a magazine angrily flipping through the pages. 'I knew you would say that. It was Ted who insisted upon us coming back here "to ask permission", as he terms it in his little old-fashioned way.'

'You need our permission until you are twenty-one.'

'You wouldn't know, of course,' Marie replied, heavily sarcastic, 'but there are places in the world where we could have been married. Then you would have just heard of it by letter. I told Ted that would be the better way; you would have had to accept it then. We have *done the right thing*, so don't be awkward, Mother.'

Katy's mind was fogging with rising panic. How could she suddenly announce that Marie could not marry Ted because he was her father. What effect would it have on the overwrought girl, she wondered, studying the petulant face as she slung the magazine across the table.

She thought back to the day just over a year ago when she had reluctantly agreed to let Marie go with Ted as his secretary. Like thousands of others she had been unable to find a job, despite a year's intensive training at Walsall Commercial College, with certificates to prove shorthand speeds of one-hundred-and-sixty words per minute, and that she could type faster than most. She was daily becoming more bored and disillusioned when Ted turned up out of the blue during one of his occasional visits to his family. Whereas Marie irritated everyone else by her rudeness and inconsideration, she made Ted laugh. He admired her outspokenness and became fully aware of her for the first time. Since he had seen her last she had grown into quite a beauty with a tall perfectly-proportioned body.

'If she comes with me she will have to work hard,' he said. 'But she won't be bored, I promise you that.'

'She is very young, Ted,' Katy had protested.

'So! It is far better for her to travel with me than alone, which she *will* do, Katy. You won't keep her here. Marie will follow her instincts.' He quirked an eyebrow playfully. 'Unlike the young Katy Brook! You know that privately you would have loved to do what she has the chance of doing now. If it hadn't been for the way your father behaved toward Mary Ann you would have come with me like a shot. Didn't trust me, did you? You still don't.'

He took her worried face between his hands gently. 'I won't let any harm come to her,' he said with unusual seriousness. 'Give her a chance. I shall care for her like a father.' Katy recalled how her heart had missed a beat at that. 'Because she is yours,' he added softly.

Even Walter, tired and ill, knowing what no-one else except she and Sally knew, said, 'Let her go, love.' So between the three of them she had been persuaded.

'Anyway, you have your own life. What does it matter to you what I do?'

Marie's impatient voice jerked her back to the present problem. How rigidly Walter and herself had stuck to the pact agreed with Sally. Even now it seemed wrong to break it without her consent.

'It matters a lot what you do, because I love you, Marie.'

'No, Mother,' Marie replied scathingly. 'You only *think* you love me. Oh, you have tried, I grant you that. But you've never loved me like you love Mark.' Katy knew the truth of this; Mark had been so easy to love. 'We are totally incompatible, you and me. We can only take each other in small doses.'

It was like a voice from the past; Sally, talking about her relationship with her mother, on the day she first offered her unborn child to Katy. 'We can't bear to be together for more than five minutes,' she had said. 'You are just as likely to be incompatible with your own mother as anyone else.' She had also said: 'Just because you are born to someone does not mean you own them; or they you.' She had certainly never tried to own the child born to her, choosing to ignore her existence when she wrote, yet never failing to mention Mark. Now it was Marie who was voicing the hurtful words, 'We are totally incompatible.' The daughter she had wanted so badly! What went wrong? How cruel fate could be.

She mustered all her wits. If only she could persuade her to wait, things might sort themselves out. 'Ted has been married before.'

'Do you think I don't know? That was all over years ago.'

'So he could end his marriage to you in the same way. Wait for a while, Marie,' she pleaded. 'One of you might feel differently in a year's time. I know this age gap does not seem to matter now, but in ten years' time Ted will be fifty-three, and you will still be young.'

'So will he. Some people always are.'

'Do you love him?'

'Love? What is love? I have never found out.'

'You might, later, with someone younger. There's lots of time. What if you fall in love later, Marie?'

'What if I do? I don't want to marry some inexperienced pauper in his twenties still attached to his mummy's umbilical cord. Ted's good fun. We like to be together. And he has plenty of money. Oh, what I can do with money!'

'It isn't the most important thing.'

'*Really?* I seem to remember it was manna from Heaven to you when that woman in India decided to share some of hers. When she decided to give Mark the house! And you could realize your dream. To fill the house with children. None of them your own,' she added cruelly. She shrugged. 'It's no use, Mother. I shall marry Ted, and that's that.'

'Leave it for now, Marie. I shall talk to Ted.'

'Please yourself.' Marie jumped up and walked to the door, where she turned and looked straight at Katy, her face filled with defiance. 'You won't change his mind, if that's what you think.'

'Are you jealous?'

'Ted! You know it's not that. She is too young.'

'Oh, come on, Katy. I bet Marie was grown up at ten. She knows exactly what she wants, you are bound to realize that.'

'Are you in love with her, Ted?'

'I have loved only one woman, Katy, and she wouldn't have me.'

'Then *why?*'

'Why? Because I am very fond of her, we are happy together, she's a damn good secretary, she wants to get married, and so do I.'

'Wait, Ted. Please, I beg of you, wait a while.'

'I can't keep waiting for you, love, can I?' he replied flippantly. 'First it was security you wanted, then Walter and the babes. Now it's a Children's Home. I can't fight a Children's Home, Katy. If I can't have the girl's mother . . . '

'Stop this Ted. Stop it! You *can't* marry her.'

'Why, Katy!' He was amazed to see her face wet with tears. Katy did not cry as a rule. 'Does it mean so much to you? Don't let's deny her a bit of happiness. Not knowing who her own parents are has mixed her up terribly. Some people can take that, and others can't . . . '

281

'Ted!' she interrupted him, 'Stand beside her in front of a mirror and *look at her.* Can't you *see*? Oh, Ted, can't you see who her parents are?'

He stared at her, uncomprehending. 'What on earth are you talking about?'

'You and Sally, that's what I am talking about.'

'Sally? Sally who?'

It was her turn to stare disbelievingly. He could not even remember her name. Her voice was hoarse with emotion. 'Sally Dilkes.' Forgive me, Sally. He has to know.

'Sally Dilkes,' he repeated stupidly; then suddenly remembering, 'Oh, Sally! I haven't thought of her for years.'

The times she had felt jealous of Sally's union with Ted! The wasted emotion she had spent on a passing affair that had meant nothing to either of them. Even now what she was trying to tell him had not registered. She had to spell it out. 'Marie is your daughter, Ted. Yours and Sally's.'

'You can't mean it?' His face was a mixture of shock and disbelief.

'Would I lie to you about this, Ted?' The secret was out at last and breaking down she sobbed uncontrollably. For herself and Walter, for Sally and Ted, and most of all for Marie.

'Katy, don't cry. I can't bear to see you cry.' He wiped her face with his handkerchief. 'Come now. My love! All these years!' In a moment she was in his arms. Oh, the comfort of those arms as he took her gently to him.

He laid her head on his chest while he stroked her hair tenderly until the sobs subsided. After a time he lifted her chin and kissed it lightly. 'Why didn't you tell me? We could have shared her all these years.

'When you asked me why I wanted Marie, do you know what I longed to say? Because she is part of you. Because you want her to be happy.'

'So this is how you talk to Ted, is it?'

They sprang apart as they realized the door had opened without them hearing a thing. How long had she been there? How much had she heard? Marie stood watching them, her eyes wild, her body shaking with rage, her voice cynical.

'I might find someone younger, did you say, Mother? You were *so* concerned. Of course you were. You wanted him for *yourself*.'

Her voice rose until it was almost a scream.

'You asked me to wait,' she shouted. 'How long would you like me to wait? Until Walter dies?'

She grabbed Katy, so much smaller, and shook her savagely. 'Are you waiting for him to die? Is that it?'

'No, Marie. No!'

'Don't do that to her, Marie.' Ted's voice was raised as he pulled her away. 'Don't do that,' he repeated sternly, holding her off from Katy.

She rounded on him, mad with jealousy. 'You want me because I am part of her, do you? I have never been part of her. Take your hands off me,' she screamed. 'Liars! Both of you!'

'What is going on?' Walter stood at the open door, his dressing-gown hanging loosely on his thin body, his face hollow and strained. 'What's all this noise? The children will . . . will . . . hear . . . you.' His voice was rasping with breathlessness.

Katy fetched him to a chair. 'Walter, sit down, love.'

'Oh yes. Sit down, love,' Marie mimicked. 'Sit down and hear how I found these two in each other's arms. I expect they have been carrying on for years, unknown to you, Dad.'

'Marie! Don't!' Katy's voice was sharp, her eyes fixed on Walter's grey, hurt face, as he began to cough. 'Can't you see what you are doing?'

Marie laughed wildly. 'Want it all ways, don't you, Mother? One man isn't enough, is that it? Go on, ask her,

Dad. Why doesn't she want me to marry Ted? Why does she want me to wait?'

'Marry? Ted!' Walter swayed in his chair. Only Katy's arms prevented him from falling. His breath became even more laboured. 'Tell her, Katy, love. It's time to . . . ' His voice gave out, as he fought for breath.

'I will, Walter. But first let's get you to bed.'

When Katy returned, Ted was breaking the news as gently as he could. 'It's no wonder we were so happy together, from the start, dear, is it? No wonder we cared for one another. I do care for you, very much, Marie.'

Angry tears welled up in her eyes. 'So you, and *her*?'

'Not Katy, no. She did adopt you as a baby, as she has always told you.'

'Who, then? Presumably if you are my father, you know who my mother is?'

He glanced across at Katy, who nodded, so he went on to tell the rest.

'Sally Dilkes! You mean that woman in India Edwin is potty about?' She began to laugh wildly, like a person demented. 'Sally Dilkes, my mother! And she gave this house to *Mark*. Not to me, her daughter! To Mark!'

Katy watched in agony as Marie's face crumpled. She had been jealous of Mark, because of the value of the house bestowed upon him. Now she was experiencing the intolerable hurt of being passed over for someone else by her real mother. 'My poor child,' Katy murmured.

'Your child! I am not yours. Nor hers. I am nobody's child. Nobody's!' The awful laughter gradually changed to deep, dry, gasping sobs as she ran from the room. Ted put out a restraining hand when Katy would have followed her.

'Leave her. Give her time. She has a lot to come to terms with. As we all have.' He took her hand gently. 'Stay here with me, Katy.'

Walter died early next morning, his remaining lung collapsing. It had been a long slow death sentence the pit had inflicted on him, more cruel than the instant annihilation of a man by a rock-fall witnessed by Paul.

Marie sobbed unrestrainedly when she heard of Walter's death, and at the funeral. 'He was the only one who ever really cared,' she told Ted as they sat together afterwards in Katy's little sitting-room.

'I would like to carry on where he left off, if you will allow me. You know, it's rather wonderful, discovering I have a daughter. We have years to catch up on, Marie. I would like to do so much for you.'

'Such as?'

'Well, let's see. First and foremost I would like you to feel you can always come to me when you need help.' He smiled mischievously. 'Then there is that car I was going to give you as a wedding present. No earthly reason I should not give one to my daughter, is there?'

Mm, it could be almost as advantageous having a rich father as a rich husband. Perhaps more so. The double row of thick lashes so like his own veiled her eyes completely, but she could not hide her thoughts from him. He watched the cunning little smile play around her lips and laughed aloud; it was not long before she was laughing with him. They had learned quite a lot about each other this past year.

He talked with her about the future. He could pull a few strings to get her a job in the London office, he said. A flat, too, if that was what she wanted. He would be in London himself for a time, so would be able to take her about, to restaurants and theatres, introducing her to people; or alternatively she could continue to travel around with him as his secretary. If that was her choice she would never climb beyond that, whereas the London office would offer opportunities for advancement. Maybe she would have her own secretary in a few years' time. His firm believed in opportunity for women.

It seemed incredible that in a time of mass unemployment and poverty he could arrange all this. Not a bad father to be saddled with, Marie reflected. Things did not look so bad after all.

'Take time to consider it carefully,' he advised.

She decided she would take lots of time.

He also talked to her about Katy and himself, from the time they had played tip-cat together and waded into Billy Button's Brook, she with her dress in her knickers, to the time when she had opted for security and children. 'In one way she was a bit like you. Suspicious of marrying for love, was Katy. Her father had seen to that.'

'Seems like she backed the wrong horse,' commented Marie drily. 'Will you marry her now?'

'Would you believe she's turned me down again? You are the most important person now, she says; seems to think you would resent it if we married. She wants to see you happy. That's her priority at present.'

Incredulity showed on the girl's face.

'You see, Marie, she does care for you very much.'

'Not as much as she does for Mark.'

'Maybe not. What's new about that? Boys are always the favourites with mothers. I know we were in our family. You were Walter's favourite.' He grinned. 'As you would have been mine. It works the other ways with Dads.'

'Attraction of the opposite sex?'

'Yes.' He took her hand gently. 'You see, you have been inclined to make a very ordinary situation into something extraordinary, my love.'

The problems that had plagued her seemed less insurmountable as they talked. There had been a comfortable rapport between them from the moment he took her away to work with him; it helped now.

A little frown appeared between her brows.

'Something else bothering you?'

'Yes. How could my real mother give her home to

someone else, knowing she had a daughter?'

'Well, I suspect, partly because she would not wish to intrude on Katy's mother-role, which she herself abandoned, and partly because of her feelings for Edwin, Mark's father. Nothing personal relating to you, dear. Anyway, you do not need a Sally-benefactor now, do you? You have won money-bags me.'

That was true. She decided she would make the most of her prize while the going was good. She might end up richer than Mark.

Mark was at the funeral of the gentle, quiet man who had been such a good father to him while unselfishly sharing him with Edwin. Dear, calm, loving Mark. It had been a therapy for Katy to have him near during the last two days after the recent traumas. It was agony to say goodbye when he left, after the funeral, for a pre-arranged concert in Italy, where he was becoming well known as a concert pianist. Ted and Marie left together, Marie having decided to stay in a London hotel for the time being.

When they had all gone Paul joined Katy in the garden where the dusk of evening was stealing in quietly. Mingling with the bird sounds they could hear the occasional shouts of older children playing in the distant orchard, the younger ones already in bed. It was a time for reminiscing. They recalled the day Walter had not turned a hair when Katy had spent the whole of his savings on a piano. 'If that's what you want, love,' he had always replied to her every request.

They talked about Heath End. Paul had sold up the stock of his bicycle shop some years ago to a Walsall dealer. For one thing, he needed the money to plough into the mine: for another, trade in Heath End was at a standstill since Rushall Lane had been widened and re-made, as a major unemployment relief scheme, and buses ran through the village, linking Pelsall with Walsall. The penny each way bus fare could easily be recouped by lower town prices.

Sarah's shop had closed, and the barber had found rented accommodation in town. Slowly the Cod End they knew was dying.

Once again they looked at the photograph Paul had received last month of Laura, a miniature Meg, dimpling with pride as she held the reins of her pony. On the back of the photograph was written: 'Laura, on her sixth birthday'. Paul had sent a little silver bracelet with hair slides to match. She was wearing the slides, one on each side of her hair.

'I shall be seeing her soon,' Paul announced. 'Tomorrow I am off to Thomas Cook's to book a berth to Canada.'

'You have done it at last! About time.'

Yes, it was about time. Yesterday he had finally wound up the mine, leaving it safe and ready for future development if ever he, or anyone else, had the chance. He had waited until, one by one, his men had managed to find some form of employment; it had been a long slow harrassing process. He had not been able to replace the fireman whose injuries prevented him returning; since that day there had never been anyone he could have confidently left in charge. Despite the heavy maintenance costs and low coal prices that had plagued him all these years he had never lost faith in the mine's potential. Yet it was with overwhelming relief that he had worked his last day yesterday.

What had meant so much to him seemed as nothing now compared with the aching longing to see Meg and Laura. For a time, after Ben went, they had hardly corresponded at all, Paul considering it best until the police lost interest in Raish's death. After that it had been impossible to pick up the threads. He had attempted to write of his feelings for her, to explain his remorse at what had happened, to regain the old familiarity, but he had failed miserably. Not until he held her in his arms would he be able to convince her.

'It is all forgiven and forgotten now, Paul,' she wrote briefly, but never a word about coming home. Mac was paralyzed down the whole of one side, she explained, and could hardly speak. For the first time Paul considered seriously the tragedy of Mac, finding it difficult to picture him as anything but the big, bluff, commanding figure, dwarfing all the other farmers, as he and Arthur steamed into Moose Jaw station. He could understand how impossible it was for Meg to abandon him. 'Can't imagine how we would have managed without our extra help,' was how she referred to Ben.

Paul was weary of the emptiness of living without her. Soon he would be hearing her laugh and sing again. He did not mind if she wanted to stay in Canada for ever, provided he could be near her. It would feel good to see Ben as well.

After Paul left, Katy continued to sit in the now still garden, pondering over the past few days, feeling frighteningly lonely. They would all be gone, Mark and Ted, Marie, and her three brothers. Always before there had been Walter to care for, Walter by her side when she slept. The last few nights the old nightmare had recurred; again she was running, panic-stricken, afraid to glance over her shoulder to discover who was chasing her. When she did make herself turn, because there was nowhere else to run, there was nothing but an empty meadow, an ominous silence and a little jenny wren. That silence seemed to close round her now, all the children having gone indoors. She was going to miss Walter, yet he had been so ill she could not wish that he had lived; only that the unhappy doubt she saw in his eyes before he died had not been there. He had tried so hard to make her happy.

'Penny for them.' It was Lucilla holding the ten-month-old baby placed in their care while his mother was in the sanatorium. Since Paul had closed his shop Lucilla had worked full time for Katy. She loved the work almost as much as Katy herself. 'He was protesting so loudly I decided to give the others a bit of peace.'

Katy looked up gratefully into Lucilla's plain understanding face. Poor Lucilla. She had long cherished an aching love for Paul. She would have done anything for him, but had resigned herself to the fact that his heart belonged to one woman and always would. Brave, kind, hard-working Lucilla.

Katy held out her arms to take the baby. He immediately began to bounce and chuckle, despite the tears lingering on his lashes. The awful emptiness in her breast receded a little. 'We shall take a nice walk tomorrow, my little lad,' she said as she hugged him close.

Tomorrow. Who could tell what tomorrow might bring? She must take it and be grateful for it, and every tomorrow. Tomorrow Paul would be buying his ticket for Canada and she must be happy for him, even though she would miss him very much.

The next morning there was an envelope from Canada. Eagerly Paul tore it open. Two letters. As he read the first he sat down heavily, weighed down suddenly by a stone where his eager heart had been.

The letter from Meg was longer than usual. In it she asked for a divorce so that she could marry Ben. The words began to bounce about like a flickering Davy lamp, and he had to read them again slowly to make any sense. 'Ben has been like a father to Laura since the day she was born, and she loves him very much. Dad's eyes light up as soon as Ben appears; he is so patient with him, spending long hours working on exercises to get his limbs moving. He manages the farm as if he was born to it, instinctively knowing what needs to be done . . . a load off my shoulders . . . ' Ben's dreams were all coming true. 'I'll dream about owning a farm while you dream about owning a pit,' he had once said. Paul's eyes blurred as he read on.

'I shall never come back to England, Paul, and we both feel it would be best for Laura if we were married.' She ended by saying, 'I have developed a very deep affection for Ben, as we all have.'

He re-read the letter several times, searching for some clue that might leave him a little hope, some indication that she did not really mean it.

At last he opened the other letter. He was surprised by the surge of emotion that swept over him as he recognized his brother's untidy scrawl.

'Paul. You said ask her to come home. It was no use, I saw that from the start. She could not have turned her back on the situation here. I have tried to care for them as you would have done. Please help us to find happiness together. P.S. I love them both very much.'

The letters fluttered from his trembling fingers on to the floor. Deep hopeless sobs racked his body as his head fell on to his arms. It was the first time he had cried since Mary Ann died. This time there were no loving arms to comfort him.

CHAPTER

18

At first Paul thought he would go mad with despair and loneliness. It never occurred to him to refuse their request; he it was who provided the necessary evidence for the divorce.

'Keep occupied. Work every minute,' counselled Katy, finding him jobs to do at the big house, gardening, repairing, decorating, never allowing him to stop for long enough to brood. She was reminded of the time they had all tried to keep Edwin busy, while Paul recalled his mother's poem, 'Must work, in order to forget the magic that is you.'

In spite of busy days there were often sleepless nights when he re-lived the agony of finding Meg in his brother's arms, followed by the insane jealousy that had struck him like lightning on a summer's day. When he did drop off to sleep he would wake suddenly, bathed in sweat, hearing again her breathless pleadings and little sobs of protest as he brutally humiliated her the following morning. His shame was almost more than he could bear, and when the long drawn-out divorce proceedings were complete, it seemed like an act of punishment he fully deserved.

Strangely, after her marriage to Ben, they were again able to communicate in their old relaxed manner. It was as if the relief of being able to legitimately start a new life put back the sparkle into Meg's inimitable style of writing, making it easier for him to respond. Occasionally there was a brief postcard from Ben; he guessed she cajoled him into writing it. Once he wrote: 'Every day is a happy day now, thanks to you.'

Paul knew what he meant; such happiness had been his. Now it was Ben who held her in his arms each night. For Ben she would laugh, and sing, and chatter as she once did for him.

She wrote of all the 'first times' in a child's life; of how Laura could hold her own with Arthur's five boisterous boys; of Mac's slow progress; of development in Moose Jaw; of life on the farm.

He was able to keep her up to date with news of Katy's ever-changing family, of postcards from Marie as she travelled the world with Ted, of Mark's success in London. He told her how once Ted came home alone, arranging with Lucilla to hold the fort, while he took Katy to hear Mark play. After spending a day in London with Mark they motored to the south coast, from where Katy returned refreshed and starry-eyed as she described great pounding seas on craggy rocks, which reminded her of a painting she had once admired at Lawson's Sale. She was curiously pensive for a few days after Ted left again for France.

He told how Sally had reported to Katy that Edwin was often sick and weak but refused to leave India. 'We love each other,' Sally wrote, 'but Edwin has always been far too timid to ask me to marry him. Now I regret not asking him.'

Their exchange of letters, although no substitute for flesh

and blood, helped tremendously in returning a sense of normality to Paul's life. To be in touch with Meg, to be able to imagine her merry face as she wrote, was in his opinion more than he deserved.

He regularly enquired at the mines for a job. Even if there had been one available they would have had to be desperate to offer it to him, for he was the brother of that trouble-shooter, Ben Brook, to say nothing of the fact he had opened up in opposition to them. Thought he could go it alone, hadn't he? Let him suffer the consequences.

He was beginning to despair of ever working again. Then one day as he was leaving the office of Five Ways Colliery, someone shouted, 'Paul! How's it going, mate?'

In the sidings were several coal merchants' lorries backed up to huge coal trucks, each driver furiously shovelling coal from truck to lorry as if his life depended on it, for after three days, rent was charged daily on the trucks.

Perched high above him was Jackie Lee, his former stall-mate at Conduit when they had both been saving to get married, an incentive resulting in higher earnings for them than for any other face worker. Paul had heard that Jackie owned his own lorry. The black grime covering his face, encrusting even his eyelashes, could not hide his obvious delight at seeing Paul again.

Paul immediately grabbed a spare shovel, hopping into the truck alongside Jackie, via the lorry. No words were wasted until the job was finished, and they were heading toward Jackie's home in Norton. Jackie had kept on the house after his wife died of TB, he explained, and his two children were looked after by his married sister across the road. Once home he made a pot of tea and filled two mugs to the brim.

He took several appreciative sips before asking again, 'How are things going?' He had heard of Raish's death, of course, and about the bitter fight of the two brothers. The issue was still debated regularly, whenever the topic of conversation in pubs or clubs turned to the marlhole, Ginny, or fights. Folk never ceased to speculate why neither Ben nor Meg had returned home. Oddly enough it never occurred to anyone to link the two. Meg's love for Paul had shone like a beacon, so was never for a moment in doubt.

'Things could be worse,' Paul answered non-committally.

'How about the mine? I was surprised when I heard you had jacked it in. All that new equipment you installed! My dad used to work there years ago; he said it should never have been closed. Reckoned there are hundreds of tons yet, for the fetching.'

'That's my opinion.'

'Then why?' Jackie was frankly puzzled. To give up, no matter what the difficulties, was completely out of character, according to what he remembered of Paul's dogged persistence.

Paul hesitated. How could he begin to explain the consequences of a sailing ticket which he gave away, resulting in him giving up the mine because he had hoped to buy another? So he simply replied, 'Lack of funds.'

Jackie considered this quietly for a moment or two, eyeing Paul keenly as he finished his drink. 'I have some money saved. How about me coming in with you?'

It was sufficient to focus Paul's whole attention.

'Not just with cash,' Jackie continued, 'but with this.' He flexed his arm muscles. 'I am delivering only three days a week, and I could spread that out if need be. The rest of the time I could work in the mine with you. We could share my coal round as well, combining the two businesses. No middleman's profits to pay that way.'

Paul could not hide the stir of excitement he felt. Jackie listened intently as he explained how he had sunk a shaft three or four miles from the original workings, and had gone deeper than ever before, where there was plenty of coal left. It was hardly an economic proposition at the moment, though, he cautioned, what with low prices and rising stocks.

Jackie was not to be put off. He was looking for a long-term investment. 'I have two lads,' he stated simply. 'There's another war brewing, Paul,' he added seriously. 'They will want more coal than they can lay their hands on.'

Paul arranged to meet him at the mine next day, where he was careful to point out all the snags, but Jackie was still keen, and soon they were in production again. They each invested the same amount of money, opening an account at the bank which combined their two names, Brooklee Mine. They set on Percy, Ben's old mate, and his brother, both experienced unemployed miners who agreed to a profit-sharing scheme instead of wages.

This time, Paul felt, things would be different. This time he was not alone. There were four men, each with a stake in the success or failure of the venture, each one prepared to work his guts out.

Jackie was right. War came the following year, 1939, and every ounce of coal was needed. Coal mining became a Reserved Occupation. They even recruited men into the pits, Bevan Boys they called them, and jobs were offered to those who opted to transfer from the forces. The pits begging for workers instead of the other way round; it was incredible!

Brooklee Mine gradually increased its workforce to thirty men, every one of them working flat out for as many hours as they had strength. Paul found there was no time for looking back, or looking forward for that matter. Each day unto itself; that was as far as anyone dared plan.

Suddenly everyone in Cod End was working, including the women, some in Walsall munitions factories, some on the buses. They had money to spare for the first time in their lives and nothing to spend it on, everything being rationed, food and clothes, bed-linen and furniture. Carpets, rugs and lino disappeared speedily from Dickinson's store, not to be seen again until after the war.

Cod End had a comparatively easy war, with just a few incendiaries to cope with and countless nights spent shivering in Anderson shelters as the bombers droned overhead on their way to Birmingham or Coventry. Katy's large house was crammed full with evacuees from those two cities, mostly children, but sometimes mothers came too. She and Lucilla worked from dawn to dusk, cleaning, washing and scheming how to produce nutritious food from the meagre rations allowed. Their spirits soared or sank according to how long it had been since they had heard from Mark or Marie.

Mark had joined the R.A.F. and Marie became a W.A.A.C. driver, mainly ferrying officers about. It was a great relief when they heard, during the second year, that Mark's musical talents had been discovered, resulting in him entertaining the troops. Katy offered a prayer of thanks; she had found it impossible to imagine him killing anyone.

Soon after the war started two sad letters came, one from India saying that Edwin had died in Sally's arms, and news from Meg that her father had been killed by a second stroke. The impact of both letters was less than it would have been in normal times, wireless and newspaper announcements being so crammed with news of loss of life every day.

At last the end came: May 1945 and V.E. Day, and everyone could relax. They could pause to laugh or cry at news they had forced themselves to be stoical about. Katy could begin to look forward with enlightened heart to seeing Mark and Marie again. Her mothers with children returned to their own homes; others collected their offspring or arranged for them to stay longer until they found somewhere to live. There were some who had been orphaned by the bombings who would never return to their own homes.

Both Mark and Marie managed to telephone. The joy of hearing their voices and knowing the danger was over sufficed to renew Katy's flagging energy. Marie announced she had plans to marry a rich Colonel who owned homes in Berkshire, New York and the Bahamas.

No one knew where Ted was. His company had been involved in supplying vehicles to the forces. He had been in France at the time of its occupation and since then they had heard nothing from him. Marie was convinced, like Katy, that he was alive, and said she would postpone her wedding until they could all be together; she very much wanted Ted and Mark to be there. She sounded different, more human; Katy was overjoyed at the thought of their relationship improving.

The war had been over for nearly a month when the awful news came. Mark had been killed by an unexploded bomb. A friend of his wrote to Katy to tell how, minutes before, he had been walking along a quiet beach, enjoying the sunset. She could picture him, with his easy relaxed stride, listening to the music of the waves, the sound of the gulls, a melody born of nature in his head. How he would be looking forward to the peace, the peace he had always appreciated, the life he loved. Now there was no more life for him, no more music, no more love for her to share.

'It had been such a perfect summer's day,' his comrade wrote. On such a day Mark was born, the day her tears dropped silently on to his little face, the day she had first taken him into her arms and into her heart, her grief mingled with the joy of anticipation. Now her silent tears smudged the words the young man had been kind enough to write, and she had nothing to anticipate.

Nothing left of Edwin, nor of Charlotte. It was as if when Mark died, they died again. The dear sweet son they had given her; she had loved him so much. Why did it have to happen to him? Every sleepless night her aching heart asked the question that mothers all over the country were asking, and to which there was no answer.

CHAPTER

19

Paul WOULD NEVER forget the day Laura came. He was walking home from Katy's one sunny afternoon, and there she stood on the doorstep, her finger on the door-bell, her suitcase at her side, as bright and lively as if she had just walked up Rushall Lane. He thought at first she was a mirage, born of an old longing.

'Oh, there you are,' she said, as he approached. 'I'm Laura.

It was as if they had known one another from the day she was born. She was Meg all over again, the same ease of manner, the same merry eyes and humorous little mouth, the same irrepressible laugh. She was about the same age as Meg had been when she and Paul first met.

She stood beside him in the kitchen as he poured boiling water into the teapot. 'You didn't get the letter?'

'About you coming? No.'

The war had been over for only a few weeks and the mail was haywire.

'They told me to go to Aunt Katy's; she would have room for me. But I wanted to see you first.'

'I should think so!'

He carried the tray into the attractive living-room her mother had furnished. She looked around as she settled herself comfortably into an armchair, gazing long at Edwin's pictures.

'Can I stay here? Until I have sorted myself out?'

'As long as you like.'

The letters to himself and Katy came a few days later, explaining that Laura wanted to finish her nursing training in England. She had asked to come for ages, but they had refused to consent during the war. 'She is determined to see you, Paul,' Meg wrote. He could understand that, remembering Marie's curiosity about the parents she had not known.

After a week it was as if she had always been there, a Peter-Pan Meg who had never grown any older. They chatted a lot, as he and Meg used to in those precious far-off days, filling in for each other the events of the long years apart.

'Mom told me all about you,' she said one day, laughing. 'How you came to Canada and swept her off her feet, carrying her off to England; or rather, enticing her to follow.'

'I didn't have the good sense to hold on to her, did I?'

'She loved it here. It seems to have been the big highlight of her life. She has never forgotten the folk she made friends with. All my life I've known about Ginny, Gert and Sarah, my grandmother who died, and all the families in the village.'

'Does Ben ever talk about it?'

'Oh, yes, they often chat together about this place. But they talk about you separately,' she added frankly.

'They do? Why is that, do you think?'

'I reckon it's because Mom still carries a banner for you. Every time your name's mentioned or a letter comes from

301

England her eyes light up in that sort-of special way. Best that Uncle Ben doesn't see it, I guess.'

'Why?' he asked again.

'Because she is his life,' she answered simply.

'As she was mine.' He remembered Ben pointing that out to him on the day Mac's letter arrived.

'Uncle Ben told me what you did for him, on that night . . . '

'There's not much you don't know, young lady, is there?'

'He wasn't guilty of anything wrong, you know.'

Paul gazed into the trusting hazel eyes. She had grown up with a man granted happiness in circumstances that could have been tragic for him. He doubted if she knew anything about that *other* night. He doubted if she had ever known the Ben of old, often bitter and angry. Ben with his farm would be a different man to the Ben who worked down the pit.

As if reading his thoughts she said, 'He is very quiet and brooding sometimes. We call them his black moods. Only Mom can coax them away. She says how close you and Uncle Ben used to be. Have you forgiven him for stealing Mom and . . . '

'There is nothing to forgive, Laura. I loved them both.'

'Have you been lonely, Dad?'

It was the first time she had used the term, and it seemed the most natural thing in the world, so it was odd that it brought such a lump to his throat. 'Very,' he admitted.

'But not any more.' She put her arm round his neck affectionately, 'Since you have me.'

'Not any more.'

She was a ray of sunshine chasing away the heavy shadows that had hung around him for what seemed an eternity. He took her about as much as he could, so proud to say, 'Meet my daughter.' Many of his old neighbours who remembered Meg thought they were seeing double.

302

They often talked well into the early hours. She gave him a full description of each of Arthur's five sons, and told how Liddy ruled them all with a rod of iron. It seemed they were each different in temperament, yet all were happy to be farmers. Five sons! Arthur's own little empire. If Liddy ever allowed them to get married Arthur would have a brood of grandchildren, all with their roots firmly planted in Canadian soil. Laura said that none of them showed the slightest desire to come to England, even for a visit. They had heard a completely different report of the old country from their mother than Laura had received from hers; you would think the two sisters had visited two entirely different places, she said.

'Whom do you agree with now you have seen for yourself?'

'Who do you think?' she laughed merrily.

For a couple of weeks she was there every day, polishing and cleaning his house, cooking him delicious meals as Meg had done, until she was installed at the Sister Dora Hospital in Walsall. She had written to them before she came, explaining she was anxious to attain her midwifery certificate, a training not so readily available in Canada. She slept at the Nurses' Home, but came to Paul whenever she was off duty. He tried to arrange his times at the mine to be with her as much as possible. Life was worth living again; he felt he had much more than he deserved.

Often Laura helped Katy with the children at the big house. Mark had made a will leaving the house to Katy; his few possessions, including Edwin's pictures, he left to Marie. To Katy's surprise Marie seemed delighted about the paintings and came to collect them. She propped some of them against the wall, scrutinizing them in detail. They all depicted life as it had been for pitmen before the war.

One portrayed a misty morning, a long boat heavy with coal moving along the canal, as two boys hurtled the lock arms, their faces set anxiously toward the distant pit shaft.

The contrast between the slow boat, the speed of the runners, and the menacing blackness of the shaft produced an eerie awe-inspiring picture. Edwin had entitled it 'Five Miles to Run'.

Another, called 'Pay Day', showed a long orderly queue of blackened miners at a pay window, weary, resentful, humiliated by the domineering presence of a stern-faced policeman watching over them, intent on keeping order.

'Beating the Deadline' illustrated the scene Paul had witnessed when he met Jackie again, a row of coal lorries backed up to a line of huge grey trucks, drivers working furiously with their big square shovels. The lorries in the picture were painted incongruous reds and yellows and purples, standing out sharply from the general gloom of the yard.

'Free to Fly' was a happier picture. A group of excited pigeon fanciers were registering their pigeons for a race. At a scrubbed table near the entrance to a public house two men importantly recorded the details, their glasses of ale frothing bright gold in the sunshine.

'All of these show a way of life fast disappearing for ever,' Marie predicted. 'Some day rich people will be clamouring to buy them.'

She wrapped them carefully in some lengths of cloth she had brought with her and loaded them into her roomy luxurious car, before gliding away.

Both Katy and Marie had tried repeatedly to trace Ted, writing to the firm he had represented, as well as to the French and British Authorities. They were informed there were long lists of missing persons; they would take years to trace, if ever, they said.

Marie decided to marry her Colonel and the wedding reception was held at his impressive Berkshire home. He was much older than she, another father-figure, a scintillating man with a sparkling sense of humour. Katy guessed he would enjoy indulging Marie, as Ted had done, while having no difficulty in coping with the moods that would always be part of her, in spite of the welcome new maturity the war years had endowed. She was elegant and composed as she glided down the aisle on Paul's arm, nearly as tall as he. How Katy wished that Walter, Ted and Mark could have been there to see her; they had all loved her, despite her tantrums. Of the three Marie had stipulated must be at her wedding there was only herself. Where was Ted, she wondered? Any number of things could have happened; another little French lady, perhaps; or maybe he needed help. Wherever you are, stay alive Ted. If she thought positively enough . . . Stay alive, Ted. *Please,* God.

Soon after Marie's wedding Paul was escorting his own daughter down the aisle of St Michael's, where he and Meg had been married. Laura was marrying Jackie Lee's younger son, Ian, a student doctor at the hospital. As soon as their eyes met they had known they were in love, to the incredulous delight of both their fathers. Another Brook-Lee merger; it seemed too good to be true. His daughter married to his friend's son, to live here in England, near the hospital, only a few miles away. It was more than he had ever dared hope; more than he deserved.

On her wedding day Paul carefully removed the heavy gold chain and pendant from Meg's jewellery box and placed it round the neck of their daughter, this precious girl they shared. She wore it proudly as Mary Ann had done. He told Meg about it in his letter describing the wedding; he could tell from her reply that she was pleased at the thought of their daughter wearing the present he had brought from Canada. It seemed a unifying act, linking two generations and two sides of the world.

Ten months later he was able to write excitedly about their mutual grandson, Mitchell Benjamin Paul. From the start they called him Mitch. During Ian's long working hours Laura would bring the child to see him, and when she

305

helped out with emergencies at the hospital she left him in Paul's care.

Under the new Labour Government all pits were being nationalized. Paul thought how pleased Ben would have been at that. The compensation they were paid for Brooklee, which had been producing a gratifying profit for some time, was little enough if set against all the graft and unpaid hours they had put in, but Paul readily accepted it and agreed with Jackie, ten years older than he and eager to retire, to turn the management of the mine over to Jackie's elder son who had worked with them since leaving school. Percy and his brother were also ready for a rest.

It surprised Jackie that Paul surrendered the reins so easily. This time he had no intention of putting the mine first. For now there was something in Paul's life far more important than any mine. Not everyone had a second chance of happiness. To have unlimited time to spend with Laura and Mitch was more precious to him than black gold. Every day they were near, he felt he was growing younger. Now he had all the time in the world to devote to his grandson.

Soon Mitch was a sturdy little lad who stood out among playfellows of his own age; he was so much taller than they. Intent upon running faster and jumping higher than any of his companions, like Ben had been, it was important for him to win. With his flaxen hair, far-seeing, clear blue eyes and the typical cock o' the north tilt to his head, he was every inch a Brook. Like Mary Ann and Ben he always seemed poised for flight, his heels permanently raised from the floor, his movements swift and determined.

Now it was Paul's turn to describe all the 'first-times' to Meg: the first tooth, the first faulty steps, the first time Paul ran behind, holding the saddle of the two-wheeler bike he had bought for the little lad's fourth birthday. Mitch was a quick learner, and often they would ride side-by-side to visit his other Grandad in Norton. Jackie was past cycling, but he would drive them on to Norton pool, where Mitch could sail his model boat. They were long happy days, reminding Paul of the joys Mary Ann and her little grandson, Mark, shared. Having a grandson seemed almost better than having a son might have been.

Now it was possible for Laura to speak to Meg on the telephone. If Paul had been able to speak to Mary Ann on the phone in the days when Ben's urgent postcard arrived in Canada he might have never come back. Mitch was fascinated by the disembodied voice of the unknown Grandma who laughed like his mother. He often asked when he could see her. 'One day,' Laura promised.

And one day she broke the news to Paul that they were soon leaving for Canada. 'Of course you must go,' he said, 'Meg must be aching to see her grandson, in the same way I used to ache to see you. How long will you be gone?'

He was startled to see the pleading glance she flashed to Ian, who took her hand reassuringly. 'Ian has been offered a job there, Dad, at a Medical Research Centre near Winnipeg. Exactly the sort of work he has been hoping for.'

Paul stood staring at them both, alarm bells ringing in his head. This could not be happening again! Not Laura! She could not be planning to leave him now, with the little lad. She would not take Mitch away from him, would she?

'You are not going for . . . for good?' He did not recognize the hollow voice as his own.

The answer was in their faces. He felt an upsurge of unreasonable anger toward Ian. 'You are taking her away? *For good*?'

'It's not like that at all, Paul. We shall naturally come over to see you and my father when we can. Canada is not the inaccessible place it was. There is air travel now, you know.'

Paul sank down heavily, his eyes never leaving his son-in-law's face. He could wring his neck as he stood there smugly talking about air travel. Laura had married an

307

Englishman and he was taking her to live in Canada! All his dreams were once again being smashed to pieces. And by Jackie Lee's son!

A little shiver ran down his spine. It was as if he walked over two graves. He was once again glibly suggesting to Mac and Maisie that he bring their daughter to England. Never had he fully appreciated their sacrifice until now.

Laura left Ian's side to gently fold her arms around him. 'Come with us, Dad,' she whispered.

'No!' The word blasted from him like an explosion from a pistol. Go with them! And see his Meg married to his brother? No, he was not brave enough for that.

Laura stroked his face gently. 'Don't look like that, Dad. I did only come for a visit, after all. I have stayed far longer than I planned. Five whole years!'

Of course! She only came to take a midwifery certificate. Five years! Had it really been as long as that? It seemed no time since that wonderful day he had found her on his doorstep, smiling at him with Meg's smile.

There were tears in her lovely hazel eyes now, the first he had seen there. He must not make her cry, this precious darling girl. He had made her mother cry; he must not be guilty of this too. Ian's thin studious face was anxious and apprehensive. Remembering Mac he chucked Laura playfully under her chin with a gentle fist. 'You are right, my love. We have had five good years,' he replied brightly. 'A lovely long time together.' He smiled reassuringly at his son-in-law. 'It's an interesting job you have landed, is it, Ian? Well done, lad. Sit down, both of you, and tell me all about it.'

As they talked, he wondered how a light that burned so brightly could suddenly go out. Like a dream too wonderful to last.

CHAPTER

20

Soon after Laura left, Paul had Notice to Quit. His house was to be demolished as part of the Heath End Redevelopment Scheme. Double Row and The Gulley had already gone, their sites like grey, flattened graves; it seemed impossible that so many homes had existed in such small areas. Little Cott and the two tall houses were just a mound of dusty rubble waiting to be carted away. All the occupants had been re-housed in new council estates in Pelsall or Rushall. Heath End would soon be like a gaping toothless mouth.

His house must come down for the road to be straightened, the official notice explained. He was offered alternative accommodation, a little council bungalow in Pelsall, resembling a rabbit hutch with its tiny living room, galley kitchen, one small bedroom and bathroom. At first it filled him with revulsion. He hurried to inspect one of the good solid houses near the church that Mary Ann had bought all those years ago, now on the market at three thousand pounds. Three thousand and she had paid about a hundred apiece for them!

People were clamouring to buy houses these days, even going into debt for them. A bit different from when Mary Ann was the only property owner in Heath End. Way before her time she was, none of her children having bought their own properties since. Not Edwin, Katy, nor Ben. Now he was dithering at the idea of tying his money up in something as non-productive as a house. That money might come in handy one day for Mitch's education. He would accept the rabbit hutch for the time being, while keeping his eye on the market for something cheaper. The bungalow would certainly be useless when they came from Canada to visit; he would have nowhere to put them up.

Paul spoke to Laura and Mitch on the telephone for a few minutes each week. It was better than nothing, but always it left him longing for more.

Katy once again helped by keeping him busy. In the same way as the Council had decided to annihilate Heath End, claiming his house in the process, they decreed that the Children's Home must be run by them, and plans were in process to take it over. Katy, with typical practicality, decided to convert an old orangery at the bottom of the orchard into a self-contained flat for herself. On her suggestion Paul set to work to build internal dividing walls and to add a bathroom. When that was done there would be fruit trees to thin out to make way for lawns and a vegetable patch. There would be greenhouses to move, paths to make. 'Must work, in order to forget . . . '

He worked every spare minute until it was dark, and in the evenings they sat together reminiscing about the village that was being destroyed and all that it had meant to them. They talked about Mary Ann and Raish, the father whose dictatorship had affected all their characters and their lives. His cruel bullying had resulted in Edwin's lack of confidence in his painting ability and in his relationships. His treatment of their mother had been the cause of Katy's insistence on security for her children, preventing her following the dictates of her own heart. Paul's nagging anxiety over money, born of his observation of Mary Ann's early struggles, had caused him to neglect Meg and finally to lose her.

Ben had reacted with truculence and aggression, resulting in Raish losing his life. Yet of the four, Ben had come off the best, Paul concluded, for he had Meg. What a waste of human emotions; Edwin and Sally, Katy and Ted, himself and Meg. He hoped Laura and Ian fared better.

Always he looked forward to their promised visit. When it came two long years later he did not need extra accommodation, for they slept at Jackie's.

It was wonderful to see them all, but things could never be the same between himself and Laura. There was not the time during their brief visit for the intimate chats they used to have, for Ian was always there. First and foremost she was Ian's wife, Paul reminded himself. She was as openly concerned and loving toward her husband as Meg had been toward himself; it was good to see her so happy and to hear her singing, as she used to, as she did jobs for him in his little house.

Mitch, now a six-and-a-half-year-old schoolboy, was touchingly overjoyed to be back, flinging himself eagerly at Paul. He often chose to stay with him when Laura and Ian went visiting friends and other relatives. There was so much to tell about school and about his visits to the farm, when he stayed with his Gran and Great-Uncle Ben in the school holidays, now that Laura was nursing full-time. He still managed to ride the bicycle he had left behind, for Paul had raised saddle and handlebars as far as they would go. On fine days they rode together to the Arboretum or up on to the Chase, where they would sit quietly on a log, watching for deer.

Their time together was so fleeting that when they left it was as if it had been just a short wakefulness from a bad dream. Laura phoned as soon as she reached home to say it went far too quickly for her too, and she wished she could have spent more time with him.

'Just go on being happy, my love,' Paul told her. 'We can look forward to next time.'

Thank you, Mac. One day I may be as brave as you.

Ian was making great strides in his career. Promotion followed promotion; good news, except that his involvement meant that they were not able to arrange another visit to England. He had to take his vacation when he could. It never seemed to tally with Laura's or with the school holidays and Laura would not come without Ian. She wrote Paul sweet little notes, sometimes enclosing photographs and letters from Mitch, but it was from Meg's regular correspondence he gleaned most news of them. Meg's happiness when she had Mitch to stay fairly bounced from the pages. She described how Ben took him fishing and riding; how he taught him jobs on the farm. She meant only to keep Paul in touch with his grandson's activities, but it was like a sharp knife turning in an old wound and left him feeling dispirited and lonely.

Not only did Ben have the privilege of raising his daughter, he now had charge of his grandson for three months each year. Oh, Ben, his heart cried, that sailing ticket was not intended to include all this. Not Mitch as well! God, how it hurt.

Katy had never lost faith that Ted was alive, and one day, as they neared the completion of their building project, she had her hopes confirmed. She was informed that he had been recently moved from a hospital in France to a centre for war disabled in Derbyshire.

She looked so eager, sitting up straight, her bright eyes dancing with anticipation, as Paul turned his car into the

long drive of the converted manor house in a quiet
Derbyshire valley. She had hardly spoken throughout the
journey, too excited, too occupied with her own
thoughts. The warm autumn sunset was as golden as the
leaves carpeting the lawns and drive, muffling the sound of
the car. Paul scanned his sister's pale face anxiously. The
glorious crown of golden hair Ted would remember had
turned to silver overnight after Mark's death. Losing him
had tested her indestructible spirit almost beyond endurance.
He hoped there were no more sacrifices for her to make.

Most of the patients had already gone in for their evening
meal. In one of the remaining wheelchairs on the open
balcony sat Ted. A nurse approached to take him inside. He
put a restraining hand on her arm as he saw the car; it was as
if he knew who would step out of it, although he had not
been told of her coming.

Katy was out of the car before Paul had switched off the
engine, running toward the balcony, her arms held wide,
oblivious of the nurse, of Paul, of everybody except Ted.
There was no need for words between them. Ted's
shoulders and arms were as strong as ever. They clasped each
other tightly, kissing and laughing and crying at the same
time.

The nurse quirked an eyebrow as she and Paul wheeled
the other patients inside, each of them cracking jokes about
'that dark horse, Ted Willis'. 'You would think he would
share what he has with the rest of the old crocks club.' The
joke fell on deaf ears, for Ted and Katy, holding on to each
other as if afraid ever to let go, were in their own private
world. When Paul returned they were talking non-stop.

They never did stop talking, through four more
operations Ted had to have on his shell-shattered hip and
leg. Katy would be there, holding his hand right up to the
moment of the anaesthetic, and by his bedside, talking
soothingly, as he regained consciousness. They continued
talking after Ted came home, first in a wheelchair, then on

two sticks, and finally limping around with one. They argued about getting married, this time Katy doing the proposing and Ted the refusing.

Why did she think he had not been in touch during the lost years, he enquired. At first he had been too ill, but later, when he could have written, he had decided he must go it alone, not willing to accept anyone's pity. He stressed he would not let her tie herself to a dreary cripple.

'I shall divorce you the very second you become dreary,' Katy threatened. 'Playing hard to get in order to get your own back, are you? Haven't you meant all that blarney you have talked all these years?'

She had an answer to every objection and at last won her way. They married quietly at a registry office, with Paul as witness, and moved into the dwelling he had helped to make ready.

Before long Ted was in touch with his old firm, personally supervising the manufacture of a special car they offered to make for his needs. When it was completed to his satisfaction, he drove Katy to London to see Marie, who proudly took them on a tour of the chain of art shops she now owned.

Occasionally they went to the coast for a few days, but always Ted was eager to return home. Paul thought of the wasted years he could have taken Katy round the world. How his sister would have loved that.

Now Ted was content to watch the tiny figure with the shiny silver hair dart about as she tended the garden. Often as Paul approached the gate he could hear them arguing good-naturedly about where to plant what. There were many lively exchanges of varying points of view, all ending with laughs. Ted was as much of a tease as ever, and Katy as swift with her humorous back-chat as of old. This was the Katy who had altered the birth certificate, who had thrown a chamber pot at Raish, who had bought the piano. It was good to see her so happy.

Sometimes they just sat on their small patio, holding hands, their heads close together like a couple of turtle doves, catching up on long years of separation.

Lucilla had accepted a post as housekeeper for the Children's Home. At long last Katy had had her fill, happy to devote herself exclusively to Ted.

Seeing them so close increased Paul's yearning for Meg. It was a physical pain in his heart that filled every waking moment. Having Laura for those five years had helped to heal a gaping wound. Now the wound had re-opened and was far more painful than before. If only he could see the lad! Meg's letters promised that one day they would send him to England during school vacation.

Meanwhile Paul rang Mitch at the same time each week. When he rang the farm during the school holidays Mitch always answered himself. What if Meg or Ben should answer? How would he talk to them? But they never did.

The first time he heard Meg's voice on the telephone was when she rang to tell him that Ben had died. He had had pneumonia, like Mary Ann.

'The last thing he said, Paul,' she explained gently, 'was to thank you.' She went on to say she had not forgotten their promise to send Mitch. 'I am sorry it has taken so long. I suppose we have been a bit selfish. We missed Laura so much, and when she came back she was married. You will understand, Paul.'

Yes, he understood. Laura had stayed with him for five years. In that time she had married and become a mother. After that things were different.

'I do understand. Everything. My dear Meg,' he whispered as he replaced the receiver.

He had hardly been able to respond to what she was saying, so riveted was he at the joy of hearing her voice after so long, exactly as he remembered it. As his heartbeats gradually returned to normal he was able to ponder on what she had told him.

It was over at last. The thing that had plagued him more than he had ever dared admit. Ben's marriage to Meg. Over at last.

The following week he received a postcard in an airmail envelope. It was written, a few days before Ben died, in large spidery writing. It contained one line only, typical of all the correspondence Ben had ever sent. 'Paul. She never stopped loving you. Ben.'

He must have known he was dying. Poor Ben. Was that the cross he had had to carry? Was the message true, or was it a last attempt to make up for all that he, Paul, had lost? Yet Ben had never lied to him. Paul read and re-read his brother's last communication. Was he clutching at straws, or could an impossible dream even now become a reality?

He would wait until his grandson came. Mitch would be sixteen soon; Meg had promised a plane ticket to England as a birthday gift.

Yes, he would wait until Mitch came. After all these years he could wait a few months more.

EPILOGUE

MITCH, BACK FROM his tour of all the important English cities, sat with Paul in his tiny bungalow, where he had joined him for the last few days of his holiday. He talked mostly about the Edwin Brook Exhibition of paintings in London. He had met Marie there.

'People were scrambling to buy, Grandad,' he exclaimed. 'And no wonder! They are marvellous. Edwin had sure got a great gift.'

Paul listened in amazement. It was incredible the astronomical sums people were willing to pay for Edwin's paintings.

'Is Marie short of money?'

'Not for herself. She is sending it all to a charity in India.' Mitch glanced round the room. 'Where are the paintings you had, Grandad?'

'I have packed them. For your grandmother. She won't want them sold.' He had packed her jewellery too.

They talked well into the early hours, about Mitch's

impressions of the cities he had explored; about the Computer Studies Course he was joining when he returned to Canada. 'Gran always said I was not cut out to be a farmer. She's right.'

'What is she like now, your Gran?'

Mitch considered for a moment. 'She never looks any older, if that's what you mean. She moves faster than most people her age.' He drew his brows together, as if wondering how else he could describe her. Suddenly he smiled. 'She laughs a lot,' he added.

'She always did.' His Meg. Merry Meg, Edwin used to call her. It would be grand to sit together, chatting like Katy and Ted. It would be lovely to hear her laugh.

Paul turned to his grandson who looked so much like the kid brother he once had. 'Tell me, lad. How much does it cost to fly out to Canada?'